WRITE & DIE

Satsvarupa dasa Goswami

Other books by Satsvarūpa dāsa Goswami

Prabhupāda Meditations

Living with the Scriptures

Devotional Practices

New Writings

WRITE & DIE

Satsvarupa dasa Goswami

Gita-nagari PRESS

Persons interested in the subject matter are invited to
correspond with our secretary, c/o GN Press, Inc., P.O.
Box 30, Philo, CA 95466, www. gnpress.org.

Write and Die
©2006 GN Press, Inc.
All rights reserved.
ISBN # 978-0911233-85-8

GN Press gratefully acknowledges the BBT for the use
of verses and purports from Srila Prabhupada's books.
All such verses and purports are © Bhaktivedanta Book
Trust International, Inc.

Library of Congress Cataloguing-in-Publication Data
Goswami, Satsvarupa Dasa, 1939-
Write and Die / Satsvarupa dasa Goswami

1. Spiritual life—International Society for Krishna
Consciousness.
2.

Cover design by Blake Farley
Book Design: True Faust (Bimala devi dasi)

CONTENTS

CHAPTER ONE

HE ASKED ME IF I WOULD rather write or get headaches, write or die. I said of course I would rather stay alive, but earlier, on a checklist in a book *A Writer on Writing*, by Margaret Atwood, there was a list of why writers write. One reason writers had given was that they would die if they could not write, and I had underlined this sympathetically. Some of her other quotes garnered from actual writers: "Because I knew I had to keep writing or else I would die..." "Because to write is to take risks, and it is only by taking risks that we know we are alive..." "Because I was possessed." Someone said, "To defend a minority group," and that appeals to me as service to the Hare Krishna movement. And Samuel Beckett's statement that "writing was all he was good for."

It is serious talk for me nowadays because I had "a nervous breakdown" in my nervous disorder syndrome which one learned person diagnosed as "possible senility." They thought that might be coming to me because I generate such inner pressure in order to do steady writing. Of course I have no intricate plots or characters to assemble, yet even what you see in my books requires a great strain, to keep the wheels moving, the semblance of order in the apparent chaos, the momentum, or even plot, the right balance of remembrance of Krishna and the material world experience.

So I promised them again that I would not write any more books, not for awhile. And here I am disobeying. Maybe I can do it at a slower pace. Maybe I will die writing. In any case, I will die, so why not die writing?

Even as I start this new one, my brave Godbrother Srila Bhaktitirtha Maharaja has undergone amputation of his leg because of cancer, and he is still making phone calls and writing e-mail. Before his amputation, he was traveling over the world constantly, an ambassador for Krishna, nonstop in his unique form of presenting Krishna consciousness. So he is dying. Krishna in the form of the preacher. One could say he is dying of cancer, or whatever the particular unique situation in his heart, and the answers to his prayer. But dying is passing, and we're all dying. In my case, why not leave as many *good* books as possible?

Another point is my manuscripts are accumulating, and there's no money to print them. Why add to the unprinted pile, which also adds to my anxiety? But someday they will be printed, and if not, so what? Some artists have sculpted in stone (although it still fades away), and some have printed on pages that fade, on the memories that fade. But you can pass it down through many generations—"because you have sought me, therefore you have found me."

It's life-*giving* not molding your own,
because your feet are cold
and it's early. Looking for the supreme.

Phone his friend, thank him for holiday gifts,
forgive yourself for your core art.
Look back at it—Subhadra's
footprints in the sands of Mendocino,
and find me a nice picture of her
mother alone. A picture of Suta and I
walking alone, snapshot of me
holding the milk bottle downward
into eager Laksmana's mouth. When will
I see them again? Graffiti,
tattoos, New York? Wish them
happy Christmas.

You don't need to phone Madhu-mangala?
Go ahead, make someone happy.
"Don't miss the nectar, be greedy."
It's extra and Christmastime.

But in reality what
you actually do, the Lord through you,
may never see daylight of publication.
Some other poets may get a chance.
Be happy at that too.

Sannyasa clothes and a Santa beard. Thump like
the rabbit at the bottom of the

cloud. Hey bro, how many
rounds to go today?

Nanda visited. He said, "I take his words and make them more alarming or extreme then they were intended." He never said I could not write anymore, and only rest. He said I could write, but then rest, write and then rest. He never said I could no longer paint. He said I could paint, but when I feel myself getting tired, then rest. He's also still inclined for working toward the miracle of printing and publishing and distributing my books. He asked me what I wanted. I said, "Like Hemingway or D. H. Lawrence, to have all the books printed and published."

"Well of course," he laughed. "What writer in his right mind wouldn't want to publish his books instead of just sticking them in a corner of the room?"

I laughed. "Yes, and I know it's hard, very hard. I have so many books, and we haven't found the audience. Working away from the 'certain religious movement' to ….?" To—the searcher, the mystic, through the looking glass (I actually did it several times and lived to tell the tale)—the writer of truf, de Principal whose voice is changing, who is heterosexual celibate and is not homophobic. Great. We can go on trying against the great odds. Keep holding on to the paddle. Excelsior!

"When did you begin writing?"

"When I was 17. I would write on the walls of men's rooms in the bars, in the Naval Reserve when I had the guard duty booth, when it was my turn to salute arriving and departing officers and make a gesture with my rifle, I would spend most of the cold evening writing on the inner wall of the booth or in those 'ecstatic notebooks kept for your own joy' recommended by Kerouac, carried and used on trains, ferries, buses, cafeterias, under any light bulb, daylight.

"When did you get your first inspiration?"

"I remember Jean Shepard when I was still in the womb of my parental home and frequent, private 'debate' papers between my dear drinking buddy, John Young, and I. He'd write, say, five pages on why Nazism is valid, and I'd bombast him in a gentlemanly way. He then wrote back (we both assumed a pseudo-professorial tone, as if we were junior instructors or journalists): 'Mr. Swamiji, your last paper against Nazism had some excellent points, but I would like to point out a few remises which render your argument useless in the end.' And so it went, week after week, ranging on any topics we wished. After awhile we switched to semiautobiographical fiction in the mood of Jack Kerouac, talking about going on the road, meeting girls, getting drunk, etc. We were both confirmed Jean Shepard fans and knew enough to laugh at our feckless selves. These were some beginnings before more 'serious' attempts in junior college."

So my counselor says I don't have to quit writing, like a dead mollusk. He appreciated the choices I noted from Margaret Atwood's reasons writers gave why they couldn't give up—because I was possessed, because I wasn't good at anything else, because I'd die, etc. But Nanda held firm that his job is to try to reach a cure for my migraines so that I can work normally. To gain your health so that you can write. I'd have to write a little slower and not be so obliged and obsessive with each book, and I *thought* I heard both he and Ollie say *no* painting, but now they say they never said that but paint some, not so passionately, and then rest. Rest is first. And I say *sadhana* must rise. And I know, from my own side, rest must prevail.

Because I did step through the looking glass last week. I saw things as in a dream and I acted as in a dream for several days. I completely forgot who certain people were, and I thought chairs were lamps and I thought extra people were in the room. When they asked me who I was, I said, "Steve," but to this day I don't recall people who said they were there helping me into bed and not believing my paranoid tales of a woman sharpshooter (she could hit a bull's-eye at forty yards) who was out to get me and was going to spread a new dirty lie about me. I'm just coming back to the real world with permission to write.

I realize it will be very difficult to publish so much. New reality. But right now that's not my problem. This is my ejaculating, my thumping against the dark cloud of unknowing. Please, Krishna. Please, Radha. Please, Prabhupada, reveal your love to this poor, wretched soul.

> Book, poem. She lost her faith.
> Went to talk to a psychiatrist about
> it. He brought in another person.
> She mentioned suicidal. He said you
> might like to visit our Shady Grove art

colony. Before she knew it, she was
in an enforced condition,
day 2 was art. "Color in your emotions."
She colored a Ratha-yatra cart. Plenty
of color for the RY cart,
stick-figure pujari and black
lines on both sides of the street for
onlookers. He asked, "Paint
the color of your emotions." She
respectfully took a new page and
colored with the crayons black and black
up and down over and over.

Oh I am fortunate indeed if I can
just move my bowels and joke my way
out of it. My Christmas nephew Narada
received a "spongeman" suit and his older
brother, who is already an accomplished
magician, received a DVD of a man
doing advanced card tricks.
I received a two-volume biography of Yeats,
which I cannot read. Received
lots of sweaters and pants. I'll
share them with the men.

What about a bump forward
toward Krishna? Didn't get yet.
They come only when one feels
very humble and ardently cries tears and
happily helps others. I want to do that.
Not just my own
achievements. Bob Brookmire, Joe Schmo,
the TV, the death of
overrated clowns.

Tell me quick, what are the colors
of your tears?

"You just tell me by what
authority you have locked me in the
nuthouse and when you'll let me
out. Allow me to phone my
lawyer. I'm not seriously crazy.
I simply told you too much.
Such intimacies should only
be shared between close friends."
Please release me. I have no intentions
of curing this body. I want to
go back to Anderson Valley,
you have no habeas corpus or
warrant of arrest. I was
just joking. I'm a Democrat.
I never vote. I am a poor
chanter but you are even worse,
we are all locked under the
dark cloud of unknowing,
worth repeating again and again,

Krishna, I'm allowed
to write books, must pass
stool at least once a day,
still working,
rest and write and drinking water
and chant. I'll get there.
Where? Better. Better better.
Let me go.
"He's got some connections. Knows a
swami. Better let him go."

DREAM

There were many many people taking part in an examination. Chaotic kind of scene. I was there, and I was doing well. It was a question-and-answer sort of thing. High authorities were questioning us. The types of questions had to do with goodness, like religious but nondenominational. Rapidly yes, no, what would you do in this situation? How would you take care of a little child if you found him like this? If you had a house and you had a portrait of Brahms and a child and the house was burning, which would you save? Questions like that, on and on and on and on.

Finally I passed the final exam along with others, and we were top winners among many who didn't pass. Just to make sure that I was one of the winners, now that we were all being taken care of very well, my man looked for my luggage and he found it all and now we were going to somewhere. I thought, "Oh this is great," but I couldn't speak. I was now polyglot, glup gluppa glup glup gluppa glup gup gup glupa glup. I couldn't speak coherently because I had somehow put together all the different religions and languages together, but that was all right with him. He got all my luggage together. But then I said coherently, "This is wonderful, and we'll have money enough, too. We can take a canoe trip, do some good-type service of protecting endangered species," and so forth. He said, "Yes, but there's trouble, because they are stopping at the airports because of so much international trouble and war. But when there's a chance, we'll go forward."

Aside from winning the prize, I was actually feeling so elated in the dream that I was going toward goodness. I was feeling happy. My foot was touching the cat. Lately she's been very nice. All night long she's touching my foot where she and I lie, and I think there's an infusion of goodness and mercy coming back and forth as we sleep and I'm coming closer to goodness and goodness is coming to me, like I'm the cloud of unknowing, we're getting closer to goodness, Godliness that is, of course, goodness means Godliness. There's no goodness without Godliness, and so we were being picked for those who were coming closer to Godliness by the mercy of God. Goodness comes by the mercy of God to those who ardently strive. "Because you have searched for Me, therefore you have found Me."

I thought he complained to me and said I was a jazzman and not a writer. But that's not what he said at all. This is from an actual letter from Dainya dated December 27, 2004:

First, please forgive me for somehow suggesting that I do not think you are a writer. When I said that you were a jazzman whose improvisational jazz music is created through words, I did not wish to imply or to suggest that you were not a writer. (You write continuously — clearly, if

15

ever there was a writer, you are!) In truth, I would say that the aesthetics of the literature you create is singularly unique.

A reader of, say, Dickens or Dostoevsky finds himself entering the world of nineteenth-century London or the world of Raskolnikov. Your readers do not find themselves entering a world that's different from their own. Rather, through your literatures, readers find themselves having a concrete experience of being with another person, a person who through the pages of a book has come into their world. And this is an aesthetic experience that is both ineffable and cathartic. I know of no other literature that offers this particular kind of aesthetic experience.

There are other literatures that give readers views toward other persons. For example, in reading the poetry of Allen Ginsberg or Frank O'Hara, you have a very tangible sense of the personalities of Ginsberg or O'Hara; you have a concrete sense of who these persons are — their tastes and sensibilities — and this experience is certainly aesthetic and cathartic. But I would say that the catharses that arise through perceiving the personalities of Ginsberg or O'Hara through their literatures is not exactly rooted in an experience of being with Ginsberg or O'Hara.

The views that these men's writings afford of their personalities might be compared to the views that telescopes afford of distant objects. When you observe, say, the planet Mars through a telescope, you may have a very tangible sense of what that planet looks like, even to the point of recognizing geographical features or weather systems, but I don't think the person generally feels that the planet has come into his world and that the planet is now there with that person. In my view, the aesthetic experience that arises within one while reading your books is genuinely and uniquely distinctive, and it somehow is rooted in the psychological experience of being with you.

Excelsior!

What's that "Poem" that William Stafford said his six-year-old daughter Kit spoke while they were driving home from a family trip to the beach? The others in the car had gone to sleep and she was talking to help keep him awake. The road wound ahead and she bubbled along, composing with easy strokes, imagining a way of life for the two of them:

> We'd have an old car, the kind that gets
> flat tires, but inside would be wolfskin
> on the seats and warm fur on the steering

wheel, and the wolf fur on all the buttons. And
we'd live in a ranch house made out of
logs with a loft where you sleep, and you'd
walk a little ways and there'd be the farm
with the horses. We'd drive to town, and
we'd have flat tires, and be sort of old.
>(from *Writing the Australian Crawl,* by William Stafford,
>Michigan Press)

POLYGLOT

Will you go with me? I'm bound for the promised land. We can chant our own Hare Krishna mantra. Hear renditions of *Vidaghda-madhava* and *Hari-bhakti-vilasa*. I'll teach you mystic pen. I'm 'umble. I shall be forever blessed. Oh will you go with me? Will you come? I don't want to write just for myself. But you have to try hard. It is for the institution members. And frogs. I can hear them too here in December (or are they crickets?) on high hills in northwest CA.

I am asking you to come with me. I'm not just one. And yet it is one to one. But sometimes there will be several loving in company, tongues in cheek, fingerlicking *prasada*.

I get the royal treatment. But it should be spread around. We were reading *The Path of Perfection*. Maybe it's too much strict instruction to the sisters. I heard there is a heavenly prose-poetic Internal Castle. Shall I ask for one? Don't worry, brothers and sisters, as I said, each night we are getting heaps (like big dollops of ice cream) of *Lalita-madhava* and *Vidaghda-madahva* sewn by a powerful orthodox Godbrother. (How can dollops be sewn?) Each night is a cliffhanger with Radha and Shyama; although I heard it before, he has fluffed it out nicely.

I have to write on the sneak. They won't allow it. If they hear me use the Dictaphone, they come and note it, and I get a dressing-down later: "We heard you working when you should have been resting. We gave you a green light, but that wasn't a flag wave to start the race at Daytona." Live and die. Write, Horseman, give a cool eye as you pass by life and death. Spare a little time for classical and blues, for the paint and polyglot.

XYZ

Nobody's fault.

He's got a Bible. I've got a *Gita* and a clicker and a migraine. And I was the best *japa* man, and boy, I could give a straight lecture.

This is for you, you is me. The libations of a guitar between us. The wall we share, so thin. Love, Lord, I call for You. Nobody's fault, but You help me, I know. There will be good times.

> The man is still alive, he plays his way
> Through the day light blue, he lists as he's
> been told but more on the health chart goes
> the truth about nearer he played when he could have had
> the ring around his finger and whisper
> the blues of Hare Krishna.
>
> Which is Hare Krishna, blues or joyride
> or Anglican-like stiff prayer or pure
> Vedic recitation, ISKCON whole governed
> by saffron giants like Hanuman?
> We've got Prabhupada on tape but they say
> that was during fire-*yajna* and not
> his usual relaxed period.
>
> You're falling asleep "writing"
> X-rated scripts while you
> *japa*—heading for boiling ocean of ghee.
> Nobody's fault but Brooks Brothers pants
> don't save nobody. At least *tilak*.
> Phone your friend and ask for all his
> money so your confessions can save the world.
> While you're at
> it, why don't you improve?

He said if you want to write a gargantuan autobiography (argh!), it will take planning in advance, the stages and strategies, the audience, and then within that structure you can go wild.

The most important single thing is to say a hearty *bon journo* to your comrades and bow down. "Oh!" Don't bow down to him, he's only a fourteen-year-old boy learning card tricks, his hair in long Shakespearean locks, but no hair on his chin, page boy. Water, water in a pot, but the cat no longer drinks from it, too many foul fumes emanating. But that's good. Early, 3:30 A.M. I'm in the painting room touching up, hoot holes, the red dot on Radha's forehead, a garland, white teeth, just a few things. I will send this one to Bhakti-tirtha Maharaja. If he has no place or taste to hang it, he can give it to a friend or leave it in the roll. The gift is my part and an ending note of his courage and even humor within the fortitude. "I'm a world leader!" he tells the nurse, but she treats him like an ordinary body with one foot missing and insists he finish his exercise.

A world leader, a king in Africa, a guru, a Princeton alumnae, an author of many books, an old friend, adored by many disciples, but to the nurse he's just patient number 6425, cancer still in the body, he must exercise to learn how to function with the new one-footed body. Indeed he is a world leader.

> Adversity when he can't get a taxicab
> on the Lower East Side, wasn't hard
> for the thin white boy who had enough
> money in his wallet. "South Ferry."
> Although in the other way, "Sheridan
> Square, 10th St." Boom, boom. They
> didn't refuse you because you had
> privileged, innocent looks.
>
> Just lucky they didn't mug you.
> I think that was ahead. Once on
> LSD, I had no idea how much
> money was being handed
> back and forth.
>
> Once in Avalon I was lost
> among those respectable little beach houses—
> which home is the Guarinos'?
> And saw ahead the police car stopped with red

dome revolving. Somehow
I walked through the trouble and found my
folks' home. That was a weekend
they weren't home. I sat
on the floor and saw skulls
and a family emblem, a big
fist like my dad's.
Meant to tell him the
next day that I knew the
secret but couldn't inherit it.

Bought blintzes from the Jewish place
near the Bowery, brought them to Avalon
as my gift. That was near the end.

This is hardly a strict autobiog.
This is writing to live. "Hey taxi!"
"Where to, pal?"

"Oh man!" A bro left standing
left standing on the downtown street.

This is not the big auto epic. There is no way I could hire the producers and the sets and most of all, the star, the self, the main actor, me, stressed. A real production would demand he be on the set five hours a day and at night working with editors, arguing for changes, thinking up new scenes and hearing the monotonous voice of the engineer: "Boy playing marbles playing marbles in the Queens gutter, take 17." No, I can't do that until I'm cleared of meningitis of the brain. The trio of authorities have to release me from their unanimous private health care decision. "SLOW." Until then, writing and dying. And this is as good as that.

When the man flexes his arm then
other things may happen in the
few hours left today. Any interruption
in time is in motion. I wanted
to take a photo of a painting for

a book cover, a second toilet
dumping, no more headaches,

more meditation (as if I ever did any)
of ardent naked sing love for God,
bury everything else to the side, even
thoughts of the pastimes, this is
the simplest, truest meditation.

I must have a calling for it.
drawn to it. By his mercy.
not displeased by it, it doesn't wane.
If it ever goes away it comes
back with more force and joy.

Then he may get fit
for it. Hope more.
not a heavy materialist who needs
pride and recognition and ritual
like I did.

When you fell, what was it
like? Oh, nothing. Just some
tears, and I lost two or three or four inches
on my heels, and never showed up
anywhere in saffron underwear.

And how to get used to righteous
officials who say you can't enter here for
five years, three years, forever, spider cat,
and me changing duds any old
way and hairy chin which

is permitted for *sannyasa*.
They checked me out and said he was
okay for now. You'd better keep writing while
you can.

Knock baseballs from the bat but
not on human steroids. Hey,
what punishment are those big
homerun hitters going to get anyway?
Call Suta and find out.
He's a sports ace.

Care packages from a patron.
we wear the clothes
we want and *tilak* too, Emerson
Avila, Krishna Rama's *Vidaghda-
madhava* and *Lalita-madhava*—
don't delay writing him a letter so
he won't chase after your disciples or
whiplash you.
And it's true he's done a
marvelous job, best writer
of *rasika* right in Prabhupada's
groove.

That's all for now, only a few
hours to supper, and I have to rush
to the bathroom now.

If you read something—fiction, nonfiction—that is dirty, it will stay with you. The next day it will be in the bathtub with you and in your thoughts. If you had avoided it, it would not be there and you could press against the cloud or your simple desire to love God. Instead, you've had the Beat poets. Their main concern is the Female and drinking whisky or taking drugs. Because they are Beat poets, they are not ethereal and don't yearn for God. They don't have that calling. They say to hell with God, He is dead.

You don't want to think that way so why ever waste time and show academic curiosity in them? Their turn of a phrase, their tough-guy stance, their revolution, use of words, defiance of the system — you have some similarities. *Ecrasez l'enfame.* Wipe out the infamy said

Voltaire, and that is the goal of Krishna consciousness. But what is the infamy and how to wipe it out? We are for Godhead and all *that* rhetoric in action. It is not just sitting and meditating; there must be action, but for the Lord. Or get tainted by their brush?

A group of people listening to jazz but you
each have to say

it in your own way?
There's a clean way? You heard, "She was sexy
but sad." I mean he's only
sad the mercy is not
coming down and that's her fault.
And that's nobody's fault but hers.

You will right yourself because
you've got good friends like Mukhi and Nanda—
Yeah, that's Keith Jarret's next
tune, "Mukhi."
Just make it Krishna-ized.
You can do it, and that's your
greatest joy.

Phoned up Suta at past eight
last night, his daughter did the automatic
answering service, all asleep I guess. Why'd
I call? Because I love the
guy and on impulse I
phoned to ask what would
happen to Giambi
and Barry Bonds. I knew
he'd know, and wouldn't mind
talking. Is that
pursuing love of God?
Somehow I think it is. And so far
I've missed it
by not making my yearly call

23

to Madhu in Ireland
just to say I love ya.

In the great Italian film "Jesus of Nazareth," by Franco Zeffirelli, the smirk on the face of Simon Peter, the fisherman, when he first encounters the soft-palmed, not rough-and-ready Jesus at the fishing dock. Peter covers his smirk with the back of his hand, partly out of some intuitive reverence. In the Baptism scene, John was scantily clad, hairy, muscular John the Baptist. He had hair in his eyes, shouting for the sinners to come forward and be baptized by a splash of water from his hand. "Repent! In the name of the Father and the Son and the Holy Spirit, your sins shall be forgiven!" Shouting at the top of his lungs so the mob can hear and be convinced they need salvation. Suddenly from a different direction, walking toward John, comes a figure taller than John but not as strong in physical build, his thin body fully covered with a long robe, which gives him a unisex appearance except for the beard and long curly hair. He does not out-dynamic John at first; he has come to be baptized by John. But the Baptizer recognizes him at once and says, "It is you who should baptize me. As you appear, I should diminish."

There's the committee meeting this morning to discuss my health (I almost wrote "death" instead of "health"). I'll produce Dainya's recent letters: one where he praises my unique writing (always an encouragement to hear), but number two, the other letter, where he proposes that we get down to the foundation of an autobiography (despite the fact that hundreds of pages have already been written) and decide, as if for the first time (maybe in committee?) what kind of a book we want this to be, how to structure it, whom it is written for, and let me go free in those perimeters. I shall strongly present to the committee today that I am in no condition to plan a blockbuster *Gone With the Wind* or *Mahabharata, Lord of the Rings*, etc.

My health advisors have prioritized (gulp) my life so that first should come Rest. Writing is allowed only in a small degree, like one of those books W.C.W. wrote, *Kora in Hell, Spring and All,* and my own string of books—*Under Dark Stars, Love and Hate, The Boy Who Cut the Gordion Knot, Subpar Japa,* etc. Those books range "only" two hundred to four hundred pages but are important to me. At sixty-five years old, I'm still at an apprentice stage, setting the foundation of the Krishna conscious writing craft. Waiting for better health, the autobiography will have to be on the back burner. And each suggestion to do it now, a little at a time, does not appeal to me. To do the autobiography, I think you have to put on your hip boots and sun hat, physically live with your editor and slash away in a marathon samurai spirit, chopping and adding. You must be allowed to be afire with it all day, not confined to one writing session and then go to bed or dose yourself as soon as the twinge of oncoming exertion headache is picked up on your revolving state-of-the-art radar.

"Pain situation in band across forehead. Moving quickly to entire dome of skull." (We're trying to avoid meds which make you constipated, so we try first wet rag, lie down, gut it out. By now all hope of writing has stopped and we are coping with the H.A.) *"Moved to right eye. Promptly in place. Plodding. No bowel movement, so I'll have to take a pill.*

You can't call for a whole film-making inspiration rewriting group to gather for weeks of autobiography *He Could Have Done Better* and then call off for two days. Wow, your anxiety builds.

Write and write. Write and limp. Write in Levis or pajamas. Lie down and sleep that you are a murderer of a woman in a book you shouldn't have been wasting time on. All roads lead to Krishna, directly. Don't "wanna sin in Berlin." Happy New Year they falsely cry, cheer straight from a bottle of booze. Turn off the radio and sleep with your cat.

> Love God every minute. There are
> so many prayer books on the market
> but you don't know what love is until...
>
> you have to be a man or a woman and they
> cry out sincerely
> please don't give up on me!
> How many times does he mean it?
> The heart pumps each second.
> He means it but the flesh is weak.
>
> How many times will the *audarya* Lord
> allow, forgive? One hundred times?
> No end of giving her chances

as long as she is trying to be
good. Little Stevie to mom:
"I'll be good." Yeah, con
boy, he'll be good. He knows
what you're supposed
to say.
Does he want to be good
or just do his thing and
get his mom off his back
with his aphorism?
Please, please don't leave me,
Give me another chance.

I'm no cynic. I'm for nonjudgment and
turning the other side of the coin. Tell 'em
"Let he who hasn't sinned cast the
first stone."

We just need to clean our eyeglasses and
get an accurate estimation of our *own*
position. Glass house. Wretched one.
Plead again. Mean it, you
really wish to be good, please
Please, please Lord, I don't
know what love is.

I don't know your suffering.
I want to get through a day
without pain in the rainy
season of north CA where
the roof leaks.

You don't know, no wonder
you never move your hand in prayer.

CHAPTER TWO

I WAS INVITED TO A JANUARY 1 COMMITTEE MEETING. I said yes. Not knowing what committee meetings were about, I asked, "What's it for?"

"Today's is about you and some basic attitudes and schedules."

It sounded suspicious, five people in a room talking about me, but I went along with it, of course. Anything to promote harmony, humility, embrace.

But as I entered the room, and if I had known what the meeting was really focused on, I would have begun with a garbled version of the blues lines,

As I come before you today, you will find me wrong, wrong, wrong. I am guilty as charged. But before you judge, if judge you must, let he who has not sinned cast the first stone. And just remember the other side of the coin.

They readied a special seat for me, and I turned to the opening speaker as if to say, "Well, Mr. Swift Executioner, what have you got to say? You all seem well prepared from separate meetings. Let's get on with the business so I can absorb it kindly and true. And take away the hurts without too much anger or shame. Without too much feeling of injustice."

They were well prepared and had it boiled down to three topics: (1) Retirement. (2) Boundaries. (3) Vacation. Retirement sounded all right to me. But then one point was that I don't need driving myself, but I am driving my voluntary workers, disciples. "He who drives too hard drives both himself and others." They said they did not want me to retire the patient or the guru or the person who they call "Steve" (because in a fit of delirium, when asked who I was, I had once replied, "Steve"), but they wanted me to retire the workaholic. The guru goes on, and the patient too, but the worker must retire. Ollie said, "RETIRE—RETIRE-MENT."

Nanda then put it in an emphatic way, saying that they were not as good as I was in many respects in my long service in ISKCON. I was used to receiving orders and carrying them out promptly under Prabhupada's strict direction and the direction of the other devotees. That was the rule. Don't be lax. Work like a dog or be looked down upon as lax. "We are not ISKCON—right now. We are limited." They certainly are ISKCON, but tired out from many many years of strenuous work on my behalf, work in which they have not been recompensed or even given much thanks for, so they've had enough. Nanda said he was about to leave tomorrow for Washington to go back to the work grind, where he is head manager in constructing a skyscraper. So this was his last afternoon. He likened it to the halftime break in the football game, with the team battered and behind and the coach giving a last desperate talk to the men to get it together and push on before it's too late.

So the message was that the workaholic in me sabotages them. I asked, "What about me giving ideas that can be put on the shelf or on the agenda to be done in the future, such as my ideas to rotate the items in the Web page more quickly?"

"Yes, yes," said Mukhi. But the others emphasized, "Don't come back 'pushing' on it." Let it be a vision that they can carry out when humanly possible. There are only four of them. No one else is helping. "And we are too-little devotees. Please don't push us to work to the point of sabotage. We want that voice-worker to go and retire."

Ollie: "RETIREMENT!"

All: "But not the guru / visionary!"

I said I am a writer, and at this retirement stage, I have to write at a retirement pace. I'm a writer of pieces, and I can keep doing that, but I cannot do big, big projects in my present health and under my present mental pressure. I then took them on a bit of a digression about my exchanges with Dainya, where we began to talk about the herculean project of an autobiography. I told him that I could not do it for now. All I can do is write my "little things," books of about two hundred pages.

Nara said, "May we have a while to catch up our breath?"

Nanda: "Yes, you are Steve in charge of taking care of the patient, and the guru will be protected. Retirement means retiring the 'worker' in your head. But if you push yourself, then others will be pushed. But please keep pushing upon us your visions and ideas. Kick the former tyrant workaholic out of your mind."

I'm a slow thinker, but I began to catch on to their message. They were presenting it somewhat aggressively, desperately, and sometimes with an edge to it that I found not so respectful. But it was all with love. I began to understand that my suggestions are welcome, but not with a time period, and not even with the guarantee that they will be accepted. This goes for any kind of demand that my new books be published within any time period.

BOUNDARIES

Mukhi said that I am generating so much work that they do not have "enough" to properly deal with it. They cannot process all the orders I give them. After her polite words, I thought to myself, *Thus I intrude, invade, overwhelm, disrespect their space, privacy, and individuality.* But I did not exactly understand the psychological jargon of boundary, so I asked, "Whose boundary?"

Nanda said, "Each of us has our own 'writing shack' (something they are building for me). We have to say 'no' sometimes. No for now. But we still love you and want to do everything. I would like 'Steve' to have boundaries with the writer."

Nara then talked about a big squabble he had with Ollie establishing their own boundaries over the use of the car. At one point, Nara had to shout, "You're not my guru!"

Nanda said, "Sustainability is the word!"

I interpreted to myself, don't give us so much work that we break down and don't want to work anymore and quit as others did in the past.

Nanda: "We want to learn from mistakes—take care of ourselves. We want you to take care of us."

Nara said that when they were making the audio this morning and editing out some names from the past, they made some bad jokes that perhaps some day in the future they'll have to make another audio and edit out the present names and say, "Nanda is gone, my Nara is gone, my Mukhi is gone, my Ollie is gone..."

Out of nowhere I asked, "Am I cruel?"

Ollie answered promptly, "Yes, you have the tendency not to see the tribulations others go through—but you focus on your own writing projects, overlooking what has been done and seeing only what has not been done."

I replied, "This means ungratefulness also, not only cruelty."

Mukhi said, "I don't want to ever quit."

Nanda: "Sustainability—as a devotee."

Nara: "I want to have another chance. I found it very painful when I presented to you all the work we did in reprinting your old books and giving them new beautiful covers. You looked them over with light praise, but what you really wanted to see was your new books. You're not aware of the infrastructure and the legalities that it takes to keep this publishing firm going. You're not aware of all the work it takes."

Swamiji: "But I thought I'm supposed to retire and not see all this work."

Nanda: "Retire, but be cognizant of the infrastructure being dealt with—painstakingly—by us."

I then indulged in my literary voice and gave the example of Rainer Maria Rilke, the long-time formative favorite of mine. I said that many criticize his life because he never worked except at his poetry. He used to cultivate various mistresses and wrote of their experience. But he's also defended by those who appreciate that even if he mistreated or neglected others, he always did it in the service of the Muse. He was working for the highest principle possible, angelic poetry spoken by the gods. He worked on a higher ethical principle. Many people think this is hogwash. As Berryman said, "Rilke was a jerk." But others respect the choices and sacrifices and loneliness that Rilke chose in the most difficult life of the lonely poet. He gave up everything to create what some think are the greatest poetic works of the twentieth century, *Duino Elegies* and *Sonnets to Orpheus*. Is literature higher than life? Is it worth stepping on someone's toes to attain? Should we be sympathetic to the writer who holds his ethics of writing above all else?

As I spoke, I was aware of the "Rilke is a jerk" axiom and of those who tear him to pieces, but I wanted to get a biography of Rilke to find some passages of empathy. I also told them of James Joyce, who was accused of doing something similar, always looking for people to help him promote his literary life, so much that they said he looked at people only as possibilities for service in the "Joyce industry," promoters, donors, people who could help him sustain his herculean tasks of writing monumental literature, and in a not-quite-relevant way I brought up his motto for living when he left Ireland. He declared war against the bourgeoisie who would stop him, but he said his only weapons would be "silence, cunning, and exile."

Nara again found us wandering outside the curriculum and

dragged us back. Nanda said that the persons in the room were sold out to my books. He again defined boundaries, taking care of ourselves so that we can serve in a sustainable way over time.

I asked for a headache pill.

VACATION

This was the third and final topic. It sounded like a good one. It turned out it mostly meant that everyone in the room is contemplating a vacation except me. Ollie is going to India. He said that it was nothing personal with me. A line he once quoted as coming from *The Godfather*, the mafia guys. They execute a job and say, "Nothing personal." But he said he meant it's nothing personal but it's meant to improve his relation with me.

We had a conception that a vacation is a bad thing, but it is fun to take a vacation. They invited me to take one too, but I couldn't think of where to go.

I said I would like to go to Suta's.

Ollie claimed I once said, "Vacation for me is writing."

I am too weak to go anywhere. I need the care program. I can't even go to San Francisco. The travel is too far. The community acknowledged Govinda's contribution to the team, and he graciously honored the opportunity. He's going to Italy soon to get married to Magdalena and should return in March.

So both Ollie and Hari are going to India. Nanda is leaving tomorrow for a long stretch in Washington. Rasa dasa, a disciple from Britain, is coming to fill in for awhile to do the cooking while Hari is gone.

I entered the meeting by saying how I would like some improvement in the supper menu, replacing Indian items with things I actually like to take that are nutritious. Peanut butter and jelly sandwiches?

As I went to sleep last night, I felt hurt by some of the body language and loud voices raised by Nara and others and the cool, aloof attitude of Ollie, and even the last-minute, almost giddy expression by Nanda, who said, "I think you are a *paramahamsa*." Things don't seem exactly the same. I guess the surgical operation had to be done. And if I'm a good boy and retire from work, give others their space, show respect for their work and so on, we can probably sustain and bit by bit "eat an elephant."

Dream: I'm wandering around different giant metropolises, confused, doing nothing. Somehow Prabhupada appears in the background. Perhaps some others were accusing me. And I *was* doing nothing. Getting into some fight with urban men, wandering around. Why wasn't I doing anything for Srila Prabhupada? Then dimly, dimly, coming to me as if returning to consciousness, oh…that sickness, that migraine. Maybe he can get better and take up regular work, but the books he's been writing—are they valuable?

> Well you needn't rub it in—"it was fun,
> it was love, could have been, should have been."
> The most important thing is *sa vai pumsam*,
> call it by any religion. We admit all
> religions contain great saints and slug
> nickels. We want that name.

> I suggested he go to the local Catholic church in
> Philo and tell them a new parishioner from
> Italy will be joining them, an ex-nun,
> Okay? Cool? You don't object? She's not going
> to take advantage of this county's allowance
> that each property can grow twenty-five marijuana
> plants. She'll attend mass and communion every
> Sunday. Her husband is a Hare Christna
> but he will bring her to church and stay the whole
> time and enjoy it. Please don't put obstacles
> in our way. We've heard Anderson
> Valley is laid back and accommodating,
> second-generation hippies run the businesses.

> We live on Sparks' plot, where the
> monk with the headache is in Private
> Healthcare. Yeah. So we're just
> informing you and expecting it's
> cool, a happy thing. They'll get married
> first in Italy, and he has to talk to
> a Bishop there. That will be his

acid test. We hope to be seeing
you in church by early March.

The monk? He always stays at home.
Lapsed Catholic, reads Catholic books
and Sufi too, even read of Gnosis
today, god, that was a trip!

He's got a little beard, face gradually
will become like crushed sugar cane.
Walks with a cane. Protects his young cat
from the bigger cat next door. They
say it's not necessary. They say...
let's leave it at that.

Suta told him Willie Mays was the godfather
of Barry Bonds but disowned him
when Bonds started using illegal steroids.
He told me yesterday.
Both types of pills and all day
in headache. Poor Krishna dasi
can't even take walks,
the Haribol cat is ready to pounce on
her, that's how I saw it.

Last minutes for your praying.
soon we start *Chaitanya-bhagavat* and
another religion's book.
Will it be passionate prayer and love for
God alone, T of Avila?
Or would you
rather read to the group
about the whirling Sufis for a change?

I am waiting for my invitation to one of the nine presidential inau-
gural balls. It had better come soon because it's only four days away, on
January 8, President's Day, corresponding with the disappearance of

Mahesh Pandit and Udharan dasa Thakur. A woman who interviewed the director of the ball said, "Why not just have one ball for the military men and send all the other money overseas for the military effort?" The ball director replied, "No, there are many worthy people serving in this country who also deserve the award and recognition, such as the firemen, policemen, teachers, postmen, disposal workers, entertainers, educational people, teachers of all variety, artists, friends of the President, and so on." No, there's no way I'll be invited. And even if I were, it's too late for me to get ready. I don't even have a blazer jacket, what to speak of a full suit, and if they require tuxedos, I'd have to rent one, and we're short on money for the whole affair, travel to Washington, etc. And what would I do there in my anti-Bush, anti-Republican Party attitude, unable-to-dance wallflower. I could keep a little notebook of joy for my own ecstasies, but that would look foolish, and even subversive, scribbling down notes while the bands played on. Some security official would probably approach me and escort me out. You're supposed to drink champagne, dance with the ladies, and have some credentials.

I think it was St. Augustine who said that a man of God can find joy even in the smallest things in the world because they are all reflections of God Himself. That's a very joyful point of view, very broadminded, too. Not just the Catholics can do it, but anyone, anywhere. Surely you've seen a ladybug—orange body, black dots—crawling up your arm. Isn't it a wonder? Oh but some things are hard. But there's beauty there too, on the other side of the coin, as you see starkly, right in your face, the mortality of all things. That's something that will turn you to the eternal as fast as you can say Jackie Robinson.

Speaking of the President's balls, there's a poem from *Cold Mountain*, in ancient Chinese, by Han Shan:

> *The wife of Lord Tsou of Ti-yen,*
> *the mother of Sutu of Han-tan,*
> *both of them well along in years,*
> *both of them women with pleasant faces,*
> *yesterday happy to go to a party,*
> *but, their clothes being shabby,*
> *they were shown to the rear.*
> *only because their hems were frayed,*

they got nothing to eat but some leftover
cake.

> —Poem #15 from *Cold Mountain,*
> by Han Shan, translated by Burton Watson,
> Shambala Book

Ah, but at least I have my poems, my novels, so there's no need to hanker for Presidential balls. I will be well known soon by all my books. What does Han-Shan say about that?

Here we languish, a bunch of poor
scholars,
battered by extremes of hunger and cold.
out of work, our only joy is poetry;
scribble, scribble, we wear out our brains.
Who will read the works of such men?
On that point you can save your sighs.
We could inscribe our poems on biscuits
and the homeless dogs will deign to
nibble.

> —Poem #10 from *Cold Mountain*

But here's a poem I was particularly looking for, to ward off attraction to pretty girls, not put their pictures on my cork board and say "she's a nice devotee."

A curtain of pearls hangs before the hall of jade,
and within is a lovely lady,
fairer in form than the gods and
immortals,
her face like a blossom of peach or plum.
Spring mists will cover the eastern
mansion, autumn winds blow from the western
lodge
and after thirty years have gone by,
she'll look like a piece of crushed sugar
cane.

> —Poem #9 from *Cold Mountain*

35

The other day I saw in a religious book the word "comfortable" used in a derogatory way. A religious person should never be comfortable. That's sense gratification. But that doesn't quite line up with Augustine's statement that we can see God in every little thing. I like to sit in the Jacuzzi bath and ease my sixty-five-year-old limbs, which are tired and ache, feel the water massage my limbs, and the white bubbles come out until they overflow. And then stand and dry yourself standing before the mirror as if you were a strong man. I like my radio and phonograph. When I get so tired that I feel I'm going to swoon, I can lie down on a "memory foam" bed. I have a cat, who is sometimes more trouble than she's worth, but we moved her last night to the other house since she was so disturbing, and now I'm waiting for her to return. No, I'm not going to the *dhama* this year, I need to be more comfortable. My clothes, my food, my chairs, my friends. They tell me that I'm in retirement and to spell it with all capitals, RETIREMENT. And I should not push others to work. Books will come out eventually, they say, but don't crack the whip. They say, "We are not as good devotees as you were all your life. Don't expect us to respond to your sharp command. And show more kindness for what we have done, to what we are doing. There are so few of us. If you don't want to drive us away, then be easy with us, commiserate, empathize." I had heard this fault of mine uttered before, again and again. When will I learn? I bark commands. "I want this done tonight." That's how Prabhupada taught. But I think I got the message now. I'm no Prabhupada. And they want to worship Prabhupada, since I've already shown so many flaws.

In reading the autobiography of St. Teresa to me while I ate lunch, Hari (who's delighted to read the book) asked me what "venial" meant. I told him in the Catholic church, venial sin is not considered so serious, but mortal sin would drive you to hell. We left the discussion at that. Are my sins mortal? Have I gone to confession? Teresa of Avila worried because she could never find a confessor who understood how advanced she was. They told her she was of the devil, and so she began to shudder more and became very anxious about what she was experiencing until finally she found a guide who understood and encouraged her. How much harm, she writes in her autobiography, is done by incompetent spiritual masters and confessors.

When the great *tsunami* suddenly rose from the water, a fifteen-foot tower of water rose from the ocean and proceeded to wipe away much of Indonesia and surrounding lands. Everyone was helpless, but some American fishing boats went out in the midst of the wave. They expertly turned their boats not to flee from the wave but right into the wave and passed through it to the other side. They picked up a few survivors, as many as they could fit in their boat, and sailed safely out to the ocean. No doubt they were praying all the time, "Oh Lord, please save us, oh Lord, please save us."

We're gradually coming near the end of Krishnarama Swami's *Krishna-samhita*. We used to read from two different books at night, and after the *Krishna-samhita* we're going to do that again. One will be a delicious mango we've been so long waiting for, the last three volumes of *Chaitanya Bhagavat*, and the other will be some ecumenical choice, or maybe two ecumenical choices. Govinda says the *Qur'an*, if read just for a few minutes, is a nice prayer book. He's checking out some other books of prayer method by Teresa of Avila, and I'm looking at a book by Professor C. G. Jung, *Memories, Dreams and Reflections*, which I've already read. I recall it has some fantastic anecdotes, which would certainly keep the guys awake.

> We will go down underground
> or burnt, you better take your
> choice and make it orthodox. I
> want to be humble but not something
> concocted. "*Sannyasis* are buried." Why
> avoid it?
>
> He can play both melodies at once—
> well you'd better get an ear examination
> to hear the transcendental sound
> from a sleep worker.
> He'll get there some day.
>
> Some say Dvorak was a black man.
> The white people say he was white.
> "*What do you say?*"
> I don't give a damn!

No ball dance for me, take a
walk with your metal cane.
I'm not going to break up fights
anymore between the cats Krishna and Haribol,
let them hash it out.

I get too nervous and others say
just leave them alone, they'll
work it out.

"Passionately at every moment,
think of God." Shouldn't that be
the book we read out loud as most nutritious
for the students—as long as it's not
too *technical*?

Baby let me shake your tree.
This is too incoherent like
Satan's babel
to pass the test.
Throw it in the file,
circular.

We want monk's pure
minds and habits
not allowed dirty habits
with women, just want
to be happy and thank Maharaja Nimi as I
told him.

"What is the conclusion of *shastra*?"
It's to please God and His devotees.
So you're doing that mighty fine.
I am very grateful for the shirts
and the money.
And if you ever read my mind

and find my treasure, please sir,
publish those new books,
That would make me your happiest
daddy of all time and I'd ride
in your BMW anywhere you
want to go—oh ho.

You know what I am talking about—
Cal Gold, Search, Dark Stars,
Love and Hate, Resting, Saints, those
books where I turned a corner where
I'm a human at best.
May you dream of that.

Prabhupada quotes the English translation by Thomas Cleary of the *Qur'an,* but it always seemed like a Prabhupada-ism. Just say "Krishna, God is as close to you as your jugular vein."

In Chapter 50, Section II, the *Qur'an* states,

We did indeed create man
and We know what his ego suggests;
and We are closer to Him than His jugular vein.

Prabhupada used to say that he recalled the little Muslim children in Calcutta singing and chanting from the *Qur'an,* and he felt it was very nice. He was speaking of the harmony that existed between the Hindus and the Muslims and how this was the norm. The neighbors of the two religions would invite each other to festivals, and there was no question of violence or riots. That happened only occasionally on a small scale. The big rioting occurred only when the British split India from Pakistan as their "departing kick" when they abandoned India in their reluctant surrender of the jewel of the British empire. Since then, the division of Hindu and Muslim has been exaggerated and riotous. Not before then. And not before King Aurenzeb.

Srila Prabhupada's answer to me when I asked if there would be schisms in ISKCON is a bit cryptic. He answered with force and anger, "Schisms?" He said it as if there is no such thing as long as one is sincere. "There are no schisms, only lack of sincerity." A sincere follower will not cause such trouble. He will follow the clear instructions of *gurudeva*. Even if in his heart he finds something that's being done differently than what Prabhupada taught, he will not make it the cause of big disruption and split. He will abide by the GBC. He may voice his difference in carefully worded letters of opinion, statements of loyal disagreement, like the Supreme Court Justice Warren, who was known as the loyal dissenter. Many times he expressed a minority opinion but followed in a law-abiding way the majority decision. It is healthy that a country or society allows the expression of dissent, but dissenters should not form a new party of rebellion and actively disobey and flaunt the decisions of the governing body. Sounds ideal? It seems to be the only way to keep some semblance of order. And within one's own life, there's still space to live as one wishes, not with cheating or conspiracy, but with a quiet stepping on his own path. In the introduction to one of his diaries, Thomas Merton wrote that in this book he may not have used the right theological terms of the fathers of the church or always appear to agree with them, but all people, all souls, have a right to express themselves in their own words.

Oh, you talk too much. We already know what you mean. Why don't you say your *gayatri* three times a day with attention? Put your money where your mouth is. Thomas Merton indeed. Quoting the *Qu'ran* indeed. Who do you think you are? A cub reporter for the Vaikuntha Press? Henry Thoreau living on the edge of Gokula? Swamiji Salami? Never heard of him. Solomon Burke? He's been around a long time. He just published a CD on Fat Possum.

When the *gopis* first heard Krishna's deeper explanation of *aprakrta-lila* with the *gopis* in Vrindavan, they threw off their sadness and became happy. He did this while speaking to them intimately in a private talk at Kuruksetra. They understood better that Krishna is always in Vrindavan, and since they never wanted to leave Vrindavan, nor did Krishna ever leave Vrindavan, all they had to do was meditate on Him with love, and they would find Him, see His full presence, personally. The milkmaids looked at one another with renewed hope. Previously, they had heard these messages as pure *mayavadi* talk, as empty *jnana*. They thought Krishna was trying to trick them by saying that He would not come to Vrindavan, but as a poor substitute, they could think of Him. They responded like Shakespeare's Romeo to the solace-giving friar, "Hang up philosophy if it does not produce a Juliet!" But Krishna was going further this time in telling them of an exclusive *aprakata-lila* that only the *gopis* could have.

He assured them that they were not simple cowherd girls. They were better than any *yogis* or *jnanis*, and therefore He was not speaking to them of ordinary *aprakrta-lila*. And yet it was based on the same principle, that Krishna is everywhere. But where is He most? Vrindavan. And in Vrindavan, where most of all? In the hearts of the yearning *gopis*, especially in the heart of Radharani. So they should take advantage of their hearts' yearning.

The *gopis* on their side wanted to assure Krishna that their greed was not based in any way on sense gratification. They knew that He wanted them in Vrindavan, and so they yearned to make Him happy, and the only way you could actually revel and be free, be *sat-cit-ananda, was to be in Vrindavan*. Why should He have to plead that He had to go kill some demons? He had so many expansions and warriors who could do that, from Balarama to Parsarama, from Lord Nrsimha to the thousands and thousands of warriors, the Pandavas, and other great champions, *maharatas*, who would gladly fight while Krishna enjoyed His sports in Vrindavan. Therefore, He should not give that limp excuse that He needed to fight and could not enjoy with the *gopis*. Was He saying that He agreed with them now and that He would always be with them in Vrindavan? Not exactly. He was saying both, that He would have to leave, but that He would have to stay because of His love for them. He could not bear to depart from them, or else He would dry up like a crushed lotus, just as they would. And He also had to personally tend to some of the affairs on the battlefield, at least from time to time. Sometimes away, sometimes back. But even when He was away, he was there whenever they thought of Him, because He was all-pervading, and He was especially present in the *gopis'* hearts, because they had conquered Him forever.

As Krishna went on speaking like this for hours, and for the most part winning the *gopis'* sympathies, Srimati Radharani looked down at His lotus feet. It occurred to Her that She wanted His feet, just like She had them now, and even more so as She had them in Vrindavan, planted on Her breasts. It did not seem that Krishna could be lounging so peacefully with His feet on Her breasts in Vamshivata or one of the familiar Vrindavan *kunjas* while He was simultaneously fighting sword in hand in a distant place. Of course, Krishna was omnipotent and could do anything. But She was just a village girl and could not comprehend how all these things could be accomplished. She felt He had betrayed them before, or fate had cheated them in that His absence had been real, tangible, and grievous. How could his proposal for *lila* be anything different? Krishna assured them it would be different. He would marry them in Kuruksetra and go with them to Vrindavan, and if He had to sometimes leave, He would always be with them body and soul, even in the *kunjas* and the flower-petal beds and their hearts and souls, provided they wanted Him and cried for Him.

For us, it is like a melody, haunting. We do not quite understand, theoretical. It repeats itself in cycles, waves come and go. There are four more chapters left. We will seek out devotees who know more about this and ask them for explanations. Teresa of Avila says that reading is very, very important, especially in the beginning, especially when you do not have an expert spiritual master to talk with. Read and read again, thoughtfully and slowly. It will come together because Krishna is very pleased with your inquiry and does not want to leave you in the dark. As to the four chapters, our attentive group will leap to Nadia and supplement a Krishna reading with a reading of the teachings of Teresa of Avila on prayer. We'll even open with a short prayer from the *Qu'ran*. But Krishna and the *gopis* are the base and foundation of anything we read. The other day I heard two devotees arguing about who would use a car, and he said, "Oh well. Just as Rukmini gave up her sole proprietorship to Krishna, so I will give up and allow you to use the car also." What analogies pass through our minds. Better that than ransoms and police corruption.

> Heeded the seeker, complaining the country
> isn't free, and he's right. But what to
> do? Protest music. Savage. Like a
> bird caught and the seeker might be
> a bogey man, he might be right
> he might be wrong.

His eyes are tired. Sounds like the wings of a
bird, or rattling of a paper bag.
Play orthodox. Can't you stay mainstream
for two minutes before you stop
and start your rap about what's wrong
with this country and vibration society?

That's what Prabhupada did.
And pointed out exactly what to do,
not just another ethnic stance
or a dog who had nothing to bark but give
me food and sex.

Close your eyes to meditate and you'll
fall asleep. Better you end or run around a house.

Let's face it, I'm not getting an invite to a President's ball. And it's
just as well ("John Milton never went to a Hilton hotel; just as well."—
Auden, *Intellectual Graffiti*), because I'm either constipated or inconti-
nent. Although I think myself better than the celebrities who will attend. When I would recognize them, my mouth would open (I'd suck
in air for suction on my dentures) and think, Wow, there's George Will,
the intellectual rightist. Oh my God, there's the famous ex-Secretary of
State. What's he doing now? Holy cow, Bill Clinton dancing cheek to
cheek with his own wife!

Probably a security guard would ask to see my invitation. It would
be so embarrassing. Maybe I'd say, "I'll give you ten dollars if you stop
coming around and asking me if I was actually invited. I'm on the list
because I'm a penetrating writer and holy man and somehow the President and the FBI and CIA know all about this, even if you don't." He
looks closer at my card, holds it up to the light from the chandeliers,
and then passes it under a handheld counterfeit-detector his buddy
hands to him while dozens of people and perhaps even the President
glances over at the scene. But it's thumbs up, and he hands me back the
card.

"Please excuse me, Mr. Goreeno, some frauds *do* crash parties, so
we have to be alert. Also, our computer detects that you haven't had

any beverages or danced yet. Don't be shy."

"Is it okay if I don't drink liquor?"

"Sure, help yourself. Cokes are ten dollars over at the veggie bar. But…you're not…?"

"I'm not gay, if that's what you're thinking. I wouldn't be here if I were, would I? I'm just a little shy, and I'm not such a good dancer. You see, I'm like a monk in regards to women."

The security man frowned, and I felt as if I was in trouble again. "Here," he said, "you can tell this to one of our bright coeds from Bryn Mawr." He hailed a girl over. *Then* he noticed my cane. "Was that instrument checked as a possible weapon?"

"Yes sir, it was. But it is not possible that I walk, or dance, without it."

He clicked his heels, saluted, and let me go, but the coed, an oriental chick with a big smile to match my false one, slid into my arms.

"Oh! I'm sorry. You're…crippled."

"It's just arthritis. I think we can slide around gracefully to 'Satin Doll' if you can keep my little hop step in mind." Obviously she wasn't going to fall in love with me, but I think I looked rather cute with my gray-white beard, freshly trimmed and waxed moustache, my big hazel eyes enlarged behind large shades, and my cool, well-fitting clothes, my decent, almost tall height. My bottom lip, decent odor, chic manner, cool, experienced from the 1960s.

"I used to know an oriental girl just like you."

"Was there a big age difference?" She looked to me, bare brown arms, brown, slanty eyes, hair in bangs.

"That wasn't the problem. We had to be apart sometimes, and she used to complain that I didn't answer all of her letters, although I answered every one on time."

"Hmm, that's strange."

"It's just the mail system. The other thing was that we both changed. I'd rather say that she changed, but I guess I changed too. Anyway, our relationship wasn't what you'd call a 'conjugal' one. It was a spiritual one. We were in a spiritual movement together, and I was her guru. So what happened is she got disappointed in me and broke off the relationship."

"Why was she disappointed?"

44

"I'd rather not go into it...To err is human," I said. "I just made some mistakes, and she couldn't forgive. Or to look at the other side of the coin, she got more interested in a different teacher. So she wrote me a letter that I 'formally end the relationship, and I only request to keep my name. I give no reason other than to pursue my path in a way that inspires me.'"

After I said those words, Basie's "Satin Doll" came to an end. It was a very smooth band playing at the President's ball. The girl seemed interested in the talk, something so unusual as a spiritual master breaking off with a disciple. But she didn't want any more talk and courteously backed away. Anyway, the band was taking a break, and so a juke box came on, blasting away with Dizzy Gillespie's men shouting, "I'll never go back to Georgia! I'll never go back to Georgia!"

The President began frantically waving his arms to stop the chant of Dizzy's men, which was so politically improper, and they switched to something else. I also felt politically incorrect. But I don't think I said anything wrong to the girl, and at least I had come out of my corner and had spoken something real. But that was enough for me. I would have liked to have given out some Krishna conscious books, but by the closed-in atmosphere and the encounters I had had with the security guard, I was afraid to even move. What I really wanted to do was go home, but the guard might say, "Why are you leaving so early?" But that's just what I did. I headed for the exit, and he asked me, "Why are you going home so early?"

I said, "I had a very pleasant dance with that girl, but I think it's provoked my arthritis. I'll have to call it a night."

"Oh, sorry Mr. Goreeno. Give my regards to the people at your monastery."

"Thank you. And all glories to the President and the balls."

> Except for the President's balls, it's all true,
> I lost a disciple from Bryn Mawr
> and decades of pain she underwent
> kicking the habit and disliking mixing too
> closely with people she didn't like
> and maybe my letters not
> reaching her on time. Then worse,

45

all my scabs starting showing as history
is recording in various ways and people
are taking new paths away from the
path I chose, the path less traveled
by, and that has made all the difference.

Stardust? Rain. No electricity in
Anderson Valley. A person could go lonely
at night, but I don't because I have
friends. Lost dear ones because I
was cruel and didn't acknowledge
"thanks for all you've done." It's too
late now. You—have—they
are gone.

Please, please don't give up on me:
It's too late for that song.
Save it for the ones still with
you. I know I've done wrong.
No, she says. I'm submitting my
formal break with you, I just
want to keep the eternal name,
if you don't mind. The only
reason I want to give is
I'm going where I'm inspired.

Geez, I'm hurt, but I hurt you,
I'm learning everything too late it seems.
Don't you see the other side of the coin? No?
You've heard that one? E Pluribus Unum,
the gnosis people, the
ones who say No and their Helen
comes falling from heaven declaring
free love.

So why should I be respected? The
plump little women and respectable big

men turn right face, about face, however they
need to place their face to Prabhupada, the rock
greater than Gibraltar (which will crumble)
and salute, crying, "He tried to take your
Place!"

Daddy. Abba, please, please give
me another chance. I know I've done
wrong, but consider the other side
of the coin and please, please,
don't give up on me. I love you,
just between you and
me, all these books are for you,
to capture footprints in the sand,
in the snow. Follow them
running, who touches this
doesn't touch a
book, he touches a crying trying
man of *gurudeva*.

CHAPTER THREE

IN *ROMEO AND JULIET*, Romeo's effervescent friend Mercutio is given a fatal wound in a duel with the enemy. Romeo rushes to his side and asks, "How bad is the wound?" Mercutio replies, "It is not as wide as a church door, but 'twill do." How is that for poignant hangman's humor? My stocks are crashing. Some men jumped out of the windows after the great stock market collapse. Cold Mountain would have laughed at them. He's living happily with rags for clothes, no companions but his flute, weeds for food, atop a tall mountain above the clouds, and he would not change his place for the macadam jungle where stocks grow bullish and bearish every day. A devotee doesn't worry in that way but holds on to Krishna or changes, but always for the better, *anandam buddhi vardanam,* growing in an ocean of bliss. Take a tip, invest yourself in Him; there will be no loss and the gain is very great.

This is not a huge epic. I'm not ready for that, I told you. They took me on an outing to Ukiah today in the pouring rain. Didn't it rain, rain, rain, Lord didn't it rain day and night. Umbrella rain. Some was crying, some was praying, some was running, some was sitting, some was moaning, Lord, didn't it rain, rain, rain for forty days and nights? To Staples to pick out a small desk and chair for the writing shack. Over three hundred dollars. Then I went to the Mendocino Bank, and with Nara's help I signed a withdrawal check for three hundred dollars. The girl was young, wearing tight, faded denims. Other bank workers also wore denims. Only I wore Brooks Brothers pants from Maharaja Nimi dasa. They were already muddied from the journey. The young girl was puzzled by my withdrawal check and took it to her elder supervisor and to other ladies. Nara guessed, "She's new on the job. This is probably her first job." Sure enough, that was it. She came back smiling and admitted she wasn't familiar with my type of check. It was a new form. The rest of the procedure was smooth. I had my passport turned face down, but she didn't ask for any ID. She gave me three hundred dollars in cash and smiled and said, "Is there anything else I can do for you?" I smiled spontaneously, in the glory of my mature beard, and said, "No thank you. You've been very sweet." More smiles, and we departed.

As we got into our car, I asked N. if what I said was all right. "Yes," he said, "it was fine." I said, "I was thinking of asking her to walk again to her supervisor's desk and walk back again." Half-serious, he cautioned me, "If you say something like that, you could get into trouble." Maybe there is a little worry that I'm not completely in control. What if I said something proselytizing about Krishna consciousness? No, that could also lead to trouble. An innocent "Hare Krishna" would be bold but harmless, wouldn't it? It could be taken as kooky.

Stopped at bookstore for Bob Dylan's *Chronicles*, Volume One. It's the genre I'm interested in. Can it help in my task of glorifying Krishna? Narcissism dovetailed. I was feeling a headache. We stopped at a pickup place for vegetarian sandwich ingredients, and I had the same thing I have at home, some sandwich cut up into small parts speared with toothpicks, tomato, lettuce, cheese, and a bottle of carrot juice.

Despite the headache, I began speaking in broken Spanish with Nara's help, and we rehearsed a conversation I will have with the two maids who come once a week. I will ask them, *"Que es el nino a los pies de la Virgin de la Guadalupe?"* We'll do this as we stand before her picture. N. says they will then gabble away quickly, and he'll translate to me. Then I'll ask, *"Que es los hornos a los pies de la Virgin?"* Again they'll answer and he'll translate. I'll ask, *"Que es la ocasion por lavisitacion de la Virgin a de nino?"* He'll correct all this broken Spanish as I stumble it out. Why did she descend? He said another time when they come, they could cook under his direction, making sure the preparation for the Principal be not too spicy. And then I could try to explain how we offer our food to God. *Su religion y nostros, muy similar, Krishna es el Padre, y Jesus Cristo es el hijo de Dios. Uno Dios por apor todos al mas. Los deferences es minor porque deferences de tiempo persones, inteligentes, crimetos, etc. Pero todos religiones de verdad* 'teach' *amor de Dios. Amor de Dios. Santos en Catolica, Teresa de Avila de Espana, Antonio de Padua in Italia, y Santo Francesco de Assisi in Italia, Santa Teresa de Liseux de France, y los original apostolos de los gasperos, Pedro, Tomas, Marco, Juan, Luke, Jesus Cristo que es hijo de Dios, y su madre Maria y su padre Josefo, y Santo Paula — todos santos en India tambien* "teach" *amor de Dios. En Christiano, el officio lingua es Latino, y in India es Sanskrito. En Sanskrit, el palabra por amor es bhakti. Bhakti por Krishna signify amor de Dios.*

So let us make food offering *con priyas Ave Maria en tres linguas,* and then *Dios accepto,* and we can eat as holy food called *prasada, prasada de Krishna.*

Sounds like fun with those Latinas and Nara, but I can't take too much of it if the cooking takes a long time and their eyes and lovely teeth are flashing with excitement. I need peace, brother.

The trip back from Ukiah became too long, but a head bath soothed my pain, and it was good to see my girl, Krishna dasi, awake. I lectured to her, "Stay awake during the day so you can sleep at night and not disturb me." Change into pajamas. Subpar *japa,* write this, glance at the *Nation* on U.S. torture of detainees. Now it's supper and hearing time, how St. Teresa openly denounces herself as a sinner. But she doesn't give as many details as I do.

We finished the scheduled readings before we had finished our dinner and dessert. I lead the talking astray into mundane topics about Gandhi in India and speculations about how they drove the British out. How naughty, how foolish. And now too I will not spend every minute chanting my *japa.* In the little time I have left, I will pick and choose as if eating forbidden chocolates before going to bed. Teresa of Avila says if you fall sometimes, do not lose heart. Keep striving to walk your path with integrity. God will draw out the good even from your fall.

He's telling about himself, about himself, about himself, about himself, about himself. That's what's in *Chronicles.* It's all about himself. I'd rather tell about the Virgin Islands or even Anheuser Busch. At the officer's dinner table, you are not allowed to speak of women, politics or religion. Imagine a junior officer trying to talk about himself and how he made it to New York and changes his name from Zimmerman to Dylan and was the greatest, just as Ali says he was the greatest. Or me doing that in competition with guru and Gauranga. Zonks if I've already been doing that and the only thing that saves me is a few jokes and cartoons. And love for words. You delight in trusting them, as in *Dream Songs,* in which no one can even understand them: *Bright-eyed and bushy tailed woke not Henry up./Bright though upon his worship shone a vice/ central moved in/ while he was doing time down hospital/ and growing wise./ He gave it the worst look he had left.* (From *The Dream Songs,* by John Berryman.)

That's just cut and paste, stealing a homerun from Maya with brilliant catches made running at the 410 foot mark at Yankee Stadium: "The *sannyasa* ashram is meant for complete freedom from all anxieties, and is meant for uplifting the fallen souls, who are merged in materialism. But unless a *sannyasi* is freed from all cares and anxieties, like a white cloud, it is difficult for him to do anything good for society." (*The Light of the Bhagavat*, no. 32)

Yes, I said it before and I'll say it again rather than give the material leavings of "I said so."

But you can stop the eye, swamiji, because he has to see Krishna. Even the selfless lovers of Krishna wanted lidless eyes, like the fish, so they could always see the beautiful form of truth, Sri Krishna. I need eyes to see the false and the possible truths, so inevitably I talk of self, not just reciting from the *Qu'ran* or Zimmerman's own tale—"I hitchhiked on a boxcar (not even true)—I can't remember when I began to write my own songs." Was it before you were born? What's the expose on Wal-Mart picking on the bones of the poor? And if the *sannyasi* doesn't pray, who is he to say? Zimmerman delivers the goods. God's in command in all cases, so let's hear more about Her. Sorry, it is *He*, Paloosa. She, Radha, however, has a will that can overpower Krishna's. Stick around and learn these *lila-tattva* truths, spiced with lemon juice and kids' sandwiches. I ain't no poor *sannyasi*, blessed with oratory, so there's no harm in using the first person singular if you hitch him/her to the topics of the Lord, who is real because Mahalia sees Him in her heart, *and I believe her.*

> 0 [?]
> If you don't have a bank account,
> you're considered in dire poverty.
> So on welfare check day, Wal-Mart
> advertises for jobs. Discounts
> keep the people poor. Read and make
> sense of the inequality
>
> and sexist oppression in America.
> Why does God allow?
> He's got more important things to do—
> apportioning out the total

equality of requital is
no small job. So from here
it may look like someone
innocent is getting shafted
and the guilty is living off the
fat of the lamb,

but Lord Jesus and Abba
have it all equally dispersed
and at the right time
rewards and dues will occur
 like magic and there will
be joy and moaning.

No newspaper journalist has to tell
us. A most powerful reformer has
every ounce weighed out and at
the exact right time

The saints will come marching in,
the blind will follow the blind and
fall into the ditch—

pray says Teresa, even if it's faulty
and you slip. Slippery chanting
does wonders for healing
and curing. Never give it up.

Someday it will taste
blissful to come out of a session in
a disgruntled mood just
to know you didn't give up
and even better than that,
God's pancakes in Vrindavan.

We're in the rainy season. The artist Andy Goldworthy works with
found objects. He said he's been living in the same house in a neighbor-

hood in Scotland for seventeen years. He and his wife have raised four children. He likes seeing the same children waiting for the school bus, and then he notices some of them are growing older, brothers and sisters growing up and people living and dying, the men growing older, and all in the same neighborhood. Everyone knows everyone else. And he too will die there. He goes out every day and by intuition works with the river and the tides, placing rocks and trying to make something that will not be washed away. Sometimes his work is destroyed by the tide, but sometimes it stays permanent, like a cairn or mound, like a beehive. It stays all year, solid and beautiful. Sometimes covered with water, but sometimes covered by tall weeds, like free love, like legends. He doesn't like to look at it after it's done, but he takes pictures of it and it becomes part of the landscape, part of the life of the land. He adds to God's creation. As he speaks on the film, he seems to be a very sensitive man, but what is he doing?

The images were lovely, and so was he a lovely man, but the thing that grabbed me the most was his incidental remark that he liked living in the same place for most of his life. It struck me and made me think that maybe I would live here in Philo for the rest of my life. Of course, I have to visit Vrindavan sometimes if I get well, but to see the seasons change in the same place, and the same few people, getting to know them, and the same animals, seeing them grow up and die, and the changes, and the things that stay the same. Disciples, and your painting, getting better in the same place. Defying the idea that you have to go to different places to get "material." Emily Dickinson stayed upstairs and wrote universally with more experience than a ship captain who circled the world. She didn't have to mix with some celebrities and publishers and big-timers in order to get recognition and learn how to write to suit the world's taste. She remained a barefoot writer and actually came to please more people than almost any other poet with her letters to the world that never wrote to her.

And for a life of prayer I think it would be good to stay here, gradually, gradually reading books of prayer, relating them, I might get a tiny inkling of what it's all about. I might learn to chant *japa* and get rid of a headache by resting. It might really be best if you don't get agitated or bored, smile at fate, greet the few people in your life with warmth, get new life and write nice. Hmm. What do you think?

Living in One Place—Benefits
You may live in this one room, it's called
house rest, they all know if you ever
step one foot out, just Krishna never leaves.

No I won't *aprakrita* appear to leave
but he does go rain or shine nothing
like that.

He must be in this small space, and the
heart or everywhere you'll find Him
and you'll find Him smiling or He'll
turn away.

They have a flat of a thousand cars
so if He's around somewhere

He can't even keep His eyes open to
see Radharani, baseball cap on backwards.
Expecting *Sunday Times* any moment. That
will scat me out of my
head. Please mama, buy me a briefcase
with a lock on it for all my
accumulating documents and a
cherry-centered chocolate and a CD
and a book and new eyeglasses and a
stets idea, CA, requiem
mass, all the passive stuff
my brain is off kilter.

I built a stone house along the
well-cared planet done and the
nun couldn't smash it with her
ruler and the blue doesn't push it over
suddenly so we made a barbed wire face
out of black spring weeds
that poodles don't like the smell of

and can't bite through. The ingenuity of
man over both
was due to his praying
at play. Bye bye black
bird. All have died
and the rest will have to follow
but some of the art will last
for many tides into the future
until Sankara says
who's that, let's wind it *all* up,
and divide souls into their requisite camp, before
the Eveready batteries run dry.

Where did it come from, Bobby? I don't know. Where did it go? I
don't know. God, I hope my little gift doesn't go away. I can pray then.
You've got sex urges still at sixty-five and have had them all along.
What can you do with it, swamiji, so that the same energy can be used
in approaching God? That's a lot of energy required, yours is running
down, time-wise, wise-wise, keep your energy centered on God, who
is real. You haven't seen Him in your soul? That means you've got seven
out of seven circles to go through before you reach the brilliant circle
glow of the energy castle.

Sex? He's a quick-looker. But then he looks down at his feet as
H.D. Thoreau did walking across campus at Harvard "as if he had some
serious conversation going on with his feet"—against the oncoming
maya. You dream of gypsy ex-wives who are like Baul-dancers on a
train in India with eye mascara and eyeliner, like Mirabai, crying out
love songs to the blue heroic lifter of Govardhan Hill, whom they want
to embrace. When they finish a song, they pass around a tambourine
for donations. I thirst in the West. "Was Abe Lincoln gay?" "Is there
anything else I can do for you?" They train them up to be flirtatious like
that. How can I sublimate my charge? Maybe it will fade away. Dove-
tail it into humor, blast it into *mayavadi* jokes or harmless romance, re-
morse. But it's *here now*. Then I don't know what to tell you. Just keep
cool and edit out anything X-rated. Funny your Vesuvio should still be
smoking at sixty-five years old. I think it's a good sign. Better than Monk
just shutting down all tunes and not touching the piano for ten years,

or Dylan turning to a dull prose autobiography. Better to keep your love of words even if they become elusive, as with Berryman, who *himself knew what he was saying* (and Lewis Carrol, too)—"through the forest, vowed, Henry made his chickadee was struggled, small marks, smiled / on his swift passage…" (from *The Dream Songs*, no. 116.)

It's so hard to remember it comes
back in broken shards Dead Sea
scrolls linear, not like a jig
saw puzzle, "Oh here's Maine, here's
Florida." It's painful, like pulling
endless teeth.

This table is sticky from honeyed tea.
What was that dream, darn it?
Talking with Govinda about Picasso and Rodin and
Cezanne, people whose inspiration lasted long.
but some are *eccentrico*, persons who live
just for themselves. "For their art," I said.

What did Rilke live for? Make the best poem
before he died,
his salvation.

We talked about Rodin "Work! Work!" ethic and then
finally I got again onto the phone and told him
I am anxious when so many caretakers
take their vacations.

It will be all right as long as I can write coherent
gray rabbits and run behind Krishna
coherent linear—the Govardhan?
We can't walk on that holy mount after *Him!*
What a clever boy. Oh yes we can.
Who is to stop us? If He does it, then I can,
because I'm a brahmin boy, said Madhu,
and this may be needed for *yajnas*, although

you others must stay behind
and protect the cows.

That is proper. They hooted at him but
stayed in their places, except for Sudama
and Sridama, who made some excuse
and bounded up the hill, "in case some cows get
lost or Krishna needs protection."
You're over your heads, bros, said Uddhava
with a smile.

You have to breathe constantly to live. You have to drink water at
least every few days. You should drink two and a half liters a day. In
any case, even if you eat regularly and drink water regularly you will
die. Contemplatives should call out the names of God urgently, *every
moment, and they may not die!*

Compared to that, this obsession you have to write and die is pid-
dling. Therefore I haven't been writing very much lately. Nor eating
pumpkin pie.

No, no sirrah, don't trifle so with writing. Consider the great poems and how they had the urgency of the contemplative saint:

It is difficult
to get the news from poems
yet men die miserably every day for lack
of what is found there.
(William Carlos Williams, from *Asphodel*)

And Emily Dickinson:
I dwell in Possibility
a Fairer House in Prose
my more numerous of Windows—
Superior—for Doors—

of Chambers as the Cedars
Impregnable of Eye
and pull an Everlasting Roof

the Gambrels of the Sky—

Of Visitors—the fairest—
for Occupation—This—
the spreading wide my narrow Hands
to gather Paradise—
(Poem No. 129)

And so many more of Ms. Dickinson's poems:

Wild Nights—wild Nights!
Were I with thee
wild nights should be
our luxury!
Futile—the Winds—
to a Heart in court—
done with the Compass—
done with the Chart!

Rowing in Eden—
ah the Sea, might
might I but more—Tonight in
Thee.

Oh but it's good literature, entertaining. Not everyone is a contemplative. There are so many types of people, and they need varieties
to bring them to God. How about if within a thump, thump, thump,
silently the word of God, but since many people would bring me to the
Inquisition, I spread God consciousness and tell with many many tales.
I tell them Teresa's early dilemma. When she prayed, she had visita-
tions from the Lord, and yet she still saw herself as a sinner being
tempted for the occasions of sin and womanly vanities. How could the
higher visionary life coexist with a low woman's life? A few confessors
were frightened to hear her and thought that she was possessed by the
devil. She was vulnerable and wanted to be careful and knew that her
visions were real. She cried real tears. They advised her to go to a Jesuit
with much experience. He at once diagnosed her and concluded that

certainly her visions of God, locutions, seeing Him, etc., were bona fide. But she had more to learn of mortification in her life, and that was causing her pain. At least now she had some clear understanding of a corrective path.

Do you see why I am using these words and not just "fire"? Help!, God. We neophytes need early coaching, and it takes some explanation.

Ah, I don't believe it. I think you're just a garrulous drinker in the pub who doesn't know what he's talking about except that he's talking.

Oh you shall see, Fergus, one day I will be as silent as a great contemplative but still able to help friends on the path who need minute instructions, and I'll join in the *kirtana* of the glories of the Lord in the mantra that pleases Him most.

Pariksit Maharaja's wife, Betty, did not much benefit from their trip to Vrindavan. She concluded that Krishna was not her ethical God. Too bad. I would like to encourage her that she still can believe in God. She can read St. Teresa, and even more so, *The Dark Cloud of Unknowing,* wherein the anonymous author teaches us to call His name with any word like love or God or beloved. I would like to chant Radha-Krishna, the crying being reduced to one word. But we can't chant Krishna alone without Radha. Call His name. How little we can know of Him, but we want to increase our love for Him and decrease our sin. There is no use in trying to ponder over all the many sins. It will just agitate you and confuse you and tempt the devil even more, "the devil" of sin. Just roll it up in one lump and say, "wretched sin," or something like that. Disgusting too, spit down your face whenever you think of it and turn to Krishna. Even when you don't feel the ecstasy, do it. You don't need to attend the long mass in a church or the similar rituals in the synagogues and temples and mosques. They are not as important as a simple calling to Him, to Her, the lump of your yearning love. Make that effort.

> Oh it's frustrating when your tune gets
> tired-tuned and your synopsis can't utter the
> sublimity and light touches you planned is
> the Supreme Lord deliberately holding you back
> because your sermon is vain? Your imitation Teresa?

59

You don't pray at all but you grasped
her theoretical dilemma and you theoretically
heard what heights she reached as in a fairy tale,
and in public company
as if you are also a saint, you cried tears.
One who knew the highest
but couldn't explain it because of a
hang-up of mortification.

Hey, let's hear what that Jesuit
says to her. I may hear a breakthrough
for my own soul. I'd take it if it came
as Catholic, Muslim, and I'd
place it at Prabhupada's feet somehow, that photo of him relaxed with his hand
on his lotus foot.

The preacher has to push sometimes
in forty minutes how you can pray
silently in a one-moment prayer.

Convinced you don't need to be
ceremonious of votive candles,
robes, organs, holding hands. Yet it will
be all right.

It's just all balderdash if you don't
actually practice.
Be all right if you can stay awake
and behave and be content.

All right, stop and bathe and dress
do some practical moments,
and God will see that you're at least
on the more devotional side/honest talking.

You wake up with a headache, and the first thing you should do is take off all the layers of your shirts and sweaters and take a head bath but instead you write. Write and die. You write only one line and then take the head bath. Write and die. Nothing can revive you from the dreaded disease. Telling Rasa dasa, a new arrival here, how my ankle has deteriorated. He tells me his aunt has an ankle that is misshapen, just like me. She got it from jumping off a castle wall. The gate was closed but she jumped over it anyway. She was with an irresponsible person. My Supersoul was also irresponsible at that time. Write and die. You mean it doesn't make any difference whether you write because you're going to die anyway?

No, I explained that in my little essay *Love and Hate*. Loving is worthwhile even though it can't save us from death. And it *can* save us from death if it's love of God and if it's intense enough. Love of God can save us from death, if not in this life, then by accumulation in the next life. "Oh Death, where is thy sting?"

Picking out where he shall be buried. Lots of confusion over who shall do it, who shall pay for it. Shall it be the Queens property, the Long Island property, as in *The Great Gatsby*, where he talks of the vast cemetery plots? Shall it be Mayapur or Vrindavan? We have ruled out burning. A *sannyasi's* body is not burnt. I am a *sannyasi*. Why get burnt in Vrindavan? Don't be an exception to the custom, as suggested by the GBC. Get in line. From the queue as it winds around the *pukir* (a Bengali word for "little pond"). Right near Prabhupada's grand *samadhi*. Next to Tamal-Krishna's. He has two of them, one in Mayapur and one in Vrindavan. You could do the same. A special room, like the Christian Science reading room, set up in Vrindavan with books and paintings. Yes, you could have two. You can write and die, and yet your books and paintings go on. "Now he belongs to the ages." How long would a painting last? We bought the best canvas. How long will they tolerate it? The books are on the best paper.

Twiddle your thumbs, twiddle your toes, write and die. I know a man who had a habit of twisting his fingers as if in agony. I know another man who has a habit of masturbation. He can't go a day without doing it. So he joined the armed forces, where there's more discipline, and somehow he avoided it. A military career, but still some kind of Krishna in him. Writing, writing, writing "until the last breath." There are my books on the shelf.

"You mean he wrote all those?" Well, with the help of editors and patrons and layout people and artists and supporters, but yes, he's responsible for the scribbles and for the pictures. They let him get away with it. He had the karma to convince them that this is writing for Krishna. He had that gift given by Prabhupada, because he wrote during Prabhupada's time under Prabhupada's authority.

Yeah, but those were straight essays from the *Bhagavatam*. These are straight essays too. They just look a little different. They've grown up in a new garden. Same wine. They're growing on a different hillside. Same varieties. Write and live.

I know a man... I know a woman... I know a bearcat... I saw a black bear... The lights are clicking off and on because we lost power while I was sleeping. Is it important to write these things down when they won't really save anyone? That's a good question.

Has any book saved anyone? Oh yes. Consider the Bible, consider the Vedas. They teach you how to be good. They teach you how to be close to God.

You mean there's a God? Do you believe in Him and Her? Yes, we believe, and we believe our writing is a reflex, an automatic reflex. We like to catch on a baseball team, and we're glad we haven't been retired. Here comes the next pitch. Thud. Strike! Right into my mitt. Write or die. How many more years in the majors for you? I just got a new pair of shoes today. Thump. Write or live.

Peanut butter and jelly for kids. Eat something healthier. Here comes the next pitch. Punch! You can't save it. At first he prayed that his prayer could be accepted by the Lord, like the prayer of Vasudeva Datta: Take everyone's bad karma and place it on me. Later, he phrased it a little differently, give me a year and *then* put me through tests to make me perfect (and save all souls). Courageous utterance, but the Lord didn't give him a year, not even a month, he moved in with deadly cancer. He's still hanging in there, a foot amputated, but one percent or two percent chance of surviving, less than a year since he made his prayer. He offers his motto: "trite" he calls it, but so much almost reckless bravery behind it—so much it leaves us all behind him, rooting for him, praying for him. "Blessed by the best, would not settle for anything less, and I continue to pray to be able to pass the remaining tests."

It seems impossible that this man will fail. We are all behind him, rooting for him, praying for him. Luckily I had a phone call with him, clearing up a misunderstanding, restoring our love.

Write or die. What does it matter? Well, just think, if I hadn't reached him with that last phone call…, we would have both died, but with so much loss and misunderstanding. Continue your songs and writing. They can clear the heart and help you eternally. Yes, write *and* die, but if you hadn't, it could have made an eternal difference. That unheard melody you refuse to sing or hear, that apology, that standing firm, that opening, opening up. That tender cat. Oh Lord, be with us. Now we're getting somewhere.

> Chop the dop/handstands too
> this man has no one understood. Do you
> do it for romance or because you *have* to?
> It's a master music.
> It's as form of love to God,
> thanks to guru, who turns
> everything I do and turns
> the ship's bow headed to Krishna,
> knifing through the waves.

> *Letters*
> Let's call this, I must write at 8:45 P.M.
> Everything we did with four.
> Let's call this private health care.

> He wants to call it something else
> like new bandana banana for
> *all* hearts, not just one
> fall, once called cool. One
> coddled. Love for all. Watch
> your step. Don't ask for anything.

> I opened the bag and found a
> shoulder bag to carry
> my social security, old age,

old ID, state of CA non-driver's ID,
a little money when you drive to Ukiah.

Are you really going to talk
to those Spanish maids and
ask the question *se ver la Virgin de la Guadalupe*?

Write and die. No matter how
many times you push or tilt
it, it's not write *or* die.
But chant and be happy
is validated on the charts
if you do it sincerely and attentively.
That's our method of prayer.
Haribol. He just took the Deities to bed.
Wore a yellow *kurta* and *dhoti*,
first guy I've seen
wearing one today.

We tease, play, work hard.
I am quiet and I don't push
too hard to get things done.
It's too early to discuss your tomb.
Put it off.
Talk of increased prayer,
love all, don't be attached,
be humble, most important
for the life of prayer.
Read every day.

"What did you do today?"
"Not much."
"That's good."

Longevity is another thing. Yogis can extend their lives. Cats have
"nine lives." But these are petty things. Even Brahma's longevity (311
trillion, 40 billion earth years) is fabulous and true, but it comes to an

end. Many valuable things can be accomplished in only a short life-time. Lord Chaitanya stayed only forty-eight years. Jesus Christ left exemplary teachings in 32 years. So the adage "write and die" is not futile. We are disappointed that Prabhupada at eighty-two years of age could not finish his giant opus of *Srimad-Bhagavatam*. He wanted to do it, but he also had to sustain a worldwide movement with not many intelligent managers, and he traveled constantly to keep the movement alive, construct temples, mediate battles. Now we wish he had given us more books in his own hand. Some complained, "It was not enough, it's not the same when his disciples translate them. I wish he had writ-ten more and more." Yet his disciples have become qualified, and they are putting the most precious Vaishnava literature into his mood and standard, so we don't have to stray to other gurus and *sampradayas*.

Write and don't die. Read what he's given and what his followers have given again and again. Chant always.

Are you speaking ambiguously? No, I'm sure of what he has done and the general character of *Brhad-bhagavatamrta*, *Chaitanya-Bhagavat*, etc. There's enough or too much. In the first weeks I met him, that tan monarch told this Lower East Side smartass who thought that the swamiji had only one book. "No, no, we have many more books than the *Bhagavad-gita*. We have so many books that if you read for twenty-four hours for the rest of your life, you couldn't finish them."

It's a *personal* question, and I answered it confidently with my pen-nants flying. Question: Do we have enough of your books? Has your literary volcano exhausted itself, as some say? Your physical sickness has depleted your spirituality, you have waned to the point of hope-lessness and materialism, just telling what's going on with yourself and your pals, fixing the washing machine.

Now I've plowed you under with excellent trilogies and oratories, and this is state of the art, this is what the world needs right now, everyman's Krishna consciousness, old wine in new bottles, the Porsche over the oxcart, new readers who love, some of them isolated, some of them in communities, who are not straggling behind, not knowing what Thelonious is doing. But I hope you will find out. In any case, it is al-ready solid. Moanin'.

The only thing is I sometimes doubt, as St. Teresa did. Am I a schmuck? Am I wretched? Am I the lowest of the low? Have I written too much already? But then suddenly I feel Jesus beside me, right there. I can't see him, but I know he's there. I go to my friendliest priest and he tells me, "This vision is so high that even the devil can't tempt it, so it must be right." And so I write on, and I'll die, leaving you a nice big library shelf of literature. Pardon me for speaking up. Somebody's got to do it.

> All you do is talk about yourself and
> preventing death. You think you are
> St. Francis holding
> up the pillar of the whole collapsing Catholic church?

> A man who writes about himself is an ego
> maniac, not a Vaishnava *kavi*, right, isn't that
> what you wanted to hear? This seat is reserved
> for everyone. Everyone has the same heart
> and gonads if he's male and if woman
> she can carry a child in her belly, very complex
> embryo. They put it in a museum.

> Similarly, a soul has got unique
> features. Like baby's book of life,
> especially when tots, but as they grow old
> the karma becomes manifest.
> The Supreme Lord is ever
> changing but relentlessly the same
> in the most important, all-knowing,
> all-beautiful, all-powerful, wise,
> abilities, all-purest,
> ubiquitous, wealthiest,
> wisest—most compassionate

> for the past, present. He can change
> His pastimes. He can marry the *gopis*
> or He can be more exciting and
> be with them in *parakiya* (unwed) love.
> He's the freedom suite.

If I talk of myself, it's just because
I want to use my eyes for Him before
they dry out, as is already happening.
My memory is already fading,
at last try for some sound,
as has already been missed—
as messed up in psyche and food
and head and sex.

I will talk of Madan-mohan.
Don't leave me out of the loop.
This is not a *mauna* cult.
Whoever you meet,
Tell him about Krishna.
But not about how you
bought new sneakers and CDs,
about your teaching for the better,
be kinder, Christ may I be
making a mistake? Just a
venial one—I
wait to be called by Him.
Would He hear me
and take me in His swan carrier?

TORTURE

The U.S. Army admits torturing the detainees (prisoners of war) captured in Iraq and taken to Guantanamo Bay, kept and tortured there. Gory pictures in *Time* magazine. They don't make much apology for it. Torture is torture. You torture us and we torture you back. The Iraqis torture their own men who go against them and torture the American journalists.

You can just kill him or you can sustain torture unto death in many many ways, which I won't put in this book. How God is disturbed by his *jivas* torturing one another. We've been reading their *Qur'an*, and there's much mention there of how God will give torment to the sinners after death. We think God is very punishing. But take it another way and see how torturers are the *jives*, and so they must get an acquit-

67

tal of some sort, even if it's not eternal. Or should everyone just be let free without any punishment, even after they've harmed so many innocent creatures? God comes most likely in the *tsunami* in Asia, killing 40,000. The magazine cover: Does God Want Us To Be Happy? Brave expose journalists write against corruption, point out bad doers, risk their lives, lose their lives. Write or die to protect the penguins in Wales and the underpaid and the high-rise bandits, the drug dealers, the high-ranking politicians, baseball players who take steroids, speak at the risk of your life. Writing suite.

This is a more important *tsunami*. I don't know, it seems so. It outlasts all the empires and the corruptions. Talking about God, getting your record straight. You can laugh if you think it's not important. Those are old tales, mythologies. Sure, there are many religions, but they are split up into different sects who fight against one another and just add to the trouble. Many people, important, soulful, intellectual people, people who are asleep and dumb have been awakened by important messages. Not just the scriptures but books by writers with alert souls and open hearts. The books I read in my "search through books" that made me sensitive and ready to approach Srila Prabhupada.

> It is difficult
> to get the news from poems
> yet men die miserably every day
> *for lack of what is found there.*
>> (From *Asphodel, That Greeny Flower,*
>> by William Carlos Williams)

CHAPTER FOUR

SWAMIJI HAS BEEN A PREY to migraine for over thirty years, but now he has more coworkers and helpers than ever before. He's fighting with Maya and the demons on the subtle platform. Swamiji usually takes about four naps a day, and on waking, he usually has four headaches and they are the smashing result of four nightmares. Rather than immediately take a pill by proxy, which always causes constipation, the first attempt is to take a sudsy, foaming "Kiss My Face" head bath, and then before any pharmaceutical, he tries to reach his counselor in Washington, D.C., on the telephone. He reached him yesterday and told him two shocking dreams.

In the first dream, he was racing, racing, racing. It was like he was in the Boston Marathon, with blocks and blocks of people running, running. But it was also like a religious ritual, and he was running after young attractive Priya dasi. He had decided he wanted to marry her. She was primping up to make herself look as attractive as possible, wearing Indian sari-type clothes, which exposed a large part of her back. Yes, he had made a decision. Most of the people in the marathon knew this, and so they were running along in a somewhat jolly spirit. But it was not so easy to catch up to her. They had to forge rivers and break through forests, and so the decision did not guarantee the actual catching up to her. Running exhausted, a sixty-five-year-old man after the prey. She looked back like a deer to see if he was still coming, blinking her eyes, willing him on. This is what she wanted. This is what he wanted. But now the play of love had to be consummated. He got closer to her, like passing through subway cars, broad-ways—be careful that the door doesn't close on you and then you'll never be able to catch her. It'll be many, many stops before you catch her, but somehow he managed to keep on track without the door closing, and so it went on until finally he caught up with her, like catching up with someone after a hundred-yard dash on a football pass. He grabbed her, just like a footballer at the one-foot line. He grabbed her at the ankles and threw her down in a matrimonial crush. But then now that he had her, suddenly—although still in the dream—he didn't want her, and in a Humphrey Bogart manner he said, "Go powder your nose." It was as if he had suddenly woken up to the fact that he was not a New York

Yankee but a Boston Red Sox man. She was on the wrong team. At last, "Go powder your nose." He left her there.

He hadn't been able to catch the counselor. The second dream had come later in the day. That was also a dream with mass numbers of people running like in the Boston Marathon, but it was scarier. It was all running, running in a great mob. We were heading for an auditorium, where most of the people would be in the audience but a few people would be Hare Krishna speakers. My assignment in this was menial but very important. I was to hold one end of a string and Pandu was to hold the other end of the string. That would be a boundary to keep the people contained as an audience, and then on the stage, a few speakers would speak on scientific aspects of Krishna consciousness. Without the rope, the people would not be contained and would mob the stage. We had known from the past that Indian people had a tendency not to keep any order and or listen to a lecture but instead to just create a chaotic scene. And yet one string had the effect of a strong rope, and they would all just stand respectfully behind that string. But we had to arrive there first, or else it would not be effective. So the first thing was to run fast with the string. I was doing that as fast as I could, just as in the first dream I ran as fast as I could to catch Priya dasi. With the extra speed afforded me by my dog and new sneakers, I reached the stage a few feet before any of the mob. Pandu had reached the stage even before me because of his long legs. He posted himself on the left side of the stage and directed me to go to the right. But now I was completely flattened out. The effort was too much. I couldn't run further. "Go ahead, go ahead," he said, "just take the string and walk a few more yards to the other end and stand there and then we'll be secure." But I couldn't. I started walking a few feet and then I collapsed. I tried to get up and walk on my knees. People were screaming, and some of them were starting to mob onto the stage.

"Quick," Pandu's authorities were yelling at me with foghorns. "Swamiji, *get off your ass*. This is it. This is your moment of truth. You've got to do it."

Externally, I knew I could do it somehow. I thought of St. Anthony the Great from Egypt, one of the early, early Christian saints. You remember? He heard in the Gospel that one should give everything to God and travel light. So all I had was the string. Traveling light. I threw off my clothes so externally I had nothing to carry but the string. I had a spirit like that of St. Anthony the Great. You've got the spirit now, it's turning you free. Yes, I thought, just like St. Teresa did it. Now for the rest of the way. I don't care what they think.

"Look, that man is naked, and he's the one who has to carry the string." But I fell down. I remember hearing the broadcaster yelling in vintage style from the 1960s, like when Floyd Patterson went to fight for the championship against Ingmar Johansson. People expected Ingmar to flatten Floyd, but Floyd had a new style. He had Ingmar walking like a sleepwalker. Floyd was bobbing and weaving, and he slammed Ingmar, who went down unconscious. He couldn't even get up at the count of ten. His leg began twitching. It was a serious thing. They interviewed Floyd, but he answered only a few questions and then he said he wanted to go over and see if Ingmar was all right. He was still unconscious. Floyd didn't want to hurt the other guy. Before the fight, Rocky Marciano, who was in the audience, said he had favored "the puncher," meaning Johansson, but it looked like the puncher had lost. Floyd Patterson interrupted his interview and said, "I have to go see how he is, he hasn't come to consciousness yet." Later, Patterson spoke in an interview that when he noticed that Johansson's foot was twitching, he never wanted to see that again. He did not want to hurt a man so that his foot twitched. It sounded like that fight took the pure killer instinct out of Patterson.

In her book for writers, *Writing Down the Bones,* Natalie Goldberg advises that one go ahead and write, even if it makes you cry. Don't be afraid to write through your worst feelings. In this connection, she said, "No one was ever killed by writing." But I wonder if that's true. What if you were killed by writing? Or what if you killed someone else by writing? Someone said that John Keats was killed by a bad review someone gave him. To write or kill. Two men dueling with swords. I am a writer. Like Floyd Patterson, I would not want to kill anyone. And it's true you could never kill yourself by writing. Or could you? My caretakers make the point that if I write too frantically and don't rest enough, I could kill myself, like taking a drug or something, pushing too hard instead of resting. I won't do that. But I won't stop either. You have to keep alive, and whether you could save the world by writing, that can only be done by Jesus Christ or a Vyasadeva. They solve all riddles and give us the blessings. If you follow what Krishna writes, you can be liberated from birth and death. Now *that's* writing. But from what I write, you can't get such a benefit. Or maybe...following the link, the trail where the seeds have grown up into tall daisies leading you to Prabhupada's cabin... where he teaches Vyasa... isn't there a connection?

I was worried when Nara said, "Unless you connect your free writing to something, it's just a lot of babble babble." A few hours later, I asked him what he meant. I had been saying that I was happy about my new books, which had more shape, like themes, or even novels, but on hearing him read the EJWs (*Every Day, Just Write*), I saw my books for what they were and accepted them happily and peacefully. That is, they are bona fide diaries, and a diary certainly has a shape. It's a day-by-day account of a person's life, indicated even by hour and day. And although it may not be peak-by-peak adventuresome, like an exciting movie requiring stunt men and lots of sexy girls, it's very understandable and quite comfortable too. Also, EJW was always *more* than a diary. Each prose passage was followed with a poem that often had nothing to do with the prose diary, and the prose was sometimes just an Emerson-like essay (wow! this guy has got a swelled head!). In other words, they were power-packed diaries.

So I went back to Nara and said, "What did you mean by free-writes being gobbledy-gobble?" He said, "Oh no no no, I didn't mean your writing was like that, because when you do free writing, you always go around in a curve or tangent. You bring it around to some sense again. You don't just go perpetually out and out on a wing."

"Oh yes," I said, "I see what you mean." I see what he means. We do welcome free writes, and that's why we sent those boys to automatic writing school for a while, but they didn't learn anything there. It was too dry and séance-haunted, talking about spirits and writing things that come down from we know not where. We just like the break from the *raja-govinda,* and we always come back to our story. And in fact we were digging for gold when we went for free write, digging for the gold of better *sadhana,* closer to Krishna, in that format. Like picking up a different pick or baseball bat, trying out something new.

Now I have to hurry because guess who's pushing? But let's make it clear that we've got our theme: write and die. All the miniscule and big fat rocks and pebbles, brainwaves, little and big things, from *tsuna-mis* to dried-up wells, all things must pass, even this youngster. I must pass. Funny word, because they're always asking me to pass. They want me to pass in the sense of moving my bowels, but also I must pass on into the next world. Pass on, throw the football pass, catches it for a 40-yard run. Pass on. What body do you get next? Pass. Pass so rudely in your car and you may get road rage from the fellow you pass. Always afraid of some revenge or retribution from the fellow you pass. Pass with excellent honors, *magna cum laude*. But it doesn't matter unless Krishna comes down to you and says, "You've passed." Not like when Uncle Mickey came down the stairs in the house in Brooklyn around 1945 and said, "Pop is dead."

He said those three words with such poignancy it knocked everyone over. I mean the small clan in that room. Knocked them over like a tidal wave, even though they were expecting it. Pop is dead. Pop, patriarch of the whole Guarino line. Now everyone was on their own, separate families. They were liberated from the strong hand of Pop, the dear guidance of Pop. I don't know how they felt about him.

But getting back to the subject at hand, unless I write, something in me dies, some spark. Pop is dead. I don't ever want to say that. Let me die, but before then, let my writing-pop live on to praise Prabhupada in my indirect way, to draw people to him. Let me Google on the Internet thousands of times. Did you hear about this fellow? He had some trouble. He got reprimanded. I know his weaknesses, but still I love him. Ask your correspondent what he sees as your weaknesses. Talk about pain with him, something we share. Ask him what he thinks your weaknesses are. Tell him you don't think one of your weaknesses is that you don't like to hang out with people because there are *babajis* and there are people who like to mix. And there's always been two. The cloud of unknowing favors the *babajis*. But you don't follow that book, do you? I mean, not officially. But we like to follow it.

We like the saying, "The best preacher is a *gostyanandi* who preaches. A *gostyanandi* is a person who is very broadminded and preaches. A *babaji* is one who is caring mostly for his own liberation and who is disgusted by the *mlecchas*. But if he is willing to go out and preach, then you've got a good preacher. Or if he remains in his position of *babaji* but preaches by writing books, like blessing with a wand,

[*bhajananandi*???—Haridas]

by doing something. Of course, writing books, serving *prasadam*, giving out his kind of might, reaching people with it, by hitting a homerun, then you've got some potency.

You just can't go out now. He's got only one foot, and the other guy's got practically only one foot, and the other one's a cane. And headaches as soon as he strains.

That's why Krishna is perfect, and the *gopis* are the best judges of that perfection. But all the Vrajabasis know that perfection, and they want to be with Him always. So maybe He'll marry the girls, although that's against the *parakiya rasa*. We'll have to see what they say. Rum de dum, rum de dum, rum de dum, rum de dum.

What fools these humans be. I've heard one say the best rendition of "Rain or Shine" was by Ray Charles. Isn't that silly? I immediately think of Art Blakey's rendition and how superior that is, and John Coltrane has a pretty good rendition too. Jazz and faith. This is Martin Luther King weekend. Rum de dum. January 16. Don't forget the price you have to pay. That's cited very severely in the *Qu'ran*—torments, torments, torments. So do the right thing. Behave and strive. Stay with the good guy and ask him to bless you with some of his unmatchable strength.

> He told me wherever June bugs go
> Don't be sorry. Dhruva Maharaja was attacked
> by the astral weapons of his
> *rakshasa* enemies. They were *illusory*
> but they could kill you! The Lord
> came to him and said this shit and puss
> and meteorites they are throwing at you
> are not real but be careful! Watch
> your step. Fire back Hare Krishna mantras
> at them or you'll die!
>
> 'Twas a fiery battle! Dhruva and his
> soldiers repeatedly were covered over with
> clouds of oil and pitch and puss I said,
> a multitude of spears, but they
> ducked and together chanted at the tops of

their seared lungs Hare Krishna! Hare Krishna!
Krishna! Krishna! And the demons were dissipated
and fell dead in wave after wave
until more demons came like a *tsunami*.

His invincible arrows sped up and he fixed
the mantras to it more rapidly
and they died in speedier
measure until it appeared he would wipe out
the entire race of vipers of all kinds,
those breeding, middle-aged
and champs. Whoa, their leader
pleaded to Lord Brahma,
please ask Dhruva to spare our race, we
surrender, we are defeated, don't make us
extinct.

Brahma did so and Dhruva, like a good
obedient son, relented. "Just don't keep
attacking our people, that's all."

Forgive. Forgive. He could do that.
I told him about St. Anthony the Great
and his temptation
painted in many galleries. He didn't know.
I told him the story
not in a sentimental mood.
Anthony heard the gospel where
the prophet said give up everything and go
to the desert and pray, cast off all demons.
He literally did it. He sent out a challenge
to all demons and they came flying to
him in his cave, tempting him as beautiful women,
as vampires to bite his neck.
He fought them all with deep prayer
in full surrender
and was saved.

Have you seen or heard of the temptation
of St. Anthony? It's a scary picture.

Other monk reclusives came to live near him
But when there were many,

Too many, St. Anthony the Great
Escaped in the night to a deeper solitude,
But they found him out and another group
Lived around him and he escaped again
To a more remote place and then to another
More remote until he finally found an utter
Solitude with God in His hermitage
And had a long life
Before he went back to Godhead.

Quero escribir algunos partes pequenos de este libro en espanol. Some in Italian. A little bit in pidgin-French. But I can't fake any Greek as James Joyce and Ezra Pound wrote in. I *can* write in some "Engfish" as Joyce wrote in *Finnian's Fake*. But it is best to be plain and simple with as much Sanskrit as you know (along with *devanagari* script, Roman transliteration, and English-American translation).

They want me to keep a sincere, ardent, Krishna conscious theme. Just one theme? In diaries, the themes would change from day to day according to what happened externally and according to my internal life. I admit that *Every Day, Just Write* was a diary. The internal life was not planned, it just happened. Of course, in a book like *Twenty-six Qualities of a Devotee* or *The Sixty-four Qualities of Krishna*, I simply followed a given trail and wrote mostly inwardly, with scripture, like giving a lecture, but it was actually an essay on the them, "Krishna is gentle," and then, as free as you like, on the next given topic, "Krishna is true to His word," etc.

But the last seven or so big books just start out in search of a plot or theme and pretty soon find one *and tightly keep it*. Well, at least half of them keep it, and the whole point in being a writer is to be edifying, inspiring, and purifying, both for your readers and for yourself. It is a type of *kirtan* or *bhajan*.

It is not just for temporary, secular kicks. So when I say "write and die," I've got the metaphysical implications in mind, which I've already explained. Explain again?

Okay. The body has to die, and my writing cannot prevent that from happening. The soul never dies but transmigrates from one body to another. When a person reaches perfection, at the time of death, he or she doesn't take another material body but transcends to a spiritual body of eternity, knowledge, and bliss in the spiritual worlds. An uplifting spiritual book may help him to reach the path of liberation and transference to the spiritual abodes to be with the Supreme Lord Krishna and His consort in a form in which the reader desires to be with the Lord.

Write and die or write or die are purely personal statements meaning I can't live if I'm made to stop writing. Is this literally true? I don't know. I haven't been forced to stop writing. God has been kind.

> Show, don't tell. Here is Sun Ra's
> golden disks. Here is Krishna's mercy.
> Show me the foot imprints in Vraja
> the temples and *murtis*. The ancient
> trees. Do the ponds at Kuruksetra
> prove they are the blood of the *Ksatriyas*?
>
> Is that Govardhan? Yes, every *sadhu*
> for thousands of years has pointed
> it out and made *parikram*
> even though it's getting smaller
> because of a curse.
> And here stop, hear *sabda*,
> bound in a modern-day binding
> by the exact facsimile
> of Vyasa's words and Krishna dasa Kaviraja's—
> *Srimad-Bhagavatam* and *Chaitanya-charitamrita*.
>
> Here is the *Srimad-Bhagavatam*. Can you read
> in Sanskrit? Oh you're not so intelligent, are you?
> Yet you want proof. Here's a monkey

bite fresh on your arm. Take off
your eyeglasses and squint before
the monkeys steal them as living
proof.

I believe. They said hug this
banyan tree and your wish will be
fulfilled. I hugged it hard, desiring to truly
deeply love my spiritual master. But what
came out? I fell in love with
him like a lusty woman for an
ordinary man. I try to chase him
and he barely got away. Ran to
the U.S.A.

I took to the degraded life when
I heard he too was a man
of clay. Pulled down his statue.
Wanted him perfect, wanted
him flesh, when he stayed I…

You are off the track, six train cars fallen
in the grass bent zigzag
fifty people reported dead. No, say it didn't
happen. It's only an exercise because
he wants to write.

They were trapped inside and all crates and surly
Krishna Krishna and the paramedics came
and dug them out. No one
died. Everyone saved. Doom—doom,
let's go to bed I says to me self, you're
sufficiently on the track.

You want to write and find God
if your writing-blowing may be a
way. The people here are nice.

Sweet rice. Not overeat but eat please
so you'll be ready,
that's all.

But what if you lost the ability to use your right hand? Would you still praise Krishna in writing? I heard that once Ernest Hemingway was in an accident that impaired the use of his right hand. For a while he thought that he couldn't even write, because it was his habit to write by using his right hand. He couldn't just switch over to his left hand or dictate the material. Not being able to use his right hand meant no writing, and that meant Ernest Hemingway would have to become something other than a writer. Imagine. So if I couldn't be a writer-preacher, what would that mean to me? I'd be like the walking dead. I couldn't be so ingenious as to be a speaker? Be a manager? Of course you could, but it wouldn't be your druthers. It would be very hard on you. And maybe they would say he has died again. They were in so much debt they put the house on a mortgage. They sold his Schaeffer pens. They put away his plotting notebook, where he tried to keep the continuity. It was all in his head. He had to keep going, even with a broken hand or without a fancy place to live.

Why don't you draw a picture here of icicles melting eternally? Why don't you do something wonderful? Why don't you be quiet for a long time, like Buddha, and come to a conclusion worth calling Nirvana and spreading to thousands of people as a religion of sorts? Why don't you die for everyone's sins? Why don't you declare yourself the last prophet and say that all previous prophets were all right but now they're invalid and you are the last one? Anyone who claims to be a prophet after you is invalid and should be killed. Why don't you set up a hot dog stand and call it Nathan's? Somebody already did that. Then open a hotdog stand without using any meat and call it *bhakti* dogs. Advertise that they are karma-free and filled with love. Say the profits go to lost souls and then prove it.

Why are you so absurd? Why are you so clerical, like a quartermaster or a clerk in a store, always checking on the stock of your clothing and counting what's in the boxes and seeing if it fits you or the customers? Surely that's narcissistic, self-indulgent. All you need to wear are simple *sannyasa* rags. See if you can get into a concert wearing them, presenting yourself as a humble monk. You could even press your *dhotis* for the night.

What I really mean to ask is why this emphasis on writing? He says he'll write or else he'll have to die. Shouldn't the big question be about your attempt to reach God? You've chosen writing as your way to God, or it has chosen you. It's your calling and vocation. A man selling bananas could say it's his vocation. He would say it's the way he earns his living. You know the story about the man who was a banana seller by trade. He was a poor man, and it was the only way he knew to earn his money. A big commercial opportunity was provided by the Ratha-yatra at Jagannath Puri, so he took advantage and went to Jagannath Puri to sell his bananas. At the same time, he knew it was a spiritual advantage to go to Puri and see Lord Jagannath. He was aware of the double advantage and took them both. It's not exactly the most pure thing, but as a banana seller, where else to go on Ratha-yatra day but Jagannath Puri? He didn't go to a cricket match, which perhaps drew just as many people. He wanted to see the Lord of the universe at Nilacala.

But still I want to reprimand you. You shouldn't be primarily writing about writing. You should be writing about Krishna. That's a defect. You say you worship this way because it's the best way to capture the minds of the young, seeking generation. That's your defense, your argument. The hip way is the best way. Old-fashioned preachers will not gain as many souls for the Lord. Is it true? "Give me that old-time religion, give me that old-time religion. It was good enough for Moses, it was good enough for Jesus, it was good enough for my granddaddy, and it's good enough for me."

Don't change a word of it. Don't meddle with it. But you *are* a banana seller, and that's a given, your karma. Sometimes you even boast as you hawk your trade, "Karma-free bananas! Step up and get 'em! Organic, *bhakti*-filled karma-free bananas!" The fact is, it's your karma to sell. You're a *vaishya*, but somehow by contact with Srila Prabhupada, you're like Kolaveca, you sell bananas, just as he sold banana leaves, and you give half of your measly income to the Ganges and keep just a little bit for yourself.

You think you're a writer. In your youth, you were whammied

into thinking that to be a literary fellow was the best. Prabhupada convinced you that to be a *bhakta* was the best. So you gave up all writing in the artistic way and wrote his way, repeating the *shastras* word for word. You threw away your own original works down the incinerator at 26 2nd Ave. Nothing original. He was with us for twelve years. Then gradually, gradually, the ISKCON vise began to crush you with its corporation blues, and you took part in defending it and leading it, but gradually you were being crushed by it yourself, and guilty, finding out later, later that you were guilty of sitting on the *vyasasana*. While all the qualified Godbrothers and Godsisters sat on the floor, you were Gurupada. And the children suffered in the *gurukula*. Might as well write your own way and tell your story of what *you* went through. You're a victim yourself. It wasn't just one or two. You may have been a guilty one, but also a victim. And so you wrote true as you could, and it's getting truer. And that truthfulness will help others to be true and to stay in ISKCON in some way, preserving their truthfulness, being who they are. So that's my banana selling.

Therefore, maybe I don't reprimand myself when I say I'm not exactly a prayer-maker or a book distributor or another kind of preacher, but I depend a lot on selling bananas as my way to worship my Lord. And that's why I talk so much about it, to defend it and to encourage those who are coming along behind me, at least behind me in time.

> *Srila Prabhupada:*
> *Keep on with this business of writing articles: in the midst of your heavy duties, go on writing something glorifying the Lord, and put our philosophy into words. Writing means to express oneself, how he is understanding this philosophy. So this writing is necessary for everyone.*
> —Quoted from the epithet of *Shack Notes*

Kolaveca Sridhar, I mentioned him.
For that you get two points. If you say
Lord Chaitanya or Lord Krishna
you get one hundred percent for each poem.

If you say "I must write or I
may die," you don't get any points
until you link it to something like, "I

must write for Krishna or the penning
will have been in vain."
Buy two thousand dollars
from Land's End and send them—
clothes with slight defects—
to the poor in India. Some of the shoes
are perfect but are "overstocks," etc.
So he did it and the children seemed
as happy as they do in America
when receiving a new pair of sneakers,
and running around the *parikram*
trail. Girls in Western dresses
and pretty, can't even notice what's
wrong with them and it doesn't matter
compared to what they were wearing.

Two photos taken for "Food from Krishna"
propaganda so they can get
more donations. Smilingest
kids. Their inner minds would smile anyway
if they actually knew
"I'm a resident of the holy *dhama*."
but if a pair of Nike sneakers does it,
fine.
We Americans have the shoes and
no happiness for residing in Vraja,
no feeling except to be an outsider rain or shine.
no sense, we don't want to leave
in any case. We talk Vraja,
we laugh and cry Vraja, we know
all the birds and seasons and we don't
envy tourists,

We don't really know much about
the Supreme Lord's book
but we know He's Krishna,
God, and Radha too—

that's a whale of learning
and *rasa*. A trillion light-years away
or millions of years passed as
the astronomers claim when they
look at a planet through their
telescope, life existed on Mars
and other burnt-out planets,
but now it's gone. This
is the only one left.

I'm like that in the distance from the *dhama*
In my small friendly heart
from Krishna's heart
of love.

Lord, will you reach down to me?
I'll ask my sports coach how I can balance my
exertion headaches with my need
for exercise.

I'll ask my counselor how to increase.
There seems no big way
the medical doctor says you
are already chanting by whatever
you do. But none of the others
really believe that. They say
it's too naïve. But Krishna may forgive me
or give me strength,
determination
to revive taste
for moving those old
red cherries through my
worn fingers. Used to rip holes through
the bead bags and pronouncing clearly.

Teresa of Avila said it's very important to have a learned director
or you may indulge in "silly devotions." She sought out learned men,

[Spanish for "in the heart of the body,
the tingling soul."]

even if they weren't advanced in prayer. At least they knew theoretically the right directions and would not lead her wrong. She yearned for knowledge to give foundation to her soaring visions. This seems contrary to *The Dark Cloud of Unknowing*, where one is advised to put knowledge aside while in meditation and simply yearn in devout passion for one word, like "love" or "God"—yearn for lover, for penetrating through the cloud of ignorance that you have allowed to come between you and God. He is merciful and wants to come to you. Hearing your ardent, desperate, persistent thumping from beneath the cloud, He will descend and embrace you. You need not be a scholastic. Simply a lover. An "ignorant" lover. A bulldog who won't give up. Your prayers are imperfect. Your knuckles are bloodied, "Please Krishna, have mercy on me, a sinner."

See how these words are serving, by imagination. Here's a metaphor. We have a nineteen-foot boat. The water is a bit choppy, but the cork bumpers are protecting the sides of the boat when it hits the dock. All aboard, four of us. Start up the inboard engine. Hit throttles. A Johnson motor, three hundred horsepower, kicks foam. Throw the rope from the dock into the boat. Our captain starts the engine, backs up, we slowly maneuver our way through the docks and boats and into open water. The water slaps against the forward part of the hull. Is it too rough to go out? No, not so bad. We will not go speedy. Delicious spray. I wear protective mask-glasses over my prescription lenses. Put my rubber hood over my head. Smiles to one another. We are not on a killing expedition but trying to find God once again, *en el alma de el querpo*.

> "I know I've done wrong, wrong, wrong, Lord,
> but please, please, give me another chance."

> *Over the Waves*
> Over the waves, the foolish crew
> are serious. If you could see
> all their intentions
> but so many lapses, and with little time
> left he chooses frivolous, the comfortable,
> the healthy, since they have told him
> not to stress at your age.

Oh what on earth is more appealing?
Why are you attracted to the governor's daughter
and your own cat and the meeting about
how to keep your bank accounts?

Shouldn't you be out on the docks at
6:00 A.M. jogging a prayer to a young
Supreme Controller? Leaving the
book behind, breaking in a new man,

arrested for store theft. You thought
jail time would be a peaceful monk's cell but
it's hell. Fear of rape and beating.

Stay where you are, as miserable and unwilling,
lull in count as they are in their *japa*s,
The man called
the police and you were in trouble again.

Put it aside, say the punchy prayer where you
say again and again
Krishna Krishna Krishna until
in the last round with Ali the greatest
on the Chris Craft. Don't give up. Eat at least
one crumb, one health drink and
hear your own vocal chords recite
the *Qu'ran* because you want to
know why Krishna is best but
not to quibble, just to be with
Him.

Sorry I fumbled four
times in the last six plays without
rhymes, at least it's better
than falling asleep or
thinking of embracing women
I have known and others

on the hot pitchfork or embracing
the hot metal form
of a woman in hell.

Those are metaphors, similes, *yajnas*
In wordage. It is another cheering way
to punch and punch against
the cloud of unknowing,
another way, just like
any of the nine absolute ways
of *bhakti*
but each one must be tested—
how sincere
would you put your hand in the fire?
Will you die for it?
Could you live without it?

There is something beautiful about sex. When a hunter of ancient times killed a pair of *kalinga* birds who were mating, this act of cruel interruption brought a cry of grief to the poet, who felt grief by his killing. From his heart came a poetic meter of grief that had never been used in Sanskrit. It was called *shloka*. Thereafter, all the Sanskrit meters came to be known as *shlokas*, originating from that first cry of grief.

But in the *Srimad-Bhagavatam,* Srila Sukadeva Goswami explains the introduction and purpose of each of the senses to the living beings. He says that the pleasure of the sex act for the human being (Srila Prabhupada refers to it as the coating of pleasure on the genitals) is so great that living beings will be driven to commit it repeatedly for the single purpose within the cosmic scheme—to ensure procreation of the species. The animals are regulated by certain seasons of mating built into their bodies. The human beings are free to have sex at any time they wish. Sex should only be used, however, when the mother and father are prepared to beget another offspring and are prepared to raise the child with responsibility, love, finances, attention to its needs, etc. Sex should not be committed with contraceptive devices, deliberately avoiding pregnancy or childbirth by abortion. These are great sins. To-day they have become mere political issues, right wing, left wing. But they are very great sins.

Stick it in her, Charlie, enjoy while you can. The counselor diagnoses swamiji as being straight heterosexual but with a streak of homophobia. Why can't he like the gays in their harmless joining? God has created all sorts of bisexual mates such as males who really want to be women and women who want to be men, and so on, bona fide transsexuals. Sometimes they even undergo a surgical operation. The "queer" becomes a lady, Christine Jurgenson was the first big attraction, "ex-G.I. becomes woman." She went on television wearing a gown. The "queer" becomes a lady. Real transformation, however, is to become a soul. Unisex angel, or a male and female *gopa* and *gopi*. We have so many piles of chronic bad reaction piled upon us that it is difficult to discern whether we are actually a man or a woman. And so if someone gets just a little bit of dirt chipped off, he triumphantly thinks, "Now I have discovered who I really am." But you can't find out so quickly just by a few thousand dollars worth of visits to the psychiatrist.

You have to go deeper. The important search is not to find your sex but to find God, to find your self who is beautiful and desires to give to others the enlightenment of Krishna's wisdom.

The Seeker
The seeker walks up a long white road
by himself, no one behind or ahead.
He hears so many teachers,
who to believe?
The one with long beard, no hair,
long ear lobes, a woman Sikh dancing?
The oldest man, the youngest child?
The grand oldest traditions?
The newest tradition just arrived?

Helicopters disturb his mountain-peak sleep,
suddenly beside him in his sleeping bag
in the Himalaya, a sheepdog. He
talks to me. He's been on all the great pilgrimages
for centuries and knows the story
of Christ marrying Mary Magdalene and the

American Red Indian being the first
and wisest, met a Jew in a delicatessen
on 55th St. in Manhattan who met
Swami Bhaktivedanta in 1976, who
told him Radha, a woman, and Krishna
equally rule all the planets but
actually Radha is the highest by Her
love. "Krishna likes it that
way."

The dog knew it all. I became confused,
anxious, gnosis,
couldn't sleep anymore,
couldn't eat. Since my
lover is gone, I've got anorexia,
bought good tickets to hear Branford Marsalis
and Ravi **Coltrane** for the fortieth anniversary of Trane's
A Love Supreme in San Francisco. The doctor says
it's good for me to go to outings

But I don't know if I can walk around.
my feet go cloppity clip. It's like
I am flatfooted and weak-legged,
like a fawn, like a ninety-year-old man.
but why let that disturb the merriment,
you dig?

Afterlife will come, but why not have
some fun in the meantime?
That was never forbidden
as long as it's clean and you don't forget
Hari.
It's even recommended as Rx.

Cry, baby. Crybaby, soaked in tears. But it is nobody's fault but
mine. I'm laughing in the meantime, joking about...
Am I claiming I have a direct link to God? A scholar of this prose,

looking at it scrutinizingly through a big microscope, would say, "Yes, he is making that claim. Just see these sentences like 'I delight when I pipe my flute' and 'My writing pleases Him' and 'He does like the offering I make Him' and 'I write to the people on earth how we are one and we are not doing well. We are testing Vishnu's patience and Sankarshan's rage!' and 'He forgives me' and 'I am blessed by the best, wouldn't settle for less—I pray to pass the tests,' etc."

And then at night, talking in bed when he should be asleep. He thinks it's so significant he turns on the light and writes, but in the morning it's incoherent. This boy received a B.A. *cum laude* diploma from Brooklyn College, but he could have done better, *magna cum laude*. Here is what he wrote, and it might as well have been invisible ink, or shall we call it incoherent ink?

Cry, baby, crybaby and soak the couch. But it's nobody's fault but mine. I'm laughing in the meantime, joking about the presidents, the Parthenon (imagine). I write Ollie to where I was not indeed, no God. But don't hope for the chains of life's make up, come life me? (The previous sentence could have also been, 'But don't love for the claims of next life's make up, come guess me?') And as I did, woman man was but to finger all red bob in audit plan and anybody one hundred and one. There is no way they you true. Or they are plush in pure panthers. Dear Srila Prabhupada, but you turned your back on him. Surely you did, and where are you now?

There was a maid where she stayed angels tried 'twas a gift of such a person how was the angel on the trunk? Any for moth and I tried energy a little to this. You are from my invalidity. Cry, baby, wish you would, but you're dry as wood.

Man, that seems like rock bottom. But I didn't "mean it." I mean the highest things, the best things in my conscious mind, not the slush running through the sewers of the unconscious. Please lift me up, Lord, I want to go above the cloud. I want to be with You in one of Your holy *dhamas*, just as I am meant to be with Krishna. My holy trend's in Krishna, You Yourself, and Radha, and the boys. I must not indulge in it too much but take it as it comes, and we must work together. I must not assume to be the Principal. Yesterday when the Latina maids came, we sat before the picture of the Virgin of Guadalupe. I asked them who was the *niño* at the feet of the Virgin. She said he was a saintly boy Juan

Diego, to whom the Virgin appeared in 1840. He was about sixteen years old. The Virgin asked him to build the church right there, a basilica on the north of Guadalupe. The boy ran to the bishop and told him what the Virgin had said but the bishop disbelieved him two times.

Again the Virgin appeared to the boy, but the boy told her the bishop didn't believe. This time the Virgin gave the boy a huge armful of roses. At that time and season in Mexico, there were never such beautiful roses to be found. He wrapped the roses in his poncho and ran to the bishop again. This time, when he threw the profusion of beautiful, scented roses before the bishop, the bishop believed, and they built a beautiful basilica.

Since then, all of Mexico accepts the Virgin of Guadalupe as the mother of all Mexicans. That was the message. She asked them to build many different churches for her and that she would take care of the Mexicanos. On his last visit to Mexico a few years ago, Pope John Paul II made Juan Diego a saint, to the great happiness of the Mexicans. The cleaning ladies told this and then had to rush off to another cleaning job at a restaurant. If you pray nicely, you will get roses.

> We'll build a stairway to the stairs
> or rather one will be lowered by this
> method, if we "say our prayers."
>
> It can't be a forced ritual but
> a heart-giving. At the beginning
> it is the hardest. "Go to jail.
> Do not pass go. Do not collect $200."
>
> You need a guru. Did you forget
> you had one who helps you?
> Man, your amnesia has bent you
> in the shuffle when the gang fights
> clubbed you in the head.
> Maybe you need another clubbing
>
> or an easing, a retiring to consciousness
> through the looking glass return to

who you were, "Steve," as Swami called you,
then "Satswarup."

Patched what cracked just like
our neem Nitai *murti* has a
widening crack in His head but
they say don't worry it can be fixed.
Jesus, I hope so. Not much time
in this life, already am an official
senior citizen entitled to certain benefits
like a state I.D. card,
two hundred dollars a month.

CHAPTER FIVE

SWAMI JUST BEGAN DISCOVERING that he was being kept under confinement at the private medical estate. He'd been there sometime, but it had never occurred to him. He thought he was there on his own free will, happy as a hermit. Sometimes the doctors and his counselor would suggest different things to him that he might do. Sometimes he'd do them and sometimes he wouldn't. But he would always obey them about medicine. But yesterday, they said, "Tomorrow we're going to go on a little outing to Fort Bragg, where there's a beautiful view of the ocean, and you can go to the botanical gardens, and there's a little house that you can go into and do some writing, and we'll have a picnic. People from all over the world go there to take a drive through the redwood forest, and we'll have a great time."

This was the first time he had realized from the intonation of their voices that they were telling him that he was going. Earlier, they had suggested possible trips to Ukiah for shopping, and his doctor, whom he'd only spoken to on the phone, had increasingly suggested that he take outings as a sign of good mental health, but he hadn't done it yet. But now this outing was just something "he was going to do." It was an agreeable thing, so he went for it, as they say, but with a little uneasiness about whether he was doing this on his own free will. He said nothing about it and looked forward to the day.

Unfortunately, despite much advertisement by Nara about how sunny and beautiful it was going to be, it turned out to be a very foggy day. The million dollar trip through the redwood forest was very dark and very chilly. Swamiji didn't wear enough clothes, and he was uncomfortable. They had trouble finding the place, and when they finally arrived, they entered the botanical gardens and started walking. But he couldn't walk after awhile because his left ankle started to hurt. He asked Nara if he could run back to the headquarters of the garden and see if they could get a wheelchair. Surprisingly, Nara came back on a battery-propelled wheelchair. Swamiji took the handlebars and following the directions, he went off, leading the group. This was fun.

Although the sky remained overcast, they could see the breakers crashing in over black rocks and sea gulls hovering near them. Quite exciting, even for a dullard. They finally found a little shack, nothing more than that. Swami was very happy to find that no one was there. He jumped in and started singing songs he made up about San Francisco waves crashing over the rocks, Nara crashing too, now we'll have some fun, we'll picnic and then we'll write…, but shortly after they got there, a large tourist group, which they had passed on the road, joined them, and everything changed.

Our group had been eating sandwiches and making small talk, but mostly enjoying silence and chanting *japa*. This huge group of about a dozen people came in, and their leader pointed across the ocean to a house on the other side, which he said was the house that Jack Benny once lived in. Fortunately, they only stayed for about five minutes and then they left. That was a great relief.

I, Swamiji, began complaining that my hands were very cold. Nara put his big hands around mine, and they were so warm and big, like catchers' mitts. He said, "I can't believe how cold your hands are." I bathed in the warmth of his fleshy, big hands. I said, "Doctor's always telling me that my extremities are very cold because I have poor circulation there." Rasa dasa, who was along for the trip, said that his wife also had cold extremities due to poor circulation. My hands warmed up quickly, and I got ready to write. But what is there to write about?

All these preliminaries, but now I'm stuck looking out at a picture of an overcast sky, Jack Benny's house on the other side of the bay. Oh, I can tell you one thing. As soon as we arrived here, I felt an urge to defecate. I ran into the men's room, but it was too late. I defecated some into my underwear and had to scrape it off with the toilet paper. I had arrived too late. But I managed to scrape most of it off, and I dumped the rest of it into the toilet bowl, like a good boy. Two dumps in one day.

Oh dear Lord, is this what we had planned for? Happiness on the run? Happiness steering the motorized wheelchair, which I will now be happy to drive back? I thought I had something more to say, something about being a book writer and devoting it all to the Lord. When will that day come when tears will come to my eyes by chanting Your holy names, and my voice will be choked up by uttering the name Krishna? This world is vacant without you, I shall cry. And it will feel that way. There will be nothing. She is unhappy without Krishna, and then when Krishna comes to Her, She is unhappy again for another reason. Radha and Krishna, Radha and Krishna. It is hard to understand. Just try to be a good devotee. Try to say your prayers, try to say your prayers. Try to say the name, naked, thump thump thump, with the very beat of your heart, thump thump-thump thump-thump. You don't have to think of those difficult pastimes, just thump-thump, thump-thump, thump-thump. Hare Krishna, Hare Krishna, Hare Krishna. You don't even have to keep your eyes open. When you open them, you see you're in a cold shack all alone. It's so nice to be all alone.

Oh, they want me to write different kinds of books with less reference to Krishna. Make it so you can throw it out of the ballpark, the confines of Yankee Stadium, way, way out there, so that everyone in Mexico can read it, where they worship their Virgin of Guadalupe, or they don't worship anybody. Way, way, way out there, where the *tsunamis* are hitting the beach, way out there into the heart of Iraq, Baghdad, South Korea, 55th Street, New York City, California, the smart kids, the one individual who is my reader, whom I am in love with but don't need to ever meet, but I'd like to hear from him too, that sweet pie, that porkpie hat, although he's passed away, he can read from the dead. He's a one hundred percent American who'll be remembered before we're all dead. That's what they want me to do.

Do I have to remove Krishna's names to do it? No, you just have to be stronger in all ways so that they can't say in their crotchety ways, "Oh, this is Hare Krishna stuff, this is fatally parochial, this is running into the canon." No, I'll stuff it back into their pipes so they can smoke it. I'll stuff it back into their rear ends. I'm mad as hell. They won't keep me confined. I'll tell them where to get off. They've kept me so petrified by those remarks. I mean Murray, who said, "You too soon wrap it up in the canon. You should read Rumi. He's fearless," and Kowit with his remark, "You are fatally parochial." I'll keep Krishna and not be fatally parochial. I'll prove that He is everywhere. Right, Walt Whitman? I am the locomotive, I am the woman in labor, genital to genital, lopping off the soldier's gangrene arm, but doing it the right way, the Krishna conscious way, everything is everything, the sun is the sun, a book that's Krishna conscious but doesn't proselytize itself. It's not a born-again fundamentalist book but it's a fundamentalist fundamentalist fundamentalist. As fundamentalist as the rocks and the waves pouring it. Hallelujah, *Haribol*. I won't hide my cards, but I won't be a preacher to bother your ass.

94

Why do you think you're confined? That's your paranoia.
The only thing holding you back
is yo' self, baby.

Yeah, I think so. You cats got to be upright.
You'll be flying high and you'll read
the right books
and spare time for Piere pierse.
In any language, here comes dat determined lad,
the **tercerio** time to the bishop whose
annoyed—but this time Juan has a big apron full

[THIRD in Spanish, research]

of out of season roses
from the Virgin Mother of Guadalupe
who said bishop you'd
better heed this boy and build me a big
basilica on the hill of Mexico City
and I will always protect Mexico.
Now the *parikrama* to see her continues with thousands
of people proceeding on their knees all times of the year.

The fellow in the mature beard is
just a pint-size pipsqueak.
He never read a slick *New Yorker*
story and doesn't know how to untangle a participle
or dramatize, make character or drama,
dénouement. He just shoots ISKCON
bullets, giving what he learned in the streets
and apartments of his youth and even
his later age. I'm telling you the
friends he's got can go
a long way to pushing a KC hit
for the modern age if it
pleases Lord Chaitanya.
I think so. Do you want it, Lord?

What does it matter if I'm confined by force? Where would he go
anyway if he had freedom or free will? He'd go where the divining rod

95

led him, where his passions wanted to go, or his intellect, confused mind or whatever. Where the shadow wanted him to go all along, where the dreams lead him at night so consistently, back to his ex-wife, into the interior castle but never getting far, stuck in a mote, stuck in a motel.

I mean seriously, where would you go? Just now you said out loud, "This is my house. I'm home." It felt nice. Is that what you meant? But you can't stay here forever. Tear the boards down, tear the doors from their hinges, as Whitman said,

> Unscrew the doors themselves from their jambs! Whoever degrades another degrades me, and whatever is done or said returns at last to me. Through me the afflatus surging and surging...if I worship something more than another, it shall be the spread of
> My own body or any part of it
> Translucent mold of me it shall be you.
>
> —Walt Whitman, *Song of Myself*

No, that's not for me, that supermaniac of ego. He can't tell self from Self and doesn't know who God is. I don't believe Walt, I know so much more, but still I fall shorter.

Where do I want to go if I am free? Hold your divining rod steady. Where does your free will want to take you? What does your accumulated passed karma say? Can't you correct it? Can't you go where the Lord wants you to go? Hold steady, don't veer to the right or the left, don't go where the modes of nature call you.

Go then right. Find a way so that on your own judgment day He will say, "Come to Me, I see in your heart your real desire is to be with Me forever. You've passed the tests. Just barely, but you've passed, and that's mostly due to miraculous 'chance' of being linked to Prabhupada."

Now what's this talk they want you to package your books in a way that it won't be too obvious you're a Hare Krishna man, because it might not sell books to those who are not inclined? What shall I do about that? Should I describe myself as a "seeker," and I'll tell them whom I am seeking? Shall I leave it to guess? But all the fun is in the particulars, all the angst is in the real. I know a person, and he knows me, and all the truth is there. He does know me, he gave me a name, and to my great shame, I've almost disowned him and disobeyed. But still I'm sure he knows me despite my disappointments, and I'm still writing for him. So I shan't take out his name, although I've changed my clothes and grown a beard. I shan't take out the *sampradaya* words just in the hope of catching a new audience who we think may not like to hear the syllables *pra-bhu-pada*. They've swallowed down Paramahamsa Yogananda, Vivekananda, Maharaja Hrsikananda, Deepak, Maharishi, Ravi Shankar, Ravi Coltrane, Mahavishnu, Elvis Presley, U2, the Ides of March, Cher, Madonna, George W. Bush by fifty-one percent—"We're going to smoke them out!"—so anything is possible. Just throw that curve ball fast on the lower inside, on the lower outside, on the high outside with changeups and more speed for nine innings at a stretch. *California Search for Gold, Write and Die, Sanatorium,* collections of poems, put an elephant in a bag—there's no way. Do what you can, so why not this? Italian-American served down dish. He said he's All-American, original as can be, to be remembered long after everyone's gone.

But surely he's dipped into W.C.W. and way back then it was e.e. cummings and Thomas Wolfe and Kerouac. At least in some way they lured him on, although not a trace of it is left. He went through those phases, and the *Bhagavatam,* of A. C. B. S. P. running through his veins.

I mean that's the meaning. When my teacher said, "You write very well, and I say this not just because you're in a small school. I've taught in big schools too, and you're really first class. But you seem to lack a meaning. What is it you want to say?" I had no answer. What is it that I wanted to say?

But now I know. I want to say we're not this body, we're all spirit soul. The body is a covering, and when you're born, your dying begins, and when you're dead, the soul goes on to take a new body. What kind of body? Depends on your karma, the kind of acts you've done during this lifetime, whether you've turned your back to the Lord or ardently sought him and pumped and pumped and pumped against that dark cloud of unknowing and helped others as hard as you could without embarrassment, helped them to come. Worked, in other words, as a servant of the Lord to spread His name and glories.

If you've done that to everyone you've met, then you might just go to Him, to Lord Chaitanya, to Prabhupada, and help push on the movement, telling people how to get out of the corruption, the sensual fleshpot, the awful torture of human to human, of human to tree, of

97

animal to animal that goes on every day as if it were right. Oh Doctor A. I've got plenty to say, and conviction in it, too. So I know what to write, but I just need to say it in a way they'll accept, and I'm trying that out with these poems and frames.

And I'm trying to work out my own solemnities and wise cracks and troubles. This year they slapped me on the wrist. People don't look at me so much as one to be trusted. I have to get it together, cure my aches, become more pure and fit in the body. Oh I know *what* to say and have learned how to say it. That's why I want to write until I die. That's why I want to write and die, and that's why I have to write or die. There's nothing else worth doing.

So let them confine me as long as I've got a pen and some paper and as long as I can sweetly cajole them to publish these books, and we can think of a way to spread them.

And that's hard. That's hard. That's really hard in this market of junk and trinkets. It's like trying to sell Manhattan again for twenty-four dollars. But we'll die trying, and Krishna will be proud of us. Maybe sometime in the future we'll find these manuscripts in a clay jar and realize you're the answer to the sexus and the plexus and the nexus. We've got to try anyway and not give up.

Writing is okay, and he says he can't live without it. But what about chanting?

Oh I know that's the tops, but I can't do it.

What's your excuse?

The medicine makes me sleepy.

Really?

Yes, and I've got other excuses too. This prolonged period of sleepy *japa*… you see, I could use that time to do things in *awake* Krishna consciousness. I could write or I could answer letters or I could talk to people, make a phone call, be nice to someone, give them some instructions, instead of just nodding in my head or trying to chant 1,728 times. And you know what that's led to? It's led to lack of taste. So that's the worst position.

I thought you'd reached your quota back when that book came out, *California Search for Gold*?

That was a different time. Things have slipped, and they've rooted now, too. Way down.

You don't believe it when your doctor says, "Everything you do is chanting. You don't have to chant anymore in this lifetime"?

No, I don't believe it. I think he's just being very soft and gentle. He's trying to say, "Don't worry, stick it out. The time will come when you'll chant again." But literally speaking, he can't say something else is a substitute for chanting.

So what will you do?

I spoke with my counselor, and he gave me some good practical ideas. At first we were going to settle for not chanting and doing other spiritual things, things that even brought tears to my eyes, like reading about Teresa of Avila and the dark cloud of unknowing. But then we got back inevitably to chanting *japa*. He said to me, "It's between you and Prabhupada." When he said that, I said, "Then I have to chant." Prabhupada wouldn't be satisfied with my reading *The Interior Castle*.

So my counselor suggested that I forget counting in numbers for now. Give up the clicker and use the beads. I told him my difficulty, which I think is due to my nervous disorder. When you begin chanting, you start from the head bead and go counterclockwise, right? Well when I start that way, an hour later I still won't have reached the end of one round. Something happens where I lose my sense of direction and start going back and forth, back and forth, within one round and never make it to the end of a single round. It's a dysfunction. Very frustrating, and that's why I took to the clicker. But he advised me, "Well, just chant on the beads anyway and don't care about the number." This seemed like a liberation to me, because Krishna doesn't really count, and even if I don't reach the end, I'll still be chanting the beads and reach "the end." I'll still be chanting the beads, adding them up. The main thing is not numbers but ardent love for God.

So my new plan is to always wear my precious faded red beads around my neck in a beautiful bead bag that Mother Yamuna dasi gave me. It shows Lord Chaitanya chanting His beads. The other part of the plan is to not count the beads but chant on them whenever I have an inclination. Also, try to chant at least a little bit every hour. I may find that there are some parts of the day that are better for chanting than others. That's all, a simple plan.

When I first came to Krishna consciousness, I was a good chanter, and now Krishna has taken the taste away. He has some plan, and I don't want to react by turning my back on Him and giving up the chanting. In one of her books, Teresa of Avila gives an example of a gardener pulling up water with a bucket from the well. When there is lots of water in the well, the work is easier, and it's even easier if the garden gets regular rains or has an irrigation system. But it's hardest of all when the well is completely empty. But even at that time, the gardener should go every day and lower the bucket and pull up the empty bucket. What? That sounds absurd. Why go through the ritual of lowering and raising an empty bucket? But used as an analogy for prayer, she says that God appreciates her act of prayer even when we lower an empty bucket—mechanical, arid prayer—and raise the empty bucket. Although it appears to be useless, we should be confident that God is pleased with it. And so here I go, arid, with my bead bag strapped around my shoulder. The others will see. Oh I'll be so proud and have my fingers again in contact with those precious faded beads from Tandy's, after almost forty years still not broken. It's like Bill Evans wrote in his song, "Yet Ne'er Broken."

> Weep for me, red beads, I ain't quittin'
> for purgatory yet. Those beads were well
> worn down when I stopped using them
> a few years ago. They are sitting like Rupa
> Goswami's relics or Al Capone's hat in
> a museum now, unused and gathering a bullet hole of dust.
> Not as famous as Carl Perkins'
> "Blue Suede Shoes."
>
> So who cares who is counting them?
> I'm picking them up and wearing them always
> like the doggies in Iraq
> who keep their automatic machine guns
> always wrapped around their bodies
> pointing from their chests.
>
> My bullets are not for terrorizing
> innocent Iraqi citizens. They are for

punching holes against the dark cloud
of unknowing.

Another
for my brother, for all souls
what does it matter if you don't like
them? You can pray for them. They
are the same as you. Souls of Govinda.

You are so dry you lower the bucket
and the well is empty but Krishna says,
"Go on lowering the bucket. I appreciate
your dry work." It's senseless you
say with your logical bearded brain.
Go on lowering and picking up
the empty bucket. But it's dry, dry!

I appreciate it, says Krishna.
You get credit for it. It's on your side.
Soon there will be
water. *Haribol.* He who laughs
laughs last. The last cry for the resurrection
of Almas
as possible by the power of the holy beads,
write or write.

Your Honor, so far the defendant has admitted that although it
gives him great taste to put pen to paper, so that he more or less cannot
live without it, it is more imperative to follow the first order of the spiritual master, namely, to ardently say the holy names of God. He can
now write with taste, but he can neither say the names with taste or
even mechanically. But he believes it is better to say them mechanically
rather than neglect to say them at all.

Objection. I think the chanting attorney is confusing two things. We
never said that writing should supersede or is more important than chanting.

Judge: Objection overruled. The discussion of chanting *is* proper within a context of writing or "write and die."

Prosecuting attorney: Let me continue. I also am not trying to make an exclusive boycott on writing. I'm just saying that there must now be no exclusive boycott on chanting. It must have its place, and that place I am not mandating except to say the bead bag should be worn as much as possible. The clickers should be all put away in drawers. All attempts at counting the number of beads should be suspended. The point is to chant as much as possible or whenever possible. These "laws" will have no deleterious or undermining effect on writing sessions. They will only increase chanting. It is a win-win proposal. It will only eliminate those horrible sessions of falling asleep while chanting or the equally horrible proposal of complete stopping of chanting. The actual number of rounds chanted may be more or less, but we are asking that the beads be worn and that frequently they be touched and the holy name be said. Perhaps as much as every hour, that is all. We feel that it is certainly true that the medicines make one sleepy while chanting, but if we experiment to try a little bit of chanting very frequently, we may find there are some parts of the day when chanting is more amiable and one is able to stay awake better. You give it more of a chance.

Judge: Any questions?

Writing attorney: We have not really begun this proposal, so I don't know if the big beads will actually be possible. If not, I will use the smaller beads and the Auckland bead bag. I am certainly willing to make the experiment.

Judge: All right. Meeting dismissed.

> This is strange music.
> We don't know if we can sustain it.
> Krishna wound up His earthly pastimes,
> That's what we want here. Or sometimes
> He called me Sir Isaac Newton because
> I am so impractical and foolish.
>
> I was becoming intimate fast but
> I took his affectionate cuts as lacerations.
> It was a full moon last night and
> they kept telling me how beautiful it was

and told me to look at it. So I went outside but
I said, "I don't like it. It's
Too glaring, like looking into a headlight beam."
They admitted I was right, and they said, "Yeah, but
look at the lights on the shadows
around it." *That* I agreed,
it was beautiful, although too cold
outside.

We're in school, but we were supposed to let out early. It was hard for me to look back because of the pain in my eye, but I kept trying to look back, and I asked the guy next to me, "Have we been let out yet?" He kept saying emphatically, "No, no, not yet, not yet." We ran on, we ran on.

My ex-wife wife was running beside me as usual.
In her usual dream role
Trying to get me to go over to Rasika Maharaja.

Lots of people were running. The thunder was heavy
But we were indoors running upstairs running through the high school building. Again I turned with pain and asked my question. "Are we able to get out yet? We're supposed to get out early." "No," they said, "not yet, not yet."

Little did those guys know how much I wanted to get out, how much I was already out in my mind. They didn't know I didn't want to be in anymore.

What did you want to do, play the splash drum?
Don't ask me trivial questions.

I'm not telling you the truth. I can't tell you, I can't reveal that much, but I'm just telling you something. You can guess the rest.

I don't want to be in it.
Little do guys like you know little do guys like you know little do guys like you know
and I can't tell you because it's a secret.

Can we get out yet? Emphatically he says, "No, I can't tell you."

Populi? But *sadhus*
Prabhu. Don't you have to
care? Yeah. You're in that loop again.
Better stop. When I said I'm confined, not free,
I was just putting them on.
It was a way to attract the bikers.

I'm listening to Stritch on flute and applied tools,
Eb contrabass and pop guns. That may
have an effect on my chaos.
Why don't you be a sweet girl
and go home to your bead bag?
You can wear your engineer's hat.
This music is too dissonant for me.

DREAM

Woke up with a splitting headache from a dream. In the dream it was settled that I would marry my former wife. A big big festival was taking place in ISKCON. I had to step down from *sannyasa,* but it was settled. It was of course socially humiliating, but everyone was satisfied that I was doing the thing that was somehow best for me. My wife seemed to agree, but then later she came up to me urgently and said, "We'll have to have separate apartments," and she interjected all kinds of Indian expressions and expressions that I supposed she learned from Rasika Maharaja. I thought to myself, *"Oh no, this is going to be hell. I'll have to maintain two wives,"* because I had one wife, and I was going to have to have two wives. I would have to get a job or something. And I understood she was doing this to ensure her chastity. She didn't want any kind of sex in marriage, and that was good on her part and I was willing to do that, but it was going to be a hell of a lot for me. But I agreed with her, and I said, "And the benefit is that I will get the association of Rasika Maharaja." "Yes," she said. And I said, "And you'll get the association of Prabhupada." She was very eager to get that, and she said, "Yes, yes, and I will be able to get the association of Prabhupada," but she was very firm that everything had to be separate. I was to have no personal association, so if I had any ideas of sense gratificatory marriage, she was making it clear that she didn't want anything to do with me, but I would have the satisfaction of some kind of social status as being married to her.

I then woke up with the idea that this was completely not something I wanted, because what was unsaid, I realized, was that I did want a personal relationship. What I craved was personal. Don't call it sex union, but what I craved was personal relationship. I didn't want a distant relationship with my ex-wife, I wanted a personal relationship with somebody. Very personal. Like in other dreams where my sister is my close companion, like those dreams where my sister is about to have a child and I'm there. *Ay yai yai.*

So anyway that's that dream where I would then probably have to go around and tell everybody that the marriage was called off, and I don't care if they don't make me a *sannyasi* again, but there's no way I'm going through with that marriage to live separately from her and maintain her and have all her shit, meaning the way that she would come by and want something from me socially, and we get the benefit of Rasika Maharaja as my only reward, and her demanding something from me as a wife and me getting no entitlements of a very personal relationship. Hi-ho Steve-oh. I'd rather write than die. But if you've got your ex-wife as a new wife, maybe you could chant sixty-four rounds a day. How about that?

The "dream or die" myth is a very subjective one, my personal religion. It goes back to my seventeenth year and grows to fullness on the Lower East Side. There I was the monk worshiping at the altar of poverty, holy poverty in the cold-water flats of Suffolk Street, then Avenue A, then 11th Street, and so on. Funny odds that I was never mugged or violently attacked, although I was constantly robbed in my 11th Street apartment. I had no possessions at all but pills and one suit, which I hid under the mattress when I wasn't actually wearing it. As I say, it was a myth that I lived and believed. I held onto it tenaciously. I didn't want to do anything else, such as go back and live with my folks. I did not want to commit suicide or the near equivalent of it, reenter the military.

If I had lived in another world and someone had arranged it to my liking, I would have accepted a marriage and worked at a job to support it. But we were already in the time of the 1960s, when no one did such things. My parents wanted me to get married, but we were already at a time in our society where you had to go out and get your own girl, just like we see in the Vedic marriages where the red dot is put, just a dot of vermilion now, to signify that you have drawn blood from an opponent to win your bride. I could not fight to win a bride. I could not aggressively woo any girl. She would have to aggressively fall in love with me and drag me to the altar. And she would have to also worship my writings. I have heard vague accounts that Nora Joyce was something like that to James Joyce. "She made me a man," he said. But she did not worship his writings. She didn't need to.

Other data: the approximately three-year period of living on the Lower East Side, LSD, etc., made a deep imprint. Life is mostly lived out. It *is* confined, if not by some state authorities, then by the very nature of the body, bones and flesh and by the fact that we all have a certain longevity and nobody lives more than a hundred years. At least this specimen is not going to live longer than that. The longevity is not the real thing. Therese of Liseau yearned to die early and go back to Godhead. Teresa of Avila, in her childish play, practiced for martyrdom. They wanted to go to the other world. Yes, they believed there was such a place, and the data we have on this man is that he screamingly, clutchingly believes it so. He has an image of himself crying and hanging on as one would hang on to the feet and to the *dhoti* of the spiritual master A. C. Bhaktivedanta Swami Prabhupada, asking for atonement and asking, "Please, please, don't give up on me." He doesn't really know what it means to die, so in that sense, this book and talk of death is shallow.

Hasn't even been near death. That's not true either. He's been near there but came out of it. And when he was near, he was not "himself."

Further data would mostly be material—height, weight, how many points he makes in a game, and that's not important unless you're an athlete being written up in *Time* magazine.

Makes rhymes, realizes dimes, or worse, almost nothing, compared to the old days

When they could buy you a Coke.

> Lately he's been crying
> emotions coming quick. He likes that softness
> and wouldn't trade it for a John Wayne fix.

Let him cry, let him cry
let him burst into a dam
of cathartic flowing down
unashamed, unabashed
not changing a line to suit the publisher, the packager,
the audience. If their idea goes against the realization
of the soul.

Yes he's been quick to cry and not afraid to show his face
and grab a hanky and look right in the face
of a companion and say, "This is what it was like,
this is what they did to me.
this is how I felt.
This is who I am" and blows his nose
and everyone knows it's a kind of show
of the emotions
that even Prabhupada let flow in torrents
near the end of his life.

It's good to cry and I know why
because tears cleanse, just like those "tears"
that flush out the eyes when they sting too much
and you need relaxation
or a headache will come.

Or when you get too nervous
and hung up
when the phones don't ring
or the phones don't work
and things don't happen like they're supposed to
and people tell you, "Don't push on me,
don't give me so much work,
you're supposed to be retired,
don't cross over my boundary,"
and I tell you so many things
how they want you to be
and then they walk out the door

and you're alone again
and you sleep and dream of women,
unattainable women who you'd never want to have
who you never want to have
you used to spit and turn your head
because what they want is not what you want
and you'd be a fool to take them back.
They're only Maya's housewives,
paramours, witches, secret angels
of the secret service, whereas all you want
is ardent love of God.

Now where did I leave those beads?
Oh here they are, right around my neck,
just where they belong.

They're coming back from India.
They went to India. Strange place, but
"in my village no one goes hungry." She sent
me an album of photos of her second pilgrimage.

He sends the sad notes of starving
tsunami-hit peoples' houses and jobs
swept away. He hits the drum pedal in NYC
to emulate his own feelings, Elvin Jones,
he's dead now, dead in the *tsunami*
of death that washes over every mortal
being wherever he lives. It's a big unstoppable
wave. Crying, crying against the American soldiers.
"Allah! Allah! He will send
retribution against you. You cannot
kill and get away with this! We are
living peacefully in our house and you
come and bomb us calling us terrorists.
It is *you* who bring terror."

Meanwhile in preschool, poor war

free Vrindavan, the pilgrims come and go
and pile stones at Govardhan symbolizing
they would like to come back and live there
in one lifetime, and they visit within the shelter of
an ISKCON swami to guide them
and give *darshan* of his Govardhan
shila. You don't know what a *shila* or swami is?
Do you know what
Pepsi-Cola is and spaghetti
and chocolate-coated cake? Yeah
they serve it in the restaurant day and night for
the foreign tongues.

Look at the good-looking women.
Look at the old ones.
Look at the old train. The rocky
path leading up to Radha's father's house.
Do you know the story? Do you want to hear
someone tell you? One hundred rupees,
fifty rupees, pushing from both sides,
give me both sides, chasing another train
at the peak of the hill a ferocious monkey
with what ancestral lineage?—bites
your tender child on the arm
and the teeth marks remain,
the child is crying. An old Vraja
basi puts some medicine on the
sore and says it will be all right,
the monkeys are not infectious,
they are Krishna's friends, that's why
they live here. Meanwhile the kid's father
is thinking he'd like to plug the
monkey with a .22 and hang
him from a branch.

Don't. Don't get angry. Be neutral
of offenses in the *dhama*. Don't show anger.

Remember, you have a low birth.
If you could be born here you would be lucky
born poor saintly.

How much data do you have on this man? Is he another Herman Melville? I hear you've shortened his beard. So his head wouldn't look so oblong. He has some friends. Some people are disappointed in him, confused over his misbehavior. He's on the left side of the bank. So far he's fallen off the country, like Bush said of Kerry. He's a lefty. He'd like to swing with words incomprehensible like people who talk in many tongues. He was talking and he got interrupted by the phone. He's always interrupted. He'd like to live a hundred years and reach inner perfection.

He started reading a terrible book on Teresa of Avila. Interpreting *The Interior Castle*, the author said Teresa winds up making no distinction between the self and the Supreme Self and winds up a complete *mayavadi* coming back down to the earth like a *bodhisattva*, no love of Jesus. That's not how I read it. That's not how I know Teresa. Her love for Jesus always remains too, dualism, her and Jesus, that's why they call her Teresa of Jesus. Why these strange interpretations? You've got to straighten it out. We *bhaktas* have to preach. Let me go on chanting the Lord's name and go on loving Him. We never merge, we never disappear so that there's nothing but love. There's always love and the lover, love and the beloved. What is love without the two? This translator named Ms. Mirabai says that it all goes up in a puff of smoke in the seventh interior room of the castle and all we get is love love love.

That was just in the introduction so we decided to go no further. We'll read Teresa herself, let her speak for herself. Toppy dotty dote. Toppy dopy dope. Just like we would hear Coltrane for himself. No interpretations. As Prabhupada says, now no interpretations, no ill motivations, *Bhagavad-gita* as it is. And as for me, just a struggling tear-filled boy. You've got to make those feet tough walking on some *parikrama* trail or the equivalent.

In the subways I put a nickel in the slot and all I ever got was five salted peanuts.

They say self-knowledge means accurate self-appraisal, knowing you are very low, humble. Humility is a crest jewel in spirituality. If someone has mastered spiritual texts theologically but is proud, he or she is nowhere. Humbler than a blade of grass, more tolerant than a tree and free of all material desires… he is eligible to chant the holy name of the Lord constantly. Ringing a solicitor. Your writing prayers interrupted. Not convinced where all the pure devotees live.

She is stressed, try not to bother her, don't go against her. But what about my point of view? Please, let's not go through that again. I was not whipping the lone workers, I was trying to speak to a larger audience.

But you are right to correct me. I should not have said so much about the trouble I was feeling when I wrote that book. I got into it too much. I should just have said something like, "I wrote this during a time of turbulence." That's enough. And then say, "I was surprised when I pulled the poems out, they were free of the turbulence I was going through. They had their own turbulence, but clean."

Everyone seems to understand things in a different way. Please let it go through. Pass it. Understand it the way I meant it. Don't touch a hair of what I wish to say, don't touch its color. Don't change it.

Deepak took me to the writing shack and asked me where I wanted the pictures hung. He preferred Prabhupada on the right side and Coltrane on the left, so I agreed. I said I have no master plan for putting up other pictures. He said when they come, we can decide where they go. Yes, other things may be added.

He is too tired to write three coherent lines in a row. It is all due to fatigue. And that is why he cannot do the rowing machine, even though the shin-building machine is arriving soon. It will be shameful when the man sets it up and sees how little I can push. Nothing to be ashamed of. It's meant to build you up, and all he wants is his money. One hundred and fifty pound weakling. Coming for to carry me home. Build up your body physically to carry you spiritually.

She is stressed, try not to bother her. Don't go against her. But what about my part of the vine? Just be patient. You're getting more than you're due. Around here our motto is love each other.

There is false humility too. There are people who always find fault with others and report this to their director; this is pernicious. Everyone has some wrong. Frogs "ba-rup" is not a wrong, it's their natural call. But mischief is mostly from human plotting. Complaining. Picking on someone. Even someone very good. God is obviously displeased with you and you have to go back and undo it. Better keep quiet and see the good.

> Some people think this
> is the only land and sea—Earth planet
> but we believe in millions of others
> and finally the eternal ones.

> Vaikunthas. Where is your writing going?
> We suggested you make it more smoking as
> well as something rational. Not just
> fundamentalism. Room for eclectics,
> room for lefts and rights for
> gays and straights.

> For gnostics and agnostics.
> You really want to reach
> the audience beyond the book table
> at the Ratha-yatra?

> I want to reach the Eskimos
> and Hawaiians, natives and Navahos
> and Syrians and Sicilians and
> Napoleons and Swiss elders
> tired professors and hophead
> teenagers and religious seminarians.

> Like the search for the new land,
> those who never heard the word Krishna
> or Vishnu but like it when
> it comes in a joke or a solemn
> utterance of omnipotence by
> Arjuna in *Bhagavad-gita*

> from a boy whose genes are white and black boys

bend a branch he read
Lewis Carrol and steals
from Jackie Robinson's home base.

He paid life dues and still
doesn't know the art of flying
rejects as ultimate the Zen, Buddhism,
Tao, Christian, accepts the
best of all, reserves the plot
of cowherd land in Uttara
Pradesh in India but
stays in bed in CA

with pills and books because they can give him
bestseller status and link him
to Hollywood so he can refuse and
write him up
in *Sunday Times* as a
profound hermit of Gaudiya
sampradaya with a picture
of Prabhupada and Gaura-Nitai—
comparing them to Christ and Teresa,
he's satisfied with that.

They let him start initiating
again. And he does. The
bastards of execution
who cast the first stones.
"I think the judgment
was excellent." Who knows the truth?

Chapter Six

THERE IS THE LEGEND of Paul Bunyan at the place where his cooks made a batter of dough for thousands of pancakes, some done by ice-skating. Babe the Blue Ox is preserved in *murti*. Other remnants. They killed all the mosquitoes in wintertime, and that is why there is none during that season, only in summer. *The History of God,* by Karen Armstrong, is her own mythmaking because she doesn't believe in one deep God in her heart.

The Native Americans smoke mushrooms and meltdown in sweat lodges and chanted mantras and received visions in dreams and orders from the gods. They are the best caretakers of the earth and the animals and the water and the trees. They preserve what nature has given as best they can. The sophisticated men are the ravagers of the natural resources and will be punished, as they rape the earth and natural re-sources run out and they resort to using artificial goods. Krishna is the ultimate preserver and replenisher. He can restore infinitely if the hu-mans will cooperate and take their own share without taking more than their quota. But if the ravagers predominate, they will be ravaged them-selves by pests and imbalances, by great floods, disasters, wastes, deserts, *tsunamis*, landslides, global warming, and disasters worse than anything anyone has imagined. This is the picture for Kali-yuga.

So it is better to get out of Kali-yuga, to become liberated. To not come back. To return to Krishna and reach the spiritual planets.

You have only ten thousand years in which to work in devotional service before Sankarshan is let loose to destroy, before the incarnation of Kalki is let loose and everything is set to fire, and alternately there is flood and drought. That is the real history of God, Miss Armstrong, a nonpretty picture. So better get out.

> The "eye" of the hurricane is the place where it
> seems calm but it's worse—
> you can see all
> the ruination going on around you *out there,*
>
> bandmasters, bang, crash, hold onto what?
> Recite what text?

I have a scary feeling I'll be blown off this
tree with everyone else. There's no solace. It's banging
in my ears. Have you got an aspirin or a
med? Tenor sax.

Last year the contest went to Montreal,
this year it goes to no one, no resources
to avoid a prize from the Eye of the hurricane.

A state trooper gets crashed off his bike
helping no help although crushed.

No prizes. The heights are unable like
tape from the eye of the real hurricane.
Can we leave Kali-yuga
with Kalki's sword help?

That means you're beheaded.

Drink a smoothie and become
eternal-headed like Rahu—
he blocks the moon.

He don't block me. I'm praying the maha-
mantra and nothing can stop that.
You will be safe in all conditions. Eerie
sounds don't matter. Eerie name
Roonie? Collapse. Bubble of
lava, electric effects, don't

worry, it's just natural-sounding frogs
in our garden. Gal-up.
Gal-up...
The demon's name is Rahu.

Twenty million Russians died defending the front in World War II
against the Nazi invasion. Yevtushenko tells how the street bully Red

beat him up with brass knuckles. Yevtushenko bought a book on ju-jitsu, "where a weaker person can beat a stronger person." He studied and then beat up Red. "That day I learned you had to not only write poems but back them up in the world." Wow stuff. His mother was a singer but cracked her voice singing on the front to cheer up the troops.

Dhanu Swami keeps telling new details of his kidnapping by Ted Patrick and Patrick's assistant, the Black Goose, in the very presence of Dhanu Swami's parents, when Dhanu was only eighteen years old. Ted Patrick pulled the tin Prabhupada medallion from Dhanu Swami's bead bag and threw it to the ground. Patrick had memorized *The Nectar of Devotion* passage, as had Dhanu Swami. Patrick said, "If a demon blasphemes a pure devotee of the Lord, then you have three alternative choices: you can either kill that demon, you can defeat him in logic, or you can leave the place. So which are you going to do?" Young Dhanu sweated and cried, but then turned to his father. "Dad," he said, "you've told me that you would never even go to the neighborhood of the *swarze*, the black men, and you'd never hire them. So how come now you're hiring one to give your son so much pain?"

That remark took everyone aback, especially Dhanu's father. Yes, why was he allowing a black man to torture his son? He told Ted Patrick to get out at once. Ted Patrick called him some dirty names and asked for a higher fee, but Dhanu's dad, along with Dhanu and some other devotees just pushed him out. The tables were turned in the name of prejudice. As Chanakya Pandit also says, when you are dealing with cheaters, you can also cheat. This was not prejudice against the black man but clever dealing with an anti-Vishnu demon. And so Dhanu set himself free by clever thinking in the service of the Lord. Ted Patrick called them all dirty M.F.s, but they were free from his black magic power. Dave's parents hugged their son and asked forgiveness, and Dave thanked the Lord for giving him the intelligence to speak the right thoughts at the right time. "I'll be back," said Ted Patrick, "to get the balance of my money."

"If you step foot in this house," said Dhanu's dad, "you'll see the muzzle of this .45," and he pulled out his pistol from his drawer and menacingly waved it at the trembling demons, who exited quickly from the house.

Stand on queue with your dinner plate. Stand politely and wait. This is like going back to Godhead. Your angel's wings grow slowly. You are dressed nicely. But why don't you have your *sannyasa* uniform on? Well, is it required? Yes, I should think you should go back and put it on, and get your *danda*. Don't do anything that will hold you back. Hmmm. I thought it was all right to do anything you wanted and that you would be all right as long as you had the right sincerity of heart. Yes, that's true, yes, that's true. But don't be forced to stand and pray. Do it because you want to and you don't even have to eat unless you want to. Stand on line. Leaden patience. Be happy. Be happy. Your chance is coming. Your number is coming. Get your papers together for when you're called, and then you'll have to present everything. You'll have to present everything just right, the way it should be. You know what I mean? Not exactly. Do you mean I should go up to the counter confidently, give my birth certificate, social security number, age, sex, and everything that's needed to get my state identification card, senior citizen, and then just wait for it to come in the mail along with my bank account, and then pray?

Yes, it's as simple as that, and more complex too.

RETROSPECTIVE I

Ordered not to write or you'll die from the pressure of it. No, not true. Got to write a little. *Gives* me life. So many artists *had to* write.

Gives *them* life and gives *people* life.

Why is writing such a high priority for you? Shouldn't devotional service be highest? Basho lamented at the end of his life that he missed salvation because he gave his life-heart to haiku expression instead of service to One, to God's people.

It may be that your vocation to God *is* through writing. He wishes you to serve that way. Teresa wrote her life. John of the Cross built aqueducts. What does God want you to do as your service to Him? It *could* be writing, so that when you are away from it, separated from it, you wilt, and you feel you cannot carry your cross, you feel you're not preaching, not glorifying the name as He wants you to.

Time to go.

Did you get your sister's message? No, that
was your Godbrother's plumber's message—
Joe's slate roof is ready. Scott said he didn't
bother to call him back because it's premature.
He's not ready for the roof.

We are talking with stale cake at dinner. The
Moroccan went to bed early with a cold.
I told Nara my ankles hurt extra
and I need new shoe inserts, told how Ollie
would deal with it. Nara tells me
how he'll do it, a slower way but in America.
Okay, I'll go along with that.

Pray on the hill, I don't even know
where we are, but Eric cries even when
he doesn't know. He calls to God and I feel
a twinge where teardrops start. That's how
you do it. Just wail, lost boy, cause your
ankle hurts and Mingus is up to Eric
crying, the questionable authority,
the boss with a bleeding heart.
These men are real poets and I better
run to the toilet again in true
operation or can I hold it off
to tell something more that's bringing
a clause that he says he doesn't
like but they won't stop—
because they appreciate, he can't stop
it and they mean it sincerely too, no
put-on. I too mean it. I
can't reach the basketball
rim and my head hurts.
God amen.

    I saw an advertisement for a book with a pious picture Hallmark-
Christmas-card style of a man who was miserable looking, with patches

of hair and an old cloak from the ancient times. Somehow he didn't look really sad because the publishers weren't that deep about it, but the lettering on the book said, "Why didn't God, who is all-forgiving, grant forgiveness, to Judas the Iscariot?" I didn't stop my reading of the opposite page but only guessed what this other book was about. I guessed at the premise of it. Were they saying that God did *not* forgive Judas? If so, I was doubtful whether heavyweight Christian theologians held the same point of view. Maybe this was a "born again" Christian or splinter group Christian religion. And if I accepted the point that God is all-powerful, then why didn't He forgive Judas? I still didn't read any further into the book or think of sending away for it, but my mind lingered on the picture before I kept turning the pages of the *New York Times* magazine. I thought of Mary Magdalene and how she was a great sinner, but by the force of her love purchased God's great forgiveness. She had done it by love, and she had been allowed to stand under the cross where Jesus was dying. She had been allowed to stay "as one of the family members" beside Mary, Jesus' mother, and experience the agony without suffering any loss of faith in Jesus her Lord, so far had she come in her conversion. I thought also of the slight lapse in the apostle Thomas, who did not believe that Jesus was resurrected, even though the apostles told him so, because he had not been present to touch him. He said, "I will believe it only when I can touch his wounds," and Jesus came again and chided Thomas. "Oh blessed are they who believe just by hearing," said Jesus, "not people like you who will only believe when they touch the body." To this chiding, St. Thomas said, "Oh my Lord, my God."

This comeback by Thomas has been noted to be the highest praise of Jesus in the entire Gospel—"Oh my Lord, my God." And so Jesus allowed him to be the speaker of the highest praise. And St. Peter failed also on the night before Christ's crucifixion. Peter had bragged that he would never betray Jesus, and Jesus said, "Oh yes, you will, and not only once but three times before the cock crows." And so it came about when the guards started looking for allies of Christ, and an ordinary street woman three times accused Peter as being one of the friends of Jesus, and three times Peter denied it for fear for his own body. How he wailed and regretted that cowardly act and later admitted to Mary Magdalene, "We are all cowards." And yet Peter was made the rock of the church, the first Pope.

Turned the page to see what was next in the magazine, but my thoughts went on different lines before I saw what the *Times* magazine had. I thought of the Gaudiya Vaishnava line and its sinners and saints. Did we have sinners who became saints? Yes, lots of them. I always think first of Valmiki. I think of him because his changes were so great. He robbed and murdered to support his family, but after meeting Narada Muni and talking with that soul-changing saint, he was converted into a great Vaishnava and stopped all his sinful activities. He changed his occupation to becoming a mendicant and writing, by the help of the Lord, the epic *Ramayana*. The story of the incarnation Rama was all dictated through him by the avatar. From sinner to saint. This was by the blessings of associating with a pure devotee, Narada. That is the case with so many sinners. Just by meeting with a pure devotee and following his directions. It is said in the *Srimad-Bhagavatam*, a moment's meeting with a pure devotee can change one into a pure devotee. A whore monger in Bengal changed into a great *rasika* Vaishnava who went to live in Vrindavan to worship Radha-Krishna and write poetry. How did this come about? It came about when one night he risked terrible storms to go see his prostitute. When he found her, she said, "If you only had as much devotion for Krishna as you do for me, you would be a great devotee." Somehow the words struck him and he immediately left her and walked to Vrindavan. Along the way he was tempted by another woman, and to stop all visual temptation, he put his eyes out. In telling us this story, Prabhupada said to us, "But don't you try this. This is for Bilvamangala Thakur, not for you." Bilvamangala Thakur composed a beautiful poem for first-class Vaishnavas called *Krishna-karnamrita*, which was highly valued by Chaitanya Mahaprabhu. He would share it with His intimate devotees. But can we say that the man's prostitute was a great devotee? She was his *shiksha-guru* because even though she was not highly placed in terms of her *sadhana* or regular practice as a devotee, she served to give him the right words at the right time, and he was able to follow them by God's grace. So he writes at the beginning of *Krishna-karnamrita*, "This book is dedicated to my *shiksha-guru*, Chintamani."

Most of us are all still in the sinner category, certainly not in the saintly category. We must be on the lookout for fuller conversion, fuller *shiksha,* fuller *chintamani,* so that we can be forgiven by the Lord for all our remaining sins. Surely God can forgive every sin and every sinner if we just "keep on trucking."

I phoned my counselor for my weekly call and told him I had trouble reaching him since he installed his new business line, which puts off people who the machine doesn't want you to listen to, or when the man isn't in, tells him that they can leave a message. I don't know how to leave a message on his new machine. Anyway, I'll have to learn how to leave a message on the new machine.

But we started talking in my allotted one-hour time. I told him that I had talked to my doctor last Saturday, and he was out of town, so he hadn't received the medical reports for the last three days. There was a significant change in those days. For three weeks I had been going excellently with no headaches at all and no medicine at all. Three weeks! He had described it as a breakthrough. So I told him I realized he had not received the last three days' charts because he was in a new city. The report, which he hadn't received, was that I was taking a real downspin. I had taken extra medicine and had had quite a few headaches. He asked me what I thought it was due to. He already knew what the issues were. They were old issues, but I was having new reactions to them.

I'd better relate this as happening to Swami Jim so you don't think it's too personal or private. Swami Jim said, "One of them is Ollie's being sent away." You all know about Ollie's being sent away, don't you? I told you briefly that the committee members of the health board decided he was causing too much trouble by his misbehavior. This resulted in his being a bad effect on me, and I also having a bad effect on him. They described it as codependency, where one person is bad for another in their deep friendship. I had added fuel to the subject by sending a page by St. Teresa wherein she cogently points out that within a convent, there can arise a situation that is unhealthy, in that two nuns develop too much of a friendship for each other. They make it too exclusive. It is better when friendships are shared more widely, and not where they become like cliques of two. So when my counselor saw that, he thought it really hit the nail on the head. I hadn't shown it to him with the intention that it would point out the situation between Ollie and me, but he thought of it that way. And perhaps unintentionally I was giving it to him, even though I knew it was ammunition against Ollie. In other words, I don't want to send Ollie away from here, and I know he did want to send him away. But fair is fair, so I sent him the ammunition, because it was objectively coming from such an authoritative source, our Teresa. If she said it, I didn't want to withhold it from myself.

Anyway, let's get back to my talk with the doctor on the phone. He was very optimistic about my condition. He said, "There's nothing wrong with your taking a few extra pills just because of some setbacks that you had, like with Ollie gone, and you wanted to go see Bhakti-tirtha Swami, but then you were in anxiety because you knew you weren't in shape to go to see him, and you were also in anxiety because you have extra guests here who are rather disappointing persons. So the wonderful thing is that despite all these anxieties, you're taking a little medicine, which is all right. The medicine is there for you to take in these situations, and you're not being so distraught, you're pulling through well. He was being very optimistic about it, as he usually is, and at the time, I accepted it. However, about three days later, while I was mulling over things, I thought of what he said, especially about Ollie. I reversed his decision in my mind. I thought, "Wait a minute, why such optimism? I don't like it that he's not here. I want him to come back here." When it's my turn to talk again on Wednesday with my counselor, I'm going to tell him plainly that I don't like it that he's away. I'm not going to say it as some kind of definite thing that has to be changed, but I'm going to express my feelings, that's all. I'm not threatening him, because I knew that he's very attached to his plan for refusing to let Ollie come back early. He's got a lot at stake in his doing it gradually, not letting Ollie sneak under the wire but making him do things the way they should be done. He wants Ollie to get a kind of license in hospice training and cooperate instead of jiving around, and bringing this bipolar codependency on me. He does it in a way where it doesn't help me. My counselor said, "You should follow the spirit that is the Teresean, renounced *sannyasa* way, right? You don't want to have to stand with a crutch before God, you want to stand alone before Him. But if you have to stand with Ollie helping you by getting some extra money to get something you want or giving you some extra pills or arranging some gig for you, that's not going to be what you need or what will allow you to be free to stand alone before God. It will hurt you, and it won't help him either." He said that Ollie even acknowledged toward the end, when he left, that "It was good for me." Nanda was swinging hard, telling me all the other members who were in agreement with him.

While I'm talking on the telephone: "U can choose the one or the half." Three days later I see the note and try to decipher it. The whole life or the half? Is this a poem, a love song, a request? Then I remember and see the half pill is still there. Horatio. I was worried a lot that I had forgotten a plot. Nanda calls this my symptom of being "all over the place." Too bad I can't reach him by the phone right now. His phone is always awry. Tell yourself, pumpkin, you don't need a plot but always in a separate pad leave big notes as to where you're going. No, I say, I'm too lazy. This book starts off explaining in a literary way About the truth—you can't write or die; there is no choice. You must live *and* die, as W. H. Auden discovered in his poem and changed it. Auden changed it, but with despair, knowing it was too late, since the first version of the poem was already famous.

Then we took a turn and started explaining themes from Teresa of Avila in *The Inner Castle*, appreciating it. There was not much of a connection with the previous theme, except they were eternal themes about death, about writing, and about God the eternal. Write about the eternal. Then it won't be wasted writing. In other words, writing is not useless. If you say, "We must write or die," that's a useless statement, or fairly useless, and the statement, "We must love and die" is also fairly useless, although it's a better one. But once bhakti comes into the picture, then loving as an alternative to dying becomes something profitable and everlasting action in Krishna consciousness. I think we tried to talk about that in an inspiring way. Live or die, love Krishna and die in this world and resurrect in the next world. Live in Krishna and help others to live in Krishna forever and forever. Whatever you do in Krishna consciousness lasts forever. That includes writing. Write something that people will read. Just one word and it will help them in their march to eternity. Remember Prabhupada emphasizing that in an early New Vrindavan talk? "Write just one word!" he said. "Publish just one page of *Back to Godhead*. Write articles!" He wanted us to defeat those rascals who say there is no God. Very encouraging. So writers are not dabblers. They're important people in the matter of life and death. To write a good piece of Krishna consciousness is like throwing many life savers into the ocean while the boat is sinking or while men are falling overboard.

Very reli- gious [?]

Very religious has no typewriter, but would it help? He noticed his sight is worsening. Debilitating. Call to Krishna. We need more books about Krishna. Keep up the theme. How can you do that when you can't even see the page and the Sharpie pens are now odorous? Besides, you're a dork. You don't even care that much for your soul. I don't like my cat anymore, whining about it to Mukhi. Ollie wants to hash out his problems with his counselor. Either live with him in Washington or by telephone from India to Washington. Even President Bush would hesitate at the cost of doing it by telephone. You can talk to God free? It doesn't cost much in terms of life change. Mahajana sent me his latest slide show of Vrindavan. Why can't you come alive and give your opinion? Because it doesn't move me, just as my books don't move him. Too tired to think anyway.

Just use words. SK's father was a wealthy hosier. Jazz musicians never were very rich. But they were God-loving improvisers and compassionate. My eyes grow dimmer. This is not a good sign. Today's Saturday, and on Monday I will phone the optician for a Tuesday appointment. Try to get new glasses ASAP. Read good books.

Leading members of a worldwide spiritual community got dissatisfied with themselves. They wanted to make things more dynamic. They decided on making a world tour. They gathered for the tour, and I was there too. They were glad to see me and said, "All right, let's start going," but I stayed back, hiding behind a garbage pile. Pandu also stayed back doing his little Hindi things. They didn't get too angry with me because the spiritual community headed off to a state where if people wanted to do their own things, they were more or less permitted to. I disturbed some of the Indian people I was near, and some of them were twisting my arms, but in the end they allowed me. They saw that I had some papers with me.

This is all very interesting, I thought to myself, this grand, ancient land of gods and goddesses and the Supreme God. It is interesting at least to be in a land where God is most sought after and where He has descended in His various avatars, and where even I am known to have done some explorations.

When the Indian children saw that I was staying behind, not out of some whimsy but because of an illness, they were going to tend to me and give me some medicines, but they themselves were living in such poverty and filth that they had nothing to use to really cure me but probably would get me in a worse condition, so I rose out of the filth pile and started with my great gimpy limp wandering and wandering with the use of my pole.

> If I should lose you
> I would be a skeleton with
> scrambled eggs eyes
> a deer smashed by a big Mack truck
> if you go
> I have no guts. No tenderness to go on
> no bells ringing in search.
> I'd have to learn some kind of self-search pattern.
> Leaden spirit.
> "Are you okay?"
> Is a person okay if he's sick
> with headaches and he has no stick,
> he's penniless and he can't see?
>
> It's a matter of adjustment.
> So what
> if it's an amazing increase.
> I've got to take it. I need it.
> I need it.

DREAM

The end or exposé of the sister dream cycle.

My sister Madeline and I agreed to marriage, and a ceremony was conducted. We were driving away from the marriage in a car and had a car crash. Then the usual separation took place and we didn't know where the other was. I wound up in a school-institution but didn't know my identity and couldn't even speak. Perhaps my sister was here too. It was a big place. The experts there were interrogating me. Apparently they had already done a lot of work. I began to inquire from them. I gradually began to come out of the dream. I'll try to tell you at which point the questions and answers actually stopped being completely unconscious and at which point it became a conscious storytelling. But in the dream world, the unconscious story is just as valid as the conscious story, and it will be hard for me to tell the exact point.

It appeared that my sister was in that same institution, and she had confessed to them that we were married, although she was actually my sister. Therefore, she told them that we had committed incest. In my dream union with her in the church, or wherever we had committed the ceremony (there was no sex in this dream), she was all for it, but now she called it incest!

I looked down at the ground and said, "Incest," and they repeated it, "Incest." We went back and forth a number of times repeating the word, "Incest, incest." It began to sink in, as they intended it. A terrible sin.

"So now you're going to pay for it," they said.

I think about here the sheer, pure unconscious dreaming ended and I began talking the dream script, finishing out the story as it seemed likely.

They said, "You're going to have to pay for this."

I said, "How?"

They said, "With your hard-earned money."

I said, "How can I work? I have headaches."

They all shouted out, "YOU FAKE! YOU FAKE!"

I said, "I am not faking, I am not faking. I have proof of headaches."

"No," they said, "you fake! You fake!"

"No, I can't work, and I also have a crippled arthritic ankle."

"No, you fake! You fake!"

"The x-rays, the x-rays."

"You fake! You fake!"

"But my age, sixty-five."

"You can still work at sixty-five, you're not so old. You fake! You fake! You're going to go out and work."

I said, "You don't know how bad it is, how painful it is on my feet."

They said, "You'll be able to work and stand, because we've cut your feet off!"

I looked down and I had no feet! I said, "I have no feet!"

They said, "It will be easier for you. You have no feet and you can walk with these new sticks."

I tried standing up on the new feet with sticks and said, "Well, maybe these will be better," but then I fell on my back and they all laughed.

"You'll get used to it, you'll get used to it." They said, "You'll be able to get a job."

And I said, "Yes, I'll be able to get a job." I said, "I won't have to give the money to the Hare Krishnas. I'll give it to this girl. I can do with it whatever I want."

"No," they said, "you won't be able to eat anything but bread because we have punched your mouth in such a way that you won't be able to wear any new dentures."

I went to the mirror and saw that my face was all punched in so that I could not wear any dentures. I looked horrible, with a broken nose and my face broken in several places. I was a most ugly-looking person whom probably no one would even hire. I touched my face tentatively and said with some self-reconciliation, "Well, that's still not so bad. I can eat only bread." But then I broke down crying and saw that this is what I had done to myself by claiming that my sister was my wife, that she was actually attracted to me and my way of life at Philo.

He said, "You believe that the Prabhupada *murti* is actually Prabhupada, right?"

"Yes," I answered.

"So go before him and ask forgiveness."

I said, "I must have faith and pray to be brought closer to him." That's a good idea. Go regularly to Prabhupada like the Catholics do with their stations of the cross. Talk with him as my best friend and mentor. Develop a routine. I used to actually talk with him "in the flesh." It was in awe, but I was not afraid to talk with him. And I would follow whatever he said. So I can still do it. It's not some otherworldly thing. Talking to Prabhupada. I had this idea for some days, but I went to him only once with feeling. I'll try it again, maybe tomorrow morning, bring up some questions, just to talk. Some basic questions that come up. Some basic begging. Some basic declarations. Prabhupada, please bring me up to where seeking you is important. Please make it important. I have little life left and I should desire very much to clear my heart of *anarthas* and go with you. But I see that now my mind is still filled with many *anarthas*. Please show me more clearly the way to become a better, bolder devotee. Clear my path. Make me better. Establish a routine where I can come and talk to you, expose my wrongs, and ask of you and hear from you.

Book Distribution, Our Srila Prabhupada's Favorite *Yajna*, the Fastest Way to Go Back to Godhead

Prabhupada loved his book distributors. Here's one story. We were going to go in a van. It was a very quiet evening, but when we got into our van, it was soon flooded with men from the whole Northeast Zone, including some parts of Canada. They looked at me a little ironically but said, "Are you going along on *sankirtan* marathon too?" I said, "I guess so." They had a tremendous amount of books with them. It was actually more a truck than a van. I really wasn't expecting to go out, but they didn't care much whether I was or wasn't. They went out in many directions with their books, intent on selling the books in every direction.

I don't remember much about this story except suddenly these book men became my enemy and knew that I possessed something very secretive in a metal vial. What it was was the essence of my writing. They wanted to get it from me and fought with me for it. Finally, I was very surprised but they got it from me. I had not eaten in several days and so I was weakened, and I had hardly drunk, so that also made me weak. They got the vial. Somehow I had to accept the dire results of losing all this material just when I thought it was going to be published. What would they do with it? They probably considered it of no worth and went on distributing their own books. But at least they had it if they wanted to distribute it in the future. I had a headache now.

I thought of the old story from the Goswami days when they left Vrindavan with the carts and all the Goswami books to take them to

Bengal, but on the way they were stolen. It's a long, great story how they were recovered from thieves. I prayed very quickly, like lightning, and I still have a hope that I can recover that vial. In fact, I'm almost sure that I can because I think they will value it little and I can buy it for almost $24 in a used vial store. The first thing I started doing, however, is fighting with them viciously. I pinched at their bodies with the strength of steel pliers and hammered at them. I found that their bodies were soft, these *sankirtan* men, and I said, "Give me that vial back. It's not much use to you. Go on with your *sankirtan* distribution." With that, they said, "Well, you just give us the $24 and we'll give it to you," and I think they did. Yes, I think that's what they did.

We were reading unpedestrian, transcendental books pointing to the Supreme Person, the Lord and His *parisads*. But then my eyes went dim. I could hardly read or write. That's terribly embarrassing when you lose a material facility in your quest for the immaterial role. I know, because I've heard on authority that a blind man can be a saint like Bilvamangala Thakur, but it's too much for me. I feel I need my eyes to write and read. But it so happened that I would start a line of handwriting and the penmanship would just start to dwindle. It became so small that I couldn't read it. Or it would come out double lines. No matter how big I tried to make the letters, I couldn't read them later. So I got an emergency appointment for an eye examination in Ukiah.

We did a few other things in Ukiah —applied for a social security card and stopped for lunch. While in the parking lot eating our lunch, we saw a young girl wearing her hair in cobalt purple color tied with a band around her forehead, and her lip was pierced with a silver stud. I asked Rasa, "Why do they do that?"

He said, "They think it's more fun." We brushed it off and made fun of it, but it left a haunting impression on all of us. The girl was very young and attractive, and her silver stud shone clean and brilliant and her purple hair was attractive in a crazy way. I'm still thinking of her now instead of chanting. But in the meantime somewhere I heard read to me by the devotees that if a man has any attraction for a woman, it's not possible for him to be attracted to Krishna, who is the real beauty in all the worlds. One has to be disgusted at the material female beauty, at least when compared to Govinda or Lord Chaitanya Mahaprabhu. They are just like corn fritters or those terrible cheeseburgers we bought and wound up half-eating.

It seems everywhere we go the doctors have diplomas from Texas and California, and that starts Nara off talking about those states. I keep quiet about New York, New York. There seems to be a prejudice against New York out here. The optometrist showed me a neat three-dimensional model of the entire eye. A rather small part of it is the lens itself. As part of my health checkup, he first splashed some liquid into my eye and then flashed light into my eye and asked me to strain my vision upward and to the north and to the northwest and to the east and to the south and to the southeast and to the northeast until I was reeling. Then he switched the light off and said my eye health was pretty good but I had some cataracts. This meant, he continued, as I barely could make out his fine moustache, nothing to worry about. But in time, if it worsened, I might have to have an operation and have my natural lens removed and a plastic one put in. He assured me that cataract lens removal had come a long way and that it was not a big deal nowadays to have your lens removed. It had to be done because after the years so much dirt and pounding occurs to your natural lens. But after all, you're only sixty-five, so it may not be until you're seventy-five that you have to have your cataracts removed. "Uh-huh," I nodded, absorbing his peaceful manner. It sounds like a long way off. It sounds like an easy operation. Eye lens removed and a new one put in. But the worst thing of all is that my present lens, the one God gave me through the material modes, is dimming. It's just a matter of adjustment.

Early this morning we heard the turkeys screaming in the trees, first time this year. What's this? Coyotes? Oh no, those familiar Anderson Valley birds, cluck cluck, cluck cluck, CLUCK CLUCK! He says they like the rain. That's not it. It's spring coming, mating time. The garden at night, at dusk, at dawn is a symphony of frogs, same reason, mating calls. Does this bode well for me, good God-searching weather? No better on your feet, but you're not so sleepy. Maybe more resigned. Is that good? If he wants me, he'll call me. But the physical exercise sheet says, "Don't be afraid to work, but don't work too hard and risk injury."

You will be begging favors
and regretting regrets not many
reaching up for the stars like a
monkey who bit you.

Looking at your pierced skin
and hope you're not infected by that
rat bite. Oh the dangers Miss
Virginia! Maybe better you stay
At home and amass your papers
you're not sure of.

You do something to me
send me home wondering
if I should care more for
others. But how—I can't
just plunge myself into helping
the retarded or skinheads
teaching academic classes
by prepared seminars.
Do what you can do—he called
you "champion," roll
those stanzas Rollinesque
going where they do, climb,
hop over a barbed wire five-foot fence
you used to do when you
were twelve years old, be a
tough guy running away from
trouble, Dentyne chewer—
God in your sacred heart—
"don't let them get me,
I'll be good
from now on."

NOW IS THE TIME FOR ALL TO COME TO THE AID OF THEIR
COUNTRY. It is in vain, sir, to extenuate the matter. The war has actually begun. The next gale that sweeps from the north will bring to our

ears the clash of resounding arms. Why stand we here idle? What is it you gentlemen wish? Is life so dear or peace so sweet as to be purchased at the price of chains and slavery? Forbid it, almighty God. I know not what course others may take, but as for me, give me liberty.

Dozing your life away. Reindeer leap through the valley. Swami gave his cat away and he doesn't miss her at all, as long as mice don't invade. They say this house is tight. The monks are kneeling on their prayer stools waiting for porridge. Some of them wish they had entered a more reclusive order where they could pray all day long without group liturgy or socializing and working except for making wine alone (but not drinking it). Others think the opposite. They would like to get out and do some politics of liberation and take sides in a political revolution. It takes all kinds. Some might like to paint or grind away. Pass stools. Some of the invalids think they may be making a breakthrough, less medicine and less headaches, and so those voices in his dream—"Fake! Fake!"—should be killed. The thing is not to be trapped. If you want to go somewhere else, then leave this place. If you don't like New York, then leave that place. Leave a jazz concert, leave wherever you don't want to be, even Vrindavan.

Jim is very alert, even if carloads of thugs are chasing him. He can leap from cliff to cliff, leaving them behind. No bravado about it, just saving his life, but he's always able to scramble through head-high mud floes, or evade bullets and run scrimmage through pursuers. Recently he was doing this to catch up with his ex-wife because they both wanted to tell each other emphatically that they did not want to make up to the other again.

He didn't have to rush so just to tell her that, but I was most pleased to see your agility. It made me think you could be saved from death. Of course, that will be done by the Lord's grace. But it made me think he would give me that confidence and speed when I need it. Just run, escape, whatever it takes. Now you are under His protection and they cannot catch you, those satans. Even if it doesn't seem so, there will be a way out. Even if you seem subpar. You are Swami Bhaktivedanta's man. PERIOD. And it's slowly being revealed to you.

NEW VISIONS

RITING WON'T KILL YOU or despiritualize you. You simply need some good optics. Let us write to our heart's content and chant much better. You just have to write of the brilliant white underclouds at 4:30 P.M. and remember the good side of your mother. The cameo of this child praying here on my desk, whom I brought from Ireland. Now you can expect "Dear John" letters, more from Ireland than anywhere else.

And the eagle soars to the top of the Douglas fir.

God is not a dot. Not a vast, indifferent universe, not a merging of selves, not a *nada nada nada nada*. God is the Supreme Person, and He expands into many parts and parts and plenary parts. His loving potency *(hladini-shakti)* is Srimati Radharani.

Pulling out all the stops. Shine all the stars. All the lotus petals. Nevermind one fellow who can't make it. The tide flows anyway, despite his puny failure. You have compassion for the poor? So does She. Call on Her mercy for all errant souls.

Who is the good-looking man, and the beautiful young woman with him?

> Hare Krishna mantra has twice as
> many Radhas as Krishnas. Krishna has
> arranged it that way. You are
> capable of considering the quality
> of *nama* a little.

> Me? Me talk about Radha's
> radiant face and limbs for plenty
> pages? What you know, what you've
> heard. I'm shy to go forward.
> Just repeat what Prabhupada
> said. And what he said of Krishna
> and what he said *not*
> to say. Oh, like he said
> some people are like the traumatized cow in
> the barn who saw fire and
> now is afraid of any red. She's
> compared to sex mongers who've
> heard of Radha and Krishna pastimes
> and can only think of them
> as like their own sex exploits.

> Such people should
> never go into the *kunjas* of
> Vraja as long as their hearts
> associate mundane sex with
> Radha and Kana.

So write or die, have you fully explored that? What do you need to revisit? Or visit for the first time?

Your relationship with your father? All Radha-Krishna pastimes in a new playette?

Sharon Olds in an interview: "I never create characters." I rally to that statement by Sharon. I mostly assassinate any character that comes my way, including my own self, give him different names. It is a great achievement to make a Raskolnikov, a Micawber, a Holden Caulfield, a Dr. Zhivago, a King Lear, little Dorritt, etc.

Especially I don't want to make Krishna a character, or Radha a character, or Mother Yasoda, or Nanda, or Sridama, or Vrindavan or Yamuna. It can be done by great authors who make reference to the *rasika shastras* and who are themselves immersed in those *shastras* and have a vision of the Lord and His *parisads*. But I am too afraid to go there. I can occasionally pick a fruit of a Prabhupada saying or something straight from the *Krishna Book*, spoken in my own hoarse voice. But not a character of my own creation.

So now that you have proven writing doesn't kill you and that you are a writer, what have you to say? You know, you must have a plot in your hand, and if not characters, then some kind of development from beginning to middle to end. There's no way to escape that. You are now at about the one-third point in this book. You must have a subject matter, and so far it has been to prove that writing will not kill you. Now let's explore what it is you would like to say, given that writing is nonpoisonous, *ahimsa*, and good for the soul.

> I don't know if you find this
> usable, Mr. Publisher, Mr. Reader,
> but I wrote it just before supper.
> I am not a holy monk from Salamanca.
> But I have pure, pure roots
> replanted at age 26
> at 26 Second Ave. by His Divine Grace
> Prabhupada. He gave me the name
> Satsvarupa dasa, and I had to
> turn in Stephen T. A good
> deal. Smoke gets in your
> eyes at the *yajna* in his apartment.
> I dove deep at his feet
> saying "bhakti," they had to rescue
> me.

> That is not a made-up story,

> truly happened with big red
> beads. It's been a long road
> and I'm not so happy about
> where I've sunk to now. Need to
> pull up by my bootstraps.
>
> Gray hairs, beard, doesn't
> wear *sannyasa* rags, polite and write
> talk about the weather,
> grab still for his feet,
> the show ain't over
> Mickey Mouse, you're squiggly
> still alive.

I'm on board the ship Saratoga. I'm standing on a lower step holding Ghana-shyama's hand, and he's holding the hand of another devotee above. Srila Prabhupada seems to be somewhere down among the other persons, and they are all just gathering around idly to catch a view of him. I have a sensation of great happiness that I'm in the Navy so that I can catch glimpses of Prabhupada and be on his team. Suddenly he's not there, and the crowd breaks up. People get back to their individual tasks. I let go of Ghana-shyama's hand. I ask him, "Was that Prabhupada who was here?" "Yes," he says, then he goes back to his task and I go back to mine.

You don't have to be recognized or praised wonderfully. You just have to be on that team.

Chop's close friend, Shay, who was taller and heavier than him, said that perhaps Chop was no longer a mere *sadaka* and so numerical strength in *japa* was not required of him. Huh? Chop lifted his tired eyelids. "Others in the movement say this of themselves," said Shay. Chop was speechless, but then he said softly, "Thank you." He could not assimilate it, believe it, yet he hung onto it like a raft in the swift rapids. Maybe... some people are saying that of themselves...?

But when he held it in the light of cold reason, he couldn't remember Prabhupada saying that anyone could drop that. It was a very important thing. Yes, there were some exceptions—the amazing letter to

Paramananda that during the harvesting season he could drop his six-teen-round quota and work from morning to night in harvesting the hay and the cornfields. There were a few other letters like that. When you are very, very busy with some other devotional service, chanting could be put aside. But normally...when there was no emergency...

Paramahamsa, who was in some other *samadhi* mood of constant concentration and twenty-four hours *astakaliya* Krishna and Radha meditation... agriculture, behind the plow from sunrise to sundown.

But for a boy who didn't like the taste of chanting, like a boy who didn't like bread and butter and milk, to refuse it when his mother told him to drink it, could that be accepted? At any rate, it now remains "impossible."

As a servant of Prabhupada living no more than six feet from him at all times, it did not seem that he chanted sixteen rounds, at least to most material vision. He was too busy with other things. His one-time joke, pushing the counter beads, the fourth one, and saying, "Now I can do any damn thing I like," and the devotees around him laughing heartily. What was that for?

A devotee from Vrindavan wrote, "I saw Nimai dasa yesterday sitting by a big table covered with colorful books of yours. Any way that I can get to read stuff you've recently completed?" The answer is no, because none of it has been published. And what would he find in it? A stairway to the stars? He would enter the path of suffering with me. See if he likes that. It's not a twenty-four hour *kirtan* at the house of Srivasa Thakur with Mahaprabhu leaping up and down in ecstasy. It's also within the realm of Vaishnavism. In any religion there is the path of tears and search, regret and pain. He feels he is outcast, but maybe he is not. Maybe he is closer to the Lord than he thinks. Is that what Shay meant when he said, I may be closer than I think? But the only sign I see is my own distaste. Oh! I see leaves. Yes, I see leaves, wet and damp, and they seem to speak of God. And the trees, and everything in nature that catches your view. Like I said before, the white of the clouds at 4:30 P.M., or anytime. God is everywhere to the observant one. But not to the self-pitier.

And I ain't he! Little bursts of ecstasy, little puffs of glee. Little signs of progress, breakthroughs come to thee. Hope, the thing with feathers, never asked a crumb from me. Now it's 6:11 P.M. The sky is close to dark, soon my friends will return, and that's a great blessing too. You have protection, people who love you and care for you. Don't bitch, my friend, don't say, "My *sadhana* is low, this is my complaint." Say, "You're doing well. You're breaking through, although you could do better, and in time you will."

The announcer's voice boomed loudly overhead. You are coming into the home stretch. It was a close finish. Was it? You could not tell it all from the ground where you ran. You ran your heart out, but you could not tell, you and the other persons in the running, the lovers. Yes, it was just like a horse race. But in a horse race, the horses can see. In this race, so strange, you could not see. You could only hear the loud booming voice from above, "And they're coming around the last turn, and inching up from second place comes…" Will you place at all? Where are you? Why don't you wake up and see the result? Are you afraid to know? All right, all right, just run, just run.

Hari returned last night, smiling broadly. "My son! You carry the dust of Vrindavan." But his body carried a heavy odor from traveling, so I asked him to shower before putting the deities to rest. He also carries a certain odor, as if rooted to the earth of India. Or so I imagine. I'll have to overcome my little prejudices and appreciate the great, generous service he does here. At breakfast he read *The Life of St. Teresa of Avila,* and it was almost totally incomprehensible, both because of the subject matter and style of writing and Hari's pronunciation. I waded through my flakes placidly while the high talks of prayer passed like morning clouds.

Later he brought in three letters from Vrindavan, some deity *chadars* from Ollie, and a *sannyasa danda* I had asked for. I became excited to see the *danda*, and coincidently I had an urge to pass urine. I ran for the bathroom but didn't make it on time. I soaked my corduroy pants and underpants. I took them off and on a whim replaced them with a *sannyasa dhoti*, something I rarely wear. So I stood in shirt, jersey, *dhoti,* sneakers, and *danda.* Maybe it would help me with my prayers if I started wearing my full *sannyasa* clothes every day. I tried it for a few hours and then changed back to regular pants.

Ollie didn't expect a one-way ticket to India. We're telling him, "You're not welcome back, not yet." The general word is that he can come back at kartika time (next November), but the real point is that he has to change. The headmasters have to change their attitude. Hari came back from India with impressions from Ollie that the headmasters will just soften up by *kartika*. But the masters don't see it that way. Nanda says he is fiercely dedicated to making me well again, and he thinks that Ollie is being destructive by his codependency, his own sickness, and therefore he's not welcome back. Still, there's a lot of time to go. They are speaking mostly of this codependency. They want him to get a license so that he can be an official hospice worker and help others, not just me. I have no desire to possess him just for my own errands. Yet if we can have an intimate relationship of friendship, why is that forbidden? Can it be cleared up? He's taking weekly counseling from Nanda. I am opening all the doors here, or what's the use?

Weekly 11:00 A.M. call from the doctor: "How are you feeling?" I told him everything is progressing except my prayer life. He says, "The prayers are in your books." I like to hear that. He lets me off the hook. I imagine I'm a wailing Jewish (somehow) rabbi crying his prayer that he cannot reach God, but *that prayer* is the prayer of God. "It's in all your books."

Try a little just now. Advise Ollie not to stay in Vrindavan during the summer. Go to some cooler place in the hill country, like Haridwar or Hrisikesh. Direct-wave satellite Sirius radio cannot pick up the signal. The skyways are too filled with rain and clouds. You can get a little bit of Stan Kenton, which you don't want anyway, and then it's gone. But Joshua Redman sounded cool, and then he's cut off too. Turn to exercise machines. Three sets of twelve pulls of the chest expansions at weight 0.5. Hey this is hard. At the end of the direction sheet, it states that these exercises should be spread throughout the day, not that all of them should be done at once. What about prayer exercise? Yeah, I'm for a little of that. "How is your appetite," the doctor asked. They don't know I have a small appetite for everything. Hmm? For this do or die? A little throughout the day.

> Never be another supreme,
> be true to he. I want to be

the lover obedient saint.
At least the altar boy.

The fighter for, the tithe giver,
the sax player, don't show off,
don't try to grab a spotlight
but write letters and pump out
books like your father would pump
out water from the hydrant and
arc it up against the blazing tenement
and run in with swinging axe to save the
screaming tenants.

At least an untattooed 5'10"
lasting in the ranks until the
end, I imagine myself doing
many heroic things, but now
if I can just get through
decently outwardly.

As for inwardly...wag the
flag.

In the Anderson Valley today it's
so foggy you feel like a ghost
in a Japanese film.

But you know that film will
be over and so will the fog and
you will be faced with the question
Where are you? Addressed to
the *one*. He can be found only
by mystics, like Six Goswamis and
those on whom He pours His mercy.
That's His choice, not dictated
by anyone else. No government, no
law above His decision where to place it.

He can rain on one side
of the building and leave the other
side dry.

My Lord. Workers do get
recognized. Those mixed
and stuck in the modes of nature *do* get their
just rewards. There is a
system but I'm just saying it's up to Him, ultimately,
His mercy, He can pardon,
special favor or leave you
dry. I heard this on different
occasions from the wise one.

Jimji decided to start wearing his *sannyasa* clothes again. But it's still cold, so he'll wear some kind of gym pants underneath. Probably won't wear shirts but sweaters and pullovers on top. Probably won't wear the upper *sannyasa* piece. But maybe, why not? Get a little bit into the spirit. We'll have to see if the *sannyasa dhoti* doesn't drag around too much on the floor or make you trip when you go out on a walk. There's nobody to worry about, thinking you're odd, because nobody ever comes up here, and why should you worry anyway? This is Anderson Valley, a place of eclectics. Everyone knows you're the monk who lives in the valley on the little peak in the little hermit's house. Rather, they expect you to be a little exotic. You already have a beard. Now some saffron clothes, the *sannyasa* rags, as Jay has called them. It'll feel strange at first, as if I'm announcing I'm a bona fide member of ISKCON, which I am. Maybe the taste is gone of wearing those L.L. Beans and Lands End clothes. I tried it and still may go back to it if I want. I can do what I want. But if I don't want to wear those duds and look like a dude, I don't have to. I can be a little round-shouldered monk, like Prabhupada knew me, and shuffle around getting the body of my *dhoti* wet and dirty. I think I'll ask Hari to press the *dhoti* tops, the shirts. And I'll need a few more, so I'll ask Ollie if he an get them from Vrindavan. Well look at you. A uniform man again. I thought you wanted to get away from all that? But you're a uniform man anyway, in your L.L. Bean jeans, your mock turtlenecks. You can try for *tilak*, but it'll be a problem taking all those head baths for headaches during the day. Do it anyway and apply the *tilak* again and again. It's a beautiful adornment, and the books say whoever does it gets the blessings of the *gopis*. Why go without it? Get used to that wonderful routine of rounding out the peak just over the nose and making the middle part clear and clean. You're a Vaishnava, son. Be proud of it and let them see it when they look at you. Let them ask about it, let them be startled, let them know you're a "Marlboro man."

CHAPTER EIGHT

H E'S FEELING LONELY. You'd feel lonely too on a rainy, overcast Sunday with nothing you really want to do. You don't want to work out on the Body-Solid equipment, or prayer rote, have no friend or lover to share, cry to God and His texts. Can't call something for that. The Sunday *New York Times* was here, but that was a waste of precious gold. As is listening to music. Is that why you daydreamed of going to Washington, D.C., to pay homage to the great man with one foot? But it would be a great strain. And what would you say in his presence? Touch him and acknowledge, "You are a great soul. This is my last chance to touch you and be in your presence. I don't want to drain you but to show my homage, acknowledge you as a greater son of Prabhupada." Go to a holy place and see a holy person. Am I fit for such a trek?

A lonely person's pain. He could paint. He could sing the sorority songs if she were a girl at Harvard among fellow girlfriends. Find solace in the expanded lone rings of the pebble thrown into the pond of writing. Curl up with a book, even if it doesn't have the seal of the BBT or the Pope's "no objection."

Our body is old and is daydreaming about the rigors of driving all the way to S.F. and then flying all the way to D.C., taking extra pills. Extra hotel stop. Extra writing. Line up an appointment to see a great man and then come right back to Philo. Oh it will take a great toll on you. Yes sir, it will. I can think of other things you can do. You can paint the scene of this smiling man with big teeth leaning down to bless you as you touch where his foot used to be and your arms reach up and his reach down in a last embrace. But nothing can replace the personal visit. A painting would be something. Curling up with a book. Would you replace? I just spoke with a woman who said she was robbed eight years ago, hit on the head with a golf club, and set afire. "Are you Maharaja?" She wanted to talk to her son Michael, but he's at the store. She had some medicine suggestions to give me. She said, "Today it's a lovely day in Texas."

> You aren't going to do something
> adventurous, I just know it. He said
> why not try in small increments,

but how small can you get? Your
efforts are...miniscule.

Play golf on a misty day. All these
things take physical energy. I see you
like a leech. Cut out that deprecation.

I want cooperation. You have stuffed your
head with international politics and now
what can you expect to come out but
Bush and Spain and Iraq and
Republican and sports and women's
styles? What will you buy?

Further from the holiness, more
double chins. My friend went
shopping and he won't come back
all day, taking his Sunday
vacation to get away from me
and this place.

How does it feel to be avoided
and left alone on the shelf?
Isn't this what you arranged?
Do you have a billiard ball table?
a stack of cards for solitaire?

You could dance in *kirtan*
say a special mantra that opens
a world of private *bhajan* for
the secret *sadaka*—he who works
to help others gets more juice out
of his own alone hours.

BRIHAD MRIDANGA

(The Great *Sankirtan* of Chanting)

> My dear king, although *Kali-yuga* is an ocean of faults, there is still one good quality about this age: Simply by chanting the Hare Krishna *maha-mantra*, one can become free from material bondage and be promoted to the transcendental kingdom.
>
> —*Srimad-Bhagavatam* 12.3.51

> Those who are actually advanced in knowledge are able to appreciate the essential value of this age of Kali. Such enlightened persons worship *Kali-yuga* because in this fallen age, all perfection of life can easily be achieved by the performance of *sankirtan* (chanting Hare Krishna).
>
> —*Srimad-Bhagavatam* 11.5.36

Big Jim pointed out to a slim *sannyasi* that when a Godbrother builds a temple, he's praised up and down, but they seem to forget the example of Bhaktisiddhanta Sarasvati. Bhaktisiddhanta Sarasvati said that he was disappointed with the temples because the inmates fought over who would use the different rooms, who would be the proprietors. He said, "Better to take the marble off the columns of the temples and use it to print books." And His Divine Grace told our Srila Prabhupada, "If you ever get money, print books." Our Prabhupada took this as his life order and carried it out "blindly." Temple building is important, but first comes book distribution. Preaching is the essence, books are the basis, purity is the force, and utility is the principle.

In a dream, our Srila Prabhupada was invited to a program by some yoga society. He accepted it, not knowing what it actually was. When we entered their building, we saw that they were a wild group of *sahajiyas*. They wore strange haircuts. Some of these haircuts sawed off part of their heads, and they wore various strange costumes with no order to them, only whimsy. They danced about in mad nonpatterns. Prabhupada took it as a challenge and began to dance himself, showing that he had life in him, as they did, and he wasn't going to just sit still in the midst of their "dancing." But it was a useless cause. All they wanted was intoxication, which they derived from some stones that they kept in their bead bags. They fought me to get some more stones.

They had transferred some stones into my bead bag and smuggled some of their bead bags into my hands and fought me to get them. But I was acting in the mood of the agile and alert one, like a first-class basketball player, and they could get nothing from me, no matter how they cornered me or double-teamed me. My ex-wife was there trying to be the first one to greet Prabhupada as he entered the room. I was glad that she was trying to catch Prabhupada's attention and be in his group. He stayed for some time, then the fracas became so wild, like a fight, and we were all so afraid of illegalities that we left them all behind. There was no seriousness in them, and they would not listen to our Guru Maharaja, so what was the use of staying? I gave them all the stones they wanted, since they were useless to us, and we fled the scene.

> Those who are actually advanced in knowledge are able to appreciate the essential value of this age of Kali. Such enlightened persons worship *Kali-yuga* because in this fallen age, all perfection of life can easily be achieved by the performance of *sankirtan* (chanting Hare Krishna).
> –*Srimad-Bhagavatam* 11.5.36

> It could be said of these people what the ordinary people said of Nimai Pandit in the *Chaitanya-bhagavat*: "Oh brothers, I know the secret of why they close the door and perform '*kirtan*'. At night they recite mantras to bring five girls along with various palatable foods. They eat, they wear sandalwood paste and garlands, they dress in fine clothes, and they enjoy with girls in various ways. If other people saw this, they would be embarrassed. Therefore they enjoy behind closed doors.
> —*Sri Chaitanya-bhagavat*, Ch. 8, text 241–244

This was not our way. We follow the way of the Vedas and the *Srimad-Bhagavatam*, which declare that service to the Lord is the greatest treasure. Lakshmi, Brahma and Shiva are always engaged in such service. Anyone who does not believe in the words of Lord Chaitanya cannot attain Him. What more can I say?

> Oh brothers, please hear attentively about the Lord's transformations of ecstatic love, which are unique throughout the innumerable universes.
> The transformations of Mahaprabhu's ecstatic love can never be compared with the transformations of any devotee's ecstatic love within the fourteen worlds. It is to be understood that cheaters who imitate the

146

Lord's exhibition of transformations of ecstatic love in order to deceive
people are devoid of love of God.
—*Sri Chaitanya-bhagavat*, Ch. 8, text 136,
Translated by Vrindavan dasa Thakur,
with commentary by Bhaktisiddhanta Saraswati

In proper mood, Swamiji resumed reciting his books, avoiding the
sahajiyas and those who gave him no credit.

TEXT MISSING FOR REF. BELOW?
(From the general introduction to *St. John of the Cross: Selected Writings*, edited by Kieran Cavanaugh, O. C. D., Paulist Press.)
How could that be? How to understand his sensual poetry? Theoretically, how wonderful is the concept. His poetry in the book, *The Ascent of Mt. Carmel*. Especially these stanzas:

6. Upon my flowering breast
Which I kept wholly for him alone.

Their he lay sleeping, and I caressing him
There in a breeze from the fanning cedars.

7. When the breeze blew from the turret
Parting his hair,
He wounded my neck
With his gentle hand,
Suspending all my senses.

8. I abandoned and forgot myself
Laying my face on my beloved;
All things ceased; I went out from myself,
Leaving my cares
Forgotten among the lilies.

And at least we know this much of the meaning—"A deeper enlightenment and wider experience than mine" (*St. John of the Cross*)—it is necessary to explain the dark night through which the soul journeys toward that divine light of perfect union with God that is achieved, insofar as possible in this life, through love. The darkness is in trials, spiritual and temporal, that fortunate souls ordinarily undergo to the state of perfection are so numerous and profound that human science cannot understand them adequately. Nor does experience of them equip one to explain them. Those who suffer them will know what this experience is like, but they will find themselves unable to describe it.

> In discussing this dark night, therefore, I will not rely on experience or science, for these can fail and deceive us. Although I will not neglect whatever possible use I can make from them, my help in all that, with God's favor, I shall say will be Sacred Scripture, at least in the most important matters....Taking Scripture as our guide, we do not err, since the Lord speaks to us through it.
> —*St. John of the Cross*, prologue to *Ascent of Mt. Carmel*

Therefore, the description of the union of the bride and the bridegroom is a symbol of the joining of the soul with God. John tells us right in the beginning that the approach to this path will be obscure and dark, but it is a solid path, a substantial and solid doctrine for all those who desire to reach the nakedness of spirit.

Therefore, the descriptions of the soul leaving his house with a yearning to go meet the beloved is actually not something mundane but a spiritual urge to go and meet God. One has an urge, yet one is prevented and has to go through purgations of impurity.

First stanza of his poem:

> One dark night,
> Fired with love's urgent longings
> —Ah, the sheer grace!—
> I went out unseen,
> My house now all stilled;

He was lucky to escape his house without anyone noticing his departure. He was fortunate to succeed in emptying himself of his appetites in order to go to God. The nature of this dark night is a journey to divine union. All this is fascinating and profound but somehow very difficult brainwork and requires immersion into Old Testament scriptures, etc.

Yet this is just the subject matter I am speaking of for myself, for ourselves in Krishna consciousness, is it not? The words are different but that meaning is the same. Or if you say the meaning is not the same, it is only slightly different. If we could understand it by the right guidance, it would benefit us.

Tell them, tell them. Branford Marsalis. Guests coming. Dada characters cross stage: I warn you, don't get too involved with them, but I hammer home the underground artesian spring. What is it? Four foot six inch Barbara Bagley looking happy walking down Samson Avenue like Uncle Remus, taking in the oak trees and blue jays and mother nature, not noticing me peeking at her from inside our house. Why do we have to get dragged along with Mom and Dad on Lord Nityananda's appearance day to go visit our in-laws? We prefer to stay home. No celebration. No *kirtan* strain, no *mridanga*. Lord Nityananda is Sankarshan, the *sandini* potency, who holds everything together.

I love my friend Nara and the Supreme Narayan. And Lord Chaitanya. And Srila Prabhupada. So there. As I watch Barbara Bagley, so short but still happy in her private communing with nature. We are so low-profile here, he said. "It is Lord Nityananda's appearance," and I replied nothing. He mumbled.

We're happy to read about a new trend in writing away from realism, as reported in *The New York Times Book Review:* "She takes great pains to avoid specificity essential to the allusion of realism, as if she's warning the reader not to get too invested in her characters, to look elsewhere for the meaning of her stories."

She's influenced by Kafka, often establishes a farfetched premise, and treats it with deadpan literalism. "What if a family kept traveling salesmen imprisoned in a pen, as if they were farm animals? What if a deranged Civil War surgeon planted amputated limbs in a field?" The reviewer actually prefers realism but admits that this new kind of surrealism is the trend again. It's more like what Swami Swims is swimming in. So there's hope.

One time, when I was alone in our family house trying to get high on nutmeg and reading a book about Nietzsche, I understood that he was an ascetic. That's what the guy writing the book said. Our parents had us lined up to make a holiday visit way out in Rosedale, Long

Island, the next day. I really didn't want to go, packed up in the Dodge and having to spend a whole beautiful weekend day mingling with cousins and aunts and uncles. So I wrote them a note and said that I was an ascetic and that was why I didn't like attending such gatherings. And then I went to sleep for the night. My parents were out somewhere. The next morning, my mother woke me up. She was outraged about my note and told me to get ready as soon as possible for going to Rosedale. My father also thought I was a blathering nonsense to say I was an ascetic. It just added fuel to my desire to get out of that house forever and be an ascetic. Now I am an ascetic and my parents are both dead. I'll be dead soon also. I think I am an ascetic. I'm not sure about Nietzsche. It's unfortunate that we couldn't make more peace or harmony or some kind of familial touching base, even though we were so different. I'm certainly partly to blame.

The plumber told the electrician that humans are more frequently meeting up with bears and mountain lions as spring approaches. The instructions for what to do when you meet these beasts are indelibly imprinted in my mind: don't run away from them, stand as tall as you can, make loud noises, etc. I wish I had the same seriousness and anticipation about prayer meeting as I have in anticipation of lion meeting. It doesn't have to be such fear of God but that indelibility, that complete faith in the method.... One wouldn't think of trying another method whimsically when meeting a lion or neglecting to act. So it should be with prayer. Rooaar...Hare Krishna, Hare Krishna, Krishna Krishna, Hare Hare, Hare Rama, Hare Rama, Rama Rama, Hare Hare. It's not a trifling thing. At least I'm on the path winsomely. Lovingly, desperately, you old ascetic. Now go pick out your pajamas for tonight and stand tall. Harrre Krishhhna, Harrre Krishhhna.

The Kurds are in control of Iraq and I had to take two pills today because I foolishly read *The New York Times* with my poor eyesight and old eyeglasses. You get the reaction of your acts in karmic evolution.

Ken Couttoms Typewriters and Printers just phoned. I jumped with great alacrity to catch it on the second ring. He wanted to speak with Mike Kelly. I knew what it was about, their fascinating proposal of making your own books at home with materials he'll supply. But Mike is in Ukaih today. "Does he have a pager?" No, he lent it to Blake. So Ken Couttoms said he'll send the materials in the mail. Very glad for that. We'll take a look at it. Just as good as going into his store. We are fascinated at the idea of making our own books at home, sounds good.

Why don't you paint? Why don't you exercise, at least take a walk? Yes, I shall do it. I wish we could take a look in that Ken Couttoms. If Nara only knew about it, he would stop in at his store, but there's no way of reaching him for that.

Why do you think of these minor things instead of chanting Hare Krishna mantra? The mantra is rated as the most important thing by Lord Chaitanya Mahaprabhu and Srila Prabhupada, far more impor- tant even than home book making or new eyeglasses. Honestly. And it is accessible, in one sense, right here.

Right now Acharyavana is walking in the garden chanting on his beads. His Moroccan French accent is so heavy I had to ask him to stop reading to me at breakfast, but that does not stop the Lord from receiv- ing his *maha-mantras* from his sincere heart. It is sunny out for the sec- ond day in a row. Get thee out there for twenty minutes.

Oh but maybe my eye hurts. Nara says his mother has a new doc- tor, and he says that his mother is maybe a hypochondriac.

Jimsy has fallen into a second day of right eye pain, and he's guess- ing why. It cannot be stopped despite extra meds. It may be that he wanted to go see the heroic footless *sannyasi* and then realized he was not strong enough to do it. It would be a heroic act for himself to go see the hero. Then he decided that it would be heroic to paint pictures of him going to see him, and a picture of the hero being with Prabhupada, but he could not do that. Could those be reasons? And then today Nara left, and he tried to get in touch with him and could not. Anyway, the Lilliputian world of pain surrounds him, and even his lips are chapped, as if he has a cold to go with it. Even a pill cannot do it, and he sleeps in a dark room, like a typical migraine man, helpless. He does not try prayers. Oh well. Yet he does, and waits. The prayer of waiting, the prayer of quiet. Is that Nara returning? He'll eat a little something and go to bed again, hide in a corner of the eye. Nara will have his new eyeglasses and new sweatpants. Things to cheer you up.

We're too tired to think of gaining eternity. Tomorrow we'll get on that again. Nara brought home hip eyeglasses, blackish frames, makes my eyes look bigger, blend in better with the grayish hair and short, dark beard. Modern swami look, I'm glad you dared to step forward from that golden chandelier look. Tight, snug, don't feel like they'll fall off, carved fit. What about Krishna? It's only 7:40 P.M., you can't acquire a radio signal. Too much rain. Are you wearing your miraculous Mary medallion, your Lakshmi-Nrisimha medal? *Maha-mantra* tattoo in Sanskrit? Too much anxiety to make sense of the long day of pain and poor meals. I missed you, I missed you too.

CHAPTER NINE

WHILE TALKING WITH THE COUNSELOR, I calmed down my offensive, but I continued crying tears. He said my crying was good and I should look deeply into that love, into that dark well of love that I have for Ollie. He said it was a precious ornament. But he said it can be purified and be a beautiful thing rather than a sick thing. I can't completely understand how it is a disease at present, and yet I do believe what they're saying. It's just that at present, I feel dry and lonely. I also feel especially lonely in my relationship with God. I know my relationship with Ollie, a sick Ollie, is not going to help a lack of relationship with Krishna. A relationship with Ollie was full of fun and love. But nothing replaces a relationship with Krishna, and that has to be done with austerity and seriousness, like the seriousness of chanting and the seriousness of searching for Him, and not letting up on seriousness. Yes, writing—that's a big part of your seriousness. So go to it. Now go to bed.

New York Elegy
At night, in New York's Central Park,
chilled to the bone and blowing to no one,
I talked quietly with America:
both of us were weary of speeches.

I talked with my footsteps—unlike words they do not lie—
and I was answered with circles,
dead leaves uttered, falling onto a pond...

to the trunk of an evergreen
and sleepily rubbing its cheek against the sky; onto someone's
forgotten glove,
onto the zoo, which had shown its guests out,
onto the bench with its wistful legend:
PLACE FOR LOST CHILDREN.

Dogs licked the snow in a puzzled way,
and squirrels with eyes like lost beads
flickered between the cast iron baskets,

amidst trees lost in the woods of themselves.
Great juttings of granite stood about
morosely, preserving in mineral calm
a silent question, a reproach—
lost children of former mountains.

Behind a wire fence, zebras, munching hay
peered, at a loss, into striped darkness.
Seals poking their noses from the pool,
caught snow in mid-flight on their whiskers;
they gazed around them, quizzical, confused,
forsaken children of Mother Ocean
taking pity, in their slippery style,
on people—lost children of the Earth.

I walked alone. Now and then, in the thicket,
the crimson firefly of a
    cigarette
floated before an unseen face—the staring pupil
of the night's wide
    eye.

And I felt some stranger's feeling of being lost
with searching embarrassed
for a feeling of being lost at my own,
not knowing what this is what I longed for.

At night, beneath the snowfall, its whispered secret
having made us
    one,
America and I sat down together
in the place of lost children.
    —Yevgeny Yevtushenko

I've Been Lost Too
    Macy's department store all alone with a policeman, my name on
the loudspeaker, just one block over from ours, 77th Street, but it was

terror from strangers and bullies.

Many years later, taking LSD at my parents' summer home when they were not there,

I went out for a walk and got lost, encountered a police car with flashing blue lights interrogating some teenagers

I almost walked into it but turned around and walked the other way, petrified with fear, feeling lost among the look-a-like bungalows until I somehow by instinct, like a dog, found the house that was theirs and breathed a great sigh of relief.

> With all a great feeling of lostness, among
> marijuana smokers, "sensitive" poets.

When I got out of the navy I came to an ideal—cold-water flat, money in the bank, I could write all night, but no soul mate

no one to love my poems, no one to love me. One who loved me

in the place for lost children I made a tradeoff—my parental home for living alone with lower East Side dreamers. Had to work, struggled. Place for lost children, live with other foreigners. She said I'm a genius. Chase after her for that.

> *Saturday Morning Phone Call*
> Go ahead, you're doing fine, the doctor said.
> To take medicine under pressure.

Like Ollie's not coming home and you're not able to go see Bhakti-tirtha Swami. Pains are coming and going, coming and going. You have to take some extra medicines—

That's what they are there for. You're doing fine. You're doing fine.

That's one way to interpret it.

> Missiles crashing. Don't run,
> you're trapped. Be cool and rest, you're a
> senior citizen of CA with photo on a laminated card,
> Your ankle is worse?
> But you're pulling through better than you ever did before.
> I'll call you next

Saturday? Yes, *haribol*. Yes. I can't look at it as the worst.

Never Thought I Saw Anyone as Beautiful as That
I look at Radha and Krishna as Gertrude Stein first falls in love
with Alice B. Toklas, never saw anyone as beautiful

As that, never saw anything as beautiful as that. She had seen other
girls but never anyone as beautiful as that. Her hair and her pure com-
plexion. She fell unconscious by her beauty. In that way a million times
I was entranced with Radha and Krishna. I say a million times a trillion
times it is because They are supreme

Beauties of all the worlds and I am just a speck of capacity to enjoy
beauty and They allow

Me to take in that capacity the way the devotees of
Lord Chaitanya were allowed to enjoy His beauty at
Srivas Thakur's house.

He was kind and generous to allow them to see according to their
Capacity different facets of His Vishnu expansion from the view
point
Of their eternal identities of Him.
I don't know what I'm talking about but just accept it as pure utter
capacity to love.

Gertrude loved Alice as her best girlfriend for the rest of her life.
She always thought of her that way.
I see Krishna as more and more beautiful
Most generous, the richest, the most powerful, the most wise, the
most loving. One time He came as Vishnu from Vaikuntha. He came
down as a boatman to save the family of one of His devotees. They
were in great peril from the flood and the *yauvanas*, but He came down
as a boatman and saved them. He asked them—I forget which man it
was—do you remember that night?

Do up remember when I came down as Vishnu and I came as an
ordinary boatman and saved you?

When he said that, the devotee fell unconscious, remembering the
bliss of that night.

But you're always claiming that you don't appreciate the glory of the Lord. But the other is true too. Sometimes I look at Gaura-Nitai in this room and I fall to my knees.

After They change into a new outfit, I notice how big and beautiful They are, and I thank Them for Their mercy.

So my life is not *all* bad. I like so many things about it, including the medicine that takes away the headaches. Including the relief I get from Gaura-Nitai.

So it's true and worth repeating, the way the bottoms of Their feet are painted

makes me very happy. Their legs are yellowish but Their feet are red at bottom. This makes me happy, very happy, and worth repeating. I'm happy

Especially when the sky is very gray and overcast and rainy

And the boards are soaked red and the tinkles of the rain are bouncing and there's no letup in sight and I call Nara and he comes and I tell him I have a headache and he gives me a pill and says, "Don't worry, just take this." I cannot tell him then how much I love Radha and Krishna and Gaura-Nitai, but it makes me happy to say something to him like, "You know, you're a good guy. You are the best guy in this house." And I tell him that Gertrude Stein is a good writer, and I tell him silly things, and then I go back to bed, nursing my wound. But it's all because I love Radha and Krishna, at least in a little way, in a repetitive, handsome, rainy-day way. Foghorn again and again so other boats won't hit it. And you're very happy, the touch of the leaves that you won't be hurt and that you'll be safe and sound, and you believe that you'll be safe, and you believe them when they tell you that your lawyer is smart and that you will not lose, because you're a senior citizen now and you won't have to pay any income tax, and anyway, whatever happens, you love Gaura-Nitai the way Gertrude loves Alice, so there's nothing that can harm you, even if you are in jail, just chant the holy name and it would be true, you would remain happy as a lark calling in the rain, and they could print it in *Time* magazine that Stephen says he's happy as a lark singing in the rain, even in jail. He said because his conscience was simple and free he did not feel bound by the prison walls, but he was happy, although he went against the government he was truly

happy, as happy as Gertrude was for loving and being loved back by
Alice B. Toklas.

That's how I feel about my complete freedom above life from now
until the end, even though my love is small, it will grow, and I'm free
for my love so no one can stop me.

Metamorphosis
A man took his son to the
hospital where his uncle was
dying from cancer.
Did he tell him what to expect,
what was going on?
No, the uncle did that,
he did all the talking.

It made a big impression on me.
I saw him go from a big healthy man
to a skinny ravaged man in one year.
We visited once a month.
And your father didn't tell you?
No! He didn't tell me anything!
My uncle started slowly telling me
about spiritual things. With about
three months to go, he told me about Aum.

Then with about two months to go, he was
in the Catholic church hospital crying to Christ,
completely changed, crying to Jesus.
It made a big, big impression on me to see him
dwindle down like this and go completely spiritual
crying for forgiveness of his sins out loud
and praying out loud.
It embarrassed my father.
But I was ten or eleven years old
and fascinated, how he changed in
those last two months.

One Man Against Everyone
I was one against all
humanity with only a blade.
I could give them no mercy
and they spared me no quarter.
They slashed into me with their naked hands,
with their police squads, I slashed down
family shoppers, "Please have mercy on us!"
I could not. I only hoped my
trusty blade would hold out
and stay firm in my fingers to
cut through the mass of steel
and living flesh and
I could survive and find what
I wanted and they could only
pour on more resistance to
tear me apart, not caring for
what I was, that I was only one
person, no mercy, not asking
what I wanted, it was a nonstop
melee and it didn't end. It was
a typical nightmare
for SDG.

Yes, so much laceration of all young cats and dogs, to keep down the population, and strategies in the tobacco wars—stop smoking or you'll wind up dead premature. We all die, but why at thirty-five or forty years when you could enjoy a precious three more decades? Has he come to interrupt me again, the man from Porlock? I've tried so hard to get it right, but still I am boycotted (I mean Alfred Swami is) from having his articles accepted in the magazine of the Hare Krishna movement. Three years' embargo, and by then his pen may still be looked at askance... ex-felons are still not allowed to vote after release from jail sentence, or there is some confusion about it among the dwindling ranks of the Democrats. Is it that no one wants to say that he or she wants to speak out that he is a Dem but actually does remain a silent Dem? Are the Dems silent and yet because the mandate Republican president is too outrageous to speak against or for?

And therefore he writes to die in a private place listening to Robert Schumann's piano concerto and wishing he knew about classical music and its connection to heaven. He has his own homemade theology about Trane, so surely the same must be true of the peccadillo Mathkings, the centuries-old classical composers who are available now often only to snobs.

No, you are a drive-ass member who finds the twenty-four hour radio channel Sirius pretty middle-class, not playing the cutting edge, but playing to a soft audience, a little of this, then something excellent, then the excellent Mingus dynasty, then Dinah Washington, then Stan Kenton, the mediocre, Medicare, mundane, pretty good, pretty bad, prayer, excellent, pretty bad. Better you play your hand-picked—"we must love one another and die." "*Turn that off!*" shouts poet Auden, "*that's the worst thing I wrote, I disown it, I threw it away, I revised it.*" Turn off all music. I'm too lazy to "do a workout," or even take a walk. No, a walk I shall do.

Poopy-doo, Robert Schumann, will you last a little longer and come with me on a board walk promenade? I do like your choice of notes. But I don't put you between me and *harinam*. I have an agent in Vrindavan who is rolling daily in the *Vraja-raja* (holy dust of the *dhama*) for me. Can I benefit that way? He says the monkeys are getting bolder and more numerous. You have to think about them constantly and outsmart them. Think of monkeys. Hare Krishna. Hare Krishna.

Cats in boots. We shall soon get out of the rack. The waters of *tsunami* will subside. Nurses against the governor of CA, good for them! Let them kick ass! Where did I leave off? It looks like a sophisticated wrist bracelet, but don't be fooled. Behind that silver clasp and string of *Tulasis* is a *nama japa* set of fifty-four beads. Unclasp the clasp and you can say one round of mantras while going to work (while driving?) or while watching your kid at soccer then turn your beads around and finger another fifty-four and you've got one round done. You can't trick Jimmy into spending fifteen dollars for one of those. He has no hope that they will help him. Why don't they advertise for the clickers? Might as well face it; they are more functional, even though less orthodox.

And so as we wrote, 3:15 rolled by, and we promised to take a walk on the golden pressed leaves with a timer in our pocket to time about fifty-one mantras.

Why don't you come to Guyana?

Why?

Do you like it here?

Do you write, wear a small beard? Someone wrote to the magazine, "Is it better to wear a beard that has to regularly be cut or not to have a beard?" Get off my back with your piccadillos. Stiff as boards, rules and regs. Straw-man questions. Let a person show their heart if they want to wear a beard. Keep your leading questions and straw men to yourself. Even if you live without a beard, you still have to shave your "beard" every day.

Hare-Jo, a new 'zine. We shall write it in our own rime in wine without liquor but soft root beer to Krishna. It's getting late and I'm a senior citizen who doesn't smoke, and somebody loves me, that's nice work if you can get it.

> Down with drunks
> and monks and dogs on this property.
> I love the people of this world under
> certain conditions. I don't believe
> they should be ripped off by
> bigshots and entrepreneurs.
> Be good, do good, teach good,
> be one of the good who
> hears of God from
> the God-knowers.

We already told you what S.B. said when asked why he wrote. Raise your hand if you remember. It was not "for fame," it was not "if I didn't write, I'd die." Ireland's Samuel Beckett said, "I write because I'm not good at anything else." Did I tell you that answer resonates with Jiminy? He can't even run a dictaphone without fouling it up.

But he can enjoy Rachmaninov's "Third Piano Concerto," occasionally remembers rooting for the old Brooklyn Dodgers at Ebbet's Field via TV to his room. But basically, "because I'm not good at anything," and that's why he evolved to his own style. I don't mean that in a demeaning way. I could have trained myself under professionals to write the right way. But when I saw the published mavericks, I wanted to be *honest* like them and write whatever I had to say. Not like Salinger, Bukowski, Miller, or anyone, but *oneself*, without kowtowing to publishers' standards. Gather these pages, keep rocking. Mud in your eye. Organic pudding. Something.

All right, we'll all die. He said, "Be sensitive about telling the survivors of this *tsunami* the philosophy of Krishna consciousness. They're in trauma. If you shove the philosophy down their throat, it will make it worse for them. Share the sorrow with them. Don't argue with them as they condemn God. Give them practical shelter and solace. Don't "preach" karma and sins right away. But at some time, when their traumas have abated (when?), when the flood waters of time have subsided, take them gently aside and teach them Krishna consciousness. He said timing is very precious in when and how to preach to such people. Krishna consciousness is a science and a human art. Well said. Now back to the baroque. At least that article went out with smarts and timing to the choir, the preachers who may have otherwise blundered in their delivery of Krishna consciousness to those in trauma. He's an emeritus general and gave wise counsel, living until he dies with excellent statesmanship and protocol in his own forward march, if you'll hear it.

Satan said to Jesus, "Bow at my feet and I'll give you whatever you desire in all the worlds." Ahh, but everything here lacks eternity. Your old joys lack deep, profound eternity. The bell strikes one! But all joys lack deep, profound eternity. Thus spake Zarathustra. How can you "sell your soul" to gain eternity? It's a contradiction in terms.

Then there are the Struldbruggs (*stir dull blood*, from *Gulliver's Travels*), a race of people who are immortal. They do not die, but as they grow older they attain all the miseries of old age. The state makes them give up their wives at about eighty years; eventually they cannot read books, they cannot even think, they just sit around and mostly vegetate morosely. When they see a funeral, they lament, wishing that they too could die. So that is not a desirable immortality, and they're a most unwanted race living within the kingdom. They are shunned. When Gulliver first heard about them, he became overjoyed and wanted to see the Struldbruggs. He thought if he could become one, he could use his time to amass riches and learning and surround himself with other Struldbruggs and have very enlightening discourses as he watched the epochs flow by. He thought that he would stay hale and hearty. He did not understand the "Catch-22" of Struldbruggs, that one remains mortal in all ways, except that he lives on.

This kind of immortality theme is a composite of the literary preoccupation of everlasting life without youth, as in the Tithonus myth and the scientific concern with longevity. To an orthodox Christian, such a quest for eternal life was blasphemous and foolish. Jiminy Swami agrees with these opinions and would not like to become a Struldbrugg, or even meet one. So he is writing to die, writing within a normal period of years. Damn the torpedoes, full speed ahead while you've got the stamina and the semen. A big businessman met with our friend Nara while Nara was doing business in Mexico. The bigshot took a liking to our Nara and gave him a piece of business wisdom, Mexico style: "Nara, first act, apologize later."

No one lives forever. Write and die. You can die at home just from an infection by a rose thorn, as well as in a battle skirmish in Iraq or by a sniper's bullet or from a cataract in the eye while the simple operation is being performed. You can leave all your little children behind you as posterity. But Prabhupada mocked posterity. He said, "Oh yes, posterity is living on in your place, but where are you going?" The fool says he lives on in his son, but where he is going he doesn't know. All my little children piled up in manuscripts, but where does Jiminy go? He don't go where his prose goes, he don't know where his nose goes.

And what about Faust in *Mephistopheles*? The devil, with God's permission, tried to lure a soul to hell. It was Dr. Faust, a man who was already happy in his attempts to reach God by reason and alchemy. Mephistopheles went and conquered Faust by saying that he would become the slave of Faust in this world, and then in the next world—if there was such a thing—Faust would become the slave of the devil. So then Faust went wild living a life of ribaldry and greed, gaining lands, and out of lust conquering the women, purging everywhere, being consumed by every form of lust, being cruel to people everywhere, until finally he loses his own sight. But at that moment, he's redeemed because he feels the pity that other people have. As precious sight is drawn from his dying eyes, suddenly it's as though Faust could finally see. He called in excitement to his laborers to set forth and complete the work of draining the remaining tidal swamps so that he might give away all the reclaimed lands to his people. "This is the highest wisdom that I own, the best that mankind ever knew," he cried as he raced about blindly.

> Yes—this I hold to do with devout insistence
> Wisdom's last verdict goes to say:
> He earns both freedom and existence
> Who must reconquer them each day.

> *Then, in joy, Faust died.*

Just as Mephistopheles reached to take the prize of Faust's soul for eternal damnation, a host of angels descended and distracted while Faust's soul escaped; it was the devil who would taste defeat. Though Faust had sinned, even so he had struggled toward growth, knowledge, and transcendence. "Whoever strives in ceaseless toil him we grant redemption. The seraphs sang. Then with the devil still raging, the angelic chorus flew into heaven, bearing off Faust's immortal part."

This is a picture of man's real immortality, not the immortality of the Struldbruggs. The pure soul as Christians know it and as the Krishna conscious people know it. The soul that cannot die even if it has to undergo birth and death due to its folly and due to its being entrapped by *maya-satan*.

F.W.

You can't avoid death by any compact with a power less than God, or even with God if you have improper motives. He said that in the *Bhagavad-gita*: "Only by devotional service can I be gained." You can't contact the honest faithful and you have the disease of living sleepiness, moody, mood swinging moody body, working on the chain gang— cloak marks, hold it right there. Reckon that ought to get it.

> Tiny powerful spirit
> Hey, pay for that, no free lunches.
> Could it be possible

To get out of this confined bedroom
A paradise for one, locked door, just
locked?

The hundred percent compact is to give to Him
and to expect nothing in return and you will get plenty.
And here is some essential advice for Vedic
followers. Never offend a great devotee.
That's the worst. If you do offend
then even I, Krishna, chanting and even studying
the Vedas will only add to your offense.
There's no forgiveness for offending the *mahatma*.
so be careful because you may not even know
who is a *mahatma*.
Do not offend.

You say you cannot give me a ride and you don't like my poem
and you can't get me a compact to eternity, then what is the use of our
friendship? Can't you even buy me some new underwear or take me to
Santa Rosa?

I'm too tired to understand my friend. It's burgeoning and I must
call for breakfast before it's too late, before it's too late.

And I must write and die.

Daddy longlegs, like a grasshopper, catches up to every escapee.
He must get a leg-pumper, the superior flier descends upon the stealthy
fliers, swoops down like fast-as-wind hawks and takes them in his claws.
All metaphors in a potpourri for death. But this is all the material car-
rion.

When Socrates was asked by his followers how he wanted to be
disposed of after death, he said, "First you catch me, then you can put
me in the grave or talk of burning." First you catch me, then put poison
down my throat; the soul will be with God before the executioners can
say, "Take off his head," or "Strap him in the wheelchair" or "Guillo-
tine!" They go through the ritual of the gas chamber and rummage for
the golden teeth. What they had would have no connection with the
eternal gold.

WRITE AND DIE

He's a schmuck, I mean Ju Jim.
I forgive him because he's me and
people depend on him and love him, but
his eyes are so droopy today and I don't think he'll
write inspired visions of Vishnujanas coming to take him,
or the other pole, dark-faced, tears streaming
and the agony of feeling Krishna's absence.

The Sunday *Times* will be here and he won't
dwell on it, the bra ads, the Oscar
awards, the basketball,
social security, he's been all over to
Lilliput and Japan but he's a tired man,
Ludwig Beethoven.
They want some money from
him. He's a CA senior
citizen and wants to buy another shirt and
eyeglass cleanser and
as in *Faust*, before the devil
catches his mortal body he wants
the angels to swoop down, scare
Mephistopheles away and carry the immortal part
of Schmucky to the eternal planet of the Cowherd Boy.

We don't know where our uncles are going
our knuckles got scraped in playfulness which
is a happy state that is the subject of some of
his best poems, like the one of
Mini Mouse in Hollywood. I think that's
just goofing. When you go shopping insist
that Nara buy a couple of nice shirts for
himself and a pair of pants. That will make
me feel good.

Why that woman allows so much cleavage

to show is her own business. None of my own.
It could be a little cooler on the *brahmachari* if she…
but it probably is much more comfortable for her
her own way.

Get bold colors. The main thing is to lower the
headaches that come from exertion.
Holy Ghost don't allow it yet. I used to
paint five canvases in two hours. Now I can only do
two. And I'm starting to feel that dreadful
light-at-first twinge in the right eye. You know
there's nothing to do but quit, really.

Holy Spirit write and die.
Would you like a cup of tea? Where's that
cat? That dog? That giveaway?
I thought he'd just come and take me
because I did not have time to invite death.

He came to take me,
there was room in the carriage
for only him, me, and eternity.

He knew how to get there. Death doesn't mean
necessarily hell, just a round house
to an account of Krishna next time around
and He may take you back if you are good enough
or do as you need.

CHAPTER TEN

HE THOUGHT HE DID SOMETHING SWELL by kicking up his heels, not re fusing to fall asleep in the early hours. But there were two things I can quickly think of that were better than doing that type of thing. One was to walk around the outside of the building while chanting *harinam* about fifty times, and the other thing would be to read a holy book. Or I could chant indoors while keeping awake. But it is 7:15 A.M. We could fill out the order form for five volumes of Sir Winston Churchill's famous books, *The Second World War*, which are now on sale for $9.95.

He dreamt his group had to make an emergency diaspora. They did it with very little knowledge of where they were or where they had to go. They had little money or direction. He thought, "I used to be a big star and leader of this group, but now I have no knowledge of where I'm going." But then he felt the reassuring hand of his ex-wife. At least he thought it was she, and he was not abandoned. Their hope was that they could reach the country and city that they knew and then put on a show. By Jake, let's get out of this zoo and reach a safe place. Chant with the Krishnas.

What if, before breakfast, the mind is sleepily snow-ploughing through *harinams while at the same time* recalling the plot of the Charlie Chaplin film, which Chaplin himself narrates, up in the icy north searching for gold. Do you remember? He is somehow thrown together in a wintry blizzard with Big Jack, and they survive in a one-room cabin through episodes of Jack hallucinating that "the little fellow" is a chicken, which he tries to shoot for dinner, and then the cabin starts to slide off a cliff in a storm, and Jack jumps outside and finds his hidden cache of gold and allows Charlie to survive as co-partner millionaire? Is that *nama japa*? Offensive certainly. Charlie had a sweetheart, too. He wins her in the end on the boat leaving the Great North.

Cranberry juice is good for stopping emergency urinations, they say. But I tried that before and it didn't work. I'll gladly take antibiotics if I can just get a prescription, with or without a test. I wet my pants so often, surely that's a "test." My counselor keeps telling me if I don't want to go or stay at the concert, then at any moment I can change my mind and go back to the hotel. You're never trapped. But "this material body is a network of flesh and bones on the pathway to death. Somehow we have fallen into this ocean of material birth and death, and of all the senses, the tongue is the most voracious and difficult to control."

Wheat flakes, mango, milk, prayer uttered before eating, but then back into the mental pool of chaos and confusing speculation and bodily reflections. No single-minded concentration on serving your Lord.

No, you can't get medicine without going personally to the clinic and delivering your dear bodily-produced urine right on the spot. So we will do that today. And get in some shopping beforehand. John Ashbery, underwear. He's making progress saying Krishnas silently off the beads.

The Grammy Award for the voice of death, the Oscar for the picture of immortal life. The National Book Award for the fiction and nonfiction of God by believers. The Nobel for banning prize-fighting.

If you write a book that loops the loop and is alertly limber and at discount prices and that gives you the best merchandise—Nara knows the quality brands—then you enjoy picking. He refused to take any clothes for himself. The technology is so advanced that the counter boy just placed a metal meter against a pack of socks and it passed the price. Then he placed the meter against a pair of shorts and a red light flashed the price. Then he threw the clothes into a bag. Then he told us today, Tuesday, it was ten percent off for senior citizens. So that meant our socks were free. And hey, we weren't that easy to convince.

Soft and quiet, kept to himself. Didn't like the flashy ones. Didn't like the miracle makers. For him it was enough to work eight hours a day at the welfare office, taking a few hours off to type at home, and then go see the swami at night. And chanting and *kirtan*, opening the faucets, outpourings of sweat in the summertime, Lower East Side. Not a family as lovely as theirs sounded. Bhima, head mafia. Don't go back to that right now. Keep talking about life and death, the breath, how long can you last? The timer starts ringing in Jim's pocket.

"What's that?"

"It means we've been walking for twenty minutes. Now let's think of what you can do while you're here for three weeks."

Yeah, ask your momma if you can go see Branford Marsalis and Ravi Coltrane. I hear you've been chanting more off the top of your head and not counting them. I heard you've been "gettin' better" but "slippin' an' slidin'." It don't look good for a man your age. Kids one third your age are running past you. You're running on social security benefits and old-time points. Counting on that and expecting to go to heaven for service you did thirty years ago and last-minute improvements? You'd better work out on the slide bar.

Falling asleep, I remember giving a *Bhagavatam* class at the Dallas *gurukula,* early days. There was a passage about how the materialist thinks he is happy in his illusory life, happy home with gardens and birds chirping. I made a joke how in the cartoons, they depict the bird-chirping when someone gets knocked on the head unconscious. Right? Tweet tweet. Those films for kids are so sadistic. One of the worst is Tom and Jerry—nonstop torture back and forth between the cat and mouse. They try to cut off each other's heads and cut each other in half. A rapid sequence of torture to a background of light jazz. Boinnng! Tom ambushes Jerry and hits him on the head with a sledgehammer, flattening him down to a two-inch *jiva*. But then Jerry bounces up and soon flattens out his opponent with a steamroller until Tom is as flat as a piece of dough. One of them saws the other in half and stacks him into piles of logs. One has his eyes pulled up and always occasionally someone makes a hammer blow to the tweet-tweet-tweet of birds, as Mohammad Ali seems to be hearing when knocked out by the darker man Spinks.

I remember the teacher Nandini dasi laughing at my joke, and I appreciated that because I admired that. It was not a deep insight by a sage, not a brilliant interplay of *shlokas* or some much needed practical advice on disciplining children, just a joke, comic relief from a traveling preacher, which is what I was by then. Not a teacher in a school. So I could laugh.

Jim was imagining all different funny cartoons—Road Runner and Woody Woodpecker, torturing scenes, when he was awakened by the phone ringing. By the second ring he held the phone to his ear. "Hello?"

A woman said, "Charlie?"

"Charlie?" Jim said. "I think you have the wrong number."

Then she said, "Charlie Schlenz?"

And he said, "Oh yes, he's in India."

She said he applied for so many social security benefits and appointments and has broken them all. Won't be back for a year. Can you give me your name? "Jiminy Cricket."

Thank you very much. Now where shall I wander? I wanted to rest all day before the long ride and concert tomorrow evening. But can I risk going back to dreams of cartoons? That could go on forever instead of Hail Marys and Hare Krishnas and rest.

The little chipmunk is not used to going to the city, the big city of high and low streets, San Francisco. But they went, four of them—Nanda, Mukhi, Nara, and the chipmunk—to a big hotel. The computer map showed them how to go. When they finally found the place—Mukhi was driving—Nanda advised her, "Make a left here and then another left, right into the entrance. Enter as if you own the place." This is for Krishna because we're going to hear the fortieth anniversary of *A Love Supreme*, played by musicians who are inspired by the spiritual piece." [where does quote end?]

Yes, it's for Krishna, staying overnight in a big hotel. I talked some peppy talk in the truck on the way over, but then got exhausted and had to sleep. I hope I will hold up during the show or else I'll just have to leave. Remember, at any moment you can leave. At any moment you can leave your body if Krishna tells you.

I hadn't realized what a small, grizzled, rural monk I am, how far away I have been from the big city and its roughnecks. We met so many motorcyclists at the gas stations. One had "I am an asshole" on the back of his jacket, and many other things like that. Slinky girls, slacky girls, lots of graffiti everywhere, a big billboard showing a terribly dented car and next to it a marijuana crop and a big sign: "Made in California." Take the hemp and you'll wind up dead. But we haven't come for that but for what we hope is a spiritually enlightening evening.

Write or die. Smoke hemp and you'll die sooner, without any chance.

While sleeping in the hotel, I was rehearing in my mind of a *vyasapuja* lecture I would give in the future. I would sing first the Hare Krishna mantra. I would say *"touché"* to someone in the audience. After chanting I would say, "First I want to recognize the auspicious presence of some advanced persons in the audience," and then I would introduce a *sannyasi* and a few other persons. I would not assume that they were my disciples or say anything about that. I would give a straight lecture, but also do some tricks, and I would be straight because I am meant to be straight, and I would be playful because I am meant to be playful, and I would somehow talk about crying. Yes, as I lay in bed I thought about crying and saying that I may cry during the lecture and don't ask me why, but everybody cries because we have soft hearts. Everybody cries, the Vaishnavas cry because they want to come closer to Krishna. Yes, I would talk about crying and have on hand statements about crying from the Vaishnavas. It might seem odd, but I would go on about that subject and get them prepared for my crying, and then I would talk about false tears, known as crocodile tears. I would recite the Quadrille of the lobster in *Alice in Wonderland,* sung on the beach.

> *The Lobster Quadrille*
> "Will you walk a little faster?"
> said a whiting to a snail.
> "There's a porpoise close behind us,
> and he's treading on my tail.
> See how eagerly the lobsters and the turtles all advance!
> They are waiting on the shingle—
> will you come and join the dance?
> Will you, won't you, will you, won't you,
> will you join the dance?
> Will you, won't you, will you, won't you,
> won't you join the dance?
> "You can really have no notion
> how delightful it will be
> When they take us up and throw us,
> with the lobsters, out to sea!"
> But the snail replied "Too far, too far!"
> and gave a look askance—
> Said he thanked the whiting kindly,
> but he would not join the dance.
> Would not, could not, would not, could not,

would not join the dance.
Would not, could not, would not, could not,
could not join the dance.
—from *Alice's Adventures in Wonderland*
by Lewis Carroll

In *Alice in Wonderland*, Alice asks the crocodile why he cries his crocodile tears. We know that they are insincere tears. Bhaktisiddhanta Saraswati advises that we soak our couch in tears if we want to reach Krishna. Krishna consciousness is a crying movement. If you can't reach him by all the different prescribed methods, then cry. Let your hair down, baby, and cry.

Cry and die. A little bald-headed man in a Phillips-Morris suit introduced us to our room in the skyscraper hotel. He said the room included writing paper, and that made me click, thinking of Rilke writing letters in different European countries. Write and die, longhand message from the heart, and then some. Taking it as a castle to write in, and in between the lines, looking for a paramour.

Breakfast: Irish pudding and braised apples, English muffins, OJ with the window open and zigzag San Francisco view, harbor to harbor. Nara isn't feeling well, has a kidney stone. He has them frequently and has to drink lemon juice and pee for twenty-four hours. So we're all anxious to leave this Renaissance hotel and return to the farm. No matter that they have business consultants (for a fee) and a concierge to help us plan our activities in San Francisco (for a fee), and a fitness center with a treadmill, Stair Master, exercise bicycles, free weights, and complimentary fresh fruit and water available after our workout (for a fee).

Complimentary newspaper. Why aren't I happier? My comrades may want me to get into the swing and praise the drummer from last night. But I was tired. *Déjà vu*. I liked it. I could not whistle or shout after the solos, but I applauded. I think I will cancel our plans to come to S.F. again in May to see Sonny Rollins in person. I just bought a CD of *The Best of Sonny Rollins*.

I like to play with my friends. In the business world, they call it "face time" when you can actually be with someone in person, not just electronically—e-mail, telephone, etc. Chipmunk was trying to do some *japa*, he claimed, but the phone kept ringing, and he had to jump off the bed and grab the telephone. He was the operator at Grand Central, fielding calls from peoples' relatives in Australia (sixteen hours ahead)—6:00 A.M. our time, 11:00 P.M. their time—and in Texas and New York. He played the role politely for awhile but then tired. Then his friends nearby started phoning, and he made appointments to see them, face time. Treatment team tomorrow. Playing the original "A Love Supreme" to compare it with the Marsalis imitation his friends loved, all four here together, and discuss.

Meeting with Gita-nagari Press the next night. Maybe a short counseling session before his counselor travels east and you're on your own again.

> Sunny on yellow page on beach
> March. Existential man took out the pistol,
> sun as blazing in *L'etranger*
> and he could hardly see in the sunlight
> a stranger approaching on the beach and
> he thought life has no meaning so why
> don't I kill him, and he did.
>
> Just as Raskolnikov did over a hundred years
> before for the same reason:
> atheism. So what does it matter
> what you do? Take an act into
> your own hands in the meaningless
> universe.
>
> Do you want a last cigarette?
> Would you like to see a priest
> before we hang you? No he turned
> his head away. Not like the murderer who turned
> to kiss the feet of Jesus Christ at the last second
> before the guillotine. Maybe because Therese
> had been praying for him fervently as a personal

project to save his soul.

She rejoiced—"It worked!"
Intercessory prayer really
works and the world has
meaning. I mean he does it because
he believes in it still and prays
from the heart.
Chipmunk feeding, paces himself
for a weekend in the big city.

I'll tell you the truth: Jiminy is recovering from a serious disease. Tell you the truth, he's actually recovering. But he's not well enough to do what other people do. For example, healthy people can work out on exercise machines and if they are printers, they're able to print. Jim has an inclination for late-in-life keep-in-shape exercise workouts. He knows a friend who works out every day and who encourages Jim. Has even bought him some equipment. This friend has an awesome physical build. If he were to ask Jim whether he's working out, Jim would have to say no, I don't do it at all. Maybe in the future I'll get over my lethargy. And Jim has lots of hard-earned realization doing art. Is he any good? Yes, under the umbrella of outsider art. At any rate, he likes to do it, does it a lot—it was love, could have been, should have been. But for months now it's lethargy and no painting.

Now a scholarly disciple is visiting, and he should give him some time, talk to him. This devotee is the principal of a school, and he says the main thing he wants to achieve in the school is character development. So ask him, "What do you mean and how have you developed your own character?" Questions like that that come from the heart. You can't go on trying to ask him questions. It's a matter of time. If I had enough time, if I had enough bodily strength, I could do the things I want, at least one of them or two of them.

Come on, man, don't complain. You're doing one of them now. Get on the phone and call that boy and struggle through some talk with him. Something will happen and he'll be glad for it. There'll be time another day to paint. You can do it. Just paint freely, use a lot of paint. Paint quickly and don't care what someone thinks. So that's what this is. I confess—our character Jim is in an insane asylum for crickets, and he's recovering pretty well, but he's too lethargic and won't lift his finger to save his ass. To save his soul, I mean, even though God is giving him face time. Even though there are friends who mean to help him. Even though he has obligations to fulfill. Okay. I'll try to fulfill them. That doesn't mean I'll do them well or with spontaneity. That doesn't mean I can't bitch, does it?

Report from your committee: Significantly steady progress. Over the year, they hope the relaxer medicines will be reduced and pain will not come. At present, only a few relaxer medications are being used, and they wish to get rid of some of the major ones in the coming year. But others can stay. The goal is not "medicine free."

When you feel that you're on the fence between being relaxed and playful rather than being tight and feeling that your advisers want to push you forward, it is better to take the path of being relaxed and playful. That is their desire for you.

Reality check: But my desires for work and creativity cannot be kept up at a rate I would desire because there aren't enough people to carry them out.

Then ironically, after telling me to relax and that I am making progress in that way with reductions of medicines and cautious optimism, they present me two letters. One states that Bhakti-tirtha Maharaja's cancer is active all over his body and the doctors have pronounced that they can do nothing for him. He asks that the GBC remind the devotees about the prayer he asked them to make, which is basically that we ask Prabhupada to bring us whatever experiences we need that would allow us to fully please him and to take away whatever necessary to allow us to be better servants in his institution. It doesn't seem very good for his longevity. " . . . The alternative medicines do seem to slow it down temporarily. We're being very aggressive at this time because the cancer once again seems to be spreading. More important, my concern, of course, is not so much my own health but more importantly, the health of our institution, the health of my disciples, and in general how my life and my impending death can create value in helping us all to connect deeper as Vaishnava *sadhus*, how to serve and protect each other better, to live our lives with much more compassion and to live in such a way that we help to minimize the suffering of others while we strengthen our own abilities to connect with transcendence."

Why have they handed me this letter? They admit that they received the letter before we went to the concert. They didn't want to disturb me with it. How might it disturb me? Because I would probably consider again going to see him before there is no chance to see him. Then they hand me another piece of paper, an e-mail message from Gurudasi, the outreach coordinator of ISKCON Houston. "It is a once-in-a-lifetime opportunity for personal book distribution at the Houston International Festival. She describes Houston's largest festival, sponsored by the city and large corporations, with an attendance of 150K people over two weekends. Every year, the festival showcases a different country, and this year the country is India. The dates are April 23–24 and April 30–May 1. The festival has six different areas. The principle one is called 'Incredible India.' Here they have a special area for literature from India, where writers can display, sign, and sell their books. We were thinking that we could get you a table in this area to display and sign your books . . . . We believe that you have written more about Indian philosophy and culture than any of the other writers who are coming. . . . This would be a wonderful opportunity for you to get your books to people *outside of ISKCON*. They also have an artists' colony, where you could display/sell your art if you so desire. We understand that your health is precarious and that you don't travel much. We promise to arrange suitable accommodations/*prasadam* and we will not demand anything more than your presence at the festival site for as long as you choose."

Chipmunk slaps his hand to his knee and says, "Now *that's* an opportunity I can't refuse." And they plan a tour to include both a visit to Bhakti-tirtha Maharaja in Washington, a stayover at Suta's in New York until it's time for the Houston festival, and then a flight down to Houston in time for the weekend of sitting and signing books. My counselor's worried on the one hand that I might not be able to take it all, since even after the one-nighter in San Francisco I came back pacing myself and tired. It would be a challenge to see if I had the strength to make a quantum leap from invalid to active traveler-preacher. My counselor keeps assuring that if things get painful, at any moment I can cancel, and there's nothing wrong with that. My trouble is I anticipate too much, think ahead. That's why it's called anticipatory migraine. I think of the planes I'm going to get on, I think of the faces I'm going to meet. I prefer that I relax Taoistic, living by the moment. Just take it easy and don't think of what's ahead. Lie back and face the moment, that's all you have to do. As much as possible, live like that. And your best friend is the moment-by-moment writing. That's why we say write and die. Because there's nothing else to do but just that.

CHAPTER ELEVEN

A DREAM

I'M CONVINCED THAT MY MISSION is to physically fight against those who are nondevotees, *asuras*. So I go into the street and do it while singing a hymn about this. I'm surrounded by six at a time, seven at a time, and surprised as they are when I knock them down one after another. People cheer me on, but then some devotees go by and criticize me. They say, "You're not authorized to do this. This is not what Prabhupada said to do." I somehow come up with some proofs to show that it is all right, that he was a fighter and said it was a fight. Other devotees then begin to praise me and say that it's all right. I continue to knock down one after another after another until finally I collapse, but it's a happy, triumphant collapse. I realize I haven't slaughtered everyone and that now they are free to come after me. The dream ends here, and I think I'll have to get up and continue fighting back, and I'll have strength for that, but I wake with a headache. So what to do? Try to recover. Am I dreaming like this because I'm planning to see a great fighter who took a vow to fight the whole world's karma and I'm afraid to meet such a fighter?

The doctor has "mixed feelings" about the tour. But you only live once. No, you live many times. The doctor doesn't want me to relapse in the slow recovery I'm making. It may be too early for Surge Jiminy to jump from the private health care branch and fly. He may just lose elevation and fall straight down out of the nest. But the tour is well planned with rest stops and caretakers at all points to make sure that Jim doesn't overwork himself.

Swami went to a large spiritualist's festival. A fiend confronted him there, appearing as identical twins. He recognized this fiend from former days in the institution. The fiend shoved his fist up the swami's anus. It was a very painful and embarrassing position. The swami couldn't disarm the fiend, and so he turned for help from people in the large crowd. But there was no one there he could recognize, no face was familiar, and so he didn't ask anyone, "Please help me." But he did in a very low, whispered voice say, "I'm Swami Jim. Please help me."

The people could hardly hear him and didn't come forward to do something about the dilemma. He kept looking for a familiar face. Then he would turn around to look at the fiend, who was enjoying it all. In desperation, the swami thought, "There is no other help. I'll have to disengage myself on my own. This fiend is not so powerful. I must get out. It's too painful." What a pity that Swami Jim could not recognize a familiar face.

Is that what will happen at the International Book Fair? No, surely someone will come forward. Or even if he has to encounter such pain, he can press down on his own and knock over the double fiends if necessary. They are not so powerful that the chanting of Hare Krishna and applying of personal pressure cannot release you from their bond. But what a pity to have to endure their torture, even for a while. Don't worry about it, don't anticipate it. Don't run it through your unconscious. But what can I do? I see you are worrying that way. Please, take a more "taoistic" look at it. It's just a breeze, one day at a time, one moment at a time, and Krishna's name is always there in your mind and on your tongue, ready to save you. The contemplative in you can reach for <u>him</u> in love without being a show, just being sorrowful and true and loving, and Krishna will be with you, as He always is. Krishna will act and the demons will flee.

Him/
him?

> It's nothing to worry about. You can go
> out and walk. Look at your calendar and watch.
> Examine your wallet and itinerary. Who is
> dragging you where? When do you get off in D.C.?
> Who picks you up in Albany? Do you have to ask
> for laundry service in New York? Will
> someone always be carrying your pills?
> Do you know how to make a public phone call by yourself?
> What if they drop you off at an airport? Can you do it alone?
>
> Will you read a mundane book aloft?
> Can you chant airborne? If you are sitting
> next to a pretty girl, will you strike up a
> talk and then drop it? Are you suave
> and girl-shy both?

> How will you behave before the
> dying spiritual warrior? Can you be
> genuine for an hour and a half?
> Will you hold up without tripling
> your meds intake and getting very
> nervous and disordered?
>
> Just breeze through
> with Krishna the heart pacer.

Write and die. In the unconscious so many things come up. In a dream I was at an apartment. There was a big party going on, New Year's Eve. But I was just neglected, and mostly attacked by little children who were grabbing at my glasses. They were trying to tear them apart. A few people who were maternal types were trying to help me to either get the children off my glasses or get me to understand that these things happen in life and you have to accept them with more composure. I said, "Yes, yes, yes," but I decided that what I must do is bolt out of this apartment and the so-called party. I didn't know any of the people there, and anyway their intentions were all raucous and insidious as far as I was concerned. I finally did it, but I knew what the risk was. To go outside meant to go out to a world where I was completely, completely unknown and unloved. At least in that party there was some semblance of being "together" with people who accepted me, even though they didn't really accept me. Now I was in the most dismal condition, walking, walking, totally lost, like some mythical character in a Greek story.

> You better be careful, lad,
> we reach your counselor and get some
> salt to toss into that sweet rice of your
> dream.
>
> The long tongue of the snake had better
> be defanged. I know what I'm
> saying with my head.

But there's a deeper strata of sentimentalism or
is it love that wants its way,
that says don't die this way?

Open the door (the electricity just
went off). What are you going to do about
this burst of sentimental love?
You recognize your friend among strangers.
Is that so fiendish and a sure trick of *maya*?
Should it definitely be turned off?

The fates would have it that I can't reach
anyone on the phone. Even the
powerful one is busy (and this electricity is omen-ish—
it just went out, so no more phone calls).

Follow your heart, hirsute
try to put the light on but then
no power, hirsute.

Hirsute, not me. It's raining hard and
I'm shaven-headed mostly, phone calls
will be coming in and it's raining
hard now, you can't stop me
if I follow my impulse to
not be lonely. I am afraid
of myself but I intend to do it.

I met you in a dream and I intend
to follow it up, but if you
reach your counselor
first he'll roadblock
and besides, hearing Roland Kirk
is stalling me. Go and try again, see if
the phone is still busy.

If he asks me why I acted straight from the dream instead of stopping for a reality check with Reasoning, I'll tell him I was using Jung's Shadow, where you acknowledge that whenever you act in favor of one side of yourself, you're going to have to give leeway to the contra-side. We had been bashing that person. It's like being on a seesaw. When you put weight on one side, then the other side goes up. Was it Fritz Perls who refers to it as the underdog who is always trying to come to the up side? So we had been bashing that person, and now the reaction, the showdown where the underdog came up. A dream of mutual love with that person, a love of a lasting nature.

Later in the day I had another dream of my grammar school and high school buddy Phil Backoff, and I didn't want to act favorably when I woke up. Neither was he favorable in the dreams, where he was mocking me for being always the antihero in everything I did (like every antihero movie role that I got involved in). Phil is dead to me. I don't know where he lives, and I have no desire to get in touch with him.

At least keep it cool. Don't follow up on it quickly. I won't. Maybe it was a situation I didn't want to leave locked up with a "no trespass-ing" sign on it before a certain senior citizen goes to death.

Oh boy, Yadu has been reading *Under Dark Stars* and he wants me to explain it to him. It doesn't make sense, he feels. Maybe, he says, because he doesn't read literature or art. How to explain it? I started easy, saying something about New Age. He quickly said, "Free writ-ing." That was good. But he is not familiar with how this can be used in Krishna consciousness. It's a challenge to see parts of it and try to ex-plain it, admitting to him that it's not a book that some of us love best. I realize that it is not reader-friendly to those who have been reading books only of a certain dogmatic presentation, with nothing indirect. Tell him what you can. But isn't it as obvious as Stan Laurel and Oliver Hardy, except that you are unwilling to see it as Krishna conscious-ness? Isn't it really glittering in a nonlinear way? Happy, and even sad and melancholy as *Malte Laurids Brigge,* which I loved in my youth but also often couldn't understand?

You don't always have to know what's going on to love a painting or a sky. But look closely and you'll see the silken threads that tie the Deity dress to the walls, creating the floating effect. Look long enough at the episodes and you'll see them accumulating in a straightforward

Krishna consciousness effect. Like gathering snow, like the brilliant art-ist as he works through his painting to a special kind of comprehen-sible work. Maybe it's not for everyone. But we are reaching a growing audience with each word that we sling in a new fashion, as long as they are actually meant true. Have you read *Alice in Wonderland* and *Through the Looking Glass* and the lyrics of Bob Dylan? Hear them. As you savor, you'll understand better what *Dark Stars* is and the way it's moving, so that lots of new people can move with the Krishna ripple ripple and beat. From *Wonderland:*

> "Will you walk a little faster?"
> said a whiting to a snail.
> "There's a porpoise close behind us,
> and he's treading on my tail . . .

> Will you, won't you, will you, won't you,
> will you join the dance?

Or a short poem by D.H. Lawrence:

> *Song of a Man Who Has Come Through*
> Not I, not I, but the wind that blows through me!
> A fine wind is blowing the new direction of Time.
> If only I let it bear me, carry me!
> If only I am sensitive, subtle, oh, delicate, a winged gift!
> If only, most lovely of all, I yield myself and am borrowed
> By the fine, fine wind that takes its course through the chaos
> of the world
> Like a fine, an exquisite chisel, a wedge-blade inserted;
> If only I am keen and hard like the sheer tip of the wedge
> Driven by invisible blows,
> The rock will split, we shall come at the wonder, we shall find
> the Hesperides.

> Oh, for the wonder that bubbles into my soul,
> I would be a good fountain, a good well-head,
> Would blur no whisper, spoil no expression.

What is the knocking?
What is the knocking at the door in the night?
It is somebody wants to do us harm.

No, no, it is the three strange angels.
Admit them. Admit them.

The last words of *The Notebooks of Malte Laurid Brigge* are dismal: "He was now terribly difficult to love, and he felt that only One would be capable of it. But He was not yet willing." Our books do not end on such dismal notes, but we sometimes learn things from dismal masters. For example, Rilke's advice to a young poet is something that a God conscious poet may certainly take. The young poet asked him if he could ask him about his doubts of bringing an inner life into unison. Rilke replied, "It is always what I have already said: Always the wish that you may find patience enough in yourself to endure, and simplicity enough to believe; that you may acquire more and more confidence in that which is difficult, and in your solitude among others." Rilke advises the poet that it is not that he should live a life of solitude in some extraordinary way but that we all *are* solitary, and he just has to begin assuming it. There is so much more I could quote that is worthy of reflection and inclusion in the thoughts of a *bhakta's* writing life, but there's not time or room for it here. I'm digressing from my own themes.

Rilke's persona ends his book, "How could they know who he was? He was terribly difficult to love and he felt that only one would be capable of it. But He was not yet willing" (from *The Notebooks of Malte Laurdes Brigge*). Johnny Swami woke up dry-crying those lines. His counselor who said of him that he was deep in lonely existential love. But we're not calling to a lord who is unlikely to reply, we do not interpret it that way. Krishna is willing, but it is I who am greatly attached to stay in the illusory world. Not yet willing to go to He who is calling for me and sending spiritual masters. Mostly I just hang around, or sometimes I become greatly exasperated and say what it is. I don't like to go to others and talk about it. But my counselor said I should try that with trusted friends. Even if you can't find a great *mahabhagavat*, you can find a trusted, friendly devotee who will not hurt you. And much of the time you have to live alone and focus on your lack and pray to Krishna, who is real. You've got the blues, but remember, you can also clap your hands in happy rhythm while waiting for a chance to talk deeper with the devotee and also get the chance to express yourself and die.

> You should choose the best friends and
> eventually even the world-class friends have
> to be abandoned and you are solo flight
> toward Krishna. Be patient at all stages.
> Leaden weight. He's a lonely guy but he sees
> people who was a benefit to him
> and whom he has helped.
> Ultimately
> waiting
> for his own cry to reach out.
> Krishna is already calling from the other
> side of the cloud, although you're too
> attached and afraid to let go
> of your preoccupations.
> Your presupposed eclectic theme.
> You don't know how down
> and out you are, how much
> you are in need of His mercy.
> That's why you guys used human steroids
> instead of hitting natural homeruns
> at a lower pace.

Yes, at last you must let go of all your attachments, your pride in writing your own way, your comforts and security of a circle of caretakers, your façade as theological eclectic seeker, "Self Reliance" memorizer, name dropper, jazz hearer. You really have to turn "to Mecca." Or activate everything you're doing, what we call Krishna-ize your life from top to bottom. Can you do that with "Night in Tunisia" and *missi de angelais* and that new book you've heard they're sending you, a biography of Jean Shepherd? You say you just can't turn away from the world, but you know the way, the trick for turning it into light. You'd better be right. It's no small gamble, my friend.

I finally looked up histrionics in the dictionary. It means artificially overacting, melodramatic gestures, *et al*, as XY used to do in the military war room among the other generals. He did it to get his way. Others did it also, shouting, pounding fists, one jumped over a table and claimed territorial possession of the Falkland Islands so that he could hold a festival for the penguins, or just to say it was within his vast domain. Histrionics. Get angry. Receive the Mad Dog award. It's different now. Very parliamentarian, and no one has any self-interest, and no one wants to climb the corporate ladder. Everyone just wants to be spared too much administrative work. Young Turks ready to replace some dinosaurs. Some dinosaurs digging in, won't be removed till death. Revolutionary proposals raise eyebrows. One woman in the committee for five years, no more added yet. Steady flow of retirees. Steady young blood infusing from hinterlands introduced by patron patriarchs. Stern conservative atmosphere overall. Does it really matter so much? Is it the heart of the Vaishnavas? At least we need it, the dam to stop chaotic flood of schisms, destruction by lawyers. So they are Prabhupada's leading men.

FW

Palm Sunday is past. Just after Easter I travel for the first time. This invalid, Jenny Sparks Maharaja, goes with permission from doctor and counselor and with regret of his home-based caretakers for a tour of three places. Lots of airplane time. But he'll be sheltered with a companion at all times. Bobby Kennedy riding on the hood of a car on Second Avenue, New York City, the exact moment of the explosion of the volcano of Mt. St. Helens. You can buy these photos and frame them for your home. Laughing is good for you, science proves. But anxiety's not. Jim misplaced his California senior citizen's card for three hours this morning, but he was pretty cool. He just knew it would show up, and finally it did. Neither could he eat lunch they prepared, too hard on the dentures. He made an appointment to see the dentist in Stuyvesant, New York, the one with the pretty assistant. It could be a one-time checkup or turn into a complicated thing. Still reading in the dark cloud about the ascent of Christ in his physical form, subtle points, that it was not a material body yet a humanlike body. The author can't be as specific as the Vaishnavas, but he seems to be saying the same thing about the descent and ascent of the Lord in His spiritual body, and the same thing for his spiritual representatives. The *mahabhagavat* may appear to have an ordinary human body, but he is actually spiritual.

In my case, I am actually material, but I have a pure spiritual soul, and I am trying to throw off the attachment to material, both gross elemental and mental attachment. You may dream in your unconscious sleep down deeply, still attached to matter. Why then do you dare to feed the various levels of the self with subtle kinds of matter? Hemingway said a writer should know about everything. Yes, clog the mind so you can write confidently about this world. Don't be naïve about any worldly experience, such as how much to tip the bell hop, how to deal with a whore, how to watch a bullfight. So you can write books about all subjects—and go to hell, shackled by your memories of experience gathered for book writing. Better you know nothing but Krishna, write and die making simple, pure ditties of Vrindavan and close your eyes to the material world.

> Rain he don't dry his massa's PJ's.
> Why don't they make some benches in
> the men's ashram so we can sit around
> and read at supper as we
> used to?

> Better yet, why not bring a table back into
> your house? Because I want my
> privacy, a privileged man, can't
> stand people walking in and out
> with the whole spread.

> "Runnin' from the trash."
> Scared people don't want to be
> mishandled by cops and robbers
> so they make tracks for escape
> and run through the dark park
> free, breathless, hiding
> under the fire escape.

Sometimes a daydreamer peace
you could yearn for its sweetness
even though it's transient and
you heard the breath of the
flute player. We want
that dream to be the real
mark of our desire but no
it must leave us our mood swings
of lonely, bored, resentful,
so try to sacrifice, love, until
the *bhava* boat comes sailing in.

Monk's counselor said he is too attracted to friends that give him drama, sensual or mischief making, or intellectual give and take that may be negative—rather than to interactions that are truly nourishing. But he said Monk tends to think people who are mature and independent are too boring. They won't play those destructive games with him. Advice: be patient and develop the truly deep friends who can help you, don't grab for a cheap candy bar or chocolate. Hearing this reminded Monk of when he was just a newcomer in the Lower East Side freedom and Elliot said to him, "You know, I can corrupt you." And something like, "Are you afraid of that? Do you really want to get into a friendship with me?" Monk answered naively, "I don't think you can corrupt me." But a few years later, when Monk jumped off the window ledge, he felt it had something to do with his corruption with Elliot and Anna, along with other things. "I want you to talk only with angels," said Jesus Christ to Teresa of Avila after she wasted many years in the convent as a socialite mediocre nun, talking superficially in the gossip room.

So counselor advises he seek intimacy versus drama, meaning versus flirtation. Devotional feeling vs. mania and mischief. He pointed the monk to what he wrote in his own book *Vaishnava Compassion:* "We may also be afraid of the higher taste of *bhakti,* where we feel everything taken away *but* Krishna and our lives are turned upside down in love of God." (p. 105)

These friends are not boring—

Jim's book is playful, an element
prominent in Vraja. Pixie-ish
boys tease and the girls do too.

Of course their passion is deeper
than anything mundane, they're
climbing beyond Meru but I
say pixie because they are
always capable of playful when
their Lord is present face to face—
because that's what He wants.
So why not you be playful
with me as a prelude to kiss?

Ollie, the mischievous, whose chemistry is tuned to mine, said all
the way from Mayapur, "Outrageous!" when he heard Chip's travel
itinerary. "How was it possible for the headache-prone to plan such
plane trips and people-meets!"

"I just heard about the opportunities, last chance to see the spiritual warrior, at an outsider book fair to sign my books, and an in-be-
tween stop at Stuyvesant, New York, and I couldn't pass it up." You
mean you felt strong enough to try it. And you could cancel it at any
point. But I doubt I'll break down. With my meds to support me and
good counseling, think positive. I can drag my carcass to go see a man
who has suffered more than I have.

Take your shoes off *outside* the door so he doesn't protest, "Don't
take off your shoes." Enter barefoot with your cane, and no awkwardness to approach him for an embrace. Be real. Be open. Be soft, be loving. Look up to him as senior in suffering and spirituality. He's a greater
spiritual fighter.

I *am* recovering from lots of suffering. Talk as it comes natural.
Ask him that question. Why did he give up his gradual mission for the
"go for broke" prayer he made two years ago? Hear his answer sub-
missively, as best you can. And pace your own head and body. Listen to
your heartbeats. Pray to the Lord, give me strength, give me courage,
give me love to keep going through this. Give me gratitude to those
who are helping me. I want to be a spiritual warrior also. Let me look at

their faces and not cringe. Let me hippity hop in my own way. Haven't
you said you are playful? Haven't you said you are innovative? And
take time by the roadside to write or you'll die. Write *and* die. While
you move through this world, soothed by the cello of Yo Yo Ma.

You don't know what fate
awaits you. It could be a turn
around you never expected and
your plane lands flat on its
nose or fuselage.

Or as I've been saying, you could
dance through it all like a young
Fred Astaire, not a hitch or stumble.
or a stumble, like your actual self
all these years—"Pick yourself up,
dust yourself off and
start all over again."

I've got a premonition this is going
to go well, I get the blessings of the
Swami and that will be a touch-
stone. And Prabhupada himself will
carry me to D.C. and to N.Y. and Houston
and back. Heck, I used to travel
like that in the old days in
His service with not much self-
motivation but out of preacher's
duty. Now a senior citizen's carefully
planned few stops to somewhat distant places
on the wearing down
air jets. You can do it. With rests in between

his secretary said, "I'd rather
he come a day earlier." But mine said,
"No, he needs a day to rest
after traveling." He told me, "I'm your

manjari and his secretary is his
manjari. I had to protect you and he
has to protect him. See how you feel
when you arrive here."

Arrive in an S.F. hotel and get up by 4:00 A.M.
at the very latest and catch a 6:00 A.M. plane
and on the same day after
flying thousands of miles go to
a crucial personal meeting?
Can you do that, chipmunk?
That's what the host would prefer
of his visitor. Vat
pressure.

Cancer can even break the collar bone of a spiritual warrior, but it can't stop him from glowing. They say that Vaishnavas die, but the Vaishnavas never die, they live on in immortal sound. Jim Maharaja keeps measuring the few days before he leaves Philo and starts his "epic" travels. Takes his notebook with him. Write or die. You have to keep breathing and eating or you'll dry up, even if the eating and breathing isn't perfect. Same with the writing. Even if it takes you away from your reflective home-hermitage on to risk-taking journey for a nervous-disordered, easily exhausted anticipatory migraineur. It's good for a kind of travel writing, which may not be as deep and reflective as when you're living home in your routine, but it's got it's own kind of passing borders, new faces and places excitement. It's what you've wrought, grist of a traveler, and you have to write it down. Don't avoid the truth of the meeting with the spiritual warrior.

It's as if, in some imaginary way, Jiminy feels that he's down to the last few days of his own mortal life. He just caught that feeling going through his mind. It's actually happening to the spiritual warrior. And remember in the *Srimad-Bhagavatam* they asked the sage, "What should a person do with his life, and eventually, what should a person do who is very near his death?"

The answer given is that we are all very near our death. Someone has actually a few days left, and it's very dramatic for him and for those around him. But relatively speaking, all of us are *about to die*. Jiminy's feelings revolve around the fact that he has to travel within a very few days and is going to see a man who is literally about to die. And this makes him think that his estimated time of departure from this house and his estimated time of departure from San Francisco airport and his estimated time of leaving Washington to visit the spiritual warrior and his estimated time of etc., etc., are all bringing him closer and closer to the estimated very last days.

He's proud that he's a senior citizen, and he even has an ID card to prove it. He's getting social security benefits and is happy about that. Money in the bank. He smiles with his dentures and his new good looks of an older man, his goatee friend. "You look so relaxed, you look like a new man." Less headaches, more pain control. But closer to the end. Swing while you can. Listen to Sirius radio. What about improvement of *sadhana* ? Oh *that*.

Yes, it's very ironic, or I don't take it so deeply or sorrowfully. Nevertheless, it's a fact that these last days in the house here are giving me this itchy feeling, this feeling where I keep looking at the calendar and try to figure it out: When do I really leave? When does Nara come back? When is our appointment with the spiritual warrior? How late do we actually have to leave the airport in order to be sure of catching the 6:00 A.M. plane? Can we make it all? So little time is left to make these connections. So little time. And you're not using it to the ultimate benefit. You're doing some things that are too casual, that aren't purely spiritual, so you haven't caught on to the seriousness of life.

> The *Surrealist Manifesto* of 1925
> will arrive soon, with lunch. But I
> can't read all that stuff thinking I
> could transform it. However, in the intro
> to selections of Juan Frey,
> the man says many mystics give out expressions
> to their "religious
> visions" in sculpture, symbolic poetry,
> by laying bricks, gardening, making aqueducts,
> architecture, and the like. Put to

193

here the fellows and ladies applying
paint brushes to express the inner heart
in ways visible
for ordinary people or people
who can't follow all the way
the liturgical, dogmatic,
and hard journey through the
dark night but who *can* be

entranced by a stained
glass window, a fountain gushing
clear water, a little poem about wild
turkeys, or even fellowship
in a *kirtan* on Lord Gaura's
advent day. A soldier came by
and watched and accepted a fudge
maha-prasadam.

After lunch, while performing l.s.d. (taking a nap on the left side),
I drifted into comatose memories of a sex affair. I pulled myself out of
that and chanted on my darned clicker. (I can't lie to you and say beads,
buddies.) At least it pulled me out of the graphic amours. Then I thought
of the last newsletter from the spiritual warrior. They said he's in a lot
of pain but gave a "beautiful and powerful class from his new book
Beggar IV." I loved his book *Beggar II* and didn't even know of the existence of III and IV. Book IV will be called *Die Before Dying.* I hope he will
have time to see me despite the new debilitation. Somehow, we are
confident we will meet him. He's concerned his followers will have
difficulty during and after his transition. He told them that the best
way to keep anyone alive is by following their instructions and exem-
plifying their teachings, not just individually but also as a community.

In that little poem above, I was celebrating the artistic creations of
inward mystics. It makes me very happy. Here's the exact quote from
the general introduction of *John of the Cross Selected Writings*, by Kieran
Kavanaugh, O.C.D. (printed by the Classics of Western Spirituality):

Mystics may undergo an irrepressible urge toward some kind of outward expression of their experiences of God, at least of the more intense ones. The success lies in the indissoluble bond between the body and the living experience of the spirit. The outward expression prolongs in the body that which spiritually resonates within. At that time, this outward expression can so stir the emotions that these latter in turn may add to the spiritual experience. The concrete form of expression depends on the capacity and inclinations of the subject.

Having the soul of an artist, John expressed himself outwardly in a number of forms. There is his sketch of Christ on the cross, still extant. He enjoyed carving and sculpting. His architectural design of the monastery in Granada was so successful that it was then used as a model for other monasteries. Today we can still see and admire the cloister he designed in Segovia and the aqueduct in Granada. He composed little dramas that the nuns and priors performed for various liturgical feasts. At times he was known to dance under the power of strong religious emotion. On his journeys, he used to pass the time singing hymns and songs, some of which he himself composed. But poetry became John's best vehicle of self-expression. In it we find traces of his other gifts: color, form, sonority, dramatic movement. Not only do the words have their function, but also the rhythm, the music, the accents, and the coloring.

I'm no saint, but this description definitely validates my claim that writing is my *bhajan*. It's my service to Prabhupada. It's as important as my chanting, and the best way I know to serve the Lord and the devotees and the whole world. Therefore, it's not wrong for me to study forms of writing such as this *Surrealist Manifesto* that has just come into my hands and see if I can glean something from it to make my own offerings sharper (as in a surgeon's knife), more colorful, more loony when necessary to attract peoples' attention, and as experimental as possible while still strictly worshiping the Lord in *parampara* (zigzag).

DIALOGUES

"Are you afraid to go?"

"Just give me afternoon time without interruptions."

"What about the early rise at the hotel?"

"Hotels call you on the phone when it's time to wake up. Planes don't leave without you. Mad Hatter snaps rubber band on his wrist to change negative to positive thinking."

"Where is your sister?"

"The blue jays are heard in Staten Island, Ireland, and a similar bird I hear right now in Philo. My sister."

"Whence have you come here? What clothes will you wear?"

"Freud gets much of the credit for dreams. I also think dreams are very important. No more wearing neck ties, sorry. You'll go too, but probably won't recommend community life."

"Do you believe in exercise?"

"It hurts but I'll do it when I arrive there."

"What paradigm shift are we in now?"

"Thinking of things as they come. Begging for time in sneakers. Trying to remember."

"But in the first *Surrealistic Manifesto*, Andre Breton states, 'Surrealism does not allow those who devote themselves to it to forsake it whenever they like. There's every reason to believe that it acts on the mind very much as drugs do . . . Thus the analysis of the mysterious effects and special pleasures it can produce—in many respects, surrealism occurs as a *new vice* which does not necessarily seem to be restricted to the happy few; like hashish, it has the ability to satisfy all manner of tastes—such an analysis has to be included in the present study."

"Then how can it be used as the saints use artistic expressions to bring out their inner states? We'll have to find a different literary form for serving Krishna."

"Are you a surrealist?

"I follow four rules, no intoxication is one. I'm a Mahaprabhu realist. That can include lots of things, but it doesn't fall in the net of Andre Breton and company's special manifesto. That was a flash in the pan back in France, and some people still practice it today. Like the New York School of poets, John Ashbery, Ron Padgett. Not chipmunk."

"Then why are you doing this dialog?"

"It's a free country. Everything belongs to Krishna, every literary technique. It's not patented by Andre Breton. That's how come Hayagriva wrote his long poem "Chant," even after Ginsberg wrote his poem "Howl." When I said something to Hayagriva that it seems like imitation, he said, 'Ginsberg has no patent.' And he was right. It was a good poem for Prabhupada, who came across the seas to save us all, who sat on a mat in the early days on the same level as the boys who came to chant with him, who was so kind to us and fed us ISKCON bullets, who initiated us and chanted on our Tandy red wooden beads, to whom Allen Ginsberg donated a harmonium from India, who made the record *Happening uptown with Allen Kallman*, but when Allen delayed a long time in paying, he said to Allen on the phone, 'I'm always thinking of you,' and then hung up the phone and said, 'I'm always thinking of you the way Kamsa was always thinking of Krishna.' Prabhupada, known as Swamiji then, who held a fire *yajna* in his own apartment, which filled up with smoke until we were all coughing, and we had to open up the windows, and Prabhupada himself said he thought they'd have to call the fire brigade. Swamiji, in the most beloved days, who said the great philosophers and poets were not Krishna conscious except in their sincerity. Swamiji, whose first-class *Back to Godhead* editor was

Rama, but when Rama left him, he carried on without him. A few years later, Rama returned, but with a beard and the same ideas that were different from Swamiji's. Prabhupada wrote him, 'If you want to come back but keep your different ideas, then we can't have you.' Swamiji, who in the absence of a BTG editor accepted Satsvarupa's offer to take the post. All glories to Prabhupada, who accepted that name on his 1968 visit to Boston, on the suggestion of Govinda dasi, who prodded him into admitting that Swamiji was a third-class name and that spiritual masters usually had names like Vishnupada or Prabhupada.

Chapter Twelve

Why do you sleep so early, rise at five?
You only shower and fall asleep again
just when the friars are warming up their prayer benches
and their prayer beads
with religious gusto?
You need to go back to sleep.
Apply for a special dispensation
to sleep through until 7:00 A.M.

then go out on deck and wave the
semaphore flags to approaching ships:
"Keep out of our way"; "we are
busy at prayer. Don't approach us."
But then in sleepiness you drop one
of the flags. What are they going
to do with you? Demote him, give him
a bad conduct discharge, disorderly for sleeping.

"Sweet Gauranga dreams," he said to me
last night, not knowing I plunge into a
world of the unconscious deeper than
the waking state but broken into
many pieces, so I can't recall "the
dream" when I awake but know it
was more uninhibited and truthful than
my guarded, polite waking state
where I worry and play roles so
as to not insult anyone, off the mark
of my true self. Hardly do I have
"sweet Gauranga dreams"

Of Mahaprabhu playing in the Ganges
or calling His devotees up to Him
one by one in the *mahaprakasa*,
and I am there too, and He tells me

to help the banana seller Kolaveca or
something that makes me roll
in ecstasy.

"Deepak wants to say goodbye to you," said Nara as they were
ready to depart in the Marriot Hotel. I embraced him and thanked him
for the three-row *Tulasi* neck beads he had given me as a replacement
for my broken ones. I told him to keep on working in the beautiful
garden and make some arrangement so that when I come back we can
all read together in the evening. Jim said, "I chant Hare Krishna a lot in
my mind." That was an odd thing to say, wasn't it? But it's true. Did
you want to impress him that you do chant? Deepak had started chanting in the car on his beads. Otherwise, none of us were chanting. We
were pointing out different things about the Golden Gate Bridge, about
the fact that we didn't have to pay a fee because we were three in a car
and considered a car pool vehicle. Or we didn't talk. I was in the back
seat and so I couldn't hear much of the talk. And I *was* chanting in my
mind. What I'm trying to do is *depend* more on Krishna for everything
that happens. Make all arrangements such as we did—tell the person
at the hotel desk to ring our room at 2:45 A.M., set the alarms on our
room clocks at 2:45 A.M., set the alarm on the neon clock facing me at
2:45 A.M. But know that everything depends on Krishna, so you really
have to relax and know that that's where your ultimate dependence
lies. The plane may not fly, Bhakti-tirtha Swami may not meet you, you
may not be fit to go to Houston, something may happen in New York,
Nanda may . . . he may not . . . , so just go along depending on the Lord
at every step, and one way to do it is to do that chanting. Out loud is
best, but that inner churning is nice too, since you have so much trouble
outwardly. Here it is inwardly. *Hare Krishna Hare Krishna, Krishna Krishna
Hare Hare* (even below a whisper) *Hare Rama Hare Rama Rama Rama
Hare Hare*. But it's definitely something, a recitation that you pay attention to, and a dependence that you turn to, and a turning away from
other things. A turning away from other thoughts, and even music,
paying attention to the inner mantras.

Yes, we're on our way. I realize how totally dependent I am on
these grown-up men who know how to drive cars all the way to San
Francisco, who know the directions, who know how to deal with hotel

people, although it was I who tipped the bellhop ten dollars, two fives, although the two fives almost fell out of my hands. I have very few life skills. Unfortunately, now I'm a senior citizen, and an invalid too. And I get treated with some courtesy and help along the way.

Swamiji is traveling with Narayan-kavaca, the name that means the mantra that covers you with protective shields of Lord Narayan Himself. That makes you feel secure. And the Hare Krishna mantra is the ultimate shield, so headaches, embarrassments, possible crashes are all covered by the insurance of the Lord's will. Whatever bad may happen is also under His control and should not be considered a truly bad thing. That is what Bhakti-tirtha Maharaja has also been saying. There is mercy in the unfortunate, because it is Krishna's will to purify us, to make us strong, to take away the last false ego, the last *anarthas*. And so he says he is excited as he struggles through these last stages. We can believe him and make a true pilgrimage to his foot, hear his words with sincerity, without envy or ridicule or anything bad. Don't feel superior. Don't feel he's simply grist for your mill. Look up to him as he deserves. And if you honestly don't feel as much compassion as you should, as much admiration as you think you should, then don't force it. That will come later, even after the meeting. The main thing is to go there in humility and pay respects. Just going through the motions with sincerity will bring about a good result. Prabhupada will favor you for your honest attempt to pull it off.

Jiminy entered the room not knowing which way to look, and then he looked to the left and saw Bhakti-tirtha Swami lying down on a couch, as if lounging on his side. He was smiling. Jiminy went forward and made obeisances full flat at his Godbrother's body and touched his hand. The spiritual warrior said, "Forgive me, I can't get up." But then he said he would get up, and indeed he did sit up and move to a chair, and they faced each other. I touched his foot, and of course noticed his stump wrapped up in cloth. He began to tell me of his different ill spots, the cracked collar bone, the different spots where tumors were popping up. He told me of the different discomforts he has now and how they are increasing. I listened attentively to his report. I cannot attempt a full verbatim report of everything that went on, but it was a good heartfelt exchange over an hour and fifteen minutes. He was intent on telling me all of the sore spots and difficulties he was going through. But he was also intent to tell me how he felt closer to Prabhupada and Krishna than he had ever felt before. He said he felt very happy that I was there, that as soon as I had entered the room, things had changed. He said he was feeling particularly uncomfortable, but as soon as I entered, it was like a shield of comfort had come in and now he felt better. I said, "You talk about those kinds of things in your books." He smiled and said yes, that he was feeling better in my presence. I forget some of what went on before I asked my question as to why he had quit his steady and regular preaching mission of going all over the world. He said that he saw he was not really changing people. He mentioned in particular one seminar he gave after the suicide of a devotee's wife. He said many people were crying after his talks and admitted to taking medicines in their own life to cope with their miseries. And people were crying and wanted to talk with him about things. But again he realized he didn't have the potency to really change the miseries, not just in that place but all over the world where he spoke to people. He thought that it was because he was not pure enough himself to change them, and that was why he thought of his quantum change, so to speak, that he would pray to Krishna for a great increase of purification on his part through a prayer to the Lord. He prayed to the Lord, "Please, give me increased potency, but at the same time make me go through whatever it takes to increase my potency. Purify me." He asked it for himself, and he asked it for others, so that he could purify others. And about a month after that, he was immediately afflicted with his cancer. In other words, he said that he was not a very pure person, and so he referred to the demigods coming down on him.

At different points in the talk he mentioned that some of his Godbrothers had been critical of his prayer and its aftermath. They have told him to take back the prayer. They have told him, "You are no Vasudeva Datta." One Godbrother wrote to him and said, "Isn't the real way to change peoples' consciousness to purify their consciousness?"

I mentioned that that Godbrother happens to be a very scholarly one who believes very much on purification by reading the *Bhagavatam*. He said, "Yes, and there are different ways of purifying, so one way to purify is not just by reading the books but by setting an example of purification through your own body." I'm jumping around here and there.

I mentioned to him that his example seems to be something Christ-like. He said, "Not only Christ-like, but this is also like the Buddhists." I said, "How is that?" He said that the Buddhists live very austere lives, and they pray to become *bodhisattvas*, to come back in another life. They pray not to harm any living being and try to help other suffering beings, and even to do so in many, many lives. And he mentioned other religious examples where people tried to help others in suffering by their own example and by their own suffering. So he said he was following that path of helping others through his own suffering. I don't think he meant that he wanted to suffer, but that he wanted to purify himself, *whatever it took*. He didn't know what to expect, but Krishna "and the demigods" hit him real hard, fool that he was, so to speak, as if to say, "Oh, you want to become purified? Well here's what it's going to take in your case." And so they gave him the blessing, and blessing in disguise it was, because even though some Godbrothers asked him to take the prayer back, he said, "No, no, I won't take it back." He is "enjoying" the whole process, and he is feeling that it is working. Many Godbrothers are writing to him, and not only Godbrothers but ex-*gurukulis* who feel resentment and devotees who have gone away sour from ISKCON, saying that they feel inspired by his example and that they appreciate his courage and his attempt. They believe in it. I told him I believe in it too.

A number of things that he got into deeply slip my mind, so I just grasp at straws. He told me two things for my personal benefit. One was that I should not resent any persons whom I see as my enemies. He said if I do, it's like holding a burning coal in my hand. It will just worsen my condition. I should just let it go and forgive them. He seemed to be saying these things with knowledge of my actual condition. And the second thing he said was about my disciples. He said some of my disciples have left me since my discrepancies have been revealed, but many disciples of mine love me but they need more attention from me, and as much as I can, I should give them more attention without overdoing it, according to my capacity. Those were his two little tips for Swami Jiminy. I took them to heart.

As he spoke, from time to time tears ran down my right cheek, and sometimes my left cheek. His face was dry. He spoke with strength. He didn't falter, and he was fully attentive, speaking about his pains.

He did not flinch or anything like that. He said sometimes he may feel some self-pity for his pains. He said it's really rough as hell. At night he can't sleep. Every half hour he has to get up and urinate and then be placed back in bed again, and there's no continuous sleep at all, because he feels the throbbing in all the different points where the tumors are, and new tumors are being added. I asked him what he expects to do in the future and how much time he thinks he has. He said he may have three days or three months. He says his future is to go to Gita-nagari and stay there and pass away there. He said he feels too weak to travel to Vrindavan or Mayapur and also his preaching is in the West.

We discussed an article we had seen in *Back to Godhead* about a year ago which had enlightened us on the point that you don't have to go to the *dhama* to pass away. You can pass away where your favorite deities are, which may be in the West, or any place where your preaching is. One learned devotee was quoted in that article as saying what Krishna says in *Bhagavad-gita:* "He who thinks of Me at the time of death comes to Me." The *dhama* was not emphasized but the thinking of Krishna was emphasized, so that is the important thing, not to die in the holy *dhama* geographically but to die while you think of Krishna. And Prabhupada has made holy *dhamas* in places like Gita-nagari. I approved with him of his choice to do this, and he seemed quite set in passing away at Gita-nagari.

My eyes felt blurry, and the room felt warm. I took off my sweater and continued, occasionally teary. He told me that the GBC had raised charges against him just at the time of his greatest success in preaching around the world. He was really very successful getting large, large audiences. His seminars were on very wide-ranging issues, like depression and world troubles and so on, as revealed in his books, such as *Spiritual Warrior* and other books. But for some reason some of the Executive Committee members made charges against him for writing inappropriate books for an ISKCON guru and for being outrageous in his behavior. A number of times they tried to find him guilty, but they didn't. He therefore asked for an apology, and they did not give an apology. He said, "If you don't apologize, then I will resign from the GBC." They refused, however, to accept his resignation. All this upset him very much, and this occurred just at a time when he had made his prayer and was entering into his cancer. He thought maybe this was part of his fate, to be driven away, but then he checked himself and said no, he should not see it that way. At this point he brought up my own situation. He said my Godbrothers were mostly hurt by my affair with a woman, that they didn't hate me but felt hurt that a Godbrother who was so much looked up to and who had managed to relieve himself from the management and still be an ideal ISKCON devotee had had this trouble. It hurt them, but they felt sympathy and realized more that we are all one family.

Perhaps this hardly sounds like a talk with a man who is about to die. It wasn't a talk filled with death images and so forth. I asked him if he was afraid of death and he said no, but he said he was something like a baby in terms of facing physical pain. He really couldn't bear it, but he was not afraid of death itself. He felt that Prabhupada would come for him. Just as he felt sure that Prabhupada came for Tamal Krishna Goswami and Sridhar Swami, and he was sure that Prabhupada would come for me. He mentioned the great spiritual treasure I had in being with Prabhupada in the early days. I smiled through my tears when he said that and thought of what a treasure it indeed was to be there in the beginning.

The time went by without awkwardness, although I felt it was going to be about an hour and fifteen minutes and then it would be over. We bonded more by this talk. He appreciated my coming to see him, and it gave him some more strength. He knows he's certainly going to die soon. He wrote a *vyasa-puja* homage to Prabhupada and said, "I'm writing this homage, but by the time the book gets published I won't be here. I'm known by different names, like Ghana-shyama, Bhakti-tirtha Swami, and in my books, Krishnapada, but by the time the book comes out, I may have some other name, but I know I won't be here."

So he has that kind of stark awareness of his identity and his passage. It doesn't scare him. The only thing that stares at his face as most troublesome is the pains that get newly added to, the tumors, the new breaks in the body, and so on. They make life hellish, and he says with a smile that he'll be glad to go. In the meantime, he asked me to continue corresponding with him and phoning him. I suppose it's a little eerie to be talking to a man who knows he's going to die and has such an attitude. If you were talking with an ordinary person, they might have quite a different attitude, afraid of death and really complaining about their ills. He was quite gentlemanly talking about the pains, not crying out about them but getting through them by the overriding factor of knowing that Prabhupada is close and blessing him. He would take that condition that he's in rather than a healthy condition without this blessing factor.

So the original point is that he thinks he is causing blessing on his own disciples and on people around the world by making this act, and that's the short of it. I told him that I believed him, whatever he thought.

We went over again the old disagreements that we had rather quickly, just to get them out of the way—the early days of my misunderstanding him when he wanted to take *sannyasa*, but they just had to be mentioned for the sake of mentioning them. I said also, "I want you to forgive me for any dislike or misunderstanding I had for your present days of preaching, because your way is your way and it is greatly successful. I've been reading your books and I like them, and I like the fact that so many people follow you." He began to mention the great successes of thousands of people attending his lectures, and he said of the GBC Executive Committee's attack on him, that it was mostly out of envy. He mentioned something about my books and said that my situation is similar. The GBC says that my books are okay, but not for an ISKCON guru to write. He said that's what they say about him, that his books are okay but not for an ISKCON guru to write. He said that I would be surprised to know how many people actually read my books, but they don't tell me. He said my books would be appreciated after I am dead, not now. He said the GBC is trying so hard to get people to appreciate ISKCON, but they don't appreciate my books. He said the BBT is even making a proposal now to find nondevotee writers to write books about ISKCON, but they don't even know that I am writing relevant books myself. I had to laugh at that one. They'll go out and hire some hack writers to write books about Krishna consciousness and ignore the writer they've got in their own camp. Similarly, they dismiss their Bhakti-tirtha Swami, their world ambassador, for going around preaching about depression and predictions of world doom to thousands and thousands of people, being an African king and being just generally outrageous to thousands and thousands of people and being "unbecoming of an ISKCON guru," and only two days ago they sent him an apology and a letter asking forgiveness for their case against him. He said, "Yes, just on my deathbed they've finally asked for my *forgiveness*."

Of course, I myself have a physical condition. It's diminutive compared to his, but I had to pace myself also. The room was a bit stuffy and I didn't feel so comfortable physically. Bhakti-tirtha Swami mentioned my own condition, and he said how terrible it must be to experience migraine headache and that he was sympathetic to my pains over the years. Fortunately I had no headache while I spoke with him. He encouraged me to go on preaching to my disciples, giving them attention, and to other people also. As we were leaving I told his disciples downstairs that he had told me to take care of my disciples, and one of his leading disciples said, "You take care of us, too." So he really put that as a burden on me, that I should take care of others and reach to him. That's something that he's been doing, and I should do it too. He kind of woke me up to that reality, although with my doctor and my counselor and my condition, I haven't been able to do it. Maybe I'll be able to enter a new phase of doing it. So that was in the air as a new kind of thing that he was revealing to me, like, hey, why don't you take care of them a little more. That was a new thing that he was saying to me, giving me a wake-up call. That was in my mind as something new.

I was enjoying his company. Despite everything, he seemed to be his old normal self. We're two transcendentalists, and he's talking about death. I know he's going to die, but I didn't talk to him with any panic or pity

If you asked me what went through my mind, it's just these things I'm putting down in the words of Chip Swami, these things that he said and these things that I said. I can't think of saying, "My heart felt this," or "My mind felt that." I was just present as these things went back and forth, absorbing it and being present and believing it and living it. Being very present. Not doubting him or not taking him as putting on a show. It was quite real and not overdone with any histrionics. It was like he said, two old generals coming and talking together. No exaggerations. If we were tobacco spitters. we would have been spitting tobacco and talking about death and talking about Prabhupada's movement and then when the time was up leaving and saying, "Well, I'll write to you, Swami, unless you die before me." At one point he said,

"I'll get a place ready for you up there for when you come." He had a big smile when he said it. I said, "Thank you." And we say it with belief, because we believe in the transcendental world and the shelter of Prabhupada. He helped me with my faith. I think I helped him. He said so. There was no bullshit. He said, "No matter what you did in *maya*, no matter how far you went in *maya*, you couldn't get away from Krishna and Prabhupada. He's captured you too much." He was saying these truisms, and I was just eating them up. He was speaking with such faith. That was remarkable. We say these things. He's got a lot of faith. That's a matter of fact. Being so near to death, he speaks with great realization and simple faith. I might not be able to speak like that, but hearing from him, I think I can speak like that more. So there was a shock of getting near a person with such faith. It was a matter of fact. I was getting my batteries charged by being with a person of matter-of-fact faith. Just as he was matter-of-fact about his tumors, he's matter-of-fact about his faith. "Oh yeah, I'll be going there. I don't know how long it'll be before I go, but when I go, I'm going there, to where Prabhupada is."

As we left the house and got into our truck, the spiritual warriors' caretakers followed us and began chanting Hare Krishna. It was a loving gesture, just like everything that surrounds him. I asked Nanda to open the electrically controlled window so I could say something to them. I stuck my head out the window and said some poorly memorized words from Bhaktivinode Thakur: "They lie who say that Vaishnavas die, for true Vaishnavas never die but live forever to spread the holy names around." They heard me but then continued singing. As we pulled out and down the block, we felt filled with the mercy exchange. When I got back to the house, I opened the gift they had given me. It was a spiffy zippered sport jacket, which I will wear with pride. All red with black design. And I will try to seriously remember his advice to take better care of my disciples while taking better care of myself. And now I have to keep in communication with him also.

He told one of his disciples that as her kids grew up, she was losing her identity as a mom. He told her she'd still be surrounded by loved ones, but eventually, "You have to die alone." He's going to. I am too. Do you think of Krishna? All the gross things. He was telling me how easy it is to get pornography on the Internet and how many people masturbate. So when they catch someone doing it, they slam him with punishment (or not), but they're really afraid that they're going to be found out themselves. Almost everyone is guilty. He was saying this about the time he was talking of my trouble. He said my trouble was Krishna bringing me closer. "Yes," I said, trying to read his mind, "by breaking my false ego, bringing me down in the ranks." He said the devotees were *hurt* by my misbehavior. They didn't hate me, but because so many loved me as a role model, they were hurt.

I guessed that means they were disappointed. But at least I didn't blaspheme Prabhupada, run off with a damsel, and abscond with a lot of money.

Noble critter bounced back. Spiritual Warrior seems very balanced. Not Woody Allenish like me. But he acts in his extremes as I do. They are looking to hire a pro writer to write a book for ISKCON.

"Oh hard times come again no more."

Your books will be better appreciated after you're dead. Hmm. Prabhupada used to spoof at a man saying he was doing something for posterity. He said posterity (or your grandchildren) may benefit, but what about you? Where will you be? And yet work for future Krishna consciousness is not wasted. Srila Prabhupada wrote for the future. Built his Bombay personal quarters, he said, not for his own enjoyment. *You* disciples, future people will enjoy it.

Spiritual Warrior is trying to die in a way that will inspire people of the future, empower them. He could not be potent enough just by his own preaching, so he prayed for more potency, whatever that took, even if it was his own life.

Eeps. We have been reading surreal works and trying to apply them in Krishna's service. Weeps, I have to keep going.

Baseball players all their lives, friends, retired, then one of them died. He later appeared as an angel to the survivor and said, "I have news from heaven, some good, some bad. In heaven they have baseball!" "What's the bad thing?" "You have to pitch next Wednesday."

Did you notice how much small talk there is when devotees gather for a dinner—baseball, movies . . . but Krishna consciousness also. We talked about Bhakti-tirtha Maharaja. But a lot of worldly talk. We are *worldly* people. Within ourselves we are more Krishna conscious than when we talk.

When you write, I abjure you, fatty, tell of the Ten Commandments. "Spiritual Warrior, you are going in a Christ-like way. Are you praying to God? Tell me more how you feel close to Srila Prabhupada and Krishna." I should have asked him that. Foggy in tears. Ask him in your next letter. Something I wanted to ask you.

Beeble. We three guys are each writing three pages of surreal writing or just three pages. Nanda just announced that he's finished his three pages. I said, "You S.O.B." I was angry, as if he must have been cheating. How could he write so fast? He said something back like, "Well you started it." Maybe he wrote gibberish. My mind is flowing in sense, I can't just make spaghetti. Nara is ahead of me. I like the comfort these men give me in my feebleness. Next stop, Albany. I'm glad I've got them writing.

Nara found a great quote in the Vaishnava verse book by Narottama dasa Thakur, whom we both love for his lower-than-a-blade-of-grass attitude. They won't let me look up the verse, but I guess that it's something like, "I have no love for the holy names, even though they're the most wonderful thing—Hare Krishna Hare Krishna—and they will bring you gorgeous love of God very soon, easily, because I am most wretched." He is—he seems to be—one of us by these verses.

Oh, oh, we are in Nanda's building hanging around. Chip got rid of a migraine by a pill. We read some John Ashbery, but the poems made "no sense." Nanda has records by Paul Simon. We played Charlie Mingus. Hadai Pandit prabhu came and joined us, then his wife came and cooked, and their son joined us. So I was extending myself as the Warrior advised. I can't think of things to do.

The airplane to Albany is a small one. Then in New York. I will be building my muscles and reading some books and writing this one. I do wish to return to painting. We have selections of *St. John of the Cross* and Vaishnava verses. Turn to God. It's madness to leave that out of your life and fill it up with lots of other things. I had wished to be a hermit in California and concentrate on prayer, prayer, prayer, like Jesus prayer. For myself and others. Prayer. Become more potent to others. *The Cloud of Unknowing* favors *bhajananandi* but states that it helps other people. Read that book again with Govinda when you return to Philo, or sooner, even in New York. It's a unique, astounding book.

Bring on the clowns in their pajamas. Write in an epic walk on a tightrope typewriter. Don't fix anything. I am the last one to finish. They don't last long. They don't last long. I value their words. You have to clamp your teeth and stand up for *espiritu*.

Continues all right. Tumors increase, he's closer to death. St. Francis added a stanza to Sister Death near the very end. Then when his time came, he lay down on the earth, with loyal brothers surrounding him. He said, "I have led my life for Christ, now you lead yours." Directors can help us. Did you understand a little bit of *John of the Cross* you read together? It was only a prologue but we hung in there. It took three of us.

They said, "When you wrote that we talk about baseball, you meant, 'But underneath we are deeply Krishna conscious people.'" Is that what I meant? Or did I mean that we are actually worldly to a fault? They said we made easy conversation, allowing the young man present to take part. Relax, don't be uptight. Be who you are. You have forgotten all your Sanskrit verses anyway. Yeah, but I can paraphrase them. I could talk about spiritual problems or what the Spiritual Warrior said last night as a context for heavier talk. I talked about grief honestly with Hadai Pandit dasa, connected it with my loss when the Brooks lost the Pennant in 1951 after being twenty-three games ahead in first place. True loss for a ten-year-old boy, hard to handle. And couldn't turn to Krishna. Krishna or lack of Krishna is implied in all of our talks. He said his daughter has more "athletic grace" than his son, but both are serious players. She's in high school, a catcher, and plays fast softball. The ball is not as soft as it used to be, and the pitchers are fast. You can't catch a ball without a glove.

Hare Krishna. Nanda insists that, unlike what some Vaishnavas say, John of the Cross's bridal mysticism is definitely *madhurya*, not something less. It is in his heart. I don't know enough about it, but we do gain gifts from ecumenical exchanges. They read the statement by Bhaktivinode Thakur from his *Sri Chaitanya-shikshastakam*, quoted in my book *Entering the Life of Prayer*:

When we may have occasion to be present at the place of worship of other religionists at the time of their worship, we should stay there in a respectful mood, contemplating thus:

Here is being worshipped my adorable highest entity, God, in a different form than that of mine, due to a different practice of a different kind, I cannot thoroughly comprehend this system of theirs. But seeing it, I am feeling a greater attachment for my own system. God is one. I bow down before His emblem as I see here, and I offer my prayer to my Lord, who has adopted this different emblem so that he may increase my love toward Him in the form that is acceptable for me.

Two days later Chip Swami sent an e-mail to the spiritual warrior, as follows:

Dear BTS, intimate brother and spiritual warrior, please accept my humble obeisances. All glories to Srila Prabhupada.

When I was with you, there were things I could have asked you that are harder to ask in a letter, but time is short. I want to ask for clarification of what you meant when you said your body is feeling miserable but you are feeling very close to Prabhupada and Krishna. Could you please tell me more of the nature of your feeling close to them, since I so much desire this myself. Do they talk to you? Do you just feel more their presence? Is it a greater confidence that they are waiting to take you? Anything of this sort that you would be willing to tell me, I would be grateful to hear.

Although you said to Patni, 'Vasudeva Datta I ain't,' you told me that you made your prayer for increased potency so that you could decrease the suffering of all people in your preaching, and you prayed that the Lord do whatever He need to do to make you more potent. This seemed to include your willingness to take on peoples' karma, as well as to take away your own karma at once. As I told you, I fully approve of this mighty sacrifice, and we discussed how it is practiced in many religions. But it *is in the mood* of Vasudeva Datta, is it not? I don't think that there is anything to be ashamed of. Have those who have been criticizing you made you change your prayer to say, 'It is not in the mood of Vasudeva Datta?' I feel I need to know this before you go so that it is clear in my mind what you are doing.

But your motives are grave, and if you do not wish to share them with me, I will have to accept that. At any rate, I love you, and I believe that you are going to Krishna and Prabhupada, and I believed you when you said you are preparing a place for me. I hope we will have time for further exchanges on this earthly plane, and even after you are gone. With love, your slow brother, Chip Swami.

Although he was in no physical condition to back pack e-mails, he wrote me right away before heading for his final resting place of Gita-nagari. He appreciated the time that we spent together. He answered my questions and said that Prabhupada has different ways to make himself available to his special servants.

> Some of them need to see the physical presence of Srila Prabhupada from time to time, and so he will flash in and out to give some solace and messages. Some will feel or hear him speak to them through his *murti*. For many, Srila Prabhupada will give his association through dreams or visions. Others will make the special connection through prayer. Some will feel solace and encouragement from tapes and books in a very special way, and for others, Srila Prabhupada will communicate with them through someone else. I am personally familiar with all of these cases that I have mentioned. Throughout my illness, I have tried the best I can to fully offer my body to Srila Prabhupada's service.
>
> When I look at a picture of Srila Prabhupada, I can feel his merciful and compassionate glance more than ever before. It is almost as if he is sad about what I am having to go through, but pleased that I have made myself available and have accepted an early departure, even earlier than I'd initially considered. In other words, he's made a decision to resituate me. He sees that even though it's very hard for me, I've accepted it. As the pain increases every day, it does become more frightening, especially when I think of how much more I may have to endure before I depart. But when I realize that everything is already arranged, I know that I just have to find ways to persevere a little longer. Prabhupada has somehow blessed me to let me know a little bit about what my original *swarupa* is, and what kind of services I'm likely to be doing when I return, so perhaps this is one of the main things that allows me to maintain a certain level of dedication and enthusiasm in spite of my complexities.
>
> Yes, without a doubt my prayer is in the mood of Vasudeva Datta, but my point was that such a prayer can be received in different ways according to one's purity. I am not trying to present myself as a high-level devotee, but the fact that I did make such a prayer perhaps shows that I have a certain intense level of compassion for others, even if thousands of Godbrothers and Godsisters ask me to change or take back the prayer, I would say thank you, but refuse. You see, the prayers that I have made are much more connected with my soul than with my physical or psychological identity. My soul had to reach out to help as many devotees as possible on a deeper level. My soul also wanted me to give up so much of my present identity, as it is too prone to subtle gratification, especially

distinction and adoration. However, isn't it quite ironic that I'm getting more distinction and adoration than before, but on a totally different level. This maybe mainly because many have seen how much I've sacrificed for them. There's much more I could say, but perhaps the next time we can talk on the phone, we could carry on where we left off in this letter.

Chip Swami recalls another phrase that the warrior swami used while they were together—"intercessionary prayer." Plenty of other people may have made intercessionary prayers or prayed for the benefit of others, and *not* had miseries come crashing down upon them. It seems special, doesn't it, that he has prayed and has had immediate results of miseries falling upon him. He jokes and says it's the demigods that came down and said, "Oh yeah? You want to be purified? Okay, here it is." But he also says he definitely feels Krishna's purification and nearness, and he believes Krishna is always working in all things, and he sincerely feels he's acting in an intercessionary way.

CHAPTER THIRTEEN

HE THINKS HE'S GOING OUT OF HIS HEAD, impressions, you
        have
so many things you carry to people, talking in the body
        creating
impression upon impression, the guitar player plays without
a pick, just his fingernails and electricity, his own
        pusillanimity—
what does that word mean?
We didn't have time to look it up
so it slipped by with room enough for only
three in the carriage, death, immortality, and me.

Who is the compassionate for the many other
jivas? I don't know where they went. Looking for
them I think they are in the morgue. Maybe
I could grow a longer beard, because he said,
"You have a delicate face. I tried to grow a full beard
and it just came out gruffy and irritated me."
I don't want to look like a Proustian dandy
or a Nietzschean swallowing your own mouth.

We'll try to see what grows in the next three weeks
we have here. You are my one and only love, Govinda,
of many names and forms. But one Krishna is
recognizable, no beard or moustache, blackish skin smooth
as a baby's arms, strong as a baby elephant—can't
compare Him to anything in these worlds. The words fail
but we try to see "lotus eyed," "most beautiful,", "youngest,"
"most handsome," what can be said? Inconceivably,
        incredible,
The Lord of all, and yet
appearing as a sixteen-year-old cowherd youth
who breaks the hearts of all the cowherd women

and draws the heart's loyalty of all the pious men
to stand by Him forever.

Okay, so we've come to Stuyvesant Falls, Suta's house. One dental
visit. He said that Chip Swami's one remaining tooth is getting looser.
When it falls out, he'll have to get an implant. It's surgery, like two
sticks and a bubble on top of that. Or there are other options. Suddenly
Nara is leaving for six days for real estate work in Mexico. I can take
care of myself. What do you do? Tell them, "I'll write. I'll read. I'll rest.
I'll play alone. I don't need much attention. Just someone cooking and
laundry, and I'll do the deity worship when no one else is here." Plan to
phone BTM.

The little brother wants to ask his big
brother if you have free will from the Lord
do you want to live on despite the miseries
in your bones? Is there something
you haven't accomplished? Do you want to
stay in this ecstasy and wait until He
does His work of cleaning you down to the
last grain with no signal from you
"I've had enough"?

How does it go? How do you see death?
Remember St. Francis of Assisi adding Sister Death
as a reality onto the canticle of the beings, along with the
birds and sunshine and all
of God's things in nature? He welcomed
her coming, saw her near.
No need to fear. Embrace her as another
in the family of God's canticle.

Or is he fighting her off, resisting so he can
put off the moment so he can accomplish
more good, loving while there is more
precious time given to love,

> help give the example of
> compassionate expression to others
> to live with for
> the rest of their lives.
>
> Only he and Krishna and death
> and the crush of cancerous bones
> know exactly when,
> but soon.

One of the symptoms of a devotee is that he is kind. If our Godbrother becomes ill, it is our duty to help him get the proper medicine and treatment so that he can recover. There's no question of ill-treating of our own Godbrothers simply because they are sick, nor should you allow such neglect to go on. So long we have this material body, there will be sickness, but we have to remain on the transcendental platform nevertheless.

—Srila Prabhupada, from a letter to Sukadeva, April 5, 1974

So much for the myth that Prabhupada said devotees don't take medicines, that they just gut it out and that is the most saintly way. They should be taken care of. Not doped out but remaining on the transcendental platform nevertheless. It is our duty to *help him get the proper medicine* so that he can recover. Nanda just found out from his doctors that he has extremely high blood pressure and has to take some medicine accordingly. He wants to retire in a year and a half, somehow.

I have been exercising for two days. Bones and joints hurt. Ripping muscles become "muscle bound." Why not just relax and sip a lemonade? Which is better for longevity? There is a dying man here. You think of asking him—is it better to hold on tight and somehow resist death, or ease into it? Does Krishna want you to fight down to the last molecule, or does He want you to drop assistance and embrace "Sister Death," not in defeat but in "surrender"? This body is a lump of ignorance. This is painful, maintaining existence in a smelly bag. Come Krishna, take me away to you. Different angles.
"Do not go gentle into that good night,
Rage, rage against the dying of the light."

But some go gentle, as Therese of Lisieux seemed to, tired of the coughing, wanting to return to heaven to shed blessings on all her sisters—"I will shed flowers on you." Oh, if only I could go now. But the good Jesus has his reasons for holding her back. If she had her way, she would fly to him at once.

In *The Thousand Nights,* the king believed that all women are unfaithful, so he decides to have each of his wives killed after their wedding night. One of the wives pleaded that she be spared one night by telling an entertaining story. The story was so entertaining that she was allowed to go free for telling a thousand stories in a thousand nights, if she could keep up the continuity of the stories and with such quality. She did it, but what happened after a thousand nights? No one is immortal. Did Prometheus save his life by stealing fire from the gods? They have built a bronze statue of him with an eagle tearing apart his guts for everyone to look at in Rockefeller Center, Manhattan. When your time comes, you are most likely to shiver and fliver at least as a human reflex, even if you're the bravest, surrendered to God, and as they say, "ice flows in your veins." Maybe not even those symptoms. You may just pray and call out the holy names of God with tears streaking your face, talking in tongues, falling on the ground, singing songs, calling out the names of Radha-Krishna.

Maybe you'll be in a station where people are talking in different languages, and so you think you're hearing different tongues and therefore you can't talk to anyone and your last words will get done in writing:

Well Daddy, thank you enormously for everything you have given me. I am sorry I didn't do better. I pooped out at the end.

I can go to Houston because I'm in better health. He can't even ride fifteen minutes down the road, but he can make a video for Oprah on what he's learned from his deathbed, a great vantage point. Every day he seeks another opportunity. Some have turned away from him, he doesn't stop. He goes forward. Amazing man. "Call me every few days." Gulp. I don't have that much deep and confidential to say. Today I spoke to him about Prabhupada, saying that Krishna had given him a free choice to live or not. But at the end it was actually up to Krishna. What did the spiritual warrior think about himself? He thought it was up to Krishna, but he felt there were things he wanted to do. Speak to the highest ranking.

What would he do to protect his disciples after he left so that they are true to his way? He has appointed a person to each country, but if they don't want to follow him, they can follow another *shiksha* or ISKCON *diksha* guru. The main thing is to find connection and get through to Prabhupada and Krishna.

> Had she been unfaithful to him in that short time? Oh
> No, never. A love supreme, a love supreme, a love supreme
> Up and down the scales, ask him what he thinks of his
> Lovely lovely shining books both behind a mask of a Christ
>   fast and spiritual master who may
> Be gone by then while you are preserving a little
> Longer. What does posterity consider of your work
> And what does it matter to you who are entering your next
>   body?

Shims is at Suta's house making up things, and in a few minutes he comes in to tell me it's time for us to exercise. I was "script writing" a story that a woman lawyer was in the middle of a dangerous case. The victim of two thugs ran into her house and asked for protection. She ran away from that by going to the police, but the victim as well as the two were after her. She got to the police first, but they arrested them all. She got to talk to the police first, and the others were in jail. The policewoman who was talking to her was angry because she just lost two horse races in a row. She said, "Tell me the story but be fast because I just lost two horse races in a row." Should I continue this story telling or start picking my nose? Or should I stop picking my nose? Should I stop telling this script and get back to chanting Hare Krishna? Someone called and said, "Well come on, do your exercises." I really don't want to do them, but that's what I'm here for, I guess. Two quiet weeks to chant Hare Krishna and relax and do exercises before going on to Houston. And in the meantime, keep in touch with the spiritual warrior.

Jim's lawyer friend Pariksit Maharaja came to visit him. He said he had just read the latest newsletter from Bhakti-tirtha Maharaja's camp. The spiritual warrior said that some of his caretakers announced that he only had three or four days to live. "But I may live three or four weeks," said the spiritual warrior. "I'm stubborn," he said. That made Jim want to phone him again.

Actually, Jim said to his lawyer friend, "I don't know what to call him about. I seem to have used up all my topics."

"You don't have to have special topics to call a friend. Just call and talk to him in an informal way." That seemed like a good idea. It doesn't have to be so formal. Just some warm talk, like "how are you feeling today," and let it go from there. Don't stiffen up as if you have nothing to say to a loved one in such a situation. Encourage him in his stubbornness. Encourage him in his courage, in which he believes that every day that he remains alive is a day in which he can do some good in the world. Every day do good.

You hesitate to phone S.W. You may be bothering him. May have nothing deep to say to a man who's dying. May not have a casual enough loving friendship to "just talk." Just talk as I would have with a few others. And so it would be artificial with him. But don't want to waste the benefit in his last days. I don't think he needs me.

> My one and only love
> does it have to be like that?
> A close and intimate playmate
> "the one that I put my hand in the fire for."
>
> Budge it along, improve it from
> what it is. Don't be afraid to.
>
> Be a friend to a man who said he wanted
> you to call him sometimes and who's
> in his last breaths and you are inoffensive.
> you are just an inoffensive well-wisher
> sending your Hallmark
> card and fresh flowers, dropping in
> to say hello.

His secretary said it means a lot to him when I speak to him on the phone. So on with the Hallmark free-write phone calls: "How are you feeling? Better today? Is Krishna talking to you? I've been reading St. Theresa of Avila. She had visions. But she felt she was wretched compared to what she should have been. She wasted years in her easy nunhood hanging out in the social room instead of praying. Then one day Jesus came up to her and said, 'From now on I want you to talk only to angels.' She was shocked and completely believed the vision. From that moment she changed. Tell him how Theresa has had some affect on me. Their prayer life. It is strongly *bhajananandi*, coming close to Prabhupada and Radha in prayer. ISKCON sometimes derides this as *"babaji,"* but there's a saying, I think attributed to Bhaktisiddhanta Saraswati, "The best *ghostyanandi* is a *bhajananandi* who preaches." An inward man who prays is the potent one. That seemed like what Spiritual Warrior spoke of. He was preaching all over the world but felt the lacking in potency in changing the souls he preached to. So he upped the stakes in a sacrificial, intercessionary way. "Take *me*, Lord. Take the karma due to everyone and give it just to me. Pile it on me." He did it for them, for us. Some can't believe it, can't see the capacity. He replies, "Many good things have happened, soured ex-*gurukulis* have renewed their chanting, men and women have written him their gratefulness and then returned to Krishna consciousness on account of his act. Things are happening, maybe not on the level of the reaction to Jesus Christ's crucifixion, but . . . the spiritual warrior felt he had to do it first for himself.

Write when wounded.

Got a book on the life of Jean Shepherd. The introduction was feisty, saying that my childhood idol was a liar, as are all artists. He did tell tall tales. But we worshipped him as a man of integrity. So what if he changed the facts of his childhood and told three different versions of how his old man disengaged a nail from his thumb? Those who dislike him for not being an historian instead of a storyteller miss the whole point. We kids didn't miss the point. He taught us not to be gullible to the real lives of our parents and government, and even if he stretched his own biography, so what? We do not consider that his "darker side." Monologue, jazz riff, twisted, made it up, magic, enigma, courage.

Making up his life as he goes along. He taught me how to do it.

> We have many things to do. You fill a
> calendar with appointments, big boy.
> Phone a friend and ask him to buy you
> a pair of pants because you've been
> peeing in your pants
> and as a traveler you don't have enough
> dry pants. "Sure," he says. You are visiting his
> house next week. Today you are visiting
> the house of an artist.
>
> "They took my strings away," lamented Bird,
> So many bad blows as he destroyed himself.
>
> Musicians gradually wised up and later generations,
> but how can you make decent
> money playing hip? Who'll give donations
> to pure devotees?
>
> Throw out all references but the
> *Bhagavatam* so you'll be safe at
> death, latch onto His names
> said the advice-giver.
> I write down in my rod but couldn't
> follow. The attempt. At least the attempt,
> I figured, was in my favor, like chanting
> Hare Krishna when you're scared
> of death.

Us is having incredibly good luck on this trip, health-wise. We are not getting any headaches and not taking painkillers. Filling the weekly calendar with social visits and fulfilling them in a kicked-back manner. Relaxed. There are many little inconveniences for a traveler away from his routine at home, but I'm taking it easy, adjusting, tolerating, being a new man for a few weeks. We *are* still wetting our pants, unfortunately, uncontrolled bladder suddenly trickling down the leg and you have to change your underpants and outer pants midday. Take a shower change into sweatpants. That's a strain on a traveling man's wardrobe. But there are quite a few sweatpants here to change into, and the hosts are friendly.

It's April 12; expecting income tax returns to arrive. Expecting Nara to come and go. We are not worrying about it. Lining up more friends to visit. The others are not worrying, so why should I worry? Exercising every evening with Suta. In exercise, Suta says your muscles tell you you cannot do more, but you tell them, "Yes, do more." Sometimes he says it out loud, "Do more!" and he grunts loudly for each one. We are learning that too, to grunt loudly on the outbreath when you are exerting your strength. Phone call with Spiritual Warrior, Dainya the editor to arrive here, Tad arriving here to serve—he says he wants to "do skits." Suta's family leaves for vacation in a few days. Rad and family visiting here for a day. I will go visit Pariksit Maharaja overnight in his home an hour and a half away. Later, visit an art gallery to see KK's paintings. Us will leave April 18 along with Nara for Houston, Texas. ain't that a lot of activities for a boy who was recently doing nothing but lying in bed?

Us is having incredibly good luck

CHAPTER FOURTEEN

Y OU MAY KNOW. I MAY RECOVER to consummate *japa* in a year and re cover to rereading *The Cloud of Unknowing*. A little boy who refused his mother's order to go to sleep that night and instead worked all night on writing music became J. S. Bach, but he lost his sight. His contribution to music is stupendous. Also, the classical music recordings of Mingus and Monk and so many of the bop jazz musicians of the 1940s to 1960s are still being rerecorded with technological improvements.

You could never know ahead of time. Let me help you step into the car. I couldn't have guessed you would have grown a goatee to wear along with your *sannyasa* clothes. Such an individual.

Write and die. How could anyone guess an Emily Dickinson? So there is a God, but what of that? Give us the *bhajananandi* mystic who trod with careful steps the *prema-bhakti-marga*. How could anyone know Krishna's and Radha's faces and forms are so beautiful, and Their friends can become so kind and eligible as to bring you into Their pastimes if you display the pure and humble states. You've heard this, have you not?

Pure, pure, pure. *utsaha nistayet dharyet tat tat karma nivartanat. Utsaha* means to work with Him with enthusiasm, and God is not absent. Everyone can be with Him in likeness, and sometimes close, and sometimes in parting. And what about Yo Yo Ma's cello, and Prabhupada's speeches, and the author of *Dark Cloud*? These things are so golden we call them *vibhuti*, empowered by God, a *sakti*, and that can be credit too. Best is to concentrate on *Dark Cloud* and your own pristine path. You were learning the *Bhagavad-gita* as it is from your master, even when you were learning it as translated by Dr. Radhakrishnan, but your Swamiji was the teacher, the teacher of all things. He even told you how to use the toilet room for making a bowel movement, and how to clean yourself with water, not toilet paper, and how to squat while urinating, not standing, and how to say, "*accha*," and how to mourn for the departed Vaishnavas, as began to happen more and more later in your life, and how to appreciate them before they left their bodies. Taught you not to be angry at others, even if they were

223

angry at you. He taught you to chant sixteen rounds a day every day, and there was no need to replace your red Tandy beads with *Tulasi* beads once you got to India. And Rayarama made a poster of our spiritual master with the heading, "This man has changed the consciousness of the world." He did not like it and shook his head negatively. "This is no good," he said, and I think he added, "This is an offense. One should not call the spiritual master 'a man.'"

We took everything he said as true, but nevertheless, I thought to myself, "Wow! He said 'This *man* has changed the consciousness of the whole world!' Maybe, but you cannot call the spiritual master a man. Learn how to do it right. He's not a man, he's a guru, a self-realized person."

Write and die, but learn how to write it the correct way. Don't write rubbish. Don't write some concocted nonsense but Vaishnava etiquette and the proper words. His Divine Grace A. C. Bhaktivedanta Swami Prabhupada has changed the consciousness of the world. When we did that and put the posters in the Harvard divinity school, we saw some students had scribbled on it their offensive language about the use of the words "His Divine Grace." To satisfy them, a phrase like "this man" would have been better, and not claimed that he changed the consciousness of the whole world. Can't please everyone, but it's better to please the guru, and this pleases the whole world.

He hadn't heard of St. Antony the Great of ancient Egypt. I'd been remembering him (me, Chips Swamiji) by our talk of Mary Magdalene and her constant absorption in Christ within her life at all times, and in particular in the episode where she is with Jesus and Martha. Martha complains, "Master, please tell Mary to help out with the cooking." Jesus is quick to defend the contemplative who chooses to take as her sole duty staying absorbed in her loving him with all her senses. "Martha, Martha, you are absorbed in many things, but Mary is fixed on me alone, so she has chosen the best part." So it was with St. Antony of Egypt, who stayed alone in a cave and battled all temptations so he could remain concentrated on the Lord.

Through e-mail we received a threat that someone heard I'm going to Houston. Someone has not forgotten that Chips Swamiji is a sinner, lawbreaker. He says he's coming to Houston to get Swami Chips. Exactly what will he do there? Some of the Swami's supporters have become frightened for their beloved Swamiji. He himself says he's not afraid. If it gets too hairy for him, he can leave the book-signing area or ignore the menace and go on signing books while someone else protects him. It's an exciting world. His books are also exciting.

Here is another poem by Ron Padgett, just to show you that I share poems of other poets in this book, and that many of them are not God conscious, as mine are:

> *Bluebird*
> You can't expect
> the milk to be delivered
> to your house
> by a bluebird
> from a picture book
> you looked at
> at the age of four:
> He's much older
> now, can't carry those bottles, 'neath his wing,
> can hardly even carry a tune
> with his faded beak
> that opens some nights
> to eek out a cry
> to the horrible god
> that created him.
>
> Don't think I'm
> the bluebird or that
> you are. Let him get
> old on his own and
> die like a real bluebird
> that sat on a branch in a book, turned his head
> toward you, and radiated.
>   —From *You Never Know*, by Ron Padgett

The worst line in this poem is "to the horrible god / that created him." He directly attacks the God who created all creatures, even the somewhat mythological storybook bluebird whom he read about in his boyhood. How fierce an atheist he is, making out of his deceptively benign childhood poem the surrealistic attack on all innocence. There were actually nice little books that told us about God. I know because I read some of them. My mother gave them to me. One was *Who Created Me, God Created You*. They were very good, nutritious books, better than books he received in Catholic school. They actually gave you faith and told you that God created you and Jesus was very kind. They were not dogma but truth. So Ron Padgett comes much later, battered by all his misadventures, and tries to ruin that sweet memory he probably did have from reading books in childhood that were sweet and innocent. He has put a layer over it with all his sourness, whereas if he could truly remember and be honest about it, he probably did read a nice book like *Bluebird* in his youth. He's just become such a sour guy by all his attempted sexual exploits, attempts to be truthful without really letting go the notion that he himself is God. Is it possibly true that he really read a book where the bird died while he turned toward the reader and "radiated"? Seems highly unlikely. Who would be writing such books but some sophisticated *mayavadi* or Buddhist?

But you never know.

Live and die.

You've heard of Thomas Mann? He is one of the most celebrated novelists of the twentieth century. He won the Nobel Prize in literature in 1920. I read a few of his smaller works. Once, before Chips entered the service of Prabhupada, he was sitting at the circle in Washington Square Park and a bedraggled black man came offering for sale Mann's masterpiece *The Magic Mountain* for one dollar, but no one took it. A girlfriend of Chips also once bought him *The Magic Mountain* for a birthday present, but he didn't read it that time, either. Some kind of anti-Mann genes in his body. But he does recall reading a preface in a Mann book in which the great German author says that when he was writing one of his masterpieces (some people called him a word-monger), a small magical circle of books gathered on his writing desk. He acknowledged this on his Acknowledgments page and said that these books appeared to help him in his endeavors. They were things that he drew from or quoted from or books that inspired him just when he needed them for this exact writing project. Immediately this statement resonated with me. Oh, you mean to say you plagiarize from different books on occasion? No, no. Chips means that at different times when he's writing on a theme like write or die, different authors will fly and join his flock in the sky, and then later, another genius will come to mind and come and join him. It's not like he plans ahead to steal something, or that he steals from them later, but that it's a worldwide current in which anyone can travel, and many great persons have traveled before, and the deeper one goes, he recalls the past travelers, and they come and join him, and it's all right, because the deeper you go, you remember their previous great passages through this land. Lewis and Clark went the first time, and even a tourist who goes today through that passage, if he takes it seriously, will start to remember the first passages, or the signs of the Civil War, and make a new pilgrimage. And ultimately, you will recall the passage back to Godhead, even from a rather routine or casual passage this time. Ultimately, we are meant to make every slightest movement in our lives a contribution to the passage back to Godhead, and everything should remind us of that, and we should remind our readers of it, too, so let us pull together. Let us push our shoulders against the wheel. Keep the wheels moving, as Prabhupada used to say, quoting from the motto of the railway system in his day. Do anything to contribute to keeping the wheels moving, whether it's inventing a new bookkeeping system, a new engine-lubricating system, a new system of employee relationships, or a new way to improve the mighty engines of the locomotives. Never be a moment without thinking about keeping the engines moving. Keep them stopping at stations on time, keep the efficiency, keep the power, keep the glory, so that everyone can arrive at their destinations as soon as possible and without any accidents. "At United Airlines, our first business is your safety."

Now you will note that United Airlines does not guarantee the physical immortality of every passenger (although you can take out insurance for your survivors), but they do say with much experience, hope, and confidence that your trip with them will be one in which you will not die. But die you must eventually, on the ground or in the air.

WRITE AND DIE

These last two weeks in Stuyvesant, New York, I've been recuperating from an illness, and we are basically just hanging around waiting to recover and waiting to go down to Houston for the book fair. I need the time for rest and recuperation. Mostly the people here are on vacation, and it's just me, Nara, and our jolly friend Tad. Nara has been doing our business, often behind the scenes, making arrangements for our air tickets, talking with the other partners in the venture, seeing that they get their books down there, taking prints and paintings, finding out what rooms we'll stay in, what things we may use, and so on. He's the planner and the leader of our group. Tad isn't going with us, but he's just staying with us here and helping out with cooking and entertaining us. He tells us about his brokenhearted life, and does wonderful, spontaneous satires, often with much self-deprecating humor about his flops in his aikido martial arts course, at which he is just a beginner. "Hut! Hut! *Sa!*" As a beginner, the first step he has learned is to roll over and fall down, and that's what he's practicing before our eyes, like a puppy dog. He does it quite well, because if you don't fall well, you can hurt yourself. It becomes a kind of accomplishment. Instead of knocking the other guy, you become expert at falling down, and he showed it off to the people on the block. In the past, when I stayed with him for a long while, we started doing skits, and we sometimes became fatalists. Fortunately, this is a short stay, and we won't fall into that, playlettes about the Panzer Pope and so on. Yesterday he did begin his speech about the new Pope, a kind of Hitleresque speech to all the new Catholic parishioners in the high military command tones of *Der Fuhrer*.

His listening career with Jean Shepherd was mostly late 1950s and the early 1960s, when Jean was on WOR radio. His show was from 9:00 to 11:00 P.M., and then there was a newscast by some guy whom he didn't listen to. Then we turned the radio back on after fifteen minutes and stayed with Jean until 1:00 in the morning. Jean referred to the show beginning at 11:15 as the intimate time when the women and children have gone to sleep and it is time for the "night people." You had your own room in your house, and your mother's and father's bedroom was below yours, so you had to keep the radio at a lower volume, especially when Jean hurled invectives. You pulled your little radio into bed with you, and sometimes covered it with a few blankets so that it was right next to your ear. So what that you had to take a chem test tomorrow or that you were losing precious sleep? This was too great of an education, too rare an intimacy, to be given up.

People often praised Jean for his collection of trivia and seeing mankind absorbed in absurdities. He made funny improvised skits mocking civilizations' morés, and in the late hours, he sometimes grew darker to the source of his beliefs, as to the actual nature of humankind. That was also present on my long-playing record *The Clown*, where Shepherd improvised along with the Charles Mingus Jazz Workshop. He started out, "Let me tell you a story about a clown. He was a happy guy. He had all these colors inside himself . . . ." He goes on to tell us about a truly simple circus performer whose only job in life is to make people laugh. He is so filled by this desire that Shep describes him as being filled with colors, like red and green and orange. All he wanted to do was to make people laugh, but he wasn't very good at it, so the circus managers weren't so pleased with him. But one time he had an accident during his performance. He tripped on his ladder and fell down three steps and landed on his head. It hurt him a lot. When he looked out at the crowd, they were laughing to beat the band. The clown was cheered to see the laughter, but it gave him an unsettling new realization, and he didn't like what he had learned.

So he went on doing these gigs, and one time in Pittsburgh—"a very fine town, Pittsburgh, you know," said Shep—the clown suffered a very bad accident doing his act. The whole backdrop fell down, breaking the clown's neck and knocking him to the floor. The band plays fast jazz for awhile, but then it slows down to a mournful mood, and Shepard then says his last words: "And that was the end of the clown." I liked *The Clown*, although I must admit the depth of its cynicism didn't really hit me. Yeah, yeah, I got the point, people will laugh at you when you're down. I did realize that the clown was funny only when he hurt himself, and that I too was guilty at laughing, and Shep was brave enough to point it out. I was guilty of laughing at cripples even at the moment when they were being hurt and all the colors were being drained, and only Shepherd had the guts to point out the truth about ourselves, and himself too. Look at yourself, mankind. Excelsior, you fathead! Write and die.

On the air, Shep frequently spoke of two characters, Arg and

Charlie, one a cave man and the other a contemporary man. He ran
them through comic routines. Wow. One night he said, "Did you ever
think how an old man sometimes looks like a cave man?" No wonder
we had to hide the radios under the blankets. In one sequence, Arg and
another cave man are squatting beside a lake in silence for a long time,
then Arg sees some clams. He crawls off to fetch them. He returns with
them, and both men sit silently, but after a while, the other cave man
picks up a big rock and smashes it on Arg's head, killing him. At this
instant, these two cave dwellers have risen to the species of manhood.
They have become "men." At the same moment, another cave dweller
who has been hiding starts crawling forward toward them with an even
bigger rock in his hand. Although not couched in religious terms, Jean
Shepherd's philosophy seems to bare a resemblance to original sin or
the fall of man. He rambles on to say, "Why do you think we have all
these wars, why are we always fighting?" You can imagine why these
kinds of talks were saved for the night people, when Jean Shepherd
bared his soul. And many of us feckless youths like Chip absorbed it in
like dry sponges.

So all of this Shepherdism got mixed into Chips' soup, along with
the Kafka diaries and the whole beatnik dream of girls that never mate-
rialized, romances that were like dreams that never came true. He
learned to give his life to be a writer. A pyrrhic victory, as one Lower
East Side friend told him. But he did expect to at least attain posthumous fame. Steve Kowit was an encouraging friend or buddy and liked
Chips' writing. Just imagine how elated Chip became when Steve told
him, "I think you will be published by the time you are thirty years
old." But it was Murray Mednick who Chips regarded as being more in
the mode of goodness—and who also admired Chips' writings—who
said to Chips, "Chippy, there's only so much cake on the table, and
there are a lot boys trying to get a piece. You've got to develop sharper
elbows if you want to get a book published." Murray had seen Chips'
general shyness with women and his humble ways among the predomi-
nating Jewish achievers at Brooklyn College, and he was suggesting
that Chips develop a little self-promotional muscle. It was the kind of
brotherly advice perhaps worth more than Kowit's remark. But now
let's look back at Shepherd's dog-eat-dog philosophy. It certainly makes
a lot of sense in the light of civilized history, with its wars and persecu-

tions, and although I don't know much about it, I'm sure it is as Murray alluded, even among those who try to publish their books—"there's a limited amount of cake on the table, Chips."

So add this to the debit column on the right. What are your chances of living a long time among your hostile human brethren and of continuing to write? My conclusion is that one should write as fast and as much as possible *before they get you!*

Why not add *Bhagavad-gita As It Is* to the special magic circle on your desk? If Ron Padgett is there, why not the best book of all, the ABCs of loving God? Turn to it anywhere. For example, the twelfth chapter, on pure devotional service. Take a look at the progressive stages of devotional service. Krishna begins the chapter by saying that devotional service is better than impersonal approaches to the Lord, then it gets progressively more nectarean. He says,

> One who is not envious but is a kind friend to all living entities, who does not think himself a proprietor and is free from false ego, who is equal in both happiness and distress, who is tolerant, always satisfied, self-controlled and engaged in devotional service with determination, *his mind and intelligence fixed on Me*—such a devotee of Mine is very dear to Me. [emphasis added]
>
> —*Bhagavad-gita As It Is,* 12:13

In the purport, Prabhupada illuminates Krishna's words, saying how the devotee is fixed in the conclusions of Krishna and is fixed in the uses of his senses.

> All these qualifications enable him to fix his mind and intelligence entirely on the Supreme Lord. Such a standard of devotional service is undoubtedly very rare, but a devotee becomes situated in that stage by following the regulative principles of devotional service. Furthermore, the Lord says that such a devotee is very dear to Him, for the Lord is always pleased with all his activities in full Krishna consciousness.
>
> —Bhaktivedanta purport to Bg. 12:14

Prabhupada is grooming us through preliminary steps to a very profound subject matter. There is God, and He loves you. That love will increase as you increase your love for God. It is very, very personal, more personal than anything you know in this world. You have to control yourself and turn away from attachments in this world. Stay fixed in the company of devotees and under the direction of the spiritual master.

What's all this worriment about write and die? It's all temporary. There should be no worry except making sure you're fixed on Krishna and bringing your attachments to Him, increasing and increasing.

"My devotee who is not dependent on the ordinary course of activities, who is pure, expert, without cares, free from all pains and not striving for some result is very dear to Me." (Bg. 12:16)

In the purport, Prabhupada tells about the daily routine of the devotee. He rises early in the morning, takes a bath for devotional service, clean within and without. He follows a whole list of devotional regimens, not in a forced way but because he knows they're best for his spirituality. Eventually he does them automatically, spontaneously. He doesn't get involved in any politics. Because he's not attached to the body, he's free of designations. He'll get engaged in something only if it's concerned with Krishna consciousness. He'll make money for Krishna consciousness but not otherwise. Prabhupada's purports are like little gems, just enough so you can learn what you need to advance. Oh dear Srila Prabhupada, let me learn this book some more so I can become a true devotee. Let me read some more. Write and die. Read these words as much as you can and die. Your time is limited, so you should stay close to these words before Arg or somebody else hits you on the head. Get as much *Bhagavad-gita* in there, realized and convinced. Don't get distracted. Chips prabhu was praying silently to himself, realizing what he really needed was in this one book, and that his attempts to bring other books under its sway was secondary.

"One who neither rejoices or grieves, who neither laments nor desires, and who renounces both auspicious and inauspicious things— such a devotee is very dear to Me." (Bg. 12:17)

In his purport, Srila Prabhupada points out briefly Krishna's equanimity, which we should have in this material world. Don't lament if your baseball team loses the game, or don't rejoice. These things don't matter. So what if you get a disciple or a son? So what if you lose everything? Nothing is dear to you. Nothing is worth lamenting over. Nothing is worth crying. Accept all risks for the satisfaction of the Supreme Lord. Don't worry about impediments in the service of Krishna. If you have that attitude, you become very dear to Krishna. That's what Prabhupada says, and one should carry it in his heart like a dear emblem, like a life's goal. Like that. Live that and die.

> One who is equal to friends and enemies, who is equipoised in honor and dishonor, heat and cold, happiness and distress, fame and infamy, one who is always free from contaminating association, always satisfied with anything, one who doesn't care for any residence, who is fixed in knowledge and who is engaged in devotional service—such a person is very dear to Me.
>
> —Bg. 12:18–19

Prabhupada says sometimes it's the nature of human society that a devotee gets defamed. But even when that happens, a devotee remains transcendental to it, whether it's infamy or happiness. He's patient. He talks about Krishna, otherwise he's silent. He speaks of essentials about the Lord. If he gets good food, he's happy with that. Or otherwise, he doesn't mind. He's not looking for a good place to stay. He's fixed in his situation. These different qualities of a devotee develop automatically by engaging in Krishna consciousness. And Krishna Himself helps the devotee to automatically develop them.

How does the *Bhagavad-gita* fit in with the theme of this book? Am I only making it appear so? *No, no, mon frer, mon ami.* The fact is that this book, *Bhagavad-gita,* is the theme. The longer you sit here with me quietly and watch the snow fall while listening to the book, you'll get the realizations. And even when we go out to pack our suitcase or to answer the phone, or someone comes back to this empty apartment and we exchange socially and start to pack our bags for Houston, we won't forget what the Supreme Personality of Godhead said about devotional service. Or we'll go back to it again to remember. He said a devotee is very dear to Him and He is very dear to a devotee. And that, *mon frer,* is the target of the magic circle. That is why we are hurrying up before death comes. That is why we are trying not to be afraid and praying to God to give us courage, preparing ourselves while we also write our fears.

Ever since hearing about the story of Orpheus and Eurydice, I wanted to bring the poet Rilke's *Sonnets to Orpheus* into the inner circle of books on my table for *Write and Die*. But it will be very difficult because I am not a strongly intellectual scholar or even a meticulous poet. Nevertheless, I'm going to do some patchy job on it, borrowing often from the quotes I find in a volume of *Sonnets to Orpheus*, translated by Willis Barnstone. He interprets the book in a very individualistic and personal way. He actually makes Eurydice, not Orpheus, the central figure of the poem. It is she who is always perpetually dancing around the world and perpetuating her art for all creatures, for their inspiration and salvation. Rilke borrows a lot from his own life in fashioning the story that comes from Greek mythology. Rilke's life was a series of deep affairs with women, with whom he took shelter of for love affairs and financial patronage also. After passionate, romantic involvement, he would then feel a need to break the ties and to become alone again because his ultimate religion was solitude and art. And yet he kept correspondence with most of them through amorous and affectionate letters. Some of these abandoned women continued to revere Rilke. Some of them went their own ways.. It seems that many of them broke with him utterly, and he continued to return to them from time to time. It is not that he did this in a callous way, but he was drawn by his "angels" to leave women and family behind and go off into the "deserts" of rented rooms or offered castles to live for months and months at a time, completely alone, waiting for a line to come at night to break his writing blocks and enable him to receive words of inspiration to continue his poems. He was certainly a completely committed and dedicated poet and did not settle for anything less than inspired words, as if sent from heaven.

When we attempt to compare him to the story of Orpheus and Eurydice in the original Greek myth, there is one instance in the poem he writes called "Requiem to a Friend," which parallels it closely. He wrote this letter in a typical situation where he had become enamored with a woman and married her and even produced an offspring. But then he felt the prison walls of married life close in, and he left her. Out of deep, sincere feelings, he wrote a poem called "Requiem to a Friend," lamenting his deserting her. You can hear the shades of Orpheus' sorrow at his blunder at turning back to look for Eurydice, and then lamenting for the rest of his life that she was lost to him.

Requiem for a Friend
If you are still here with me, if in this darkness
there is some place where your spirit
resonates
on the shallow sound waves stirred up by own
voice:
hear me; help me. We can so easily
slip back from what we have struggled to attain
abruptly, into a life we never wanted;
and find that we are trapped, as in a dream,
and die there without ever waking up.
this can occur. Anyone who has lifted
his blood into a year's-long work to find that he can't sustain
       it, the force of gravity is irresistible, and it falls back,
       worthless.
For somewhere there is an ancient enmity between our daily
       life and the great work.

Do not return. If you dare to, stay
dead with the dead. The dead have their own tasks.
but help me, if you can without distraction,
as what is farthest sometimes helps in me.

The editor, Willis, considers this poem one of Rilke's greatest and a prelude to his *Sonnets to Orpheus*. "But ultimately," writes Willis, "in his last exuberance, we hear both the ethereal poet and his creation Orpheus. But soon it is clear that the sonnets transcend Orpheus' vision to the other of his resurrected and lost-again wife, and take us fully into her world, bequeathing us a *Sonnets to Eurydice*."

Is this dream stuff? Poetry? Requiem? To die and resurrect and go about the world in separation from your loved one, always helping him by staying separated from him? Is that what Eurydice did for Orpheus?

But if we stand on our feet on the earth and with our head thinking clearly, as a Jean Shepherd man would do, this is not transcendental vision. Prabhupada would tell us this is concocted. Either you live or you die. Rilke was a Gnostic. He did not believe in a living God. So

235

he could conjure many things. But I am edging him onto the inner circle of my book table for *Write and Die* because of similarities for jumping-off places, interesting glimpses into the original Orpheus and Eurydice.

> *Sonnets* is a calendar of search, remembrance, and acceptance of Orpheus, the god of descent and resurrection, who is everywhere. Rilke succeeds in turning grief into pathos and ultimately into an ecstasy of absence and presence . . . it is not different emotionally and artistically from the pattern of mystical poets, such as the sixteenth-century Spanish St. John of the Cross, where the speaker moves from the burning senses, to the dark night of the negation, and to the light and union—which in the instance of both the Spanish mystic John and Ranier Maria Rilke is the evidence of the poem.
>
> —Barnstone, p. 73

This sounds like a sliver of Sri Chaitanya Mahaprabhu, *who in the mood of* Srimati, Radharani, *feels ecstatic separation from Krishna. This* is a separation of illumination because His separation is the highest ecstasy. We do not imagine that Orpheus had such ecstasy as he wandered the earth after he lost Eurydice, and yet there is an indication that he did remain in search of her and in contact with her, and she in contact with him. And that's what the *Sonnets* will tell us. Furthermore, the search was on a cosmic scale, and when he played his music, everyone could hear it, and when she danced, the whole world danced with her. And when they remembered, they were not apart but together. When she was in Hades, she was actually in the arms of her lover, and that was how he loved her best.

Lord Chaitanya was not a writer penning these things down, although occasionally He wrote and He compelled His intimate companions to recite poems of separation. Yes, He did these things to give spice to His separation, but even more, He lived it day and night in tears and strange actions, like swimming unconsciously in the water and falling unconscious among the cows at the gate of the Jagannath temple, or changing the shape of His body.

> Raise no memorial stone. Although we miss
> him, let the rose bloom every year for him.
> He's Orpheus, and his metamorphosis

is everywhere. We needn't scan the limb

of forests for more names. Once and for all
he's Orpheus when there's song. He comes
and goes.
And isn't it a marvelous windfall
when he stays a few days longer than the rose?

For you to know him he must disappear!
Though he was terrified of vanishing
and while his word transcends his being here,

He's already gone where you cannot go.
His hands are not ensnared in lyre string
And he obeys, stepping beyond us now.
　　　　　　　—from Rilke's *Sonnets to Orpheus,*
　　　　　　　　No. 5. Translation by Willis Barnstone

To Praise Is Foremost!
To praise is foremost! He emerged to praise
And came to us like ore out of a stone's
Silence. His heart, a temporal press, amazed
Thus with a wine of unending tone.

When he feels like a god in perfect shape, his voice never
　　　　falters in a dry mouth.
Everything turns to vineyard or to grape
Ripening blue in his sensual south.

Neither decay in the gray vaults of kings
Nor any shadow fallen from the gods
Will undermine his marvelous praisings.

He is a herald standing in the sod, offering bowls of fruit and
　　　　praises for
The dead concealed behind their dreadful door.
　　　　　　　　—Sonnet No. 7

It was at that dreadful door that Orpheus turned back just before it opened, and he lost Eurydice. He had almost achieved the impossible—the resurrection of both himself and her—but failed at the very last moment. So it cannot be done. Unless a power like Krishna wills it. Most of us must write and die. Is this enough with the poems of Rilke? Two more.

One offered to the tenor saxophonist, who dove on the earth, "Orpheus, whom we have torn apart."

> *XVI*
> Orpheus, whom we have torn apart again,
> This god is resting at a Site that heals.
> Our hands are cutting sharp. We want to win
> The truth, but scattered and serene he feels
>
> His place. We come with consecrated gifts.
> He doesn't care and takes no other way
> into his world. Emotionless he will not lift
> a finger as he stares unto a far ray
>
> of freedom. Out of the unseen pool, the source that we can
> hear, only the dead can drink
>
> When the god signals him. We are offered
> just noise. Out of the quieter instinct
> the land is begging for its bell.

And the last poem about the dancer, Eurydice, who danced with Orpheus on the earth and continued to dance with him in Hades:

> *XVIII*
> Dancer, O you translation
> Of all transients into steps. How sparkling clear!
> That culminating spin, that tree of motion,
> didn't you only seize the turning year?
>
> Didn't it bloom so your deft feet might swarm

around it, burst and blossom into calm?
Wasn't the sun, summer—those immeasurably
warm
days—drawn from your warm
inner balm?

But it bore fruit, it bore your tree of ecstasy.
everything in season. Tranquil. The urn
is streaked with ripeness too.

Through the pictures, the drawing, can't we see
an obscure stroke shaping an eyebrow
quickly scrawled on the wall? The dancer's turn?

    Chips overcame his hesitancy and phoned the spiritual warrior, but he was undergoing the treatment and they wouldn't let him speak to him. He asked his secretary if she felt tired. "No," she said, and added something like, "we're happy, but it is these last days . . . ." They are working so closely to their spiritual master and were aware it is his last days, even though he sometimes speaks contrarily, speaks of living longer. He too knows that it's his last days, but sometimes he refuses to admit how long. In fact, none of them know how long it is. Everyone who knows him knows (1) that he's in his last days, but (2) they don't know how long he'll last, and (3) they know that he has miraculously gone beyond the survival time of most cancer patients in his condition. I feel responsible and make my weekly phone calls, leaving it up to them whether I can talk, leaving it up to Krishna if he'll be there or gone. I'm praying to keep up my interest and love in his ordeal, his concentrated agony and prayer.

CHAPTER FIFTEEN

WE'RE ALL GOING TO DIE. There's no doubt about it. They say the present pope is a mirror of the past pope, which is okay if you like Pope John Paul. Some were looking for a more liberal, black pope. He pointed out the window and said, "Look!" A gigantic groundhog in the backyard. The cats could not kill the groundhog. Neither could the groundhog kill them. All they could do to each other would be to have a nasty fight.

This was Tad talking. He has come for a couple of days to cook for me. He seems to be very savvy politically. He told me that this is the following understanding that America has with Israel. They are speaking secretively to Israel, saying, "We know that you are close to developing nuclear weapons. If you do develop them, we know you will bomb Iran. If you do so, we will condemn you internationally for such a heinous act. But we will not take any action against you. We will not even disapprove it, actually, but we will speak against it." He said that within the last few days there have been very heated arguments between Japan and China. China is bringing up old memories of the genocide Japan enacted against China in World War II. No more forgive and forget. But there has to be forgive and forget or how can we live?

People speak of "the holocaust." When they say that, they mean the Jewish holocaust. But there are many, many holocausts. There is the African holocaust of bringing the Africans to the Americas as slaves. There is the holocaust against the seals in clubbing them to death and killing them for overcoats. There is the holocaust against the American Indians. There's the holocaust against the buffalo, and many, many more. There are holocausts on the highway and in the doctors' offices. Cigarette smoking—you name it. It's going on and on. Killing and killing. Write and die. Tell people to stop killing each other, to be peaceful, to obey God and practice *ahimsa*, nonviolence. Dharma before you die. People should be peaceful toward others and stop the many holocausts, the many more karmic reactions that you are building, multiple karmic reactions.

You never know. The new Roman Catholic pope, born and raised in Bavaria, was forced to serve in the Nazi army when he was a youth. He wore the swastika, and now wears the emblems of the representative of St. Peter, the "Rock of the Church." The once-anti-Christ uniformed soldier is now the main living symbol and authority for the largest sect of Christianity. Yet you could accurately say that today's pope once appeared dressed as a fascist when he was a youngster, when he had no freedom to choose. Still, it is shocking, and the nation of China has protested the Catholic cardinals' decision.

> *You Never Know*
> Excerpt from a poem by Ron Padgett
> 1. What might happen.
> 2. How people will behave.
> 3. Oh anything.
>
> *Three rules that live in the house next door.*
> Along comes the big bad philosopher,
> And at that door
> He hurls the mighty bolts
> Of lightning
> From his brain.
>
> The door is unimpressed.
> Behind it the rules
> Are chuckling . . . .

[I omit the last stanza of this poem because without it the poem stands a chance of making sense in context with my previous prose paragraph. But just in case you want to know what it is, the last stanza of Padgett's poem is, "I witness this scene/through the kitchen curtains/as I rinse the dishes."]

You never know what? When some mad person like Hitler will start another wave of terror that will push the world over the brink to six years of multi-holocausts in many directions? You don't know that out of it some fifty years later, a young recruited Nazi soldier will be elected pope of the Catholic church? You never know. Will you be alive to tell it? Will you have the insight to understand it?

You've been trying to take your life off the shelf these last weeks,
But are you ready for it? How many guests can you fit on your plate?

You tried to reach the spiritual warrior, but you only reached his servant, who said that his master was "completely wiped out." Try again tomorrow at 2:00 P.M. The pace began to quicken. Chips had one of those splitting headaches. Try the "Kiss My Face" lotion head bath. Try something fast. What do you mean? Go deep into dreams. Go deep. Get lost, and try to return to ISKCON. Try all methods. Go way, way outside, and find a friendly hand to bring you back. Walk through cement. See the outside and come back. Far, far circles, and inner circles, and inner circles. He's confident that he will come back. Even enjoys the symbolic distance because he's certain that he will come back. Isn't it joyful? What? To be in pain? No, to be certain that you're coming back, that you're coming back home, that you have a friendly hand, and he's leading you back.

They will suspect you. It doesn't matter because I am right. Even if they punish me, even if they lead me higher—I mean further out, to further-out circles—I will come back again. I will come closer. But why not make a direct cutting of all circumferences and go directly to the Lord, directly to ISKCON? I am going to do that. I am going to the Houston book fair in my devotee clothes and my proper haircut and my sneakers. Beep beep beepa doo. And *tilak*. Which is the Vaishnava's way of making his head into a temple, with the point at the end, a point to stick into your head.

Are you making this up as you go along? No, it is all straight from the *shastras*. I'm running, though, I'm starting to run, because time is running out. Time is running out, and we're further and further away from the buildings of Public School 8, so we're asking people who are friendly, How do we get there? How do we get to ISKCON?

They reach outer perfection in Krishna consciousness. By utter humility. Willing to be dragged through the muck of it. The truth of it. The demand is that none of it be held back. Let them know it all, let them see it all. Prabhupada says there are dry sores and there are wet sores. Sanatana Goswami had wet sores. In this dream I was filled with wet sores. They are the worst kind. Everyone could see. I did not want anything to be held back.

You gain with giving up everything for the Lord. Where is the Lord? I do not see Him. But I was willing to give up everything.

He reported in. Sore throat, headache, breakdown, feeling sick. Wants to go to Houston the first weekend, and then go straight back to Philo. But they report back to him that it will be very difficult to change all the tickets, so he says all right then, I'll just stay here and try to relax and get over this sickness. But they're sympathetic and are thinking maybe there's some way they can change the tickets. When he was reporting the symptoms, he also said hallucinations. "What?"

Jimmy said, "I mean like one thought comes after another in a crazy kind of way. Like I saw the little cute girl on the swing in the back yard, cute as a pin, and then I thought of a fox, and then I thought of a game like Monopoly, and then I thought of Jimmy Cagney, motorcycle races and fairy land, corporation witnesses, get caught and get punched, who knows whether they have tickets, I can stick it out in any case, but I'd rather go the easy route without pain.

The Lord says pain is good for you. Gets you accustomed to suffering. You mean He'd like you to suffer? He likes you to discipline yourself or something. He likes you to take what's coming to you. He likes you to purify yourself. Take your karma. A little bit of pain, much less than is due you. Take it on the chin nicely. Then you'll be cleaned, and all your bills will be paid. Then you can go back to Godhead. Suffer for others. Don't complain. Like someone in the mood of Vasudeva Datta. Pray for all their sufferings. Don't complain. Just lie back and sleep as much as you can. No, be active in it. An active contributor in gathering up the sufferings of others, and tell them, this is due to sinful activities. Now see how it was when we were nice. See the kingdom of God stretching beyond this mortal frame. You're due this, and a lot more than this.

Say more. I can't think of anything more right now. Punch 'em headache, punch 'em, Indian Chief. He says if you do this, you'll be rewarded because it's good for you. Yes, it is. People can see you, and you can give them benedictions by intercessionary prayer. Lord, I'm getting a little. Please give blessings to others. Make me be empowered, please, to take away theirs. For all the many, many bad things I've taken and done and messed up, now give me a cut for it. And a cut for the others, because I deserve it. I have an ugly head, and I've indulged in sense gratification so deliberately. Therefore, deliberately place some stingy stuff on my head. Am I saying something right? It's not hideous. It's good. Bring you closer to Jesus. But you wanted to hear some *shastra* to confirm it. Have at least enough alertness for that.

Some say there is no other world after this one, but I say there is, and I want to be with those who come marching in. Oh when the saints come marching in, oh when the saints come marching in, I want to be among their number when the saints come marching in.

> Bright and narye leaves enthusiastically.
> Peppermint leaves when it calls your name
> to leave stop laughing who ha ha also doesn't
> like to leave later. It will leave. Siksu the mushrooms.
> He says the Pithenthropus that enthralled by the
> star baby saying let
> busy man out brother sweet bananas
> at beginning of seventh round and
>
> what does it do? Do I grab you because a
> ruffin men *tilak* addresses boo, thank you just the same
> gut gut we'll oppose St. Dada Axton to be read to music
> is very over anyway.
>
> Come and rub my hat. I'm not charming Ben Gay
> that would not be fair. My mom goes only in a way
> bunny eggs and your long arm and I'm giddy
> to get out of the old and anxious and
> look out and look out at the stars and at the
> hey hey hey hey hey, the vital force
> to bring it to entry to deity duty.
> I don't feel like doing that right now.
> An enthusiastic man will leave

when it's his time to go. A leaves stop leave who ha ho hoo
    do,
Doesn't like to tutor like it disturbs the mind like he says. The
    baby
was pushing him under the safety belt song, let
the baby bug us under the safety belt at "anything you want
    to do."
Come and rub my hand but this morning be happy.
There's a man coming but not a mob, only a few men
who are nice and who can see our good intentions
to get out and out I'm anxious and
look out at the taffeta of the
ohhh, please don't force me to do duty to
deity work. Don't force that energy.

FW

He'll come around to speak cohaunt in Cardeno Street. I know
Dame Dickinson and greeted her early. He knew Hetinus. The trumples'
trumpets can taps carpet U2 relave into. Take you believe it. A T shirt
will well back and get happier, get shiny, but I do not uncover your
gun. He's starting to feel better. What is this due to? Lozenges? Prayers
to God? He wants you to get better so you get better and take your
thanksgiving to him. Thanksgiving. No harm.

It's a real thanksgiving.

Thanksgiving. Thank you, Lord. I have no thanks except my futile
thank you. It is a real thank you, sincerely. I got sick but now I want to
thank you. I want to go in and thank you. I'm a new devotee. I don't
sign the Prabhupada book. I'm inspired to do it. I want to give you a
name and get inspired. You have inspired me to know and to edit and
to partly de-edit. It's a kind of madness of being happy. I've got to get a
name now, and people, and do my duty and go to Houston and there
write books. I mean write signatures on my books as I promised I would.
Oh Lord, please let me do it because I promised I would. India and U.S.
and all those things. Look, I hope I can do it, like Narada. It leaves the
big band in the leeway of the new reason.

Thank you, I'm happy. Just like the big night fight of the jungle
trainer. It's all of them, and why release pressure? The gift has come.

Oh boy, like the sight of a big band. I can't say more, I can't understand it. Doctor, who does understand these things? You draw a decorator flown, and then you get better and you can play to flex again. I hope and I pray, Lord, that you will keep me well enough to make this appearance that I promise to give.

> "You'll be stomped out!" he said
> about the most beautiful rendition of "Lover Man."
> Who moon man he's playing beautifully.
> Nara is playing better the name happy
> to take me like in a playpen. Best friend,
> in a dim bed, dim dim, we will play to get
> writing together. I remember April and you.
> The café and a skiff, Ralph stares, the new engagements,
> They've got story telling and another way
> if the plane doesn't crash
> we'll be flying from Albany.
> How nice this time, it's a one-way stop
> and then onto Houston, Bush Airport.
> Yes, charming. Just stop and I'll meet Krishna
> people in my saffron uniform, placed
> in any uniform, my uniform and pajamas
> and my substance, I'm prepared.
> Tenderness, something that my big psycho
> and even then second plus to realize
> that if we go to You, Krishna.
> Go to the stark places and unknown Houston
> to sign books, "Satsvarupa" clap clap clap.
> Until the sun goes down
> and then find out whether the guru
> gets his donation. I'll have a book bag for that.
> Check out my hair, you didn't know
> I had a full beard, Charlie Parker,
> "Salt Peanuts," but burnt that day
> think they won't play him at a fable
> pineapple, only Vedic songs. Out of nowhere.
> the blue heaven of Radha Kund. The brown

Govardhan.
Won't that be nice. You cannot be together.
I can be with Nara, *mon ami.*

Red ropes held back the people. I recall my people. But my head hurts and my heart, I hurt. I begged off for conferences and anything requiring participation. I take an airplane trip back to Philo as soon as possible. I'm in the mood for food and lying down, hanging out and resting with my friends and saying Hare Krishna more times. Don't wet your lips like *Esquire's* old silver-haired man struggling for complete renunciation. Let them take Charlie's strings away, as he said to Johnny Griffin. He's afraid that they'll take them away, but "go ahead, I deserve it. Kick me in the rear end, Johnny. Go ahead, do it, Johnny." So Johnny did it gently.

You've found him in. He wanted to talk to you. You mentioned his grateful handling of your *faux pas* at the end of your last conversation. I had said, "I love you, Bhakti-tirtha Swami," and he had said, "I love you four times that." He's always in control, it seems. But then I made a terrible Freudian *faux pas* and called him, "Bhaktipada." He *calmly* corrected me and said, "Bhakti-tirtha ," but I felt I had to be carried out on a stretcher and sent to the hospital. It was a terrible sort of thing. I'm still thinking how stupid it was. I am still constipated, despite two Fleet enemas. Nothing seems to make it come. Tad left an hour ago to shop for some more, and Nara has been sleeping and asked us not to wake him.

You've heard this before and you don't
mind hearing it again and again? Orpheus descending
to Hades when his newly married wife, Eurydice,
died, bit by a serpent.

No one is allowed to do that, but Orpheus was
the son of Apollo, the king of all music, so
Orpheus persisted in entering the nether regions.
his horn was so sweet, like Lester Young,
and so loud-souled (like Coltrane's),

he could not be stopped. Everyone watched
and tried to attack him. A watchdog rolled over
into a playing puppy. Even Hades himself
made a soft, not stern face and said
what do you want?

I want my wife back. She died too soon.
Give her back to me for some time, not much.
Hades summoned Eurydice
on the one condition that Orpheus not look back
as he played his music and exited with her.
Go with her behind you to the outer mortal world.

So the blessed couple ascended, waltz for Debbie,
lovely stepping, waltzing the broad steps,
the beautiful performance of ascension, keep going
upward, Apollo and all the gods are rooting for you,
even the demons can't stop you.

But something in Orpheus' head caused him to doubt
although there was nothing wrong, there was no reason
to look back, but he faltered in his trust, the light
turned as they were going to pray, dust
reaching the daylight, causing four brighter sights
but Orpheus wanted to see if his darling
was actually behind him. So he stopped. He turned around
and saw her standing close behind. He reached for her
but all she said was,
"Farewell," and faded from view
as the gods prevented
him from reentering.

They pushed him aside, striking him back upward
to the material world where he changed into a blues
musician, wandering and playing blues music
universal catching everyone's attraction, "This is
how it is every day every day every day every day

we get the blues," speaking of bad luck and sorrow

everyone's got it every morning so sad
to dream of Eurydice, the original source
of the blues by the singer on the lyre
of grief for humans and gushing forth from his
tears for Eurydice.

CHAPTER SIXTEEN

Dear Reader,

This is not a book about writers or about Chips the writer. That would be far too parochial, a private book. It would be just the kind of thing that one devotee in Ireland used to object to about my lectures. He said, "I feel unless I'm an artist, I'm not welcome at one of your classes, because you always seem to be lecturing to how one can be an artist in Krishna consciousness." No, please don't read me that way. This book could just as well be titled, *Old Laundry and Die*, or *Run to the Bathroom and Die*, or *Spray Your Throat with Medicine and Die*. Whatever you do, and die. Precisely, this book's theme is carry your suitcase in spiritual consciousness and die. Ride in the back seat and die. Don't worry and die. Worry if you have to and die. Always think of God and die. Eat oat meal in God consciousness and die. Read the *Bhagavad-gita* and like it and die. Avoid reading mundane books and die. Don't be distracted by the material glow and die. Like Teresa of Avila in her later years, be always in trance, working for the Lord, and die. That's what I mean. Sometimes I can leave off the assumed and just say, tooty frooty blues at the Hot Spot, wouldn't you know it, he wants me to work out at the gym and says when adrenaline starts, the allergies will leave, and so I'll do it because he asked. Be nice to other people and considerate of them. No time for aikido martial arts, though I have nothing against them personally. Probably won't watch the Johnny Carson DVDs someone sent me. Not enough time, and I don't have the mechanical skill to know how to find a place where you left off, have to watch in between minutes. Why I shaved my beard. And die. Don't be afraid. And die.

You can savor the varieties and remain in spiritual consciousness. This has to be done under expert guidance. I am a guide with a bona fide license. Some voices say to me, "You're not humble enough." And they're right. But our definitions of how to act in humility differ somewhat. Be humble and stay *sannyasa* or be humble and get married? He's following the Society's rules. Get truckin'. Can't please everyone, and die.

The private interpretation is valid too: Chips' conviction, vocation,
to write until the last breath.

> Hey, where have you been? I thought
> you would never get out of that jungle of
> "circle of books" on your
> writing table. You'd better watch that stuff.
>
> You could become a text-referencer
> and lose your original spirit for which
> we love you. Gosh, Thomas Mann,
> and then telling us you never read him
> (except for *Death in Venice*).
> That whole Orpheus and Eurydice trip.
> Well, I guess it *was* interesting and
> parallel.
>
> It's all adding up, making you feel
> confident of connection to Krishna
> and all His encompassing band.
> "Go in like a needle, come out like a plow."
>
> But let's *contemplate* the wealth and
> polity of the world you know
> in a heads-on way. Don't just
> scatter buckshot. I'm glad you're
> back with a "Haitian battle shout"
> long Mingus bass line.
> That belongs.
>
> And so does this Spaulding pink ball
> I got for our dog Merlin at the farm.
> He loves to run and fetch any stick.
> I'm looking forward
> to surprising him with a genuine high-bouncy
> Spaulding. I'm sure he'll be able to run and
> grasp it in his mouth. It'll be a warming signal that

I'm home again after this stressing tour.

Tour-'n'-die. *It belongs*, that's a
good one too.

True e-mail from Bhakti-tirtha Swami:

> . . . the last few days I have been bordering on going into a diabetic
> coma. This is Krishna getting me ready for the final breakdown or break-
> through. If I didn't have special associates like you who encourage me in
> such a deep way, I'm afraid I would have great difficulty in keeping fo-
> cus at this time. Even though I seem to be accepting externally, as I seem
> to be experiencing pain and discomfort, all I can do is thank Prabhupada
> and Krishna while I cry. I'm glad that Srila Prabhupada has brought us
> together in this way for each other. Few people could say the things you
> say to me and have the same effect that you're having on me. In your
> case, as my older brother and one of my first teachers, your comments
> are most important. I feel almost like they are directly coming from Srila
> Prabhupada. I will try to call you before Tuesday evening. Yours in Srila
> Prabhupada's service with love, Bhakti-tirtha Swami

I would like to ask him if after he passes away we can continue to
keep in touch.

Now we have come to the writer's fair in Houston. Us was invited
to A Celebration of India, and one of many authors given a chance to
read out loud on a raised chair in a portion of the city, about 100,000
roamed through the city last weekend, and they expect the same this
weekend. Swami Chips is allotted twenty minutes' reading time in between other authors and other performances—dancers, elephants,
shows, yogis, throngs of people, sellers of saris and *samosas*. At first it
sounded grand, but now the realism of it sounds questionable. I may
be squeezed into a small amount of time. Chips is scheduled to be the
last reader of the writers on Saturday, on stage from 5:45 until 6:05. But
he will have two other chances to give longer readings to the "in group"
of his own spiritual family. He has picked out a variety from his reper-
toire of fast balls, curves, sliders, spit balls, sidearms, change-of-pace,
etc. Read while you can. They invited you to do it, dressed as a *sannyasi*
and clean-shaven. (Oh, he noticed that with a clean-shaven chin, the

old-man jowled sag is very prominent. This is another argument for regrowing the beard after the Houston high-profile weekend.)

Oh thank you, Nara, for taking me by the hand as we pushed through the red tape at the airport—something was wrong with our tickets as purchased, and we had to pay an extra $200 per ticket.

The plane is now making a rocky descent into Atlanta, and from there, onto Houston. Elevator sensations. You could die at any moment. He left his clicker behind and has a very good bead bag. A few nervous *japa* rounds, then at the airport, while Nara struggled it out with the manager of Delta Airlines. It was our fault. Then Chips underwent an extreme search at the security check. Two men and a woman swarming and touching all over his body, feeling him up. Does a Hare Krishna *sannyasi* deserve special scrutiny? Even my tin-foil-covered pill alarmed them, and they passed their hands over his crotch.

Christ. Sorry to take his name in vain but, jeeze. The flight was supposed to be a one-stop in Atlanta, but you don't have to get off. But then when we landed in Atlanta they made us get off. I complained to the officers. They apologized and said that "technically," it was a stay-on one-stop flight, but actually we have to get off. It was a long, long distance to get to the new gate, concourse A23. Luckily we took a wheel-chair. The wheelchair man pushed us down long corridors, up and down elevators, *onto a train,* and we got to the gate just as they were loading. He was a cool guy. He heard Nara and Chips complaining, and then at one point he said, "Are you guys monks?" Nara said, "Yes, Hare Krishna." Chips said, "I guess we don't sound very spiritual, just complaining. But it shows you monks are human too." Chips asked the wheelchair operator if he liked jazz. "Yes." Chips mentioned names, and they traded names. They tipped him, shook hands.

·   See the ground through the whole flight through the clear sky. Are you really going to read your writings and talk like a true person and *sannyasi*? "A pretty view of Jackson, Mississippi (winding river), at 20,000 feet. One hour from Houston."

Don't eat the remainder of the peanut butter and jelly on rye or the dark banana or the fruit-filled yogurt cup because they'll have a meal in Houston and they'll expect you to eat a lot.

He rehearsed in his mind. He has come here because he was invited to read at the festival. Also because he has early connections with

Houston and Dallas before TKG, and it's a pleasure to see how he and his followers have turned run-down temples into beautiful spiritual oases. Chip will take the responsibility to urge the congregations of Houston and Dallas to carry on the spirit of *prabhu-datta-desha* for Srila Prabhupada and TKG.

TKG created not only buildings but communities, and the devotees must demonstrate their bonding with their spiritual master not just as individuals but as supporters of the lives of the communities. Talk like that. But as soon as possible read. Claimed he would want me to do like that. He has passed on prematurely, just as he was about to receive his Ph.D. from Cambridge. Only fifty years old. His followers are very attracted to him and worship him as good as God. They do so by remaining and carrying out his order. Even when a great leader dies, he leaves his spirit, and they stay with him by promising to keep his teachings. In such cases, death is defied by love and disciplic succession. Write and die, and death, where is thy sting?

Bhakti-tirtha Swami has sent out a worldwide e-mail, which may be his last one. He introduces it by saying,

> This is probably the penultimate special message of wisdom from the groundhog, AKA the beggar, AKA spiritual warrior. So let this prepare you for the ultimate message (smile). You can see that this kind of communication that I am doing must actually come to a stop. Firstly, because it is natural, for I definitely have to get out of this body sometime in the near future, but also because if I am not careful, this sort of communication could become my biggest failure. Just consider how every time I sent out some of these messages, so many nice devotees all round the world write and call and offer me kindness and praise. Yes, this is wonderful, but can you see all the *danger* in this? One of Maya's most special tricks is to get the devotee who has acquired some little achievement to start thinking, 'Just see, I am an advanced devotee.' For instance, if I'm not careful and if I let myself start thinking in this way, then when the helpers come to take me out of the body, they'll take me straight to Brahmaloka or some place of this nature. They will say, 'This was your final test, and you accepted some certain adoration and glorification as your own, therefore go ahead and enjoy now for 311 trillion years, managing your own planet or universe.' Isn't Maya just so tricky? (Smile.) When Vasudeva the leper was healed by Krishna, he prayed very in-

tensely, 'Please do not let me become proud.' When the great devotee Madhavendra Puri was called out by the *pujari* and the Deity Kishora-chora Gopinath, he was so eager to avoid praise. We've never heard of devotees like Narottama dasa Thakur, Bhaktivinode Thakur, or our Srila Prabhupada (we can go on and on and on) being in the mood of arrogance. They were constantly writing and praying, addressing that they do not have love of God and how they are unqualified in so many areas, etc. Anyway, what I am writing now is for my own edification and purification and maybe for yours as well. Devotees like me in one sense have no qualification in practically any area but have received blessings by causeless mercy. However, pride manifesting as *pratistha* (a desire for fame) is a serious enemy.

He goes on to say that when he had his amputation, he offered it up as a sacrifice for the suffering of the women, children, elders, brahmins, and cows in the Krishna movement so that the deteriorated faith could be thrown from his own body and the unhealthy karma of it could be also eliminated from the Krishna movement. Now he wants to offer in sacrifice the rest of what remains of his body. He wants to present himself to the Lord in the mood of *sharanagati*—full surrender. He goes on to say he wants to make it specific, particularly focusing on forgiveness.

For the rest of his lengthy letter, he goes on to focus on different ways that we must culture forgiveness toward others, and he refers to a seminar he gave in 2003 and asked devotees to obtain copies of the tapes for more in depth hearing.

I find it so interesting that he has awareness that his messages are dangerous to himself and that they might create a pride. It's true that he *is* speaking from a platform of great influence, and many, many people, including myself, are caught up in his influence. We are like iron filings drawn to the magnet of his present position of sacrifice. We see him as glorious, a true saint, at the peak of his sacrifice. I so much admire his calm and control, and I so much value the last phone calls he's allowing me to have with him. He's even been asking me to give him directions and saying that I encourage him by my words. This has allowed me to actually "preach" to him how to face the last test, based on what I have found in Prabhupada's books. When he mentioned that he was afraid he might lose focus, I found the quotes in the *Ishopanishad* and the Tenth Canto where the Lord says that even if a devotee tends to forget, the Lord will remind him, and the Lord will actually grab the devotee's consciousness and keep him under control. From my own unrealized and relatively nondangerous position, I dared to give him advice. I saw he thrived on it and that it was helpful, so I took it as my responsibility.

He's the one who is actually writing and dying, not me. But now he has given this "penultimate special message." Perhaps he may not write to us anymore. He is afraid that his writing may interfere with the consciousness of true humility. He is afraid if he continues to broadcast his realizations, now that he's so near to death, it may make him a little puffed up that he's so special and able to give gems of wisdom right at the edge of death. Perhaps he's opting for silence and last examination of himself in the last few days.

I suspect we will hear from him some more, however. He repeatedly describes himself as "stubborn." He's quite convinced that he's staying in this world to do good for others, and he knows that just remaining silent is not the best way to do it. When the realizations come, he wants to share them. Now he has referred us to a seminar he gave two years ago. But day to day he's getting new feelings, and devotees are so eagerly awaiting to hear them. "Stubbornly" he continues to live beyond what seems medically possible, and even though he now calls himself a groundhog and realizes the risk in feeling pride, he may still talk to us. He's given us the warning and the realization that he doesn't want to be proud, so we can now hear from him in that spirit, not thinking that he's a greatly realized soul. Give him a break. If he wants to be silent, let him go that way now. Don't demand. Don't keep trying to pull gems from him. But if the man wants to keep speaking, we can take it from him humbly without throwing exaggerated praises upon him. Take it in the spirit in which he is speaking, that he is just a tiny *jiva*, but he's in a position to speak some things from the heart, which he thinks will be purifying for all of us. Can't we hear from him and not exaggerate? He's become so dear to us and has found a place in all our hearts. We don't want to let him go, and yet we know he should go, and probably soon. Until that time, it's up to him whether he'll be silent or not.

He's certainly already broken all records for writing up until the last moment, *and* dying. No one feels he's overdoing his stay. But no one will begrudge him his departure when he finally shuts down and his mentors take him to his next highly deserved, high position. He has certainly upstaged Swami Chips in his own book of *Write and Die.* I gladly give him the limelight.

Houston FW—giver of lecture last night in room of crawling heat, seemed to be bugs crawling on your head. Look out at the people, tell your stories of their departed spiritual master, whom they worship as good as God, TKG. Tell stories of your times with him, even when they drew sparks. They love to hear them. Talks at the outdoor festival sight against tremendous competition of booming drums and singers on microphones. Swami Chips strained his voice and even made skat sounds in the mood of "if you can't beat them, join them," along with his poems and essays. Kalakantha was there too from Florida, reading his rhymed *Bhagavad-gita.* A good time was had by all, but with great strain to the body. Back in Philo, resting and letting the chin hairs grow again, with many new books like *Jaiva Dharma* and *Brihad-bhagavatamrita.*

Back in Philo, California, with long rests and nightmares. Dreams that a man is looting from a store as I'm walking round and round the block. Each time I reached the store he was looting from, I glimpsed as I passed by. Soon a mob of people take the coincidence of my walking by while he steals as no coincidence but that I must be a cohort in the thievery. They rush and grab me. But fortunately, one of the policemen is my Uncle Sal. He takes over in protecting me while interrogating me. I whisper in his ear that my mother and aunt are living a block away. He conducts the interrogation: "Why do you always appear just when a man is stealing?," and so on. The crowd is partially pacified, but they ask more and more questions.

I often have dreams like this where I'm a fugitive running away from positions. I wake up from them with nightmare headaches. This is because I watched that action movie on the airplane. Or is this the unconscious throwing up all the strain in trying to give lectures in Houston while in the background music and dancing and singing took place? The strain of my lecturing to the audience, the strain of it all, the tour and waiting to return here, now with all coming out, but like the fugitive of sorts? A collapse, a breakdown. Whatever it is, it prevents me from doing anything active now. I can't use my eyes, I can't use my body. I'm in a delicate condition, and everything will produce an exertion headache it seems. Even *japa* would move me over the edge. So I sit or lie down, feeling a twinge or nearness to a twinge. I cannot enjoy the welcome-home feeling of those there in the background when I think, "What do I have to do next?" And the answer is, "Nothing but rest, nothing but rest." And yet there are letters to answer, writing to take up again, exercise to do, and painting once you're strong enough. Books to read, films to watch, but nothing starts yet, just watchful waiting, and even sleeping is dangerous. But at least the report on Houston is outstanding, and we can rest on those laurels for a few days.

Deepak found the last quote we were looking for for Bhakti-tirtha Maharaja about controlling the mind at the time of death. BTM had expressed a fear that he might lose his focus if he fell into a coma. A quote from a purport in the *Ishopanishad* and one from the *Srimad-Bhagavatam* assure us this doesn't happen to the pure devotee. Here is the *Srimad-Bhagavatam* quote:

Because the mind is ultimately controlled by the Supreme Personality of Godhead, Krishna, the word *"apaspriti"* is significant. Forgetfulness of his own identity is called *apaspriti* can be controlled by the Supreme Lord, for the Lord says, *mattah smrtir jnanam apohanam ca* (Bg. 15.15): "From Me come remembrance, knowledge and forgetfulness." Instead of allowing one to forget one's real position, Krishna can revive one's original identity at the time of death, even though the mind may be flickering. Although the mind may work imperfectly at the time of death, Krishna gives the devotee shelter at His lotus feet. Therefore when a devotee gives up his body, the mind does not take him to another material body *(tvaktva deham punar janma/naiti mam eti so 'rjuna)* (Bg. 4.9). [Purport to SB 10.1.41]

> "Who is your spiritual master?"
> Don't ask me or I'll cry.
> When she said it was BTM
> I said there was nothing I
> could tell her that would give her
> solace. A flat truth. But

then I said, "He is a great saint."

Later in the day a brother of mine
spoke of meteors, TKG and BTM
passing through our skies and
leaving us. Turn the stars out, but
ISKCON has many more, even moons,
drawn forth by Prabhupada's calls
and Chaitanya Mahaprabhu's grace.

It is a strong movement.
Devotees learning the *shastras* by heart,
working hard in the kitchen, selling books,
simply being true and loyal to
the founder-*acharya*.

There were many camps and tables and
tents at the festival but
you were aligned with the Hare Krishna
movement lecturing loudly over
the cinema music.

Your friend is getting "tennis elbow" from playing guitar so much,
but he learned a simple physical exercise that helped. He played for us
on our last night in Houston. It was nice. Our family gathered after two
weekend's work to hear live jazz. Live or die, burning eyes, stay awake.
Back home, but Nara has already left for Mexico on *sankirtan* mission.

The spiritual warrior very recently initiated over one hundred disciples in one day. At the ceremony, he told them this would probably
cause his imminent death, the taking on of so much karma in one day
upon his already cancer-infested body. But he's still alive. I was scheduled to speak to him on the phone today, but his secretary said he was
too exhausted and will speak to me tomorrow. But the secretary said
that Jayapataka Swami is also there, so who knows if I'll get a chance?
Will Swami Chips ever recover his confidence that he can play the
prankster and the serious village novelist at the same time? He became

so seriously immersed in the family at Houston that it put him in a different place. Can a writer be part of a great family gathering and live to tell his tale? His head and insides get jostled around in trying to please everyone, which he does successfully, but he seems to lose his identity. At any rate he returns home—and finds his tongue tied, finds himself falling off his train, rolled off the tracks.

He finds himself unfriendly to others. Finds himself hard to like. Write and die, live and die, what was it all about? How long can it last? Where is the path back to the army? It is dangerous to be separated from one's regiment. In the absence of inspiration for this project, Chips has been watching the Ken Burns film *The Civil War*, which Dainya, his editor, sent him in the mail. Dainya says the film is a cathartic and spiritual experience. Chips is not sure how spiritual it is, but it's very addictive and hard to get away from once you watch it. By the time of the Civil War, bayonets were already obsolete, the men rarely got so close but rather killed each other by their gunfire. More men were killed in the Civil War than in all the previous military encounters by Americans. Yes, it is fascinating to watch, and horrible to consider. And yes, poignant and sad how Lincoln tried to keep the nation together. But Frederick Douglas, the brilliant black thinker, said the war was useless unless it was fought for liberation of the slaves. I'm watching that, live and die. I'm watching so many innocent victims die in battle. They come from all periods of life, forced by the circumstances of the war, which in the end seems needless and yet fated by the irresistible destinies of men. In those days many people kept diaries, eloquent ones, from the heart, and the film often draws from them for resources. They are angry, pious, cynical, full of emotions, depending upon their attitude toward the war. They're all sincere in their expression, that's for sure. Their writing is not idle playing around. Many of them will write and die, like the famous letter a husband wrote to his wife that he will probably not see his wife again but that he loved her and that if he did not come back, she should know that he was still in her life in the breeze she felt, in the air, etc. This was a letter written by a man who died in one of the very first battles, the Battle of Bull Run. He wrote to his dear one, and very soon after died. His wife kept the letter for many years as something to live for and mourn over, and now it's part of the national archives, a piece of history of the Civil War.

What impels my engine? Is it important? Let it at least be sincere, like those diaries. Let it not be a literary flare or a playful force. I think I had it right, even though it was many stabs, like the eighteen unsuccessful charges the Union Army made upon the rocky heights of Fredericksburg under the eye of Robert E. Lee. I think I had it right, and I just have to get confident again. In the Civil War, Abraham Lincoln was most hampered by having no good generals to steer his large, well-equipped armies. One general after another had huge foibles. Some didn't even want to fight at all, some were braggarts, gofers, and inept in big ways, until he found U. S. Grant. I need my little general. It's false to blame it on Houston, to say you got lost in the rush there. You've had them all along, so just pick up your guns and pray for your leadership of innerness and truthfulness to lead your swamis and little men and women in this serious free-for-all.

> *Lonely Man*
> Soul brother, where are you?
> Missing you, feeling blue.
> How can I rejoice alone?
> Are you on your Vrindavan *bhajan*
> without me? I just want to be
> happier than I am now and sometimes
> even having you around doesn't do
> the trick.
>
> I'm a lonely man, and a "Bedroom
> Eyes" sax just stirs it up worse in
> me. I need some juice. Boom dee
> boom. The blues I feel good when
> I can write something that's
> going somewhere in the soul
>
> and taking a willing listener along.
> Soul sister, soul brother, sometimes
> I need you, sometimes I need to
> be alone. Always I need the Lord
> so I should call to Him in one-

word bursts, silent or even aloud,
what they recommend in *Unknowing*.

Grace and Grease
One by one the minutes roll by and he
gets his chances. Does he lose them all? No, he
grabs some line. Some are a mediocre
loss. Some a total flop. He says he's always
trying for the Lord. What do you think of that?

Why is he so tart and alone? Don't you
like the rainy atmosphere? You heard there
is mice turd in the kitchen. The food is
sometimes off. Dream of old flames, new
and strange dangers. Don't you know
who you are?

One by one the minutes and hours and
days go by, you're either a fault-finder
or a bead-chanter. "We hope you like
a tearful new tune called "Ugetsu." In Japanese
it means "fantasy." No, I want reality,
a glamorous transcendental reality above the
material world. I'll have to work for it.
That's my trouble, I don't work at
sadhana and *tattva*, so how can
I expect the fantasy-like *rasa*
taste which is the upper reality?

I'm stuck in the rain and walk
on a weak ankle on the boards
outside around this house. "How are
you feeling?" he asks me. He is not
close enough to me to
answer—"I'm feeling lonely."

Nothing can assuage me because I

don't try enough and I bash myself.
When I'm on the fence between
playful and putting pressure, I choose anxiety
and downfeel. I'll get out somehow,
by his grace and change of weather, elbow grease.

You lament of lack of close friendship. But at 6:30 P.M. each night you do a very nice thing which brings you back into the groove here at Philo. You read from two books, *Brihad-bhagavatamrita*, the last volume, by Sanatana Goswami, and *Jaiva Dharma*, by Bhaktivinode Thakur. Tonight in *Brihad-bhagavatamrita* we heard Narada Muni praise Goloka as the highest of all realms beyond Mahadhama, Mahesdhama, and Vaikuntadhama. It appears to be an "obscure" place, but it is famous all over the universes. It is rare that one can enter there and act as a friend or cowherd boy, *gopi*, etc., with Krishna. Some of the exalted Vaishnavas who revere Krishna with pomp and majesty do not believe that Krishna can have such worldly, friendly dealings. But actually it is true, and Krishna and His *parisads* in Vraja enjoy the greatest bliss imaginable. Why should I lament about anything except failing to know Krishna-*prema* in Vrindavan? In Vrindavan, all the residents do nothing but think of how to please Krishna, and their own lamentation is a moment without seeing Him. How much more real and palpable is this than Catholic mysticism? Krishna the cowherd boy with two hands holding a flute and loved to infinite degree by the beautiful residents of Vrajabhumi. In *Jaiva Dharma*, the grand spiritual master of Babaji Maharaja was teaching the *sannyasi thakur*, who was formally a Shankarite, the truths of Vaishnavism. The *sannyasi*, who is now becoming a Vaishnava, asked if the state of *bhava* reached by a Shankarite was not equal to the *mahabhava* of a Vaishnava.

At the sound of Shankara's name, the great Vaishnava Babaji Maharaja made *dandavats*. He then praised Shiva as the greatest Vaishnava and told about his historical rescue of Vaishnavism during the time when India was under the control of the Buddhists. But he said this was a task that was meant for a time, not for *all* time. Shankara's work paved the way for the work of Ramanuja and Madhva, who made the foundations of Vaishnavism, that would culminate in Chaitanya Mahaprabhu's Vaishnava teachings of Krishna-*prema*. Babaji Maharaja

263

goes on to tell about three kinds of religion, one without any love of God, a religion that has love of God but approaches it by different materialistic and ritualistic methods, and religion that is pure prema all the way. This last religion, he says, is the religion of Chaitanya Mahaprabhu, and therefore it is the highest form of Vaishnavism.

Hearing these books while eating humble *prasadam* is certainly a pick-me-up, and I don't complain. I'm not in the army or navy, I'm not in the college dorm, I'm not in these sad situations or beset with family worries. If I have a sadness, it's my own lack of religious advancement, and that sadness is perhaps a gift rather than something to be regretful of. It is at least a sign of life. I have at least not forgotten the goal of life.

Am I blue? You'd be too if you lacked Krishna.

I just spoke to BTM. He said he's now praying to leave his body in a week. I said this sounded different from what he was speaking of before, kind of that he wanted to stay as long as possible. He had been saying that he was "stubborn" and that as long as people were writing him and e-mailing him, speaking of good results they were feeling from his blessings, he wanted to stay. Yes, he said, I've changed because now I think there's no end to this. He thinks it would be a kind of sense gratification to stay any longer and receive those kind of pleas. After his last big initiation, he doesn't think he can do any more in the right consciousness. His body has already deteriorated enough, and there's no sense hanging on. So he asked me also to pray that Krishna could take him in a week in the right consciousness. I immediately sympathized—although I can't say I empathized with his mood. He's the one who's actually facing death, I'm just a paltry onlooker, a weak friend, a bedside comrade. He's been allowing me to phone him, although he's not taking any e-mails at all from anybody else, or even phone calls.

Near the end of our phone call, I said that maybe this would be my last phone call. He said, well, let us see. Maybe they'll be another one next week. And then he broke down crying. I said, we'll see if I can talk with you again. We spoke our hopeful chatter about communing after death, something we have some faith in. I asked him to commune to me to straighten me out in my mistakes. He urged me to take better care of my disciples and to forgive others for all their wrongs. As he said it, I thought of how I'd been shortened, chopped down, over the past year and a half by my big *aparadha*. So I'm already humbled by having to make a comeback.

This is the first time he has spoken so definitely of the deliberate desire to leave, and even putting a timetable on it—one week. A desire to go, feeling it's not right to stay any longer, feeling it would be a kind of showoff thing to remain. We talked about the devastation that it will bring to his disciples, the trauma that will occur, especially to his community at Gita-nagari. They will have to take it and follow his books and instructions to remain together as a community. He certainly has lectured enough to tell them they should live taking care of each other in any of the so-called secondary ways of life, not just the "Krishna-prema" aspects. Jayapataka Maharaja was there today with him and was also saying that ISKCON had to take care of devotees' needs in all kinds of basic ways before we could uplift them to the highest level of God. He also said with a little irony that at a meeting that just took place, some leaders who exactly a year ago were strongly criticizing his work were now praising it. Perhaps, he said, it was because they saw him as arrogant. Perhaps he was arrogant, or perhaps he was just so determined that they saw it that way. But now they see him as stricken down by cancer, and they praise him for his good work. Poetic justice for the almost posthumous writer who is no longer arrogant because he's almost dead. Time to praise him now.

Phone number 1-717-527-9936, Bhakti-tirtha Maharaja at Gita-nagari. Will I use it again? I think I will.

CHAPTER SEVENTEEN

A PPOMATTOX. Give up your rifles, give the
men rations, generous terms. But they
would never forget the enmity.

So much bloodshed, amputations, deaths.
Where do the souls of the rebels go,
the Union privates and generals?
Andersonville Prison–makers? General
Sherman and Lee and Grant? That's over now,
I am free to go on to something else.

How sincere were you in crying with
the warrior who faces his death?
Oh if you were in the least insincere
I damn you. You take it as your
duty to try to help him, your old
friend, but I know your heart is
hard as a chestnut unless
it concerns your own self.

And you don't think you are so near death.
Time to go. Your caretakers,
money in the bank. Tarnished
reputation. But you move on.
You hurt people by your mishap.
Can't entirely undo your "original sin."

Get on it, coherent pace.
I've lost my voice and
there is something about dying.
He's dying in a week but I've
got a long way to go so I'm
arrogant and can't even rhyme
or go assonant, pious yearning.

Chew a cigar, surreal, it's
for real. I'm in trouble
more than I know.
Got an innocent face
belong to the human race
but off the single-minded Gaudiya.
Natural, sour, *lonely*, irritable, lack-love,
neither give and take.

He was not afraid. When he came downstairs from the loft, the drunken bums got up from their prone position and let him pass. And they did the same when he returned from his walk or shopping. Sometimes they even greeted him. But once a person approached him on the streets. It was not safe. His roommate, Mr. Paul, was becoming crazy. He had to find another place. So he asked Michael Grant to help him. He went to Scindia Steamship Company and asked them when the next ship was going back to India. But by letter Mrs. Murarji encouraged him to stay in the U.S. His name was Abhay Charanaravinda, one who was unafraid because he takes shelter at the lotus feet of Krishna. Two heart attacks at sea. He continued to write *Srimad-Bhagavatam*. And the reception was good. Young men and women gathering to dance and chant in the loft. But Mr. Paul's dangerous outbursts, like a madman. Michael Grant found a storefront, 26 2nd Ave., and the Swamiji moved there, and it was much better. He began his Society.

We had a giant reunion. I was hogging the microphone and singing songs. But there were hardly any survivors, just a few cousins. In my mind and aloud, I began to go over the list of the dead, assuming whoever wasn't there was dead. Parents, uncles and aunts. I thought about why I had been rejected by and had rejected my mother and father. The cause was Prabhupada. I relieved him of any blame. He had done the right thing according to the *Srimad-Bhagavatam*. He had released me from their bondage. They had blasphemed him and Krishna consciousness. Of course I had acted fanatically. I could have bided my time and over many years tried tactics of compromise and slow approach. I could have even said that I had quit the spiritual path and approach them in civilian clothes and not even talked about spiritual things. I could have tried such tactics, but they would have drilled me to see whether there was any spiritual content left in me, and if they found it, they would have spat upon it and stomped upon it, and I would not have been able to bear that. So it was a blessing in disguise. I don't regret it. Yes, there were very few survivors. At least I guessed it was that way. I went over them in my mind, a few of the younger who were present. Death had taken its toll. But there were new people there from new walks of life to fill in for a new convention. Someone told me to stop talking too much and let it just be love, love, love. Who was I to assume to be such an orator and emcee of the proceedings? And so I stopped, and the party went on without direction. Eventually it disappeared.

Of the relatives I had tried to guess who was eighty years old, who was ninety. Was there any chance that a ninety-year-old person was alive? Who was seventy? Many of them could be alive. Were there any sixty-year-olds? I was there. I was sixty-five, standing somewhat straight. What were the attitudes? What were they serving for breakfast? No, don't fool around. Let them die. Say your prayers, and don't even go to such parties. They are pretty much nonsense. Dig for them and you'll come up with earthly skulls.

> Separation is gritty, you learn a lot
> from it, don't you, Mom? Those guys
> were crashing down my house with a
> ball and chain, but I smashed them
> back like Tecumseh Sherman did
> on his march through the South.
> No, not really. I
> just bore it. I failed to fear
> it. My lovers are not going to
> desert me, and I'm not going to reject
> them.
>
> No one will face me to abandon.
> Instead I loved them more. Give
> them more attention. Hold their
> attentions. Men in my battle corps

will tell what it was like in
Houston, stories and pictures.

I can't go deeper than I
know. Meet with people
you want to love even if
they are lumpy and you
are pointy-nosed, so what?
It's the heart that counts.

Hey, can we have a potluck supper before
you go? I don't mean to be foolish, but I
love feeling consoled. I'm learning
to reach out to others, especially those
who need me, want me. Write
those letters. Phone sometimes.

Go somewhere and say hello, wave
your hand and chant beads
with them. Your own rhythm and
theirs. Go out to them. You mean all
the way to Italy? To New York,
Gita-nagari? *Then* to Italy.

Your Chips could do it. You are
strong enough. And you'll die.

I shall fight, and my only weapon shall be exile, silence, and what's
the other one? Poetry, strategy? You forget all those things. But if you
go off at the time of death, He forces himself into your mind. He's in
charge of remembrance and forgetfulness. But it's not automatic for
every soul that He forces Himself into his mind and takes him to
Vrindavan, even if he loses his focus at the very end. You have to be a
lover, a rememberer, a desirer, so if something goes off just at the very
end—you get scared or blank—He rescues you. That's not for a drunken
confirmed meat-eating atheist. Krishna doesn't force Himself into that
person's consciousness.

269

No, it's for lovers only. Are you one? Are you too proud or sensuous? Are you too sensitive that you don't make friends? I hope you find succor in the aesthetic realm and with your friends. I heard you were going through some changes. If there is any difficulty, let me just say, "Sorry for your troubles." But I pray that doesn't stop you from going forward in exploring transcendence. If you have any fault, it's that you are too sensitive. Sensitivity like yours, Chips, lends itself to so much richness in the arts, but it can also isolate one. It makes it hard for some of us folks who are of the rough-and-tumble of the world to keep friendship.

Hey, but I'm okay. I've got Lee Risers and *sannyasa* clothes. I've got balls of clay from India and can wear the vertical *urdhav-pundra* Vaishnava *tilak* mark on my forehead or wash it off in a head bath. Full *sannyasa* uniform or full casual dress. I feel lonely sometimes, but it's mostly lack of Krishna-*prema*, not lack of material love, friendship, or lust. I do get the blues. Can't exercise, can't paint, and the sedative medicine is shit. But I have to take it. Slowly I make progress, Maharaja Chips. War is always hell. We saw a rabbit in a hurry today. The poetry of A. Ammons, he's dead too. "Since the death rate around this place is one hundred percent, I wanted to write to you while I can to ask your blessings and to express my gratitude."

No Henny Penny, a fifty-to-one shot won the Derby. They take the pot shots at the President of the U.S. in cartoons, but it bounces off his mighty power. Chicken burgers are available now; if they had them before, said Clinton on his way from the Pope's funeral, I probably would not have had my heart attack. He got to ride in Air Force One once again.

No, really, I'm not having any particular trouble. Not going through any big changes. Just nearer my Lord to thee. Nearer to death.

> You go slow when you walk but
> you walk straight and tall. I noticed.
> I noticed he's growing back a goatee,
> *Sadhana* at the lowest but people
> are encouraging him. He never went
> into the fusion and ruined his chops

and had to return embarrassed for making
a fool of himself.

But he did worse, acts unbecoming,
Some still not satisfied that
he was punished strictly enough.

Doing okay, aging like a
small tree or animal,
They can sometimes live
fourteen years or even more,
But what good is it
if they are not quality?

Black-caped stranger
called Phantom of the Opera.

Quick switch-hitter on
the Green Cathedral where
baseball players and audience
waste time.

Only thing we should be doing
while standing, sleeping, reading,
breathing, writing, if you have to fight
and the reason to make peace . . . .

No flirtations, no pains,
planters, oh sure
you want repaired dentures so
you can chew your food
better, but really,
doing one thing only
is to purely surrender to
the Democratic
Party, Krishna.

Come on, sister, get the typing done. He rapped his hand on the table, but she said, "I'll bust it up if I could, but I have too many bills to pay. I burnt out typing your manuscripts." So that era is over.

Chips said he could take the tapes back.

"If you like," she said. "I'm sorry I can't do them fast or at all anymore."

His jaw dropped. Want your tapes back? But I don't have any other typist. Seventeen tapes of *Love and Hate* untouched and ten of *New, Newer, and Newer*.

On Green Dolphin Street her family lived. They had to pay bills. She said she used to get up early, 6:00 in the morning, and start typing, loved the sound of his voice and his funny accents, then when she came home from work she would type from 8:00 until midnight. But that was all over now. She never even told him the flame blew out. The editor used to assure her that it was okay to be far behind, but she's got the only copy now of *Love and Hate*. I is scared, security-wise. Want them back, want them in my hands.

Nanny goat. You've got to get to bed. All day the original Irish cat, Haribol, prowls around this property, slow but sure. We know he's got cat's AIDS, and maybe that's why he walks slow and keeps to himself, a doomed air about him. In good weather he keeps mostly outside except to come inside for his domestic meal. Kills an occasional mouse just to show he can do it.

Sad air, why aren't you holier, cat? Blame it on the AIDS, which brought about the loss of weight and taste. You have to keep active to keep awake. But not too much action or you get exertion migraines. Someone else said he's getting the same symptoms and now he knows why Chips has always been bitching about it. Haunted by it. Will I get blamed for not busting it up no matter what?

Dat drummer can do it. I have to go to bed, even if I got only fifty-five percent on the surprise quiz.

One man was teasing Chips, not helping return his possessions. But actually they were rescued in a big truck and the jokester was among the rescuers. Meanwhile, closer to Chips, a tan man was singing in a low tune of his lifelong faithfulness to Chips. But how can we be sure if that's true? You can't be sure over the years because people change.

> Friends who say they love you
> oh dooby do they play your music.
> In that way they come to love
> in each others' arms but not causing harm.
> I want you to believe the
> truth of heaven with me.
>
> People who roam Vraja together
> eating mangoes, watch their spending
> and don't eat any food.
> Don't you like to stay
> right here on Mt. Palomar searching
> the stars and choosing words?
>
> But it would be nice to go out
> to see those who depend
> on you and give them encouragement,
> reading from the books you have been reading.
> Tell them there is nothing
> like the Vaishnava path with Krishna
> and the *gopis*.
>
> Can you really do that, or even the simple version?
> I'm not sure you are capable
> of lecturing anymore. You just
> did it by reading from
> your own books, but that's
> a different thing.

Pains from the cranium emanate like pencil-drawn sunshine rays. I phoned my friend several times for advice today. Which pill to take. We decided on one because we've been taking so many of the others. Funny. I've been so free of pain, but now a four-day crisis. Makes me see more realistically that I'm not so free to do whatever I want, such as taking a nonstop flight to Alachua to see all my disciples there, or visit

Gita-nagari after his passing away, or a nonstop to Italy to see so many affectionate devotees there. Or set up a schedule for many guests to come here. I might be way back. Not able to do those things. BTM advised me to show more loving care to those who depend on me. But maybe I can't do much more than I'm doing now. The books, the Web, the letters, some phone calls maybe, and visits. We can allow that. Allowing a visit from a woman with children in mid-June, allow other visits. Can you? Not with headaches. I do like the solitude, especially when it's all I can do. And write and die. Adjust your shoes, adjust your girdle. Adjust your schedule. Decide what clothes to wear. Growing back his goatee, now at the stage of a six-day ugly, a little Bowery bum. I shouldn't have cut it to go to Houston, that's my opinion now. Be who you are, who you want to be. You don't have to kowtow, and I'm a very poor sage, Prabhupada. He said we have some enemies and we have some friends also.

We get some inimical mail to the Web site, and we get some knockover, wonderful mail too. There's one from a Godbrother: "There's no doubt that our humble Godbrother is blazing new trails in his 'inner life' of Krishna consciousness. Some of us are on the sidelines, worried about this or saying that awful word, 'whatever,' and carrying on. But Maharaja has attracted so many of us by his courage to push on and his quest to expand his love for Krishna and Srila Prabhupada. The difference between us and him is that he has the guts to show himself, i.e., . . . 'walks the walk,' by real expressions of spiritual life, stuff that we forget we need to hear about in our condition of life, stuff that feeds us, kicks us in the butt when needed, and stuff that makes us cry like a small child for Prabhupada and Lord Krishna."

Chips says he needs to hear that, walking around the house with a headache, bowing down to Gaura-Nitai. And Prabhupada. And Nrisimhadeva, whose appearance day is later this month.

There's a black and white wild cat who's abusing all the other cats on the farm. They're going to try to catch him in an *ahimsa* cage and remove him far from this place. Lots of wildlife showing itself in this season. David appeared before the women with a long snake wrapped around his arm. Rabbits and turkeys and deer. Possibility of wild cats, I mean the big ones. Even bear.

Deep psychology, all the abuse and suffering. It comes up in dreams, sensitive poet among the gorillas in the navy. Thirty years of solitary migraines. Yearly GBC meetings amongst cunning bullies. And your own big *aparadhas,* especially the one that almost broke your leg. I mean broke your *sannyasa* rod. You're lucky you lived through it, only by the kindness of the Vaishnavas. They thought, "This guy has had a good record for a long time, so let him off easy on this one. He has no previous prison record." So much suffering that he has nightmares of being pushed through crowds, people rubbing things on him, like they do at Holi time in Vrindavan. True ruffians out on the streets, especially picking out the white people and rubbing them down with colored dyes. Uncivil behavior, no cops to turn to. They surround you and soak your clothes with liquid colors. If you don't complain, they say, "Oh, very humble." There's no chance to escape. The best thing to do at that time is stay indoors. If you go out, it's your fault.

My dreams resemble that. Quite a big mob of people pushing, everyone unfavorable toward me. They take my belongings. I try to get free. It's like children stealing your lunch except it's all adults and they're taking dear possessions, mocking me. A change in recent dreams is that I'm not so fearful of them. I fear I'll be a survivor. I'll slowly get through. It used to be that I was scared stiff that a mobster would take all I've got and rape me. Now I feel it's just a slow, slow, slow ordeal, but in the end I *will* survive and reach a goal—books will be printed. Do you mean to say you won't die?

Last night Chips was leaving a potluck dinner, and he saw, as if frozen in a photo, at the back of the house a pair of rickety steps. Some junk in the yard. A rear-end flasher light with sun glancing off it. It all formed a tableau of *the present moment.* You know what I mean. You told him, "This is your life. This is your life." And that meant *your life will end.* No additional philosophy was needed. It was just somehow was a tingling present moment to see those gathered objects and to catch his breath, for some reason or other, seeing with no extra cushion around it. The moment on a naked fork. He almost bowed in piety at the vision of arrested time given to him. It wasn't the vision of Krishna's lotus feet, but time stopped in an epiphany of ordinary stuff caught in the high-speed digital camera. Here I am and here it is. Then it broke, and ordinariness returned as they backed the car down the hill. "Do you have your safety belt on?"

In the first brief report as received from Nara in Mexico, he said his crucial meeting with the real estate millionaire went *pretty well.* The choice of words is so important. I would have preferred that he said it was excellent or fantastic. He says now he has to do a lot of footwork to follow up that initial all-important meeting. What is "pretty good"? How about my faith in God? Is it pretty good? What is Krishna's attitude toward me? Of course, in the generic sense, it's all compassionate. It's inconceivably loving and wise and in my best interests. Word-slinging is so strange. It's like getting marks on a test, A+, A, B+, B, B-, C+. We heard that his meeting went pretty well. Or maybe he said exactly, "pretty good." Pretty girl. A pretty girl is like a melody.

Perhaps it really didn't go so well. He hoped that it would have gone better, but he said it went pretty well.

Chips is lying in bed gutting it out, toughing it out, because he's not supposed to take any more medicine. But he knows how to endure this stuff so he can say, "It's okay." Prabhupada gives that old, serious joke. You go to see a man in the hospital and his leg is in traction, he's being fed intravenously, and you in your formality, ask him, "How do you feel, Joe?"

He replies, "I'm feeling all right." The man has to release his stool and urine with a bedpan. He can't even eat food through his mouth. He's in constant pain. But he says, "I'm feeling all right." What is this "all right"? The materialistic person is like that. His happiness is just a momentary relief from blows he's receiving from young Mohammed Ali or Joe Lewis. A momentary relief. And he says, "I'm okay." Pull him up from underwater just before he drowns and asks him how he feels. He gasps, "I'm all right!" I remember in our dining room we had a sign that we had bought at an amusement park: "God bless our heavily mortgaged home."

Plug up the pain by diversion. Avoid trying to pray by shaking your head in the pillows. Space out and don't pay attention. Watch the movies of flowing "Buddhism" and wait for something to end. I don't mean life, I mean this particular H.A. because brother, when it's over I've got a lot of good things to do, a lot of good things to say. So happy Chips Swamiji, bona fide disciple of His Divine Grace A. C. Bhaktivedanta Swami Prabhupada, a member of the nonprofit federal tax–exempt organization, the International Society for Krishna Consciousness, registered in New York City in July, 1966, at 26 2nd Ave., witnessed by a handful of original members, who are no longer members, and the founder-*acharya*, who has since gone back to Godhead, leaving his instructions, which are followed by thousands of new members in flowing disciplic succession.

Once any one of them dies, you will have to get rid of the body very soon, because it will start corrupting and stinking up the room. Bury or burn it, and honor it by speeches, and if he was really outstanding, proliferate his unique teachings in books, CDs, and videos. But no corpses, please.

> Mangoes, bananas, and plums won't last
> or any plant. Gold is quite permanent.
> And the alchemist's touchstone.
>
> The human soul is eternal, a finite version
> of God's infinite, all-expanding Supersoul.
> Best souls are Krishna in humanlike form
> and His friends in Goloka.
>
> There is eternity in Brahman, but
> it's formless and far inferior.
>
> The Vaikuntha forms are glorious
> but relations there are too formal and reverent
> for God's taste—He feels the reverence
> cripples the pure affection He yearns
> for in Vrindavan.
>
> So if you're looking for the bluebird
> and the prettiest song of His flute,
> it's Goloka you must go to
> where the *gopas* and *gopis* and Radhika live.
> She's the Queen and Krishna is Her lover.
>
> If there is writing to be done,
> deathless writing, it's the spontaneous

composition of the Vraja poets—
all are poets
and they sing and compose the pastimes
of their Lord, their child,
pal, lover, what He did today,

write and don't die,
that's the only way.

F.W., AFTER TAKING JACUZZI BATH, 1:22 A.M.

Did Swami Swimsji ever get headaches when he was a little boy? For example, when he received his first Holy Communion at St. Claire's church and when he was awarded the black pouch, gold-embossed, with the words, "The Happiest Day of My Life," which contained his first rosary beads, a holy missal, and holy pictures—did that pouch also contain a tin of St. Joseph's aspirin for children? No. Such head doldrums, coming from spiritual revelations or great happiness or wrestling with the boys, were dealt with by Swim's mother, who might apply a St. Joseph's aspirin. But it was not a frequent thing. If chemicals are applied too frequently, they lose their potency. The little devils of pain learn to tolerate the medicine, which therefore becomes ineffective. And an anti-venom agent like Garuda never loses his potency because the pain-bringing demons are never as powerful as he is and cannot learn new strategies, ways to outsmart him and his power. But pharmaceuticals are always fallible in their attempt to ward off the many kinds of blows that human beings are heir to. So sometimes you have to tough it out all day and overnight, and maybe the next day. A Jacuzzi bath was a nice idea, makes you feel fresh, but doesn't subdue the gargoyle-faced, tight-fisted *dolor* of the *cabeza*.

A lecturer who knows anecdotes about Srila Prabhupada is very valuable. He can tell more than just the recorded words of his speeches. He tells what Prabhupada did when a boy walked out during his lecture. He tells the gesture he made. He tells the time Prabhupada had a headache, and what he did. He tells about a time in Bombay, Dallas, London. True stories, captured in many memoirs. The arm flinches if they are not true, and it flinches for pain, and supposedly, it flinches when there is good fortune. When I told an allopathic doctor that flinching of the left arm means good fortune, he said, "Oh come on, Steve," and I realized how foolish it was to speak words like that to an unbeliever. Because it is impossible, I believe it. Come on, send your postulant to investigate my miracles and see if he can find a logical reason, rather than a miraculous one, for what I have claimed. His job is to debunk so that the Church doesn't get embarrassed by cheap miracle-makers. Some pass the test. They admit there are true saints and miracles, what to speak of pious people who may not be saints but who do wonders in helping people. They get embarrassed by cheap miracle-makers. Some pass the test. They change people's hearts. They help people.

Do I dare to phone BTM again this week, since he said he would not live another week? He said I could try. Today is Friday. I may try tomorrow. With faith. Hare Krishna. Everyone who has two hands and two feet and eyes and thinking functions is a walking miracle. He walks in the miracle of creation. If he just hears the pastimes of Govinda, a miracle occurs. If he does more than hear but really pays attention, then he breaks through to deeper revelations, regardless of his *dolores de la cabeza*. He begins to ignore the pain and to relish the universal scheme of the creator. Things begin to amuse him and sadden him. He becomes more sensitive to everyone's lot. He doesn't know what to do about his memory problem but tries to stay awake a little longer.

The happiest day of my life. When I received *harinam* and my name, Swampji dasa. Then the grandmaster said, "Say after me, '*namah om vishnu-padaya.*'"

"*namah om vishnu-padaya.*"
"*krishna presthaya bhutale.*"
"*krishna presthaya bhutale.*"
"*srimate bhaktivedanta swami.*"
"*srimate bhaktivedanta swami.*"
"*iti namine.*"
"*iti namine.*"

They were given papers with the translation, and gradually they began to memorize it so that it was not just repeating some foreign words. I offer my obeisances to His Divine Grace A. C. Bhaktivedanta Swami Prabhupada, who is very dear to Krishna on this earth, having taken shelter at the lotus feet of the transcendental Lord.

Keep talking to keep away the flinches. Some people don't talk at all. I think I shall resort to that back in bed.

    You've got a little time. Please use it well. It's like a surrey with a fringe on top. Clop clop clop. Pace your pony, slap his side, but not too hard because he's not a big workhorse. How much mail are you carrying? Charge ahead, be careful of his ankles across the stones, find a racetrack to run through. I heard your recitation of ill names this morning when you were trying to guess who said them, but it doesn't matter, it just floats in your head on the street corner because you are tired, your plans are blunt, you can't play detective or in-pursuit. Your own faith is strong in the impossible, but to convince others, like John the Evangelist, you kick their butts, tickling their funny bones, making a ramrod-straight-through plot built on scenes and characters with no digression, just flashbacks and . . . .

    Mr. Priest in Swami Swarth in Energy and Lenten, sixteenth century Voltairean symbolist chauvinist, Mr. Fox, Mr. Joy, joy, Sans Foi, the hypocrite priest, the strange fat man, I can't do that stuff, clap clap, wah wah, wing-tipped shoes are out of style, ornate sneakers are in and repair the blind girl's eye and bring her on the stage as a ballet dancer who prays to the Virgin for a miracle, three of them and you're a saint. Investigate it because it might come from ordinary causes, in which case the people are brokenhearted. and what can I say? Maybe the sick people got cured by something like faith, a sort of miracle in itself. Can you prove it wrong by science?

> Believe me, it does
> tarmac wet from rain,
> get us off the airplane,
> authorities check your IDs
> for the umpteenth time.
>
> Your hopscotcher stocky,
> expose your hairy legs,
> expose argyles and shoes,
>
> if they like they can go
> all the way and ask you

to part your buttocks
pull your top hair,
see if it's a wig.

But they can't find your
soul with a stethoscope
or MRI or x-ray—
it just won't show up.

But it's there. I wish I
could prove it, sister,
in the hayfield, in the rye,
he thought Holden Caulfield
was weird, the fifteen-year-old reader,
because he saw Salinger's name
listed somewhere as a member
of the "conspiracy theory."
What nutty stuff kids pick up
at least Keli is in a K.C.
family and has a K.C. heart,
believes in God, seems to love
devotee people. That's his best
associates. It happened as his
growing-up process.

This grass is Whitman's
this school is a Vassar
I'm too sad and mixed up
from pain to make
coherent tips for
carrying your suitcase
up the elevator, sir.

I didn't know what time it was
"in this tune we feature
no one in particular." That's
nice. Don't bother me at 7:03 A.M.,

I've chanted some *japa* and my pain is gone.
Is that a miracle? Two more and I'm a saint.
Tobias got a chest nutty heart
forty miracles in an hour but
the prefects won't count them
on their Archdiocese Geiger counter.

Who cares? Krishna sees the miracles
one each second, each mantra,
you just have to breathe and open your eyes.

Whew, Swami Chips just escaped further reading in a fiction book, *The Third Miracle*, a book about investigation into Catholic miracles, which was recommended to him by a Godbrother. It seems that in the world of Catholic miracles, when something astounding appears or people claim a miracle has occurred, along with the auspicious event, inauspicious events sent by the devil also come. In *The Third Miracle*, a statue of the Virgin Mary in a churchyard pours tears of blood every October for ten years, but when the miracle comes, it's always accompanied by the rape of a woman in the parish, by the upturning of graves, by the appearance of ghosts, by the appearance of dismembered small animals, worms in the plumbing, and a loss of faith of one of the priests. This is all supposed to mean that Satan is very near in the form of "competition" with God, who appears in the form of the miracle. He tries to sway the faithful. Just at the time that they're being blessed, he tests them most. I enjoyed the beginning of the book when the miracle appeared, but disliked the descriptions of the rape, the graves opening, etc. I became afraid of it and didn't think it was auspicious reading. And I didn't forget that it was fictional reading, either. I thought perhaps the author was capable at any moment of putting some touches in just for the sake of sensationalism, like Steven Spielberg, in his creation of a movie like *Jaws*. Govinda had been reading the book to me at breakfast and lunch, when he told his wife Magdaline, who is an ex-nun, that I had stopped reading the book, she said she was glad to hear it. When she was in the convent, she used to work for a bishop who was an active exorcist. She therefore was quite familiar with the doctrine that the devil is always near and that you have to be on guard against him.

You have to fight him. She said they didn't even call him by names like Satan or Beelzebub. They didn't give him that honor. They just referred to him in a distant way as "the horn." Don't give him any quarter, don't recognize him, don't let him into your life. Maybe that's what I was fearing and why I stopped reading the book. Too many satanic symptoms, and having to think about them later while resting or sleeping. Get thee behind me, Satan!

But it is fascinating . . . . The investigator just wants the facts, like Jack Webb in TV's *Dragnet*. The investigator or postulant is himself, however, very short on faith as he goes about his investigation. In one scene in the book, he goes into a church to pray.

> '*Credo quia impossible est*,' Frank said out loud. 'I believe because it is impossible,' he repeated. Just words, however. Empty words. What'd they ever have to do with faith? With God? With his life, to be exact? Was that what all this was about, finding a reason for his life? To Frank, his life looked like it was spread out to the horizon without any purpose: there was nothing for him to believe in or accomplish, and there was no one he loved. God was something of the past: a childhood memory.
>
> Frank stood and bowed his head. His loneliness tore through him like an axe. He felt it cutting him in two. He thought about Phalcone. [A previous case investigated for sainthood but proven to be a suicide.] A failed man. A loser like himself. The difference was that Phalcone couldn't fool himself anymore. He couldn't walk through the day pretending that when he faced his final hour, he would think of something smart to say that would negate all the years of wasted motion, wasted tears, wasted thoughts and actions.
>
> —From *the Third Miracle*, a novel by Richard Vetere

> Please be quiet so we can hear the
> uninterrupted sound. I told him I
> wasn't writing or painting so much
> but I was in the right place. That's
> good, he said. God bless you, he said.
>
> It's when only the piano is playing that the
> background noise takes over. I know
> what that's like from trying
> to read against tent music at

the Houston fair.
Krishna, You hear in such conditions
above the noise and the sincere
listeners, they come in close and
Swami Chips enunciates clear
and clipped the *shastra*-evoked tones
with improvised notes from his
own mind, clichés dropped
in favor of neighborhood favorites,
newly minted, freshly baked

from his loneliness, his lonely
look up and rest, hey I'm
okay, I'm in the right place. Ollie
is following the full
temple schedule in Vrindavan,
just as we did in the old days.

CHAPTER EIGHTEEN

SWAMI CHIPS IS NOT SO LONELY. He has friends who love him, and he loves them. He does not think of himself as a loser or failed man. As for faith in God, Sri Krishna? I mean *really*, with all facades torn away. I do hang desperately onto faith, Hare Krishna. The bodily twitch. Beyond reason. Simple attachment to Srila Prabhupada will rise and save me at the time I need it most. You believe that? "Pray for us sinners now and at the hour of our death, amen."

DREAM

From a distance, a man watches the roof of his house explode. Many people are sitting on the roof, and they are thrown high into the air. The roof and the people then descend back into place. For a second time the roof explodes into space, and the people are thrown high above. Again the roof descends, and the people come down, and again they are thrown into space, creating the effect of a trampoline, again and again. The man who is watching finds himself more concerned for his building, his roof, than for the people who are being exploded into space. Finally the exploding stops. Not so much damage has been done to either the people or the roof. The concern of everyone is more to whether the neighbors have been disturbed and are going to take any legal action. After the explosion is over, the man and the survivors take to writing poems and writing judgments about whether the landlord or the tenants were at fault.

This dream shifted to a scene where the same man is walking on a college campus surrounded by young girls. He is a mature professor. They are young students. One of them says she is getting used to living at the college and is now looking forward to writing English compositions and to feeling at home more in the day-to-day routine. He turns to her and says that this will come in time. A girl on his left says she also is looking forward to more informal exchanges. He assures her that this will come. Some of the older women see these exchanges and become jealous.

Freud says the more incredulous and ridiculous the dream is, the more profound it is. But I prefer my dreams to have a direct "ah-ha!"

perception to them. I am sorry that I have nothing more to offer in this whose taste is for matter above humanity, who likes to write words and play word games, even in the midst of catastrophe and who enjoys the company of young girls, even in an academic setting. There appears to be no clue of one yearning to render loving service to the transcendental Supreme Personality of Godhead. Therefore, it is useless. But maybe there is a clue there if we worked it to death, if we milked it on the psychiatrist's couch. We could say the exploding upward was seeking transcendence. We could say the fact that no one was injured meant it was taking place in the spiritual world and that the man's desire to write is on my theme to write and die and that the writing has not been explained in the dream. It remains a mystery. Perhaps he's writing what I am ultimately seeking to write, praises of the Lord and confessions of my falling short. If the dream itself is a confession of falling short, then that itself is stark honesty, the other side of the coin in spiritual life, the last leg of religion. It has to come before we reach the *viraja* and go over. We could say his being in an academic setting is his taking part in one of ISKCON's seminar programs, as a Godbrother just informed he was doing in a letter I received yesterday. Teach seminars on Krishna conscious subjects to women as well as men. But there is some impurity there in an attraction for women. That can be transcended, and one can teach girls and boys together, overcoming any taint and seeing them all as spirit souls in different bodies. We don't have classrooms where women are forbidden to come, but we see the souls in their bodies, not just the fact that they're women. Women's liberation movement, and a mature teacher has to control himself while at the same time answering their questions. There may be potential for jealousy or attraction, but these have to be transcended. And they can be, even by a middle-stage devotee. So you see, by sifting through the contents even of this neutral or tasteless dream, we find some remnants of Krishna consciousness, something to use for the good.

COUNTERFEIT PRABHUPADA GRAFFITI DREAM

Some youngsters had a red coloring that they would spread on any surface. On top of the red surface appeared Prabhupada cartoons in black. The cartoons showed themselves and Prabhupada in scenes where Prabhupada was acting favorably to these graffiti people. But the difficulty was that it was all concocted. I and other devotees were assigned to track down these graffiti people and stop their activities. Like any graffiti artists, their activities were very widespread, and we could not keep up with them. Their work was so fluid, it was like flowing motion, like a film. In once sense, it wasn't bad because you were seeing Prabhupada in favorable activities, but the bad part was that it was all made up. It was not *parampara,* it was all the spreading of things that Prabhupada never did, and so we had to stamp it out. Also, the bad thing was that it was so red, bright red, brighter and brighter. I was seeing a more and more intense bright color in my dream. I woke from this with a stuffed nostril and a headache. Intellectually, I am glad that I was dreaming of Prabhupada. The cartoon images were certainly of Prabhupada, but the impression was all of made-up activities, counterfeit Prabhupadisms, and it is not good to make up such things. So we were trying to stop it. And one gets a headache even in trying to be a detective to stamp out such graffiti.

> Pray for us
> our facial hairs, our wild hands
> and feet, nightmares, "may you have
> Gauranga dreams" hugs.
> He says it is Pentecost Sunday and
> the tenth anniversary of his *harinam*
> initiation, took place in Prabhupada-*desha,* Italy.
> "I'm still here," in spiritual
> life.
>
> For now it feels right to be situated
> in north California because his
> guru is here. Chipsji, his guru, suggests
> that both of them are
> growing deep roots here.
>
> "I'd like to paint again, as in a routine"
> but for now
> we cannot. Methinks he
> will return to it.

WRITE AND DIE

The prayer route, paper route on
bicycle. Don't even stop in front
of the house but reach in your bag
and grab the pre-rolled newspaper,
Throw it toward the house door,
pedal on.

Those were the days. Magnificent
agility, fourteen years old, not screwed
up in head, believe in God in a simple
way, worshipped Krishna and chanted,
played *mridanga* and harmonium,
had been to Vrindavan several times,
gurukula, bathed in Ganges-Yamuna,
served swamis.

Post-abuse ISKCON, liberated.
Going his own way encouraged
by his parents—do what you've
got a calling for. What do you think
you have in you that will please Krishna
the most?

That's not too "liberal" is it?
It's what he's been told by
the folks he loves the most
in the *bhakti* family,
the ones who attract him
by their love: "I'm doing
this for him, it's what I

like, to please the Lord
on tenor horn
or book distribute
or poem unrhymed
or bake lemon pie
or house construct

troubleshoot
car repair
money make
ain't misbehavin'
saving my love for you.

Religious life is suffering. To be authentic is harrowing, cutting to the bone. Does he really believe? He does it out of duty. But not a hypocrite. Trying, trying more. Crying, crying harder. Whoop the devil. Whoop lethargy. Write through pain and distraction, make it a tune you can love. Hear the technical value books with your mind fixed, simple above all.

It's simple for the simple, difficult for the crooked. Sit at the feet of your guru, take in what he says absolutely, and try sincerely to carry out his tasks, take care of the other devotees' needs. Be kind, compassionate to everyone, give them pure Krishna consciousness, books are the basis, read the guru's, and distribute them, eat pure *prasadam* and nothing else. This is a hand sketch.

Religious life is routine. It is also scholarly. *Bhakti* is described as perfect in *prema*, reached by always chanting *harinam*, which brings about perceiving the *guna* (quality) and *lila* (pastimes) of the Lord. Thus you are beyond time and can see Radha and Krishna in Their *asta-kaliya lila* (pastimes divided throughout eight portions of the day and night). This is theoretical theology of *raganuga* for most of us. Therefore I say religion is routine, routine *vaidhi* or routine *raganuga*. Rare souls break through, *saksad-darshan* (direct vision) of Radha and Krishna. Don't argue and theologize so much, just chant the holy name, Vaishnava dasa Thakur told his inquiring disciple Lahiri in *Jaiva Dharma*, a book by Bhaktivinode Thakur.

In *The Third Miracle*, Frank Morrow, the miracle investigator, is finding false witnesses and finding himself to be a false witness before God. The book gets sexy too, for sales attraction, a Scribner paperback fiction, published by Simon and Schuster.

Religion is shelter. True dharma is our pillar, pillow, success. Prabhupada did nothing wrong. You can investigate him. His life was that of an ideal servant of his guru and the mission of Chaitanya Mahaprabhu. He took daring chances and remained pure. He came to America at an advanced age with no money or institutional backing. All he had was great faith in his prayer, "You have brought me here, oh Lord, now make me dance, oh make me dance, make me dance!" He is our shelter, the bona fide founder-*acharya*, the giver of *harinam* and *diksha*. He sent us on hard missions to propagate the cult, but with the assurance that it is for God, not for anyone's sense gratification or self-emolument. Take shelter from the storms of vice, violence, corruption of every sort, the boredoms that breed death.

Religious life is demanding, nonduplicitous. He wants a few good men and women, like the U.S. Marines poster. No flapper, wafflers, but true souls who follow vows. If they do slip they can be picked up and forgiven, provided they don't fall again.

Religious life is demanding, austere, for *tapasvis*. In summer weather in Vrindavan, he eats only four mangoes a day. Chants and hears holy sounds, nothing else. Cuts out all nonsense. Does whatever is required to please guru and Gauranga. He meets demands, like hitting a punching bag. He's up to the occasion. He's ready. He takes joy in work and chooses it instead of sleep. He acts young for his age and fights against the cancer. His life is demanding, but he does it with *joie de vivre*, the joy of a monk or nun. That's not the joy of sense gratification but the joy of being detached from the same, the joy of meeting the demands as they come from Krishna-loka via the chain of *parampara*.

When religious leaders are involved in crime, as pederasts, child abusers, drug dealers, embezzlers, gamblers, thieves, even murderers, they are worse than ordinary mafia thugs—because they hide behind the protection of the crucifix and holy collar or the saffron robes and bowing down six times a day. They give their criminal booty to the church as if to absolve themselves of human crimes. But God never gave such orders to his men to pillage in the name of sacred appearance. The priests and monks are meant to be trusted in all matters, detached from money and sex and appetite for gross crimes. They are careful not to give religious orders a bad name. Religious criminals make the ashram stink and drive away innocent prospective recruits.

When religion is practiced *in essence*, it is the sweetest flower in the world. It is the only path worth living for. All other paths lead to the

graveyards—skulls and skeletons. Religion is the hope of living hereaf-
ter in a spiritual body. And while on this earth, religion is the path of
sacred virtues, ahimsa, nonviolence, global consciousness raising—
teaching people of the soul and God, which mostly people have forgotten, the knowledge that adds the living dimension to all other dead
emotions. Therefore, *bhagavat-dharma* (eternal religion) is the highest
welfare work for humanity. So-called liberation theology works on a
level of politics to free humanity from tyrants and enslavements in government. But these are temporary gains. Changing peoples' consciousness to God consciousness gives them eternal liberation, from which
they can never be enslaved again.

> Religious tide flows, you've been reading
> fiction mundane and it filters dirt in your
> brain. You pee in your bed. But majority
> of your reading is transcendental high still
> Bhaktivinode Thakur, Sanatan Goswami, memoirs
> of our Srila Prabhupada.

> Religion flows like the Yamuna. I should
> have asked him what it's like living
> in a topmost abode, does some of it
> filter down to his consciousness?
> Surely he's protected as he takes part
> fulltime in *sadhana* twenty-four hours
> a day.

> I should have told him more I care
> for him, it's not just a routine
> I phone him but affection underlying.
> I don't understand why we're made
> to live apart; the boss says it's needed
> and I have to read the cases
> against our being together.

> It makes a kind of legal
> and psychological sense, and as

> long as he's enjoying Vrindavan
> and I'm doing well here in
> CA, I'm content to keep it
> up and under higher orders.
> heart's a different thing.

You have to remember the face of death. Remember the face of the little child praying. She steps on the head of death, one, two, three, and into the chariot of deathlessness, the chariot to the spiritual world. How good have you lived? You've heard enough that any material birth is inferior to the Brahman oneness, and oneness is inferior to Vaikuntha in varieties where the Lord is worshipped, and Ayodhyadhama is above that and Dvarakadhama where Krishna dwells with His queens and Uddhava, but topmost of all you've heard is Vrindavan where Krishna is relaxed with his intense family members, friends and lovers in *krsna-prema*—but theoretical "knowing" of these things is no guarantee you'll go there. You may be reborn an animal on earth for all your vices, your doubts, you may be born as a human again struggling once more with the same doubts, come back to be more honest, austere, pure, stronger, more fearless.

You have no idea where you're going after write and death. Come back and read your own books. You might come back with a terrible disease and stay up nights playing jazz, neglecting God consciousness. Or come back more determined to follow your bona fide spiritual master. It's a shame because you have been given the best chance *this lifetime* with an eternal guru. An eternal Vedic path. You have to get on it and stay on it. You're writing and dying, but will that be good enough? Painting has faded out, you can pick it up again.

Your inspirations. Please Lord, pray Hare Krishna, don't let those mantras fall out of sight.

> Shine despite the rain. Hop off the
> bed in splendorous glee. You should be
> a barber, a dry-eyed dog controller,
> something you'd really admire in
> another. You mean a muscular drummer
> like old Philly Joe?

He was happy to dream of romance
without having any. They would
mock you but my stories
and prose was enough, and a few to show
them to. In the long run you'd
have to back it up with
a life lived and you were not
ready for that pain.

So you took to the route of
the holy rollers who avoid
pain they think, but it comes to them
a little later in life
when they see their ideas fade.
See what hard work it is to remain
constantly aflame to the Lord and
keep it alive, keep
the rituals or move on?
Where is life located?

Then so many disappointments in
yourself and the institution. Show
me your face. Does the minister
believe in God? Does he fall?
He can pick himself up but he gets salty
tears along his rocky path.
Joyful, mediocre.

Jims doesn't know the date. The daily calendar is set at May 18. It shows a picture of Srila Prabhupada at the opening of Krishna-Balarama Mandir. He's wearing silks and turns toward the audience, waving a big peacock-feather fan. On the calendar, the quote for the day is from a letter to Gurukripa, May 18, 1977: "Now I have come back to my home, Vrindavan. If anything should go wrong, at least I will be here in Vrindavan."

I do very little each day, says Jims. Just rest and try to avoid headaches and making it to the toilet before he pees or shits in his pants.

293

Today he dumped in his pants before reaching the toilet. He talked with his counselor how a lot of psychological mentality may be behind this. Oh shit with it, oh pee on it. Don't worry. And headaches, how do you explain them? Tied down, nervous disorder, posttraumatic anticipatory migraine. Psychological. Too late to phone anyone for root core advice. It's deeper than "oh pee on it." Certainly the causes are posttraumatic.

I was thinking of traveling to Alachua because many disciples are there. My friend advised me not to and said many of them are sour on me. "Don't go there," he said, "Go somewhere and maybe a few devotees from Alachua might come, but don't go into their territory."

Traumatic what ISKCON power can do. He told me how a swami's sentence was up after eight years but new persons on the GBC object to allowing him to go into temples or initiate. The GBC has great power to shape a devotee member, no matter how senior he is. Jiminy wants to know what his position is in ISKCON. Some places are friendly to him, some may not be. But he has his own niche carved out, and it seems it's acceptable to all. But still this does not remove his headaches.

His counselor said to him today, "If you want me to give you an answer of what is wrong with this man or what is his situation, I would express it simply in two sentences. He wants freedom, and he doesn't want to be restricted. He suffers when he feels he's being restricted and he thrives when he feels he has freedom." It's late, too late to be up writing. And you may be writing about topics you shouldn't be writing about.

CHAPTER NINETEEN

OH WHAT A WONDERFUL WORD is *bhoga*. And what a wonderful thing it is to transform material desire into the service of the Lord. There was a big coming-out party of people admitting they had material desires and converting them to the pleasure of the Lord. One great person after another was doing it in stellar performances. A man was taking credit for feeling that he knew Beethoven songs. He announced to the audience that he was sickly and had to wear two pairs of long underwear, yet he was performing despite his handicap. In a masterly tenor and baritone, he sang his songs very sternly and with great command. Everyone was mesmerized by his great performance until a group of girls in frilly dresses burst out mocking his melodies by changing the words to *"sergan sassafras hey."* Everyone burst out laughing. It was irresistible. The German interpreter of songs was completely undone. But all's fair at the *bhoga* party. And that was the spirit of it. Someone was in the middle of a *bhoga* conversion, and another could top them by making fun of it with another interpretation.

It was a very merry occasion, attended by many. It had the spirit of an Alice in Wonderland party, and there were no rules or regulations. There was no stern regulator or authority to punish anybody. It was just who could top anyone else in genuine good spirits. No one got sore if they were actually outdone. It rolled along and rolled along. Chips Swami was there, but he had a very low profile.

Nevertheless, two young girls came up to him. They were mostly German and couldn't speak very good English, but they introduced themselves by their tags. Their tags had many different names on them, and he couldn't tell which was their name, but someone helped him to show which of the many names on their tags was their actual surnames. Both of their names were very similar, but one of them teased, "Oh, you're pronouncing your name as if it's more aristocratic than mine." They both laughed and asked Chips Swami if he was dressed too coldly or too warmly. He said, "I'm dressed too cold." And then he said, "No, I'm dressed too warm." The dream stopped there, before he could make a fool of himself in trying to perform some *bhoga*. One wonders what he would do, but whatever it would be, it would be something tried in good spirit, some merry attempt at conversion, some claim of talent that could be laughed at despite his thinking it was something artistic or great in the grand *bhoga* party.

Incidentally, this whole shindig was sponsored by the United States Air Force. Gradually, they discovered that some of the main talented participants were members of the Hare Krishna movement. They discovered this gradually by noting the *sikhas* on the men who had the most talent. But you'll be surprised to hear that they didn't have any particular objections to the Hare Krishnas. Things had become so liberal that devotees were allowed to rise and mix with the elite. The main thing was whether you had talent or were willing to come forward and make a show of talent, offer your *bhoga*.

Birch trees. Where are you going to leave your body, pass away, presuming you have that choice? These are strange expressions to many people. "Leave the body?" They don't know we mean croak, kick the bucket. We mean the soul that resides in the body cannot tolerate living there anymore and departs. The body becomes a dead corpse, heart of stone, then begins to rot, and the soul immortal goes to its next place of residence, its next body, according to the law of karma.

He may go to the spiritual world if he has been very good and Krishna is pleased with him. That's rare. He or she must be free of all material attachments and absorbed in love of the Supreme. Sometimes Krishna favors a devotee to think of Him at the last moment. Krishna forces His way into a devotee's consciousness even if the devotee is not thinking of him, and thus He saves the devotee at the end.

> It goes on. The tall evergreens in
> peaceful Philo. Songless tongue
> picking up a heavy pen. Wearing
> wet pants.
>
> Changing to *sannyasi's* dress.
> That makes you feel
> better. Wear your little
> beard, don't fear the
> mice chewing at the

e-mail wires. You are
your own soul. Don't
foul it up. You're down
I know, but in your

dream today you instantly
chose the **renunciant** life
over Maya's temptation
and woke feeling good about
that: "I'm a monk."

There's no taste in material enjoying,
not for one who's
sold out to trying for
Krishna whole heart.
That's me. I may fail
to get the required grade
but I'm certainly on the
right side trying
and not with the material enjoyers.

In the chapel a man sings a line in Latin in *canto gregoriano,* then a pure soprano follows him. At first Chips thought it a bit strange that a man and woman should mix so intimately in holy prayer. But eventually, packs of men and packs of women, and then mixed women and men, and it seems okay. It's the *Missa De Angelis,* which Govinda's wife, Magdalene, brought from Italy. Chips uses it to keep himself awake in the difficult *brahma-muhurta* hours when he's struggling to stay awake during *japa*. This is not my God, but it's religious music and not disturbing. It may help. I can't understand the language.

On the cover of the CD there's a carving of Christ with his right hand held up in benediction. His left side I can only guess. It seems to be covered with many long, large keys. Strange priests on either side of him, only partly visible in the picture, are like griffins, lion-sized with wings, some angels on his shoulders. Pictures are so effective. We read in Srila Gaura-Govinda Swami Maharaja's book about *patra-chitra* art. It is a specialty on the palm-leaf manuscripts in the old traditional

Orissan style, and even the pages of the paper books nowadays are lavishly illustrated with Vaishnava art. Sri Govinda Swami writes, "The *patra-chitra* tradition is more than just artistic expression. For the *chitra-karas* of Orissa, *painting is their worship of the Lord*" [italics added]. How about that? Painting is worship. Chips painted three canvases in the last two days. No wonder it makes him happy. Now if only this *Massa De Angelis* or *something* can help his upraised voice to stay awake and attentive.

> Write and die
> hand in hand
> your favorite things until the end.
> *Gloria in excelsis deo.*
> The paintings are worship
> the choir is liturgy uplifted
> until the end hand in hand.
>
> Temple bells ring, symbols jingling,
> Last night at dusk we sang
> namas te narasimhaya.
> The family gathered, the
> *sannyasi* spoke a simple version
> from the scripture. Nrisimha killed
> the demon and his son asked
> if he could be liberated.
>
> Hand in hand.
> It was hard to stand straight
> although he received benefits at 65
> as a senior citizen you can ride
> the subways free.
>
> Sometimes you can sit on a porch
> and not do anything at all,
> just look at the tall pines
> and a high blue sky—
> I was never able to repose

like that in my life before.
But still have bad dreams.

Coming out here we saw one playboy bunny and then another hitchhiking. Dangerous for a man or for the girl. Finally we saw a man with a likeness of Charles Bukowski hitchhiking, plain dangerous. Drove through the dark redwood forests, passing huge double tractor trailers bearing logs.

Nara took Chips to the windy seashore, sand blowing across the page. Walruses flopped, sunning themselves on an inlet with seagulls that come and go. Over a hump of sand we see the shiny white breakers. Some people around.

The *patra-citra* artists worship by painting. N. is fingering his beads. The seagulls are squawking. I believe there is a mommy and young child close to my right.

Funerals. Sand. Driftwood in many sizes. Some like giant logs, smooth as skulls, too heavy to pick up. Some small and tangled, ready for a campfire, some strange figurations, combinations, white, bleached, bony, pressed orange, long plops of crushed curious shapes. A collector could spend an afternoon sifting through, choosing prime "found objects."

Funerals. Shadow of a gull maneuvering. Shadow of my pen. Foamy milky frothy of the already-dashed wave. Sun glinting off the tip of the incoming waves. Nara and I own this turf unless someone else wants to take it. It's free country, the ocean, the beach.

> Oh you're always trying to catch yourself
> daydream that life is happy
> that even the moment is pleasant—
>
> this one crouched under a big log
> hiding from the beach wind and sand
> enjoying the sun and surf.
>
> You always want to remind yourself
> "all joys want eternity"
> and my buttocks are aching in the hard sand.

You're such a spoilsport.
But they said Prabhupada disagreed with Kierkegaard
and said spiritual life doesn't
entail great suffering.

Wind tugging at my hood
sand gritting in my teeth but
in my earphones I hear my friends
the Sam Walker Trio.

Take a little time off
your nervous, disordered self
your worry and I'm glad to
see you don't even have
a headache. So Nara is chanting and you're

writing. What's the difference?
I could go to *japa*
now even though I didn't
bring the beads or clicker to
the beach. Take it so. It's a lovely
sunny day, you're a God-man.

Prabhupada used to compare the insects' life to the human. There was a kind of bug in Mayapur that used to live for one night only. At night they would gather around any light by the thousands, and in the morning you would see them heaped up, dead, ready to be swept away. Their lifespan was one night, whereas our lifespan is many years. Whether you are *indragop*, the microscopic germ, or Indra the great king of heaven, all beings are mortal. Sobering thoughts from the Vedas. Brahma's lifetime, so long we cannot even calculate it, full of enjoyments so subtle we can't even taste them on the gross human level. But after the long, long party of Brahma, after many years, it comes to an end and he dies, and then there is devastation. Even after one day of Brahma there is devastation, what to speak of the end of his lifetime. Everything dies, and the foolish don't take note of it. Their response to death is to put more money in the bank, save something for their children, without considering their own selves. How Prabhupada mocked me on a morning walk in Hong Kong when I said, "They are doing it for posterity." He said, "Posterity! You are giving it to your children, but where are you going, rascal! That you do not know." The rascal thinks giving something for his children satisfied him while he goes off into an unknown place, perhaps the body of a worm, for all the good he did for his children by hook and crook. And how are they even children of his? Just chance circumstance brought them together, and they are not even grateful for what he has left.

Look at these things straight in the eye, these facts of life. The insect dangling over the edge of the windowsill, the moth flying outside the window, beating against the screen. The more permanent things, the tall evergreens and the relatively short man with an arthritic ankle, a senior citizen now, smiling in his ID picture. He's got a nice place to live in, but not long duration. And what has he done to earn eternal residence with God afterwards? You ask yourself these questions on a Tuesday afternoon, but you don't even ask them. You just ponder them lightly and go on to scratching your neck, playing music, listening to the sounds of someone coming up the stairs to talk with you.

The best people are those who don't *ask* these questions anymore but settle for the Vedic version about Indra and *indragopa*. They therefore live in the reality of their short life and don't waste a moment. As Srila Prabhupada used to say, "Philosophy means to see death in your front." They see not only death, however, not just the skull head, but they see beyond him the beautiful form of Shyamasundar. They see and they taste the eternal. They strive for it. They know it's there. They take comfort in the name. They trust in their guru. They trust in Krishna's words in *Bhagavad-gita* that there is a world after this one, an eternal world where after going there, one never has to return to this world. They trust His words, "One who thinks of Me at the time of death . . . " and "One who knows My name and appearance doesn't have to return to this world but comes to live with Me in My abode." This is called faith, unflinching, unabated faith. The best ones live in this faith and even try to create it in others. They are very dear to Lord Chaitanya, and they write and die.

It's coming to summer, you can tell

by the traffic at the wine tasting houses
and art studios and sculpting for tourists
and the green hills and the gila monsters
chameleon-like on the rocks in the gardens.

I live quietly through the day, a
few phone calls, cat naps, scheduled
meals, a little writing and *japa*.
You hear readings from sacred
books and breathe, cancel exercise
on "Body Solid" machines
and painting canvases because
there is not enough time and energy.

Not any more. There's another weird insect
struggling to move. Suddenly he flies
as gracefully as a wingspread
modern jet but only
for a foot, then he grasps
onto the screen, appears exhausted
with crawling upward. Nature
has made it that way
by the *jiva's* will.

It's coming to summer, you can tell by the retired gentleman sitting on his chair on the porch with nothing to do and enjoying it. They tell him he's earned it, and he likes to hear that. At least a little break without pressure. I can sit and watch the trees and the sky without guilt.

May 24, 2005. I'm going to wrap this book up soon.

I think I know what dying is, in my own way. It's countdown. Prabhupada used to say when a baby is born, the parents are so happy, but he's actually one day dead, and when she's one year old, a blooming tot, and they're celebrating her first birthday, she's actually one year dead. You may say that's a grotesque reversed way to look at time, but it's the factual way. Each moment is taken off from a total, and the countdown begins at birth. The yogis say our time is measured in breaths.

They are given a certain number of breaths for a lifetime, and when life begins, they start ticking off, and our time starts running out. It's really not so frightful. It's the marching of time, and it's natural. One day after another is how we live. Looking it straight in the eye, the round of twenty-four hours, the routine of life is life itself. Keep a steady mind and the fact that the hourglass is pouring sand down shouldn't frighten us. As the poet e.e. cummings wrote, "Dying is fine, but death, oh baby, I wouldn't want death if death were good." He says that because death is unknown. Because death is the end of all possible joys to a man with no knowledge of the next life.

Bhakti-tirtha Maharaja knows more about death than most of us because he's so close to it. He has picked out the place where he will die, he has picked out the means of disposal, cremation, he has picked out the urn where his ashes will go into and the place, Mayapur Dhama, where the ashes will be buried. But even he doesn't know what death is. Not until it happens is it revealed.

So my little book has been somewhat playful. It is really meant to say only that I will write *up until* I die. It's been my pledge as a writer, my dedication, and the suggestion that others should become dedicated to do something for Krishna until the end of their life. I ventured into speculations about death and dying, but I cannot claim to know what death is. I know the philosophy about what happens after death, that you take another body according to the dogma of transmigration, which is according to your karma or quality of actions in this life. But what it feels like, what "tunnel" you actually go through, that I don't know and won't know until it actually happens. I've always wondered about that, even since entering Krishna conscious school. I've asked the question and never could get an answer. Do you lose your consciousness upon death? Does it just happen in an unconscious way? Do you get thrown into a state where you feel yourself beyond your control? Do you immediately see the personages who take control of you with great fear and trembling or with relief? How personal is it, how tiny? How does the mortal stuff get rearranged? How long does it take? *What's it like exactly?* I remember Ingmar Bergman's film *The Magician*. A man died, and with his dying breath he said, "Death is . . . " but said no more. We'll have to wait until we get there. Some believers are so sure they know just what it's like, how they'll step into the spiritual world.

They'll close their eyes and wait for the ride in a spiritual chariot, or they'll wait to fall into Krishna's arms. Or they wait for whatever it will be, just holding on with determined faith. "Thy will be done on earth as in heaven, for Thine is the power and the glory forever and ever, amen." It's not up to us to demand to know now. *Isvara parama krishna* — the Supreme Controller will take care of all that, and you need not inquire into it. Just spend your energies acting rightly now, and that's your best bet of meeting a good death.

It hasn't been my purpose so much to talk about death but to talk about living and writing and dying. I'm sorry if the book has been too writerly for some readers who don't like "artistic" books and want straight Krishna conscious textbook lessons. But these books are inevitably personal, and you can gain from them that way. Take what you can use and leave the rest. Live your way, and die. Live fully, determinately, passionately, and die. Live patiently. Live peacefully with faith. With prayer of a sort. With gratitude and love for your friends. Receive it from them and give it back to them. When it comes to the end of the day, all we have is our friends, and we are all they have. Or we are alone with God, our Supreme Friend, ready to make the solo flight. Alone with our prayers. "Our father, who art in heaven." *Isvara parama krsna sat cid ananda vigraha anadi 'adi govinda sarva karana karanam.* "Krishna is the supreme controller. He has a form of eternity, knowledge, and bliss. He is the supreme God of all gods, and He is the cause of all causes." Krishna has nothing to do. He has no worries. He plays in Goloka-Vrindavan with His dearmost residents, especially Radharani. You can go there if you have *laulyam*, greed, intense desire, and detachment from all other things. Start by hearing about Krishna's pastimes in this world. Chant his holy names.

"We must love one another or die." Boo! Auden's first version, which he later hated and revised. And yet . . .

"We must write to one another or die." Boo! Sat's first version, which he never even set down. And yet . . .

But master, prabhu, don't forget, the flaw is in the *or* instead of *and*. Your love for letters cannot stop dying.

Yes they can. They can't stop death but they can improve dying, they can improve the quality of life immensely. Why do we, even the

Buddhists, hail *ahimsa*, nonviolence, as a highest religious principle?
      Haven't we heard this before?
      Thematic strain worth hearing again at the end. And besides, re-
spected reader, I just said it in a new way.

> Stop dying, stop reading, start flying
> pick up shells and driftwood on the beach.
> Weep no more except for your soul
> and don't do that in self-pity, overflow
> for Walter Middy. Imagine you are
> someone great, a doughty *sadhu*.
>
> And then fulfill the nine prophecies you have
> made, *sravanam kirtanam vishnu-smaranam*,
> any of the nine, eight, or even one will bring
> you to the Lord's abode.
>
> I see some swells and even
> two whales very close to breakers, they're
> scraping their scales—it's a wondrous
> world, even this material energy where
> sea lions bark and sky's divine but
> it's death-bound-love each other
> and still we'll die.
> W. H. Auden wants to tell the truth
> that by loving embrace and antiwar
> we still can't live forever.
>
> But there is another way so he
> shouldn't get so angry that
> his verse misfired:
> We must love one another
> in Christ/Krishna or die.
>
> Oh mate up in the crow's nest,
> do you spy another whale?
> Do you see a fin protruding from the sea

???

or must we end this epic now?
Look in all directions before you say we're finished.
look through your spyglass and shout down the news.

The boy in the crow's nest shouts down
that he has seen Chicago's painted women
under the gas lamps luring the farm boys.
The first mate shouts up to him,
"What kind of relevancy is that
for a holy book? We are not interested in
prostitutes luring farm boys. We want monk's fare,
monk's bread. We want to see the straight spout
of a whale into the air, something
to thrill us, something to indicate
the holy movement of a boy
with a pure heart realizing God.
You know, *Moby Dick*, "Thar she blows,
a hump like a snow hill. It is Moby Dick"?
but that's only literature for boys and
studious men and women. It's actually boring.
We want the wave that is something continuous
and relevant on the theme of write and die.
You know, what came strong in the earlier pages
about Chips *needing* to write and claiming
that it was his *bhajan* and that without it
he had no life in Krishna consciousness
and claiming that it was his Krishna consciousness
just like the *patra-chitras* worship God by painting.
Are there any more swellings of that? Any more
allusions from books of the magic circle
that Thomas Mann used to keep on his desk
that inspired him to write his own book?
Anything there?

We are reading wonderful books, wonderful in themselves, *Brihad-bhagavatamrita*, where Krishna comes home at dusk with the cows and is bathed by the *gopis* and then sits for His evening meal, which is cooked by Yashoda and the *gopis*, and then is put to bed. And we are reading in *Jaiva Dharma* of a big debate between the *smarta* brahmins and the Vaishnavas, and we are reading of Orissan tales of Krishna and Radha by Srila Gaura Govinda Swami Maharaja, and we are reading reminiscences from Prabhupada's friends who knew him before ISKCON was even formed. And we are still reading the book about Jean Shepherd, with his biting satire and buffoonery. But these bring to mind nothing for your specific tale, for what you call a magic circle. They are themselves great magic circles on their own, each of them capable of pushing your book off the table.

He recalls hearing that Vishvanatha Chakravarti Thakur was writing on a palm leaf and a rat came and tugged at it. V.C. T. wrote on the leaf, "I see this rat is taking my *shloka* to his master, Ganesh."

He sees Madhvacharya in the act of writing a *shloka*, but he leaves his body in samadhi before it is finished.

It is not so uncommon for an author to die while he is writing, especially when he was prolific at his trade. Others die jogging. Tennis players, guitarists, and similar artists get "tennis elbow" because of too much action and practice. Boxers get killed in the ring. A philanthropist dies while carrying a care package to needy people. A terrorist dies on a mission to kill those people he has been taught are his religious enemies, and the "good guys" troops fighting to make the world safe for democracy are blown up by minefields set by the terrorists.

An old nun falls over on one of her innumerable sets of rosaries, and the monastery inmates say she died in a state of grace. The old priest dies while offering the Eucharist to the people and just after writing a pious, humble entry in his journal. Thomas Merton gave a lecture for ecumenical monks in Bangkok, ending with the words, "And now I will disappear." He then went to take a shower and was electrocuted to death after the shower by touching the loose wire of the electric fan in the bathroom. On hearing of his electrocution, a priest in France said, "*C'est magnifique.*" And so many go "not with a bang but a whimper." Correcting the proofs of his last book, Marcel Proust left prematurely with so much more that he could have done in an uninterrupted life. Anne Frank, Emily Dickinson, Jack Kerouac, John Coltrane—or had they said as much as they were meant to say, even at an early age? Some poets imagine an ideal setting for their departure with something like, "I will die on a Thursday, in Paris, on a rainy day." And a child's spiteful rhyme, "When I die, you will cry for all the names you called me."

The immortal sages of Vedic India who lived and learned to speak and write down inconceivable wisdom meant to last forever . . . some wrote and are living still . . . Srila Vyasadeva. Some died but left a legacy that lives forever in their books and in their followers who live with them in the word.

> Waves of loving and dying and
> Chips' little penmanship. Look upward
> amateur swordsman. He learned in
> the best school under the best master
>
> and played hard for thirty-five years,
> nothing to show but a
> crack in his Liberty Bell,
> inevitable slow down in the
> rate of words per minute.
>
> Spiritual poise and ardor?
> Increased? Does writing
> equal worship, and if so
> what kind? It's simply
> sad to deliver a
> child when he's due,
> leaving you with postnatal
> depression. But when all has been
> expressed, you have to go.
> Give her to the world with
> hope she's seaworthy
> and was a good read
> worth returning to, arguments sound
> and playful.

This is not the only one or last or best or worst. It flew the admiral's flag sometimes. Defied the so-called empowered "what's right for everyone." Prayed for Mother Earth and for preservation of private spiritual trails. Loyal to one master. This movie came out before the talkies. It learned how to rest on a summer day. It saw the disappearance of the worst in headaches. It learned how to drop anxieties, now *that's* a big achievement, although some of the critters still remain—like what will we do when we get to the next bridge? What if we grow tired of writing? What if we get bored? What if the Lord drops us from favor?

Please don't plague me like that. Our boat is flying nicely, so let's end it on a noncatastrophic note. He's the cause of all causes. Whatever He does we must abide with. His is best.

www.ingramcontent.com/pod-product-compliance
Lightning Source LLC
Chambersburg PA
CBHW020553260626
47157CB00003B/676